CHARLES DICKENS

"THEN MARCHIONESS," SAID MR. SWIVELLER, "FIRE AWAY!"

CHARLES DICKENS

THE
OLD CURIOSITY SHOP

VOLUME II

WITH ILLUSTRATIONS BY

C. GREEN

WALTER J. BLACK, INC.

NEW YORK

PRINTED IN THE UNITED STATES OF AMERICA

CONTENTS

THE OLD CURIOSITY SHOP

ILLUSTRATIONS

THE OLD CURIOSITY SHOP

THE
OLD CURIOSITY SHOP

CHAPTER XXXVIII

Kit—for it happens at this juncture, not only that we have breathing-time to follow his fortunes, but that the necessities of these adventures so adapt themselves to our ease and inclination as to call upon us imperatively to pursue the track we most desire to take—Kit, while the matters treated of in the last fifteen chapters were yet in progress, was, as the reader may suppose, gradually familiarising himself more and more with Mr. and Mrs. Garland, Mr. Abel, the pony, and Barbara, and gradually coming to consider them one and all as his particular private friends, and Abel Cottage, Finchley, as his own proper home.

Stay—the words are written, and may go, but if they convey any notion that Kit, in the plentiful board and comfortable lodging of his new abode, began to think slightingly of the poor fare and furniture of his old dwelling, they do their office badly and commit injustice. Who so mindful of those he left at home—albeit they were but a mother and two young babies—as Kit? What boastful father in the fulness of his heart ever related such wonders of his infant prodigy, as Kit never wearied of telling Barbara in the evening time, concerning little Jacob? Was there ever such a mother as Kit's mother, on her son's showing; or was there ever such comfort in poverty as in the poverty of Kit's family, if any correct judgment might be arrived at, from his own glowing account!

And let me linger in this place, for an instant, to remark that if ever household affections and loves are graceful things, they are graceful in the poor. The ties that bind the wealthy and the proud to home may be forged on earth, but those which link the poor man to his humble hearth are of the truer metal and bear the stamp of Heaven. The man of high descent may love the halls and lands of his inheritance as a part of himself: as trophies of his birth and power; his associations with them are associations of pride and wealth and triumph; the poor man's attachment to the tenements he holds, which strangers have held before, and may to-morrow occupy again, has a worthier root, struck deep into a purer soil. His household gods are of flesh and blood, with no alloy of silver, gold, or precious stone; he has no property but in the affections of his own heart; and when they endear bare floors and walls, despite of rags and toil and scanty fare, that man has his love of home from God, and his rude hut becomes a solemn place.

Oh! if those who rule the destinies of nations would but remember this—if they would but think how hard it is for the very poor to have engendered in their hearts, that love of home from which all domestic virtues spring, when they live in dense and squalid masses where social decency is lost, or rather never found,—if they would but turn aside from the wide thoroughfares and great houses, and strive to improve the wretched dwellings in by-ways where only Poverty may walk,—many low roofs would point more truly to the sky, than the loftiest steeple that now rears proudly up from the midst of guilt, and crime, and horrible disease, to mock them by its contrast. In hollow voices from Workhouse, Hospital, and Jail, this truth is preached from day to day, and has been proclaimed for years. It is no light matter —no outcry from the working vulgar—no mere question of the people's health and comforts that may be whistled down on Wednesday nights. In love of home, the love of country has its rise; and who are the truer patriots or the better in time of need—those who venerate the land, owning its wood, and stream, and earth, and all that they produce? or those who love their country, boasting not a foot of ground in all its wide domain?

Kit knew nothing about such questions, but he knew that his old home was a very poor place, and that his new one was very unlike it, and yet he was constantly looking back with grateful satisfaction and affectionate anxiety, and often indited square-folded letters to his mother, inclosing a shilling or eighteenpence or such other small remittance, which Mr. Abel's liberality enabled him to make. Sometimes being in the neighbourhood, he had leisure to call upon her, and then, great was the joy and pride of Kit's mother, and extremely noisy the satisfaction of little Jacob and the baby, and cordial the congratulations of the whole court, who listened with admiring ears to the accounts of Abel Cottage, and could never be told too much of its wonders and magnificence.

Although Kit was in the very highest favour with the old lady and gentleman, and Mr. Abel, and Barbara, it is certain that no member of the family evinced such a remarkable partiality for him as the self-willed pony, who, from being the most obstinate and opinionated pony on the face of the earth, was, in his hands, the meekest and most tractable of animals. It is true that in exact proportion as he became manageable by Kit he became utterly ungovernable by any-body else (as if he had determined to keep him in the family at all risks and hazards), and that, even under the guidance of his favourite, he would sometimes perform a great variety of strange freaks and capers, to the extreme discomposure of the old lady's nerves; but as Kit always represented that this was only his fun, or a way he had of showing his attachment to his employers, Mrs. Garland gradually suffered her-self to be persuaded into the belief, in which she at last became so strongly confirmed, that if, in one of these ebullitions, he had overturned the chaise, she would have been quite satisfied that he did it with the very best intentions.

Besides becoming in a short time a perfect marvel in all stable matters, Kit soon made himself a very tolerable gardener, a handy fellow within doors, and an indispensable attendant on Mr. Abel, who every day gave him some new proof of his confidence and approbation. Mr. Witherden the notary, too, re-garded him with a friendly eye; and even Mr. Chuck-ster would sometimes condescend to give him a slight nod, or to honour him with that peculiar form of rec-ognition which is called 'taking a sight,' or to favour him with some other salute combining pleasantry with patronage.

One morning Kit drove Mr. Abel to the notary's office, as he sometimes did, and having set him down at the house, was about to drive off to a livery stable hard by, when this same Mr. Chuckster emerged from the office-door, and cried 'Woa-a-a-a-a!'—dwelling upon the note a long time, for the purpose of striking terror into the pony's heart, and asserting the su-premacy of man over the inferior animals.

'Pull up, Snobby,' cried Mr. Chuckster, addressing himself to Kit. 'You 're wanted inside here.'

'Has Mr. Abel forgotten anything, I wonder?' said Kit as he dismounted.

'Ask no questions Snobby,' returned Mr. Chuckster, 'but go and see. Woa-a-a then, will you? If that pony was mine, *I 'd* break him.'

'You must be very gentle with him, if you please,' said Kit, 'or you 'll find him troublesome. You 'd better not keep on pulling his ears, please. I know he won't like it.'

To this remonstrance Mr. Chuckster deigned no other answer, than addressing Kit with a lofty and distant air as 'young feller,' and requesting him to cut and come again with all speed. The 'young feller' complying, Mr. Chuckster put his hands in his pockets, and tried to look as if he were not minding the pony, but happened to be lounging there by accident.

Kit scraped his shoes very carefully (for he had not yet lost his reverence for the bundles of papers and the tin boxes), and tapped at the office-door, which was quickly opened by the notary himself.

'Oh! come in, Christopher,' said Mr. Witherden.

'Is that the lad?' asked an elderly gentleman, but of a stout, bluff figure—who was in the room.

'That 's the lad,' said Mr. Witherden. 'He fell in with my client, Mr. Garland, sir, at this very door. I have reason to think he is a good lad, sir, and that you may believe what he says. Let me introduce Mr. Abel Garland, sir—his young master; my articled pupil, sir, and most particular friend:—my most particular friend, sir,' repeated the notary, drawing out his silk handkerchief and flourishing it about his face.

'Your servant, sir,' said the stranger gentleman.

'Yours, sir, I 'm sure,' replied Mr. Abel mildly. 'You were wishing to speak to Christopher, sir?'

'Yes, I was. Have I your permission?'

'By all means.'

'My business is no secret; or I should rather say it need be no secret *here,*' said the stranger, observing that Mr. Abel and the notary were preparing to retire. 'It relates to a dealer in curiosities with whom he lived, and in whom I am earnestly and warmly interested. I have been a stranger to this country, gentlemen, for very many years, and if I am deficient in form and ceremony, I hope you will forgive me.'

'No forgiveness is necessary, sir;—none whatever,' replied the notary. And so said Mr. Abel.

'I have been making inquiries in the neighbourhood in which his old master lived,' said the stranger, 'and I learn that he was served by this lad. I have found out his mother's house, and have been directed by her to this place as the nearest in which I should be likely to find him. That 's the cause of my presenting myself here this morning.'

'I am very glad of any cause, sir,' said the notary, 'which procures me the honour of this visit.'

'Sir,' retorted the stranger, 'you speak like a mere man of the world, and I think you something better. Therefore, pray do not sink your real character in paying unmeaning compliments to me.'

'Hem!' coughed the notary. 'You 're a plain speaker, sir.'

'And a plain dealer,' returned the stranger. 'It may be my long absence and inexperience that lead me to the conclusion; but if plain speakers are scarce in this part of the world, I fancy plain dealers are still scarcer. If my speaking should offend you, sir, my dealing, I hope, will make amends.'

Mr. Witherden seemed a little disconcerted by the elderly gentleman's mode of conducting the dialogue; and as for Kit, he looked at him in open-mouthed astonishment: wondering what kind of language he would address to him, if he talked in that free and easy way to a notary. It was with no harshness, however, though with something of constitutional irritability and haste, that he turned to Kit and said—

'If you think, my lad, that I am pursuing these inquiries with any other view than that of serving and reclaiming those I am in search of, you do me a very great wrong, and deceive yourself. Don't be deceived, I beg of you, but rely upon my assurance. The fact is, gentlemen,' he added, turning again to the notary and his pupil, 'that I am in a very painful and wholly unexpected position. I came to this city with a darling object at my heart, expecting to find no obstacle or difficulty in the way of its attainment. I find myself suddenly checked and stopped short, in the execution of my design, by a mystery which I cannot penetrate. Every effort I have made to penetrate it, has only served to render it darker and more obscure; and I am afraid to stir openly in the matter, lest those whom I anxiously pursue, should fly still further from me. I assure you that if you could give me any assistance, you would not be sorry to do so, if you knew how greatly I stand in need of it, and what a load it would relieve me from.'

There was a simplicity in this confidence which occasioned it to find a quick response in the breast of the good-natured notary, who replied, in the same spirit, that the stranger had not mistaken his desire, and that if he could be of service to him he would, most readily.

Kit was then put under examination and closely questioned by the unknown gentleman, touching his old master and the child, their lonely way of life, their retired habits, and strict seclusion. The nightly absence of the old man, the solitary existence of the child at those times, his illness and recovery, Quilp's possession of the house, and their sudden disappearance, were all the subjects of much questioning and answer. Finally, Kit informed the gentleman that the premises were now to let, and that a board upon the door referred all inquirers to Mr. Sampson Brass, solicitor, of Bevis Marks, from whom he might perhaps learn some further particulars.

'Not by inquiry,' said the gentleman shaking his head. 'I live there.'

'Live at Brass's the attorney's!' cried Mr. Witherden in some surprise: having professional knowledge of the gentleman in question.

'Aye,' was the reply. 'I entered on his lodgings t' other day, chiefly because I had seen this very board. It matters little to me where I live, and I had a desperate hope that some intelligence might be cast in my way there, which would not reach me elsewhere. Yes, I live at Brass's—more shame for me, I suppose?'

'That's a mere matter of opinion,' said the notary, shrugging his shoulders. 'He is looked upon as rather a doubtful character.'

'Doubtful?' echoed the other. 'I am glad to hear there's any doubt about it. I supposed that had been thoroughly settled, long ago. But will you let me speak a word or two with you in private?'

Mr. Witherden consenting, they walked into that gentleman's private closet, and remained there, in close conversation, for some quarter of an hour, when they returned into the outer office. The stranger had left his hat in Mr. Witherden's room, and seemed to have established himself in this short interval on quite a friendly footing.

'I'll not detain you any longer now,' he said, putting a crown into Kit's hand, and looking towards the notary. 'You shall hear from me again. Not a word of this, you know, except to your master and mistress.'

'Mother, sir, would be glad to know—' said Kit, faltering.

'Glad to know what?'

'Anything—so that it was no harm—about Miss Nell.'

'Would she? Well then, you may tell her if she can keep a secret. But mind, not a word of this to anybody else. Don't forget that. Be particular.'

'I 'll take care, sir,' said Kit. 'Thank 'ee, sir, and good morning.'

Now, it happened that the gentleman, in his anxiety to impress upon Kit that he was not to tell anybody what had passed between them, followed him out to the door to repeat his caution, and it further happened that at that moment the eyes of Mr. Richard Swiveller were turned in that direction, and beheld his mysterious friend and Kit together.

It was quite an accident, and the way in which it came about was this. Mr. Chuckster, being a gentleman of a cultivated taste and refined spirit, was one of that Lodge of Glorious Apollos whereof Mr. Swiveller was Perpetual Grand. Mr. Swiveller, passing through the street in the execution of some Brazen errand, and beholding one of his Glorious Brotherhood intently gazing on a pony, crossed over to give him that fraternal greeting with which Perpetual Grands are, by the very constitution of their office, bound to cheer and encourage their disciples. He had scarcely bestowed upon him his blessing, and followed it with a general remark touching the present state and prospects of the weather, when, lifting up his eyes, he beheld the single gentleman of Bevis Marks in earnest conversation with Christopher Nubbles.

'Hallo!' said Dick, 'who *is* that?'

'He called to see my Governor this morning,' replied Mr. Chuckster; 'beyond that, I don't know him from Adam.'

'At least you know his name?' said Dick.

To which Mr. Chuckster replied, with an elevation of speech becoming a Glorious Apollo, that he was 'everlastingly blessed' if he did.

'All I know, my dear feller,' said Mr. Chuckster, running his fingers through his hair, 'is, that he is the cause of my having stood here twenty minutes, for which I hate him with a mortal and undying hatred, and would pursue him to the confines of eternity if I could afford the time.'

While they were thus discoursing, the subject of their conversation (who had not appeared to recognise Mr. Richard Swiveller) re-entered the house, and Kit came down the steps and joined them; to whom Mr. Swiveller again propounded his inquiry with no better success.

'He is a very nice gentleman, sir,' said Kit, 'and that 's all *I* know about him.'

Mr. Chuckster waxed wroth at this answer, and without applying the remark to any particular case, mentioned, as a general truth, that it was expedient to break the heads of Snobs, and to tweak their noses. Without expressing his concurrence in this sentiment, Mr. Swiveller after a few moments of abstraction inquired which way Kit was driving, and, being informed, declared it was his way, and that he would trespass on him for a lift. Kit would gladly have declined the proffered honour, but as Mr. Swiveller was already established in the seat beside him, he had no means of doing so, otherwise than by a forcible ejectment, and therefore drove briskly off—so briskly indeed, as to cut short the leave-taking between Mr. Chuckster and his Grand Master, and to occasion the former gentleman some inconvenience from having his corns squeezed by the impatient pony.

As Whisker was tired of standing, and Mr. Swiveller was kind enough to stimulate him by shrill whistles, and various sporting cries, they rattled off at too sharp a pace to admit of much conversation: especially as the pony, incensed by Mr. Swiveller's admonitions, took a particular fancy for the lamp-posts and cart-wheels, and evinced a strong desire to run on the pavement and rasp himself against the brick walls. It was not, therefore, until they had arrived at the stable, and the chaise had been extricated from a very small doorway, into which the pony dragged it under the impression that he could take it along with him into his usual stall, that Mr. Swiveller found time to talk.

'It 's hard work,' said Richard. 'What do you say to some beer?'

Kit at first declined, but presently consented, and they adjourned to the neighbouring bar together.

'We 'll drink our friend what 's-his-name,' said Dick, holding up the bright frothy pot; '—that was talking to you this morning, you know—*I* know him —a good fellow, but eccentric—very—here 's what 's-his-name!'

Kit pledged him.

'He lives in my house,' said Dick; 'at least in the house occupied by the firm in which I 'm a sort of a —of a managing partner—a difficult fellow to get anything out of, but we like him—we like him.'

'I must be going, sir, if you please,' said Kit, moving away.

'Don't be in a hurry, Christopher,' replied his patron, 'we 'll drink your mother.'

'Thank you, sir.'

'An excellent woman that mother of yours, Christopher,' said Mr. Swiveller. 'Who ran to catch me when I fell, and kissed the place to make it well?   My mother.   A charming woman.   He's a liberal sort of fellow.   We must get him to do something *for* your mother.   Does he know her, Christopher?'

Kit shook his head, and glancing slyly at his questioner, thanked him, and made off before he could say another word.

'Humph!' said Mr. Swiveller pondering, 'this is queer.   Nothing but mysteries in connection with Brass's house.   I'll keep my own counsel, however. Everybody and anybody has been in my confidence as yet, but now I think I'll set up in business for myself.   Queer—very queer!'

After pondering deeply and with a face of exceeding wisdom for some time, Mr. Swiveller drank some more of the beer, and summoning a small boy who had been watching his proceedings, poured forth a few remaining drops as a libation upon the gravel, and bade him carry the empty vessel to the bar with his compliments, and above all things to lead a sober and temperate life, and abstain from all intoxicating and exciting liquors.   Having given him this piece of moral advice for his trouble (which, as he wisely observed, was far better than halfpence) the Perpetual Grand Master of the Glorious Apollos thrust his hands into his pockets and sauntered away: still pondering as he went.

CHAPTER XXXIX

ALL that day, though he waited for Mr. Abel until evening, Kit kept clear of his mother's house, determined not to anticipate the pleasures of the morrow, but to let them come in their full rush of delight; for to-morrow was the great and long-looked-for epoch in his life—to-morrow was the end of his first quarter—the day of receiving, for the first time, one fourth part of his annual income of Six Pounds in one vast sum of Thirty Shillings—to-morrow was to be a half-holiday devoted to a whirl of entertainments, and little Jacob was to know what oysters meant, and to see a play.

All manner of incidents combined in favour of the occasion: not only had Mr. and Mrs. Garland forewarned him that they intended to make no deduction for his outfit from the great amount, but to pay it him unbroken in all its gigantic grandeur; not only had the unknown gentleman increased the stock by the sum of five shillings, which was a perfect godsend and in itself a fortune; not only had these things come to pass which nobody could have calculated upon, or in their wildest dreams have hoped; but it was Barbara's quarter too—Barbara's quarter, that very day—and Barbara had a half-holiday as well as Kit, and Barbara's mother was going to make one of the party, and to take tea with Kit's mother, and cultivate her acquaintance.

To be sure Kit looked out of his window very early that morning to see which way the clouds were flying, and to be sure Barbara would have been at hers too, if she had not sat up so late overnight, starching and ironing small pieces of muslin, and crimping them into frills, and sewing them on to other pieces to form magnificent wholes for next day's wear. But they were both up very early for all that, and had small appetites for breakfast and less for dinner, and were in a state of great excitement when Barbara's mother came in, with astonishing accounts of the fineness of the weather out of doors (but with a very large umbrella notwithstanding, for people like Barbara's mother seldom make holiday without one), and when the bell rung for them to go upstairs and receive their quarter's money in gold and silver.

Well, wasn't Mr. Garland kind when he said 'Christopher, here's your money, and you have earned it well'; and wasn't Mrs. Garland kind when she said 'Barbara, here's yours, and I'm much pleased with you'; and didn't Kit sign his name bold to his receipt, and didn't Barbara sign her name all a trembling to hers; and wasn't it beautiful to see how Mrs. Garland poured out Barbara's mother a glass of wine; and didn't Barbara's mother speak up when she said, 'Here's blessing you, ma'am, as a good lady, and you, sir, as a good gentleman, and Barbara, my love to you, and here's towards you, Mr. Christopher'; and wasn't she as long drinking it as if it had been a tumblerful; and didn't she look genteel, standing there with her gloves on; and wasn't there plenty of laughing and talking among them as they reviewed all these things upon the top of the coach; and didn't they pity the people who hadn't got a holiday?

But Kit's mother, again—wouldn't anybody have supposed she had come of a good stock and been a lady all her life? There she was, quite ready to receive them, with a display of tea-things that might have warmed the heart of a china-shop; and little Jacob and the baby in such a state of perfection that their clothes looked as good as new, though Heaven knows they were old enough! Didn't she say before they had sat down five minutes that Barbara's mother was exactly the sort of lady she expected, and didn't Barbara's mother say that Kit's mother was the very picture of what *she* had expected, and didn't Kit's mother compliment Barbara's mother on Barbara, and didn't Barbara's mother compliment Kit's mother on Kit, and wasn't Barbara herself quite fascinated with little Jacob, and did ever a child show off when he was wanted, as that child did, or make such friends as he made?

'And we are both widows too!' said Barbara's mother. 'We must have been made to know each other.'

'I haven't a doubt about it,' returned Mrs. Nubbles. 'And what a pity it is we didn't know each other sooner.'

'But then, you know, it's such a pleasure,' said Barbara's mother, 'to have it brought about by one's son and daughter, that it's fully made up for. Now, an't it?'

To this, Kit's mother yielded her full assent, and tracing things back from effects to causes, they naturally reverted to their deceased husbands, respecting whose lives, deaths, and burials, they compared notes, and discovered sundry circumstances that tallied with wonderful exactness; such as Barbara's father having been exactly four years and ten months older than Kit's father, and one of them having died on a Wednesday and the other on a Thursday, and both of them having been of a very fine make and remarkably good-looking, with other extraordinary coincidences. These recollections being of a kind calculated to cast a shadow on the brightness of the holiday, Kit diverted the conversation to general topics, and they were soon in great force again, and as

merry as before.   Among other things, Kit told them
about his old place, and the extraordinary beauty of
Nell (of whom he had talked to Barbara a thousand
times already); but the last-named circumstance
failed to interest his hearers to anything like the extent he had supposed, and even his mother said (looking accidentally at Barbara at the same time) that
there was no doubt Miss Nell was very pretty, but she
was but a child after all, and there were many young
women quite as pretty as she; and Barbara mildly
observed that she should think so, and that she never
could help believing Mr. Christopher must be under
a mistake—which Kit wondered at very much, not
being able to conceive what reason she had for doubting him.   Barbara's mother too, observed that it was
very common for young folks to change at about
fourteen or fifteen, and whereas they had been very
pretty before, to grow up quite plain; which truth
she illustrated by many forcible examples, especially
one of a young man, who, being a builder with great
prospects, had been particular in his attentions to
Barbara, but whom Barbara would have nothing to
say to; which (though everything happened for the
best) she almost thought was a pity.   Kit said he
thought so to, and so he did honestly, and he wondered
what made Barbara so silent all at once, and why his
mother looked at him as if he shouldn't have said it.

However, it was high time now to be thinking of
the play; for which great preparation was required,
in the way of shawls and bonnets, not to mention
one handkerchief full of oranges and another of
apples, which took some time tying up, in consequence
of the fruit having a tendency to roll out at the
corners.   At length, everything was ready, and they
went off very fast; Kit's mother carrying the baby,
who was dreadfully wide awake, and Kit holding

AT LENGTH EVERYTHING WAS READY AND THEY WENT OFF.

little Jacob in one hand, and escorting Barbara with the other—a state of things which occasioned the two mothers, who walked behind, to declare that they looked quite family folks, and caused Barbara to blush and say, 'Now don't, mother!' But Kit said she had no call to mind what they said; and indeed she need not have had, if she had known how very far from Kit's thoughts any love-making was. Poor Barbara!

At last they got to the theatre, which was Astley's: and in some two minutes after they had reached the yet unopened door, little Jacob was squeezed flat, and the baby had received divers concussions, and Barbara's mother's umbrella had been carried several yards off and passed back to her over the shoulders of the people, and Kit had hit a man on the head with the handkerchief of apples for 'scrowdging' his parent with unnecessary violence, and there was a great uproar. But, when they were once past the pay-place and tearing away for very life with their checks in their hands, and, above all, when they were fairly in the theatre, and seated in such places that they couldn't have had better if they had picked them out, and taken them beforehand, all this was looked upon as quite a capital joke, and an essential part of the entertainment.

Dear, dear, what a place it looked, that Astley's; with all the paint, gilding, and looking-glass; the vague smell of horses suggestive of coming wonders; the curtain that hid such gorgeous mysteries; the clean white sawdust down in the circus; the company coming in and taking their places; the fiddlers looking carelessly up at them while they tuned their instruments, as if they didn't want the play to begin, and knew it all beforehand! What a glow was that, which burst upon them all, when that long, clear, brilliant row of lights came slowly up; and what the feverish excitement when the little bell rang and the music began in good earnest, with strong parts for the drums, and sweet effects for the triangles! Well might Barbara's mother say to Kit's mother that the gallery was the place to see from, and wonder it wasn't much dearer than the boxes; well might Barbara feel doubtful whether to laugh or cry, in her flutter of delight.

Then the play itself! the horses which little Jacob believed from the first to be alive, and the ladies and gentlemen of whose reality he could be by no means persuaded, having never seen or heard anything at all like them—the firing, which made Barbara wink —the forlorn lady, who made her cry—the tyrant, who made her tremble—the man who sang the song with the lady's-maid and danced the chorus, who made her laugh—the pony who reared up on his hind-legs when he saw the murderer, and wouldn't hear of walking on all four again until he was taken into custody—the clown who ventured on such familiarities with the military man in boots—the lady who jumped over the nine-and-twenty ribbons and came down safe upon the horse's back—everything was delightful, splendid, and surprising! Little Jacob applauded till his hands were sore; Kit cried 'an-kor' at the end of everything, the three-act piece included; and Barbara's mother beat her umbrella on the floor, in her ecstasies, until it was nearly worn down to the gingham.

In the midst of all these fascinations, Barbara's thoughts seemed to have been still running on what Kit had said at tea-time; for, when they were coming out of the play, she asked him, with an hysterical simper, if Miss Nell was as handsome as the lady who jumped over the ribbons.

'As handsome as *her?*' said Kit.   'Double as handsome.'

'Oh Christopher! I'm sure she was the beautifullest creature ever was,' said Barbara.

'Nonsense!' returned Kit.   'She was well enough, I don't deny that; but think how she was dressed and painted, and what a difference that made.   Why *you* are a good deal better looking than her, Barbara.'

'Oh Christopher!' said Barbara, looking down.

'You are, any day,' said Kit.—'and so's your mother.'

Poor Barbara!

What was all this though—even all this—to the extraordinary dissipation that ensued, when Kit, walking into an oyster-shop as bold as if he lived there, and not so much as looking at the counter or the man behind it, led his party into a box—a private box fitted up with red curtains, white table-cloth, and cruet-stand complete, and ordered a fierce gentleman with whiskers, who acted as waiter and called him, him Christopher Nubbles, 'sir,' to bring three dozen of his largest-sized oysters, and to look sharp about it!   Yes, Kit told this gentleman to look sharp, and he not only said he would look sharp, but he actually did, and presently came running back with the newest loaves, and the freshest butter, and the largest oysters, ever seen.   Then said Kit to this gentleman, 'a pot of beer'—just so—and the gentleman, instead of replying, 'Sir, did you address that language to me?' only said, 'Pot o' beer, sir?   Yes, sir,' and went off and fetched it, and put it on the table in a small decanter-stand, like those which blind men's dogs carry about the streets in their mouths, to catch the halfpence in; and both Kit's mother and Barbara's mother declared as he turned away that he was one of the slimmest and gracefullest young men she had ever looked upon.

Then they fell to work upon the supper in earnest; and there was Barbara, that foolish Barbara, declaring that she could not eat more than two, and wanting more pressing than you would believe before she would eat four: though her mother and Kit's mother made up for it pretty well, and ate and laughed and enjoyed themselves so thoroughly that it did Kit good to see them and made him laugh and eat likewise from strong sympathy. But the greatest miracle of the night was little Jacob, who ate oysters as if he had been born and bred to the business— sprinkled the pepper and the vinegar with a discretion beyond his years—and afterwards built a grotto on the table with the shells. There was the baby too, who had never closed an eye all night, but had sat as good as gold, trying to force a large orange into his mouth, and gazing intently at the lights in the chandelier—there he was, sitting up in his mother's lap, staring at the gas without winking, and making indentations in his soft visage with an oyster-shell, to that degree that a heart of iron must have loved him! In short, there never was a more successful supper; and when Kit ordered in a glass of something hot to finish with, and proposed Mr. and Mrs. Garland before sending it round, there were not six happier people in all the world.

But all happiness has an end—hence the chief pleasure of its next beginning—and as it was now growing late, they agreed it was time to turn their faces homewards. So, after going a little out of their way to see Barbara and Barbara's mother safe to a friend's house where they were to pass the night, Kit and his mother left them at the door, with an early appointment for returning to Finchley next morning, and a great many plans for next quarter's enjoyment. Then, Kit took little Jacob on his back, and giving his arm to his mother, and a kiss to the baby, they all trudged merrily home together.

CHAPTER XL

FULL of that vague kind of penitence which holidays awaken next morning, Kit turned out at sunrise, and, with his faith in last night's enjoyments a little shaken by cool daylight and the return to everyday duties and occupations, went to meet Barbara and her mother at the appointed place. And being careful not to awaken any of the little household, who were yet resting from their unusual fatigues, Kit left his money on the chimney-piece, with an inscription in chalk calling his mother's attention to the circumstance, and informing her that it came from her dutiful son; and went his way, with a heart something heavier than his pockets, but free from any very great oppression notwithstanding.

Oh these holidays! why will they leave us some regret? why cannot we push them back, only a week or two in our memories, so as to put them at once at that convenient distance whence they may be regarded either with a calm indifference or a pleasant effort of recollection? why will they hang about us, like the flavour of yesterday's wine, suggestive of headaches and lassitude, and those good intentions for the future, which, under the earth, form the everlasting pavement of a large estate, and, upon it, usually endure until dinner-time or thereabouts?

Who will wonder that Barbara had a headache, or that Barbara's mother was disposed to be cross, or that she slightly underrated Astley's, and thought

the clown was older than they had taken him to be
last night? Kit was not surprised to hear her say so
—not he. He had already had a misgiving that the
inconstant actors in that dazzling vision had been doing the same thing the night before last, and would
do it again that night, and the next, and for weeks
and months to come, though he would not be there.
Such is the difference between yesterday and to-day.
We are all going to the play, or coming home from
it.

However, the Sun himself is weak when he first
rises, and gathers strength and courage as the day
gets on. By degrees, they began to recall circumstances more and more pleasant in their nature, until,
what between talking, walking, and laughing, they
reached Finchley in such good heart, that Barbara's
mother declared she never felt less tired or in better
spirits. And so said Kit. Barbara had been silent
all the way, but she said so too. Poor little Barbara!
She was very quiet.

They were at home in such good time that Kit had
rubbed down the pony and made him as spruce as a
race-horse, before Mr. Garland came down to breakfast; which punctual and industrious conduct the old
lady, and the old gentleman, and Mr. Abel, highly
extolled. At this usual hour (or rather at his usual
minute and second, for he was the soul of punctual-
ity) Mr. Abel walked out, to be overtaken by the
London coach, and Kit and the old gentleman went
to work in the garden.

This was not the least pleasant of Kit's employ-
ments. On a fine day they were quite a family
party; the old lady sitting hard by with her work-
basket on a little table; the old gentleman digging,
or pruning, or clipping about with a large pair of
shears, or helping Kit in some way or other with great

assiduity; and Whisker looking on from his paddock in placid contemplation of them all. To-day they were to trim the grape-vine, so Kit mounted half-way up a short ladder, and began to snip and hammer away, while the old gentleman, with a great interest in his proceedings, handed up the nails and shreds of cloth as he wanted them. The old lady and Whisker looked on as usual.

'Well, Christopher,' said Mr. Garland, 'and so you have made a new friend, eh?'

'I beg your pardon, sir?' returned Kit, looking down from the ladder.

'You have made a new friend, I hear from Mr. Abel,' said the old gentleman, 'at the office!'

'Oh! Yes, sir, yes. He behaved very handsome, sir.'

'I 'm glad to hear it,' returned the old gentleman with a smile. 'He is disposed to behave more handsomely still, though, Christopher.'

'Indeed, sir! It 's very kind in him, but I don't want him to, I 'm sure,' said Kit, hammering stoutly at an obdurate nail.

'He is rather anxious,' pursued the old gentleman, 'to have you in his own service—take care what you 're doing, or you will fall down and hurt yourself.'

'To have me in his service, sir?' cried Kit, who had stopped short in his work and faced about on the ladder like some dexterous tumbler. 'Why, sir, I don't think he can be in earnest when he says that.'

'Oh! But he is indeed,' said Mr. Garland. 'And he has told Mr. Abel so.'

'I never heard of such a thing!' muttered Kit, looking ruefully at his master and mistress. 'I wonder at him; that I do.'

'You see, Christopher,' said Mr. Garland, 'this is

a point of much importance to you, and you should understand and consider it in that light. This gentleman is able to give you more money than I—not, I hope, to carry through the various relations of master and servant, more kindness and confidence, but certainly, Christopher, to give you more money.'

'Well,' said Kit, 'after that, sir—'

'Wait a moment,' interposed Mr. Garland. 'That is not all. You were a very faithful servant to your old employers, as I understand, and should this gentleman recover them, as it is his purpose to attempt doing by every means in his power, I have no doubt that you, being in his service, would meet with your reward. Besides,' added the old gentleman with stronger emphasis, 'besides having the pleasure of being again brought into communication with those to whom you seem to be very strongly and disinterestedly attached. You must think of all this, Christopher, and not be rash or hasty in your choice.'

Kit did suffer one twinge, one momentary pang, in keeping the resolution he had already formed, when this last argument passed swiftly into his thoughts, and conjured up the realisation of all his hopes and fancies. But it was gone in a minute, and he sturdily rejoined that the gentleman must look out for somebody else, as he did think he might have done at first.

'He has no right to think that I 'd be led away to go to him, sir,' said Kit, turning round again after half a minute's hammering. 'Does he think I 'm a fool?'

'He may, perhaps, Christopher, if you refuse his offer,' said Mr. Garland gravely.

'Then let him, sir,' retorted Kit; 'what do I care, sir, what he thinks? why should I care for his thinking, sir, when I know that I should be a fool, and worse than a fool, sir, to leave the kindest master and mistress that ever was or can be, who took me out of the streets a very poor and hungry lad indeed—poorer and hungrier perhaps than even you think for, sir—to go to him or anybody? If Miss Nell was to come back, ma'am,' added Kit, turning suddenly to his mistress, 'why that would be another thing, and perhaps if *she* wanted me, I might ask you now and then to let me work for her when all was done at home. But when she comes back, I see now that she 'll be rich as old master always said she would, and being a rich young lady, what could she want of me? No, no,' added Kit, shaking his head sorrowfully, 'she 'll never want me any more, and bless her, I hope she never may, though I *should* like to see her too!'

Here Kit drove a nail into the wall, very hard—much harder than was necessary—and having done so, faced about again.

'There 's the pony, sir,' said Kit—'Whisker, ma'am (and he knows so well I 'm talking about him that he begins to neigh directly, sir),—would he let anybody come near him but me, ma'am? Here 's the garden, sir, and Mr. Abel, ma'am. Would Mr. Abel part with me, sir, or is there anybody that could be fonder of the garden, ma'am? It would break mother's heart, sir, and even little Jacob would have sense enough to cry his eyes out, ma'am, if he thought that Mr. Abel could wish to part with me so soon, after having told me, only the other day, that he hoped we might be together for years to come—'

There is no telling how long Kit might have stood upon the ladder, addressing his master and mistress by turns, and generally turning towards the wrong person, if Barbara had not at that moment come running up to say that a messenger from the office had brought a note, which, with an expression of some surprise at Kit's oratorical appearance, she put into her master's hand.

'Oh!' said the old gentleman after reading it, 'ask the messenger to walk this way.' Barbara tripping off to do as she was bid, he turned to Kit, and said that they would not pursue the subject any further, and that Kit could not be more unwilling to part with them, than they would be to part with Kit; a sentiment which the old lady very generously echoed.

'At the same time, Christopher,' added Mr. Garland, glancing at the note in his hand, 'if the gentleman should want to borrow you now and then for an hour or so, or even a day or so, at a time, we must consent to lend you, and you must consent to be lent. —Oh! here is the young gentleman. How do you do, sir?'

This salutation was addressed to Mr. Chuckster, who, with his hat extremely on one side, and his hair a long way beyond it, came swaggering up the walk.

'Hope I see you well, sir,' returned that gentleman. 'Hope I see *you* well, ma'am. Charming box this, sir. Delicious country to be sure.'

'You want to take Kit back with you, I find?' observed Mr. Garland.

'I have got a chariot-cab waiting on purpose,' replied the clerk. 'A very spanking grey in that cab, sir, if you 're a judge of horse-flesh.'

Declining to inspect the spanking grey, on the plea that he was but poorly acquainted with such matters, and would but imperfectly appreciate his beauties, Mr. Garland invited Mr. Chuckster to partake of a slight repast in the way of lunch. That gentleman readily consenting, certain cold viands, flanked with ale and wine, were speedily prepared for his refreshment.

At this repast, Mr. Chuckster exerted his utmost abilities to enchant his entertainers, and impress them with a conviction of the mental superiority of those who dwelt in town; with which view he led the discourse to the small scandal of the day, in which he was justly considered by his friends to shine prodigiously. Thus, he was in a condition to relate the exact circumstances of the difference between the Marquis of Mizzler and Lord Bobby, which it appeared originated in a disputed bottle of champagne, and not in a pigeon-pie, as erroneously reported in the newspapers; neither had Lord Bobby said to the Marquis of Mizzler, 'Mizzler, one of us two tells a lie, and I 'm not the man,' as incorrectly stated by the same authorities; but 'Mizzler, you know where I 'm to be found, and damme, sir, find me if you want me'—which, of course, entirely changed the aspect of this interesting question, and placed it in a very different light. He also acquainted them with the precise amount of the income guaranteed by the Duke of Thigsberry to Violetta Stetta of the Italian Opera, which it appeared was payable quarterly, and not half-yearly, as the public had been given to understand, and which was *ex*clusive, and not *in*clusive, (as had been monstrously stated,) of jewellery, perfumery, hair-powder for five footmen, and two daily changes of kid-gloves for a page. Having entreated the old lady and gentleman to set their minds at rest on these absorbing points, for they might rely on his statement being the correct one, Mr. Chuckster entertained them with theatrical chit-chat and the court circular; and so wound up a brilliant and fascinating conversation which he had maintained alone, and without any assistance whatever, for upwards of three-quarters of an hour.

'And now that the nag has got his wind again,' said Mr. Chuckster rising in a graceful manner, 'I 'm afraid I must cut my stick.'

Neither Mr. nor Mrs. Garland offered any opposition to his tearing himself away, (feeling, no doubt, that such a man could ill be spared from his proper sphere of action,) and therefore Mr. Chuckster and Kit were shortly afterwards upon their way to town; Kit being perched upon the box of the cabriolet beside the driver, and Mr. Chuckster seated in solitary state inside, with one of his boots sticking out at each of the front windows.

When they reached the notary's house, Kit followed into the office, and was desired by Mr. Abel to sit down and wait, for the gentleman who wanted him had gone out, and perhaps might not return for some time. This anticipation was strictly verified, for Kit had had his dinner, and his tea, and had read all the lighter matter in the Law List, and the Post-Office Directory, and had fallen asleep a great many times, before the gentleman whom he had seen before, came in; which he did at last in a very great hurry.

He was closeted with Mr. Witherden for some little time, and Mr. Abel had been called in to assist at the conference, before Kit, wondering very much what he was wanted for, was summoned to attend them.

'Christopher,' said the gentleman, turning to him directly he entered the room, 'I have found your old master and young mistress.'

'No, sir! Have you, though?' returned Kit, his eyes sparkling with delight. 'Where are they, sir? How are they, sir? Are they—are they near here?'

'A long way from here,' returned the gentleman, shaking his head. 'But I am going away to-night to bring them back, and I want you to go with me.'

'Me, sir?' cried Kit, full of joy and surprise.

'The place,' said the strange gentleman, turning thoughtfully to the notary, 'indicated by this man of the dogs, is—how far from here—sixty miles?'

'From sixty to seventy.'

'Humph! If we travel post all night, we shall reach there in good time to-morrow morning. Now, the only question is, as they will not know me, and the child, God bless her, would think that any stranger pursuing them had a design upon her grandfather's liberty,—can I do better than take this lad, whom they both know and will readily remember, as an assurance to them of my friendly intentions?'

'Certainly not,' replied the notary. 'Take Christopher by all means.'

'I beg your pardon, sir,' said Kit, who had listened to this discourse with a lengthening countenance, 'but if that's the reason, I'm afraid I should do more harm than good—Miss Nell, sir, *she* knows me, and would trust in me, I am sure; but old master—I don't why, gentlemen; nobody does—would not bear me in his sight after he had been ill, and Miss Nell herself told me that I must not go near him or let him see me any more. I should spoil all that you were doing if I went, I'm afraid. I'd give the world to go, but you had better not take me, sir.'

'Another difficulty!' cried the impetuous gentleman. 'Was ever man so beset as I? Is there nobody else that knew them, nobody else in whom they had any confidence? Solitary as their lives were, is there no one person who would serve my purpose?'

'*Is* there, Christopher?' said the notary.

'Not one, sir,' replied Kit. 'Yes, though—there's my mother.'

'Did they know her?' said the single gentleman.

'Know her, sir! why, she was always coming backwards and forwards. They were as kind to her as they were to me. Bless you, sir, she expected they'd come back to her house.'

'Then where the devil is the woman?' said the impatient gentleman, catching up his hat. 'Why isn't she here? Why is that woman always out of the way when she is most wanted?'

In a word, the single gentleman was bursting out of the office, bent upon laying violent hands on Kit's mother, forcing her into a post-chaise, and carrying her off, when this novel kind of abduction was with some difficulty prevented by the joint efforts of Mr. Abel and the notary, who restrained him by dint of their remonstrances, and persuaded him to sound Kit upon the probability of her being able and willing to undertake such a journey on so short a notice.

This occasioned some doubts on the part of Kit, and some violent demonstrations on that of the single gentleman, and a great many soothing speeches on that of the notary and Mr. Abel. The upshot of the business was, that Kit, after weighing the matter in his mind and considering it carefully, promised, on behalf of his mother, that she should be ready within two hours from that time to undertake the expedition, and engaged to produce her in that place, in all respects equipped and prepared for the journey, before the specified period had expired.

Having given this pledge, which was rather a bold one, and not particularly easy of redemption, Kit lost no time in sallying forth, and taking measures for its immediate fulfilment.

CHAPTER XLI

KIT made his way through the crowded streets, dividing the stream of people, dashing across the busy roadways, diving into lanes and alleys, and stopping or turning aside for nothing, until he came in front of the Old Curiosity Shop, when he came to a stand; partly from habit and partly from being out of breath.

It was a gloomy autumn evening, and he thought the old place had never looked so dismal as in its dreary twilight. The windows broken, the rusty sashes rattling in their frames, the deserted house a dull barrier dividing the glaring lights and bustle of the street into two long lines, and standing in the midst, cold, dark, and empty,—presented a cheerless spectacle which mingled harshly with the bright prospects the boy had been building up for its late inmates, and came like a disappointment or misfortune. Kit would have had a good fire roaring up the empty chimneys, lights sparkling and shining through the windows, people moving briskly to and fro, voices in cheerful conversation, something in unison with the new hopes that were astir. He had not expected that the house would wear any different aspect—had known indeed that it could not—but coming upon it in the midst of eager thoughts and expectations, it checked the current in its flow, and darkened it with a mournful shadow.

Kit, however, fortunately for himself, was not learned enough or contemplative enough to be troubled with presages of evil afar off, and, having no mental spectacles to assist his vision in this respect, saw nothing but the dull house, which jarred uncomfortably upon his previous thoughts. So, almost wishing that he had not passed it, though hardly knowing why, he hurried on again, making up by his increased speed for the few moments he had lost.

'Now, if she should be out,' thought Kit, as he approached the poor dwelling of his mother, 'and I not able to find her, this impatient gentleman would be in a pretty taking. And sure enough there's no light, and the door's fast. Now, God forgive me for saying so, but if this is Little Bethel's doing, I wish Little Bethel was—was farther off,' said Kit checking himself, and knocking at the door.

A second knock brought no reply from within the house; but caused a woman over the way to look out and inquire who that was, a wanting Mrs. Nubbles.

'Me,' said Kit. 'She's at—at Little Bethel, I suppose?'—getting out the name of the obnoxious conventicle with some reluctance, and laying a spiteful emphasis upon the words.

The neighbour nodded assent.

'Then pray tell me where it is,' said Kit, 'for I have come on a pressing matter, and must fetch her out, even if she was in the pulpit.'

It was not very easy to procure a direction to the fold in question, as none of the neighbours were of the flock that resorted thither, and few knew anything more of it than the name. At last, a gossip of Mrs. Nubbles's, who had accompanied her to chapel on one or two occasions when a comfortable cup of tea had preceded her devotions, furnished the needful information, which Kit had no sooner obtained than he started off again.

Little Bethel might have been nearer, and might have been in a straighter road, though in that case the reverend gentleman who presided over its congregation would have lost his favourite allusion to the crooked ways by which it was approached, and which enabled him to liken it to Paradise itself, in contradis-

tinction to the parish church and the broad thorough-
fare leading thereunto. Kit found it, at last, after
some trouble, and pausing at the door to take breath
that he might enter with becoming decency, passed
into the chapel.

It was not badly named in one respect, being in
truth a particularly little Bethel—a Bethel of the
smallest dimensions—with a small number of small
pews, and a small pulpit, in which a small gentleman
(by trade a Shoemaker, and by calling a Divine) was
delivering in a by no means small voice, a by no means
small sermon, judging of its dimensions by the condition of his audience, which, if their gross amount
were but small, comprised a still smaller number of
hearers, as the majority were slumbering.

Among these was Kit's mother, who, finding it matter of extreme difficulty to keep her eyes open after
the fatigues of last night, and feeling their inclination to doze strongly backed and seconded by the ar-
guments of the preacher, had yielded to the drowsiness that overpowered her, and fallen asleep; though
not so soundly but that she could, from time to time,
utter a slight and almost inaudible groan as if in recognition of the orator's doctrines. The baby in her
arms was as fast asleep as she; and little Jacob, whose
youth prevented him from recognising in this prolonged spiritual nourishment anything half as interesting as oysters, was alternately very fast asleep and
very wide awake, as his inclination to slumber, or his
terror of being personally alluded to in the discourse,
gained the mastery over him.

'And now I'm here,' thought Kit, gliding into the
nearest empty pew which was opposite his mother's,
and on the other side of the little aisle, 'how am I ever
to get at her, or persuade her to come out? I might
as well be twenty miles off. She'll never wake till it's

all over, and there goes the clock again! If he would but leave off for a minute, or if they 'd only sing—'

But there was little encouragement to believe that either event would happen for a couple of hours to come. The preacher went on telling them what he meant to convince them of before he had done, and it was clear that if he only kept to one-half of his promises and forgot the other, he was good for that time at least.

In his desperation and restlessness Kit cast his eyes about the chapel, and happening to let them fall upon a little seat in front of the clerk's desk, could scarcely believe them when they showed him Quilp!

He rubbed them twice or thrice, but still they insisted that Quilp was there, and there indeed he was sitting with his hands upon his knees, and his hat between them on a little wooden bracket, with the accustomed grin on his dirty face, and his eyes fixed upon the ceiling. He certainly did not glance at Kit or at his mother, and appeared utterly unconscious of their presence; still Kit could not help feeling, directly, that the attention of the sly little fiend was fastened upon them, and upon nothing else.

But, astounded as he was by the apparition of the dwarf among the Little Bethelites, and not free from a misgiving that it was the forerunner of some trouble or annoyance, he was compelled to subdue his wonder and to take active measures for the withdrawal of his parent, as the evening was now creeping on, and the matter grew serious. Therefore, the next time little Jacob woke, Kit set himself to attract his wandering attention, and this not being a very difficult task (one sneeze effected it), he signed to him to rouse his mother.

Ill-luck would have it, however, that, just then, the preacher, in a forcible exposition of one head of his discourse, leaned over upon the pulpit-desk so that very little more of him than his legs remained inside; and, while he made vehement gestures with his right hand, and held on with his left, stared, or seemed to stare, straight into little Jacob's eyes, threatening him by his strained look and attitude—so it appeared to the child—that if he so much as moved a muscle, he, the preacher, would be literally, and not figuratively, 'down upon him' that instant.   In this fearful state of things, distracted by the sudden appearance of Kit, and fascinated by the eyes of the preacher, the miserable Jacob sat bolt upright, wholly incapable of motion, strongly disposed to cry but afraid to do so, and returning his pastor's gaze until his infant eyes seemed starting from their sockets.

'If I must do it openly, I must,' thought Kit. With that he walked softly out of his pew and into his mother's, and as Mr. Swiveller would have observed if he had been present, 'collared' the baby without speaking a word.

'Hush, mother!' whispered Kit.   'Come along with me, I 've got something to tell you.'

'Where am I?' said Mrs. Nubbles.

'In this blessed Little Bethel,' returned her son, peevishly.

'Blessed indeed!' cried Mrs. Nubbles, catching at the word.   'Oh, Christopher, how have I been edified this night!'

'Yes, yes, I know,' said Kit hastily, 'but come along, mother, everybody 's looking at us.   Don't make a noise—bring Jacob—that 's right!'

'Stay, Satan, stay!' cried the preacher, as Kit was moving off.

'The gentleman says you 're to stay, Christopher,' whispered his mother.

'Stay, Satan, stay!' roared the preacher again.

'Tempt not the woman that doth incline her ear to thee, but hearken to the voice of him that calleth. He hath a lamb from the fold!' cried the preacher, raising his voice still higher and pointing to the baby. 'He beareth off a lamb, a precious lamb! He goeth about, like a wolf in the night season, and inveigleth the tender lambs!'

Kit was the best-tempered fellow in the world, but considering this strong language, and being somewhat excited by the circumstances in which he was placed, he faced round to the pulpit with the baby in his arms, and replied aloud.

'No, I don't. He's my brother.'

'He's *my* brother!' cried the preacher.

'He isn't,' said Kit indignantly. 'How can you say such a thing? And don't call me names if you please; what harm have I done? I shouldn't have come to take 'em away, unless I was obliged, you may depend upon that. I wanted to do it very quiet, but you wouldn't let me. Now, you have the goodness to abuse Satan and them, as much as you like, sir, and to let me alone if you please.'

So saying, Kit marched out of the chapel, followed by his mother and little Jacob, and found himself in the open air, with an indistinct recollection of having seen the people wake up and look surprised, and of Quilp having remained, throughout the interruption, in his old attitude, without moving his eyes from the ceiling, or appearing to take the smallest notice of anything that passed.

'Oh Kit!' said his mother, with her handkerchief to her eyes, 'what have you done? I never can go there again—never!'

'I'm glad of it, mother. What was there in the little bit of pleasure you took last night that made it necessary for you to be low-spirited and sorrowful to-night? That's the way you do. If you're happy or merry ever, you come here to say, along with that chap, that you're sorry for it. More shame for you, mother, I was going to say.'

'Hush, dear!' said Mrs. Nubbles; 'you don't mean what you say I know, but you're talking sinfulness.'

'Don't mean it? But I do mean it!' retorted Kit, 'I don't believe, mother, that harmless cheerfulness and good-humour are thought greater sins in Heaven than shirt-collars are, and I do believe that those chaps are just about as right and sensible in putting down the one as in leaving off the other—that's my belief. But I won't say anything more about it, if you'll promise not to cry, that's all; and you take the baby that's a lighter weight, and give me little Jacob; and as we go along (which we must do pretty quick) I'll give you the news I bring, which will surprise you a little, I can tell you. There—that's right. Now you look as if you'd never seen Little Bethel in all your life, as I hope you never will again; and here's the baby; and little Jacob, you get atop of my back and catch hold of me tight round the neck, and whenever a Little Bethel parson calls you a precious lamb or says your brother's one, you tell him it's the truest thing he's said for a twelvemonth, and that if he'd got a little more of the lamb himself, and less of the mint-sauce—not being quite so sharp and sour over it—I should like him all the better. That's what you've got to say to *him,* Jacob.'

Talking on in this way, half in jest and half in earnest, and cheering up his mother, the children, and himself, by the one simple process of determining to be in a good humour, Kit led them briskly forward; and on the road home, he related what had passed at the notary's house, and the purpose with which he had intruded on the solemnities of Little Bethel.

His mother was not a little startled on learning what service was required of her, and presently fell into a confusion of ideas, of which the most prominent were that it was a great honour and dignity to ride in a post-chaise, and that it was a moral impossibility to leave the children behind. But this objection, and a great many others, founded on certain articles of dress being at the wash, and certain other articles having no existence in the wardrobe of Mrs. Nubbles, were overcome by Kit, who opposed to each and every of them, the pleasure of recovering Nell, and the delight it would be to bring her back in triumph.

'There's only ten minutes now, mother'—said Kit when they reached home. 'There's a bandbox. Throw in what you want, and we'll be off directly.'

To tell how Kit then hustled into the box all sorts of things which could, by no remote contingency, be wanted, and how he left out everything likely to be of the smallest use; how a neighbour was persuaded to come and stop with the children, and how the children at first cried dismally, and then laughed heartily on being promised all kinds of impossible and unheard-of toys; how Kit's mother wouldn't leave off kissing them, and how Kit couldn't make up his mind to be vexed with her for doing it; would take more time and room than you and I can spare. So, passing over all such matters, it is sufficient to say that within a few minutes after the two hours had expired, Kit and his mother arrived at the notary's door, where a post-chaise was already waiting.

'With four horses I declare!' said Kit, quite aghast at the preparations. 'Well you *are* going to do it, mother! Here she is, sir. Here's my mother. She's quite ready, sir.'

'That's well,' returned the gentleman. 'Now don't be in a flutter, ma'am; you'll be taken great care of.   Where's the box with the new clothing and necessaries for them?'

'Here it is,' said the notary.   'In with it, Christopher.'

'All right, sir,' replied Kit.   'Quite ready now, sir.'

'Then come along,' said the single gentleman.   And thereupon he gave his arm to Kit's mother, handed her into the carriage as politely as you please, and took his seat beside her.

Up went the steps, bang went the door, round whirled the wheels, and off they rattled, with Kit's mother hanging out at one window waving a damp pocket-handkerchief and screaming out a great many messages to little Jacob and the baby, of which nobody heard a word.

Kit stood in the middle of the road, and looked after them with tears in his eyes—not brought there by the departure he witnessed, but by the return to which he looked forward.   'They went away,' he thought, 'on foot with nobody to speak to them or say a kind work at parting, and they'll come back, drawn by four horses, with this rich gentleman for their friend, and all their troubles over!   She'll forget that she taught me to write—'

Whatever Kit thought about after this, took some time to think of, for he stood gazing up the lines of shining lamps, long after the chaise had disappeared, and did not return into the house until the notary and Mr. Abel, who had themselves lingered outside till the sound of the wheels was no longer distinguishable, had several times wondered what could possibly detain him.

CHAPTER XLII

IT behooves us to leave Kit for a while, thoughtful and expectant, and to follow the fortunes of little Nell; resuming the thread of the narrative at the point where it was left, some chapters back.

In one of those wanderings in the evening time, when, following the two sisters at a humble distance, she felt, in her sympathy with them and her recognition in their trials of something akin to her own loneliness of spirit, a comfort and consolation which made such moments a time of deep delight, though the softened pleasure they yielded was of that kind which lives and dies in tears—in one of those wanderings at the quiet hour of twilight, when sky, and earth, and air, and rippling water, and sound of distant bells, claimed kindred with the emotions of the solitary child, and inspired her with soothing thoughts, but not of a child's world or its easy joys—in one of those rambles which had now become her only pleasure or relief from care, light had faded into darkness and evening deepened into night, and still the young creature lingered in the gloom; feeling a companionship in Nature so serene and still, when noise of tongues and glare of garish lights would have been solitude indeed.

The sisters had gone home, and she was alone. She raised her eyes to the bright stars, looking down so mildly from the wide worlds of air, and, gazing on them, found new stars burst upon her view, and more beyond, and more beyond again, until the whole great expanse sparkled with shining spheres, rising higher and higher in immeasurable space, eternal in their numbers as in their changeless and incorruptible existence. She bent over the calm river, and saw them shining in the same majestic order as when the dove beheld them gleaming through the swollen waters, upon the mountain-tops down far below, and dead mankind, a million fathoms deep.

The child sat silently beneath a tree, hushed in her very breath by the stillness of the night, and all its attendant wonders. The time and place awoke reflection, and she thought with a quiet hope—less hope, perhaps, than resignation—on the past, and present, and what was yet before her. Between the old man and herself there had come a gradual separation, harder to bear than any former sorrow. Every evening, and often in the day-time too, he was absent, alone; and although she well knew where he went, and why—too well from the constant drain upon her scanty purse and from his haggard looks— he evaded all inquiry, maintained a strict reserve, and even shunned her presence.

She sat meditating sorrowfully upon this change, and mingling it, as it were, with everything about her, when the distant church-clock bell struck nine. Rising at the sound, she retraced her steps, and turned thoughtfully towards the town.

She had gained a little wooden bridge, which, thrown across the stream, led into a meadow in her way, when she came suddenly upon a ruddy light, and looking forward more attentively, discerned that it proceeded from what appeared to be an encampment of gipsies, who had made a fire in one corner at no great distance from the path, and were sitting or lying round it. As she was too poor to have any fear of them, she did not alter her course, (which, indeed, she could not have done without going a long way round,) but quickened her pace a little, and kept straight on.

A movement of timid curiosity impelled her, when she approached the spot, to glance towards the fire.

There was a form between it and her, the outline strongly developed against the light, which caused her to stop abruptly. Then, as if she had reasoned with herself and were assured that it could not be, or had satisfied herself that it was not that of the person she had supposed, she went on again.

But at that instant the conversation, whatever it was, which had been carrying on near this fire was resumed, and the tones of the voice that spoke—she could not distinguish words—sounded as familiar to her as her own.

She turned, and looked back. The person had been seated before, but was now in a standing posture, and leaning forward on a stick on which he rested both hands. The attitude was no less familiar to her than the tone of voice had been. It *was* her grandfather.

Her first impulse was to call to him; her next to wonder who his associates could be, and for what purpose they were together. Some vague apprehension succeeded, and, yielding to the strong inclination it awakened, she drew nearer to the place; not advancing across the open field, however, but creeping towards it by the hedge.

In this way she advanced within a few feet of the fire, and standing among a few young trees, could both see and hear, without much danger of being observed.

There were no women or children, as she had seen in other gipsy camps they had passed in their wayfaring, and but one gipsy—a tall athletic man, who stood with his arms folded, leaning against a tree at a little distance off, looking now at the fire, and now, under his black eyelashes, at three other men who were there, with a watchful but half-concealed interest in their conversation. Of these, her grandfather was one; the others she recognised as the first card-players at the

public-house on the eventful night of the storm—
the man whom they had called Isaac List, and his
gruff companion. One of the low, arched gipsy-
tents, common to that people, was pitched hard by,
but it either was, or appeared to be, empty.

'Well, are you going?' said the stout man, looking
up from the ground where he was lying at his ease,
into her grandfather's face. 'You were in a mighty
hurry a minute ago. Go, if you like. You 're your
own master, I hope?'

'Don't vex him,' returned Isaac List, who was
squatting like a frog on the other side of the fire, and
had so screwed himself up that he seemed to be squinting all over; 'he didn't mean any offence.'

'You keep me poor, and plunder me, and make a
sport and jest of me besides,' said the old man, turning from one to the other. 'Ye 'll drive me mad
among ye.'

The utter irresolution and feebleness of the grey-
haired child, contrasted with the keen and cunning
looks of those in whose hands he was, smote upon
the little listener's heart. But she constrained herself to attend to all that passed, and to note each look
and word.

'Confound you, what do you mean?' said the stout
man rising a little, and supporting himself on his
elbow. 'Keep *you* poor! You 'd keep us poor if you
could, wouldn't you? That 's the way with you whin-
ing, puny, pitiful players. When you lose, you 're
martyrs; but I don't find that when you win, you look
upon the other losers in that light. As to plunder!'
cried the fellow, raising his voice—'Damme, what do
you mean by such ungentlemanly language as plunder, eh?'

The speaker laid himself down again at full length,
and gave one or two short, angry kicks, as if in tur-

ther expression of his unbounded indignation. It was quite plain that he acted the bully, and his friend the peacemaker, for some particular purpose; or rather, it would have been to any one but the weak old man; for they exchanged glances quite openly, both with each other and with the gipsy, who grinned his approval of the jest until his white teeth shone again.

The old man stood helplessly among them for a little time, and then said, turning to his assistant—

'You yourself were speaking of plunder just now, you know. Don't be so violent with me. You were, were you not?'

'Not of plundering among present company! Honour among—among gentlemen, sir,' returned the other, who seemed to have been very near giving an awkward termination to the sentence.

'Don't be hard upon him, Jowl,' said Isaac List. 'He 's very sorry for giving offence. There—go on with what you were saying—go on.'

'I 'm a jolly old tender-hearted lamb, I am,' cried Mr. Jowl, 'to be sitting here at my time of life giving advice when I know it won't be taken, and that I shall get nothing but abuse for my pains. But that 's the way I 've gone through life. Experience has never put a chill upon my warm-heartedness.'

'I tell you he 's very sorry, don't I?' remonstrated Isaac List, 'and that he wishes you 'd go on.'

'*Does* he wish it?' said the other.

'Aye,' groaned the old man sitting down, and rocking himself to and fro. 'Go on, go on. It 's in vain to fight with it; I can't do it; go on.'

'I go on then,' said Jowl, 'where I left off, when you got up so quick. If you 're persuaded that it 's time for luck to turn, as it certainly is, and find that you haven't means enough to try it, (and that's where it is, for you know, yourself, that you never have the funds to keep on long enough at a sitting,) help yourself to what seems put in your way on purpose.   Borrow it, I say, and, when you 're able, pay it back again.'

'Certainly,' Isaac List struck in, 'if this good lady as keeps the wax-works has money, and does keep it in a tin box when she goes to bed, and doesn't lock her door for fear of fire, it seems a easy thing; quite a Providence, *I* should call it—but then I 've been religiously brought up.'

'You see, Isaac,' said his friend, growing more eager, and drawing himself closer to the old man, while he signed to the gipsy not to come between them; 'you see, Isaac, strangers are going in and out every hour of the day; nothing would be more likely than for one of these strangers to get under the good lady's bed, or lock himself in the cupboard; suspicion would be very wide, and would fall a long way from the mark, no doubt.   I 'd give him his revenge to the last farthing he brought, whatever the amount was.'

'But could you?' urged Isaac List.   'Is your bank strong enough?'

'Strong enough!' answered the other, with assumed disdain.   'Here, you sir, give me that box out of the straw!'

This was addressed to the gipsy, who crawled into the low tent on all fours, and after some rummaging and rustling returned with a cash-box, which the man who had spoken opened with a key he wore about his person.

'Do you see this?' he said, gathering up the money in his hand and letting it drop back into the box, between his fingers, like water.   'Do you hear it?   Do

you know the sound of gold?   There, put it back—
and don't talk about banks again, Isaac, till you 've
got one of your own.'

Isaac List, with great apparent humility, protested
that he had never doubted the credit of a gentleman
so notorious for his honourable dealing as Mr. Jowl,
and that he had hinted at the production of the box,
not for the satisfaction of his doubts, for he could
have none, but with a view to being regaled with the
sight of so much wealth, which, though it might be
deemed by some but an unsubstantial and visionary
pleasure, was to one in his circumstances a source of
extreme delight, only to be surpassed by its safe de-
pository in his own personal pockets.   Although Mr.
List and Mr. Jowl addressed themselves to each other,
it was remarkable that they both looked narrowly at
the old man, who, with his eyes fixed upon the fire,
sat brooding over it, yet listening eagerly—as it
seemed from a certain involuntary motion of the head,
or twitching of the face from time to time—to all
they said.

'My advice,' said Jowl, lying down again with a
careless air, 'is plain—I have given it, in fact.   I act
as a friend.   Why should I help a man to the means
perhaps of winning all I have, unless I considered
him my friend?   It 's foolish, I dare say, to be so
thoughtful of the welfare of other people, but that 's
my constitution, and I can't help it; so don't blame
me, Isaac List.'

'I blame you!' returned the person addressed; 'not
for the world, Mr. Jowl.   I wish I could afford to be
as liberal as you; and, as you say, he might pay it back
if he won—and if he lost—'

'You 're not to take that into consideration at all,'
said Jowl.   'But suppose he did, (and nothing 's less
likely, from all I know of chances,) why, it 's better

to lose other people's money than one's own, I hope?'

'Ah!' cried Isaac List rapturously, 'the pleasures of winning! The delight of picking up the money—the bright, shining yellow-boys—and sweeping 'em into one's pocket! The deliciousness of having a triumph at last, and thinking that one didn't stop short and turn back, but went half-way to meet it! The— But you 're not going, old gentleman?'

'I 'll do it,' said the old man, who had risen and taken two or three hurried steps away, and now returned as hurriedly. 'I 'll have it, every penny.'

'Why, that 's brave,' cried Isaac, jumping up and slapping him on the shoulder; 'and I respect you for having so much young blood left. Ha, ha, ha! Joe Jowl's half sorry he advised you now. We 've got the laugh against him. Ha, ha, ha!'

'He gives me my revenge, mind,' said the old man, pointing to him eagerly with his shrivelled hand: 'mind—he stakes coin against coin, down to the last one in the box, be there many or few. Remember that!'

'I 'm witness,' returned Isaac. 'I 'll see fair between you.'

'I have passed my word,' said Jowl with feigned reluctance, 'and I 'll keep it. When does this match come off? I wish it was over.—To-night?'

'I must have the money first,' said the old man; 'and that I 'll have to-morrow—'

'Why not to-night?' urged Jowl.

'It 's late now, and I should be flushed and flurried,' said the old man. 'It must be softly done. No, to-morrow night.'

'Then to-morrow be it,' said Jowl. 'A drop of comfort here. Luck to the best man. Fill!'

The gipsy produced three tin cups, and filled them to the brim with brandy. The old man turned aside and muttered to himself before he drank. Her own name struck upon the listener's ear, coupled with some wish so fervent, that he seemed to breathe it in an agony of supplication.

'God be merciful to us!' cried the child within herself, 'and help us in this trying hour! What shall I do to save him?'

The remainder of their conversation was carried on in a lower tone of voice, and was sufficiently concise; relating merely to the execution of the project, and the best precautions for diverting suspicion. The old man then shook hands with his tempters, and withdrew.

They watched his bowed and stooping figure as it retreated slowly, and when he turned his head to look back, which he often did, waved their hands, or shouted some brief encouragement. It was not until they had seen him gradually diminish into a mere speck upon the distant road, that they turned to each other, and ventured to laugh aloud.

'So,' said Jowl, warming his hands at the fire, 'it's done at last. He wanted more persuading than I expected. It's three weeks ago, since we first put this in his head. What 'll he bring, do you think?'

'Whatever he brings, it's halved between us,' returned Isaac List.

The other man nodded. 'We must make quick work of it,' he said, 'and then cut his acquaintance, or we may be suspected. Sharp's the word.'

List and the gipsy acquiesced. When they had all three amused themselves a little with their victim's infatuation, they dismissed the subject as one which had been sufficiently discussed, and began to talk in a jargon which the child did not understand. As their discourse appeared to relate to matters in which they were warmly interested, however, she deemed it the best time for escaping unobserved; and crept away with slow and cautious steps, keeping in the shadow of the hedges, or forcing a path through them or the dry ditches, until she could emerge upon the road at a point beyond their range of vision. Then she fled homeward as quickly as she could, torn and bleeding from the wounds of thorns and briars, but more lacerated in mind, and threw herself upon her bed, distracted.

The first idea that flashed upon her mind was flight, instant flight; dragging him from that place, and rather dying of want upon the roadside, than ever exposing him again, to such terrible temptations. Then, she remembered that the crime was not to be committed until next night, and there was the intermediate time for thinking, and resolving what to do. Then, she was distracted with a horrible fear that he might be committing it at that moment; with a dread of hearing shrieks and cries piercing the silence of the night; with fearful thoughts of what he might be tempted and led on to do, if he were detected in the act, and had but a woman to struggle with. It was impossible to bear such torture. She stole to the room where the money was, opened the door, and looked in. God be praised! He was not there, and she was sleeping soundly.

She went back to her own room, and tried to prepare herself for bed. But who could sleep—sleep! who could lie passively down, distracted by such terrors? They came upon her more and more strongly yet. Half undressed, and with her hair in wild disorder, she flew to the old man's bedside, clasped him by the wrist, and roused him from his sleep.

'What's this?' he cried, starting up in bed, and fixing his eyes upon her spectral face.

'I have had a dreadful dream,' said the child, with

an energy that nothing but such terrors could have inspired. 'A dreadful, horrible dream. I have had it once before. It is a dream of grey-haired men like you, in darkened rooms by night, robbing sleepers of their gold. Up, up!' The old man shook in every joint, and folded his hands like one who prays.

'Not to me,' said the child, 'not to me—to Heaven, to save us from such deeds! This dream is too real. I cannot sleep, I cannot stay here, I cannot leave you alone under the roof where such dreams come. Up! We must fly.'

He looked at her as if she were a spirit—she might have been for all the look of earth she had—and trembled more and more.

'There is no time to lose; I will not lose one minute,' said the child. 'Up! and away with me!'

'To-night?' murmured the old man.

'Yes, to-night,' replied the child. 'To-morrow night will be too late. The dream will have come again. Nothing but flight can save us. Up!'

The old man rose from his bed: his forehead bedewed with the cold sweat of fear: and, bending before the child as if she had been an angel messenger sent to lead him where she would, made ready to follow her. She took him by the hand and led him on. As they passed the door of the room he had proposed to rob, she shuddered and looked up into his face. What a white face was that, and with what a look did he meet hers!

She took him to her own chamber, and, still holding him by the hand as if she feared to lose him for an instant, gathered together the little stock she had, and hung her basket on her arm. The old man took his wallet from her hands and strapped it on his shoulders—his staff, too, she had brought away—and then she led him forth.

Through the straight streets, and narrow crooked outskirts, their trembling feet passed quickly. Up the steep hill too, crowned by the old grey castle, they toiled with rapid steps, and had not once looked behind.

But as they drew nearer the ruined walls, the moon rose in all her gentle glory, and, from their venerable age garlanded with ivy, moss, and waving grass, the child looked back upon the sleeping town, deep in the valley's shade: and on the far-off river with its winding track of light: and on the distant hills; and as she did so, she clasped the hand she held, less firmly, and bursting into tears, fell upon the old man's neck

CHAPTER XLIII

HER momentary weakness past, the child again summoned the resolution which had until now sustained her, and, endeavouring to keep steadily in her view the one idea that they were flying from disgrace and crime, and that her grandfather's preservation must depend solely on her firmness, unaided by one word of advice or any helping hand, urged him onward, and looked back no more.

While he, subdued and abashed, seemed to crouch before her, and to shrink and cower down, as if in the presence of some superior creature, the child herself was sensible of a new feeling within her, which elevated her nature, and inspired her with an energy and confidence she had never known. There was no divided responsibility now; the whole burden of their two lives had fallen upon her, and henceforth she must think and act for both. 'I have saved him,' she thought. 'In all dangers and distresses, I will remember that.'

At any other time, the recollection of having deserted the friend who had shown them so much homely kindness, without a word of justification—the thought that they were guilty, in appearance, of treachery and ingratitude—even the having parted from the two sisters—would have filled her with sorrow and regret. But now, all other considerations were lost in the new uncertainties and anxieties of their wild and wandering life; and the very desperation of their condition roused and stimulated her.

In the pale moonlight, which lent a wanness of its own to the delicate face where thoughtful care already mingled with the winning grace and loveliness of youth, the too bright eye, the spiritual head, the lips that pressed each other with such high resolve and courage of the heart, the slight figure firm in its bearing and yet so very weak, told their silent tale; but told it only to the wind that rustled by, which, taking up its burden, carried, perhaps to some mother's pillow, faint dreams of childhood fading in its bloom, and resting in the sleep that knows no waking.

The night crept on apace, the moon went down, the stars grew pale and dim, and morning, cold as they, slowly approached. Then, from behind a distant hill, the noble sun rose up, driving the mists in phantom shapes before it, and clearing the earth of their ghostly forms till darkness came again. When it had climbed higher into the sky, and there was warmth in its cheerful beams, they laid them down to sleep, upon a bank, hard by some water.

But Nell retained her grasp upon the old man's arm, and long after he was slumbering soundly, watched him with untiring eyes. Fatigue stole over her at last; her grasp relaxed, tightened, relaxed again, and they slept side by side.

A confused sound of voices, mingling with her

dreams, awoke her. A man of very uncouth and rough appearance was standing over them, and two of his companions were looking on, from a long heavy boat which had come close to the bank while they were sleeping. The boat had neither oar nor sail, but was towed by a couple of horses, who, with the rope to which they were harnessed slack and dripping in the water, were resting on the path.

'Holloa!' said the man roughly. 'What's the matter here?'

'We were only asleep, sir,' said Nell. 'We have been walking all night.'

'A pair of queer travellers to be walking all night,' observed the man who had first accosted them. 'One of you is a trifle too old for that sort of work, and the other a trifle too young. Where are you going?'

Nell faltered, and pointed at hazard towards the West, upon which the man inquired if she meant a certain town which he named. Nell, to avoid more questioning, said 'Yes, that was the place.'

'Where have you come from?' was the next question; and this being an easier one to answer, Nell mentioned the name of the village in which their friend the schoolmaster dwelt, as being less likely to be known to the men or to provoke further inquiry.

'I thought somebody had been robbing and ill-using you, might be,' said the man. 'That's all. Good-day.'

Returning his salute and feeling greatly relieved by his departure, Nell looked after him as he mounted one of the horses, and the boat went on. It had not gone very far, when it stopped again, and she saw the men beckoning to her.

'Did you call to me?' said Nell, running up to them.

'You may go with us if you like,' replied one of those in the boat. 'We're going to the same place.'

The child hesitated for a moment. Thinking, as she had thought with great trepidation more than once before, that the men whom she had seen with her grandfather might, perhaps, in their eagerness for the booty, follow them, and, regaining their influence over him, set hers at nought; and that if they went with these men, all traces of them must surely be lost at that spot; determined to accept the offer. The boat came close to the bank again, and before she had had any more time for consideration, she and her grandfather were on board, and gliding smoothly down the canal.

The sun shone pleasantly on the bright water, which was sometimes shaded by trees, and sometimes open to a wide extent of country, intersected by running streams, and rich with wooded hills, cultivated land, and sheltered farms. Now and then, a village with its modest spire, thatched roofs, and gable-ends, would peep out from among the trees; and, more than once, a distant town, with great church-towers looming through its smoke, and high factories or workshops rising above the mass of houses, would come in view, and, by the length of time it lingered in the distance, show them how slowly they travelled. Their way lay, for the most part, through the low grounds, and open plains; and except these distant places, and occasionally some men working in the fields, or lounging on the bridges under which they passed, to see them creep along, nothing encroached on their monotonous and secluded track.

Nell was rather disheartened, when they stopped at a kind of wharf late in the afternoon, to learn from one of the men that they would not reach their place of destination until next day, and that, if she had no provision with her, she had better buy it there. She had but a few pence, having already bargained with them for some bread, but even of these it was

necessary to be very careful, as they were on their way
to an utterly strange place, with no resource whatever.   A small loaf and a morsel of cheese, therefore,
were all she could afford, and with these she took her
place in the boat again, and, after half an hour's delay during which the men were drinking at the public
house, proceeded on the journey.

They brought some beer and spirits into the boat
with them, and what with drinking freely before, and
again now, were soon in a fair way of being quarrel-
some and intoxicated. Avoiding the small cabin,
therefore, which was very dark and filthy, and to
which they often invited both her and her grandfather, Nell sat in the open air with the old man by
her side: listening to their boisterous hosts with a
palpitating heart, and almost wishing herself safe on
shore again though she should have to walk all night.

They were, in truth, very rugged, noisy fellows,
and quite brutal among themselves, though civil
enough to their two passengers. Thus, when a quarrel arose between the man who was steering and his
friend in the cabin, upon the question who had first
suggested the propriety of offering Nell some beer,
and when the quarrel led to a scuffle in which they
beat each other fearfully, to her inexpressible terror,
neither visited his displeasure upon her, but each contented himself with venting it on his adversary, on
whom, in addition to blows, he bestowed a variety of
compliments, which, happily for the child, were conveyed in terms, to her quite unintelligible. The difference was finally adjusted, by the man who had come
out of the cabin knocking the other into it head first,
and taking the helm into his own hands, without evinc-
ing the least discomposure himself, or causing any in
his friend, who, being of a tolerably strong constitution and perfectly inured to such trifles, went to sleep

as he was, with his heels upwards, and in a couple of minutes or so was snoring comfortably.

By this time it was night again, and though the child felt cold, being but poorly clad, her anxious thoughts were far removed from her own suffering or uneasiness, and busily engaged in endeavouring to devise some scheme for their joint subsistence. The same spirit which had supported her on the previous night, upheld and sustained her now. Her grandfather lay sleeping safely at her side, and the crime to which his madness urged him, was not committed. That was her comfort.

How every circumstance of her short, eventful life, came thronging into her mind, as they travelled on! Slight incidents, never thought of or remembered until now; faces, seen once and ever since forgotten; words, scarcely heeded at the time; scenes, of a year ago and those of yesterday, mixing up and linking themselves together; familiar places shaping themselves out in the darkness from things which, when approached, were, of all others, the most remote and most unlike them; sometimes, a strange confusion in her mind relative to the occasion of her being there, and the place to which she was going, and the people she was with; and imagination suggesting remarks and questions which sounded so plainly in her ears, that she would start, and turn, and be almost tempted to reply;—all the fancies and contradictions common in watching and excitement and restless change of place, beset the child.

She happened, while she was thus engaged, to encounter the face of the man on deck, in whom the sentimental stage of drunkenness had now succeeded to the boisterous, and who, taking from his mouth a short pipe, quilted over with string for its longer preservation, requested that she would oblige him with a song.

'You 've got a very pretty voice, a very soft eye, and a very strong memory,' said this gentleman; 'the voice and eye I 've got evidence for, and the memory 's an opinion of my own. And I 'm never wrong. Let me hear a song this minute.'

'I don't think I know one, sir,' returned Nell.

'You know forty-seven songs,' said the man, with a gravity which admitted of no altercation on the subject. 'Forty-seven 's your number. Let me hear one of 'em—the best. Give me a song this minute.'

Not knowing what might be the consequences of irritating her friend, and trembling with the fear of doing so, poor Nell sang him some little ditty which she had learned in happier times, and which was so agreeable to his ear, that on its conclusion he in the same peremptory manner requested to be favoured with another, to which he was so obliging as to roar a chorus to no particular tune, and with no words at all, but which amply made up in its amazing energy for its deficiency in other respects. The noise of this vocal performance awakened the other man, who, staggering upon deck and shaking his late opponent by the hand, swore that singing was his pride and joy and chief delight, and that he desired no better entertainment. With a third call, more imperative than either of the two former, Nell felt obliged to comply, and this time a chorus was maintained not only by the two men together, but also by the third man on horseback, who being by his position debarred from a nearer participation in the revels of the night, roared when his companions roared, and rent the very air. In this way, with little cessation, and singing the same songs again and again, the tired and exhausted child kept them in good-humour all that night; and many a cottager, who was roused from his soundest sleep by the discordant chorus as it floated away upon the wind, hid his head beneath the bed-clothes and trembled at the sounds.

At length the morning dawned. It was no sooner light than it began to rain heavily. As the child could not endure the intolerable vapours of the cabin, they covered her, in return for her exertions, with some pieces of sail-cloth and ends of tarpaulin, which sufficed to keep her tolerably dry and to shelter her grandfather besides. As the day advanced the rain increased. At noon it poured down more hopelessly and heavily than ever, without the faintest promise of abatement.

They had, for some time, been gradually approaching the place for which they were bound. The water had become thicker and dirtier; other barges, coming from it, passed them frequently; the paths of coal-ash and huts of staring brick, marked the vicinity of some great manufacturing town; while scattered streets and houses, and smoke from distant furnaces, indicated that they were already in the outskirts. Now, the clustered roofs, and piles of buildings, trembling with the working of engines, and dimly resounding with their shrieks and throbbings; the tall chimneys vomiting forth a black vapour, which hung in a dense ill-favoured cloud above the house-tops and filled the air with gloom; the clank of hammers beating upon iron, the roar of busy streets and noisy crowds, gradually augmenting until all the various sounds blended into one and none was distinguishable for itself, announced the termination of their journey.

The boat floated into the wharf to which it belonged. The men were occupied directly. The child and her grandfather, after waiting in vain to thank them, or ask them whither they should go, passed through a dirty lane into a crowded street, and stood, amid its din and tumult, and in the pouring rain, as strange, bewildered, and confused, as if they had lived a thousand years before, and were raised from the dead and placed there by a miracle.

CHAPTER XLIV

THE throng of people hurried by, in two opposite streams, with no symptom of cessation or exhaustion; intent upon their own affairs; and undisturbed in their business speculations, by the roar of carts and waggons laden with clashing wares, the slipping of horses' feet upon the wet and greasy pavement, the rattling of the rain on windows and umbrella-tops, the jostling of the more impatient passengers, and all the noise and tumult of a crowded street in the high tide of its occupation: while the two poor strangers, stunned and bewildered by the hurry they beheld but had no part in, looked mournfully on; feeling, amidst the crowd, a solitude which has no parallel but in the thirst of the shipwrecked mariner, who, tossed to and fro upon the billows of a mighty ocean, his red eyes blinded by looking on the water which hems him in on every side, has not one drop to cool his burning tongue.

They withdrew into a low archway for shelter from the rain, and watched the faces of those who passed, to find in one among them a ray of encouragement or hope. Some frowned, some smiled, some muttered to themselves, some made slight gestures, as if anticipating the conversation in which they would shortly be engaged, some wore the cunning look of bargaining and plotting, some were anxious and eager, some slow and dull; in some countenances, were written gain; in others, loss. It was like being in the confidence of all these people to stand quietly there, looking into their faces as they flitted past. In busy places, where each man has an object of his own, and feels assured that every other man has his, his character and purpose are written broadly on his face. In the public walks and lounges of a town, people go to see and to be seen, and there the same expression, with little variety, is repeated a hundred times. The working-day faces come nearer to the truth, and let it out more plainly.

Falling into that kind of abstraction which such a solitude awakens, the child continued to gaze upon the passing crowd with a wondering interest, amounting almost to a temporary forgetfulness of her own condition. But cold, wet, hunger, want of rest, and lack of any place in which to lay her aching head, soon brought her thoughts back to the point whence they had strayed. No one passed who seemed to notice them, or to whom she durst appeal. After some time, they left their place of refuge from the weather, and mingled with the concourse.

Evening came on. They were still wandering up and down, with fewer people about them, but with the same sense of solitude in their own breasts, and the same indifference from all around. The lights in the streets and shops made them feel yet more desolate, for with their help, night and darkness seemed to come on faster. Shivering with the cold and damp, ill in body, and sick to death at heart, the child needed her utmost firmness and resolution even to creep along.

Why had they ever come to this noisy town, when there were peaceful country places, in which, at least, they might have hungered and thirsted, with less suffering than in its squalid strife! They were but an atom, here, in a mountain heap of misery, the very sight of which increased their hopelessness and suffering.

The child had not only to endure the accumulated hardships of their destitute condition, but to bear the reproaches of her grandfather, who began to murmur at having been led away from their late abode, and demand that they should return to it. Being now penniless, and no relief or prospect of relief appearing, they retraced their steps through the deserted streets, and went back to the wharf, hoping to find the boat in which they had come, and to be allowed to sleep on board that night. But here again they were disappointed, for the gate was closed, and some fierce dogs, barking at their approach, obliged them to retreat.

'We must sleep in the open air to-night, dear,' said the child in a weak voice, as they turned away from this last repulse; 'and to-morrow we will beg our way to some quiet part of the country, and try to earn our bread in very humble work.'

'Why did you bring me here?' returned the old man fiercely. 'I cannot bear these close eternal streets. We came from a quiet part. Why did you force me to leave it?'

'Because I must have that dream I told you of, no more,' said the child, with a momentary firmness that lost itself in tears; 'and we must live among poor people, or it will come again. Dear grandfather, you are old and weak, I know; but look at me. I never will complain if you will not, but I have some suffering indeed.'

'Ah! poor, houseless, wandering, motherless child!' cried the old man, clasping his hands and gazing as if for the first time upon her anxious face, her travel-stained dress, and bruised and swollen feet; 'has all my agony of care brought her to this at last! Was

I a happy man once, and have I lost happiness and all I had, for this?'

'If we were in the country now,' said the child, with assumed cheerfulness, as they walked on looking about them for a shelter, 'we should find some good old tree, stretching out his green arms as if he loved us, and nodding and rustling as if he would have us fall asleep, thinking of him while he watched. Please God, we shall be there soon—to-morrow or next day at the farthest—and in the meantime let us think, dear, that it was a good thing we came here; for we are lost in the crowd and hurry of this place, and if any cruel people should pursue us, they could surely never trace us further. There's comfort in that. And here's a deep old doorway—very dark, but quite dry, and warm too, for the wind don't blow in here—What's that?'

Uttering a half-shriek, she recoiled from a black figure which came suddenly out of the dark recess in which they were about to take refuge, and stood still, looking at them.

'Speak again,' it said; 'do I know the voice?'

'No,' replied the child timidly; 'we are strangers, and having no money for a night's lodging, were going to rest here.'

There was a feeble lamp at no great distance; the only one in the place, which was a kind of square yard, but sufficient to show how poor and mean it was. To this, the figure beckoned them; at the same time drawing within its rays, as if to show that it had no desire to conceal itself or take them at an advantage.

The form was that of a man, miserably clad and begrimed with smoke, which, perhaps by its contrast with the natural colour of his skin, made him look paler than he really was. That he was naturally of a very wan and pallid aspect, however, his hollow cheeks, sharp features, and sunken eyes, no less than a certain look of patient endurance, sufficiently testified. His voice was harsh by nature, but not brutal; and though his face, besides possessing the characteristics already mentioned, was overshadowed by a quantity of long dark hair, its expression was neither ferocious nor bad.

'How came you to think of resting there?' he said. 'Or how,' he added, looking more attentively at the child, 'do you come to want a place of rest at this time of night?'

'Our misfortunes,' the grandfather answered, 'are the cause.'

'Do you know,' said the man, looking still more earnestly at Nell, 'how wet she is, and that the damp streets are not a place for her?'

'I know it well, God help me,' he replied. 'What can I do?'

The man looked at Nell again, and gently touched her garments, from which the rain was running off in little streams. 'I can give you warmth,' he said, after a pause; 'nothing else. Such lodging as I have, is in that house,' pointing to the doorway from which he had emerged, 'but she is safer and better there than here. The fire is in a rough place, but you can pass the night beside it safely, if you'll trust yourselves to me. You see that red light yonder?'

They raised their eyes, and saw a lurid glare hanging in the dark sky; the dull reflection of some distant fire.

'It's not far,' said the man. 'Shall I take you there? You were going to sleep upon cold bricks; I can give you a bed of warm ashes—nothing better.'

Without waiting for any further reply than he saw in their looks, he took Nell in his arms, and bade the old man follow.

Carrying her as tenderly, and as easily too, as if she had been an infant, and showing himself both swift and sure of foot, he led the way through what appeared to be the poorest and most wretched quarter of the town; and turning aside to avoid the overflowing kennels or running waterspouts, but holding his course, regardless of such obstructions, and making his way straight through them. They had proceeded thus, in silence, for some quarter of an hour, and had lost sight of the glare to which he had pointed, in the dark and narrow ways by which they had come, when it suddenly burst upon them again, streaming up from the high chimney of a building close before them.

'This is the place,' he said, pausing at a door to put Nell down and take her hand. 'Don't be afraid. There's nobody here will harm you.'

It needed a strong confidence in this assurance to induce them to enter, and what they saw inside did not diminish their apprehension and alarm. In a large and lofty building, supported by pillars of iron, with great black apertures in the upper walls, open to the external air; echoing to the roof with the beating of hammers and roar of furnaces, mingled with the hissing of red-hot metal plunged in water, and a hundred strange unearthly noises never heard elsewhere; in this gloomy place moving like demons among the flame and smoke, dimly and fitfully seen, flushed and tormented by the burning fires, and wielding great weapons, a faulty blow from any one of which must have crushed some workman's skull, a number of men laboured like giants. Others, reposing upon heaps of coals or ashes, with their faces turned to the black vault above, slept or rested from their toil.   Others again, opening the white-hot furnace-doors, cast fuel on the flames, which came rushing and roaring forth to meet it, and licked it up like oil.   Others drew forth, with clashing noise, upon the ground, great sheets of glowing steel, emitting an insupportable heat, and a dull deep light like that which reddens in the eyes of savage beasts.

Through these bewildering sights and deafening sounds, their conductor led them to where, in a dark portion of the building, one furnace burnt by night and day—so, at least, they gathered from the motion of his lips, for as yet they could only see him speak: not hear him.   The man who had been watching this fire, and whose task was ended for the present, gladly withdrew, and left them with their friend, who, spreading Nell's little cloak upon a heap of ashes, and showing her where she could hang her outer-clothes to dry, signed to her and the old man to lie down and sleep.   For himself, he took his station on a rugged mat before the furnace-door, and resting his chin upon his hands, watched the flame as it shone through the iron chinks, and the white ashes as they fell into their bright hot grave below.

The warmth of her bed, hard and humble as it was, combined with the great fatigue she had undergone, soon caused the tumult of the place to fall with a gentler sound upon the child's tired ears, and was not long in lulling her to sleep.   The old man was stretched beside her, and with her hand upon his neck she lay and dreamed.

It was yet night when she awoke, nor did she know how long, or for how short a time, she had slept.   But she found herself protected, both from any cold air that might find its way into the building, and from the scorching heat, by some of the workmen's clothes;

and glancing at their friend saw that he sat in exactly the same attitude, looking with a fixed earnestness of attention towards the fire, and keeping so very still that he did not even seem to breathe. She lay in the state between sleeping and waking, looking so long at his motionless figure that at length she almost feared he had died as he sat there; and softly rising and drawing close to him, ventured to whisper in his ear.

He moved, and glancing from her to the place she had lately occupied, as if to assure himself that it was really the child so near him, looked inquiringly into her face.

'I feared you were ill,' she said. 'The other men are all in motion, and you are so very quiet.'

'They leave me to myself,' he replied. 'They know my humour. They laugh at me, but don't harm me in it. See yonder there—that's *my* friend.'

'The fire?' said the child.

'It has been alive as long as I have,' the man made answer. 'We talk and think together, all night long.'

The child glanced quickly at him in her surprise, but he had turned his eyes in their former direction, and was musing as before.

'It's like a book to me,' he said—'the only book I ever learned to read; and many an old story it tells me. It's music, for I should know its voice among a thousand, and there are other voices in its roar. It has its pictures too. You don't know how many strange faces and different scenes I trace in the red-hot coals. It's my memory, that fire, and shows me all my life.'

The child, bending down to listen to his words, could not help remarking with what brightened eyes he continued to speak and muse.

'Yes,' he said, with a faint smile, 'it was the same

when I was quite a baby, and crawled about it, till I fell asleep. My father watched it then.'

'Had you no mother?' asked the child.

'No, she was dead. Women work hard in these parts. She worked herself to death they told me, and, as they said so then, the fire has gone on saying the same thing ever since. I suppose it was true. I have always believed it.'

'Were you brought up here, then?' said the child.

'Summer and winter,' he replied. 'Secretly at first, but when they found it out, they let him keep me here. So the fire nursed me—the same fire. It has never gone out.'

'You are fond of it?' said the child.

'Of course I am. He died before it. I saw him fall down—just there, where those ashes are burning now—and wondered, I remember, why it didn't help him.'

'Have you been here ever since?' asked the child.

'Ever since I came to watch it; but there was a while between, and a very cold dreary while it was. It burned all the time though, and roared and leaped when I came back, as it used to do in our play-days. You may guess, from looking at me, what kind of child I was, but for all the difference between us I *was* a child, and when I saw you in the street to-night, you put me in mind of myself, as I was after he died, and made me wish to bring you to the fire. I thought of those old times again, when I saw you sleeping by it. You should be sleeping now. Lie down again, poor child, lie down again!'

With that, he led her to her rude couch, and covering her with the clothes with which she had found herself enveloped when she woke, returned to his seat, whence he moved no more unless to feed the furnace, but remained motionless as a statue. The child continued to watch him for a little time, but soon yielded to the drowsiness that came upon her, and, in the dark strange place and on the heap of ashes, slept as peacefully as if the room had been a palace chamber, and the bed, a bed of down.

When she awoke again, broad day was shining through the lofty openings in the walls, and, stealing in slanting rays but midway down, seemed to make the building darker than it had been at night. The clang and tumult were still going on, and the remorseless fires were burning fiercely as before; for few changes of night and day brought rest or quiet there.

Her friend parted his breakfast—a scanty mess of coffee and some coarse bread—with the child and her grandfather, and inquired whither they were going. She told him that they sought some distant country place remote from towns or even other villages, and with a faltering tongue inquired what road they would do best to take.

'I know little of the country,' he said, shaking his head, 'for such as I, pass all our lives before our furnace-doors, and seldom go forth to breathe. But there *are* such places yonder.'

'And far from here?' said Nell.

'Aye surely. How could they be near us, and be green and fresh? The road lies, too, through miles and miles, all lighted up by fires like ours—a strange black road, and one that would frighten you by night.'

'We are here and must go on,' said the child boldly; for she saw that the old man listened with anxious ears to this account.

'Rough people—paths never made for little feet like yours—a dismal blighted way—is there no turning back, my child?'

'There is none,' cried Nell, pressing forward. 'If

you can direct us, do. If not, pray do not seek to turn us from our purpose. Indeed you do not know the danger that we shun, and how right and true we are in flying from it, or you would not try to stop us, I am sure you would not.'

'God forbid, if it is so!' said their uncouth protector, glancing from the eager child to her grandfather, who hung his head and bent his eyes upon the ground. 'I 'll direct you from the door, the best I can. I wish I could do more.'

He showed them, then, by which road they must leave the town, and what course they should hold when they had gained it. He lingered so long on these instructions, that the child, with a fervent blessing, tore herself away, and stayed to hear no more.

But, before they had reached the corner of the lane, the man came running after them, and, pressing her hand, left something in it—two old, battered, smoke-encrusted penny-pieces. Who knows but they shone as brightly in the eyes of angels, as golden gifts that have been chronicled on tombs?

And thus they separated; the child to lead her sacred charge farther from guilt and shame; the labourer to attach a fresh interest to the spot where his guests had slept, and read new histories in his furnace fire.

CHAPTER XLV

In all their journeying, they had never longed so ardently, they had never so pined and wearied, for the freedom of pure air and open country, as now. No, not even on that memorable morning, when, deserting their old home, they abandoned themselves to the mercies of a strange world, and left all the dumb and

senseless things they had known and loved, behind—
not even then, had they so yearned for the fresh soli-
tudes of wood, hillside, and field, as now, when the
noise and dirt and vapour, of the great manufacturing
town reeking with lean misery and hungry wretched-
ness, hemmed them in on every side, and seemed to
shut out hope, and render escape impossible.

'Two days and nights!' thought the child.   'He said
two days and nights we should have to spend among
such scenes as these.   Oh! if we live to reach the country once again, if we get clear of these dreadful places,
though it is only to lie down and die, with what a
grateful heart I shall thank God for so much mercy!'

With thoughts like this, and with some vague design
of travelling to a great distance among streams and
mountains, where only very poor and simple people
lived, and where they might maintain themselves by
very humble helping work in farms, free from such
terrors as that from which they fled,—the child, with
no resource but the poor man's gift, and no encouragement but that which flowed from her own heart, and
its sense of the truth and right of what she did, nerved
herself to this last journey and boldly pursued her
task.

'We shall be very slow to-day, dear,' she said, as
they toiled painfully through the streets; 'my feet are
sore, and I have pains in all my limbs from the wet
of yesterday.   I saw that he looked at us and thought
of that, when he said how long we should be upon the
road.'

'It was a dreary way he told us of,' returned her
grandfather piteously.   'Is there no other road?
Will you not let me go some other way than this?'

'Places lie beyond these,' said the child, firmly,
'where we may live in peace, and be tempted to do no
harm.   We will take the road that promises to have

that end, and we would not turn out of it, if it were a hundred times worse than our fears lead us to expect. We would not, dear, would we?'

'No,' replied the old man, wavering in his voice, no less than in his manner. 'No. Let us go on. I am ready. I am quite ready, Nell.'

The child walked with more difficulty than she had led her companion to expect, for the pains that racked her joints were of no common severity, and every exertion increased them. But they wrung from her no complaint, or look of suffering; and, though the two travellers proceeded very slowly, they did proceed. Clearing the town in course of time, they began to feel that they were fairly on their way.

A long suburb of red-brick houses,—some with patches of garden-ground, where coal-dust and factory smoke darkened the shrinking leaves, and coarse rank flowers, and where the struggling vegetation sickened and sank under the hot breath of kiln and furnace, making them by its presence seem yet more blighting and unwholesome than in the town itself,— a long, flat, straggling suburb passed, they came, by slow degrees, upon a cheerless region, where not a blade of grass was seen to grow, where not a bud put forth its promise in the spring, where nothing green could live but on the surface of the stagnant pools, which here and there lay idly sweltering by the black roadside.

Advancing more and more into the shadow of this mournful place, its dark depressing influence stole upon their spirits, and filled them with a dismal gloom. On every side, and far as the eye could see into the heavy distance, tall chimneys, crowding on each other, and presenting that endless repetition of the same dull, ugly form, which is the horror of oppressive dreams, poured out their plague of smoke, obscured the light, and made foul the melancholy air. Or, mounds of ashes by the wayside, sheltered only by a few rough boards, or rotten pent-house roofs, strange engines spun and writhed like tortured creatures; clanking their iron chains, shrieking in their rapid whirl from time to time as though in torment unendurable, and making the ground tremble with their agonies. Dismantled houses here and there appeared, tottering to the earth, propped up by fragments of others that had fallen down, unroofed, windowless, blackened, desolate, but yet inhabited. Men, women, children, wan in their looks and ragged in attire, tended the engines, fed their tributary fire, begged upon the road, or scowled half-naked from the doorless houses. Then, came more of the wrathful monsters, whose like they almost seemed to be in their wildness and their untamed air, screeching and turning round and round again; and still, before, behind, and to the right and left, was the same interminable perspective of brick towers, never ceasing in their black vomit, blasting all things living or inanimate, shutting out the face of day, and closing in on all these horrors with a dense dark cloud.

But, night-time in this dreadful spot!—night, when the smoke was changed to fire; when every chimney spirted up its flame; and places, that had been dark vaults all day, now shone red-hot, with fingers moving to and fro within their blazing jaws, and calling to one another with hoarse cries—night, when the noise of every strange machine was aggravated by the darkness; when the people near them looked wilder and more savage; when bands of unemployed labourers paraded the roads, or clustered by torch-light round their leaders, who told them, in stern language, of their wrongs, and urged them on to frightful cries and threats; when maddened men, armed with sword and fire-brand, spurning the tears and prayers of women who would restrain them, rushed forth on errands of terror and destruction, to work no ruin half so surely as their own—night, when carts came rumbling by, filled with rude coffins (for contagious disease and death had been busy with the living crops); when orphans cried, and distracted women shrieked and followed in their wake—night, when some called for bread, and some for drink to drown their cares, and some with tears, and some with staggering feet, and some with bloodshot eyes, went brooding home—night, which, unlike the night that Heaven sends on earth, brought with it no peace, nor quiet, nor signs of blessed sleep—who shall tell the terrors of the night to the young wandering child!

And yet she lay down, with nothing between her and the sky; and, with no fear for herself, for she was past it now, put up a prayer for the poor old man. So very weak and spent she felt, so very calm and unresisting, that she had no thought of any wants of her own, but prayed that God would raise up some friend for *him*. She tried to recall the way they had come, and to look in the direction where the fire by which they had slept last night was burning. She had forgotten to ask the name of the poor man, their friend, and when she had remembered him in her prayers, it seemed ungrateful not to turn one look towards the spot where he was watching.

A penny loaf was all they had had that day. It was very little, but even hunger was forgotten in the strange tranquillity that crept over her senses. She lay down, very gently, and, with a quiet smile upon her face, fell into a slumber. It was not like sleep— and yet it must have been, or why those pleasant dreams of the little scholar all night long!

Morning came. Much weaker, diminished powers

even of sight and hearing, and yet the child made no complaint—perhaps would have made none, even if she had not had that inducement to be silent, travelling by her side.   She felt a hopelessness of their ever being extricated together from that forlorn place; a dull conviction that she was very ill, perhaps dying; but no fear or anxiety.

A loathing of food that she was not conscious of until they expended their last penny in the purchase of another loaf, prevented her partaking even of this poor repast.   Her grandfather ate greedily, which she was glad to see.

Their way lay through the same scenes as yesterday, with no variety or improvement.   There was the same thick air, difficult to breathe; the same blighted ground, the same hopeless prospect, the same misery and distress.   Objects appeared more dim, the noise less, the path more rugged and uneven, for sometimes she stumbled, and became roused, as it were, in the effort to prevent herself from falling.   Poor child! the cause was in her tottering feet.

Towards the afternoon, her grandfather complained bitterly of hunger.   She approached one of the wretched hovels by the wayside, and knocked with her hand upon the door.

'What would you have here?' said a gaunt man, opening it.

'Charity.   A morsel of bread.'

'Do you see that?' returned the man hoarsely, pointing to a kind of bundle on the ground.   'That's a dead child.   I and five hundred other men were thrown out of work, three months ago.   That is my third dead child, and last.   Do you think *I* have charity to bestow, or a morsel of bread to spare?'

The child recoiled from the door, and it closed upon her.   Impelled by strong necessity, she knocked at another: a neighbouring one, which, yielding to the slight pressure of her hand, flew open.

It seemed that a couple of poor families lived in this hovel, for two women, each among children of her own, occupied different portions of the room. In the centre, stood a grave gentleman in black who appeared to have just entered, and who held by the arm a boy.

'Here, woman,' he said, 'here's your deaf and dumb son. You may thank me for restoring him to you. He was brought before me, this morning, charged with theft; and with any other boy it would have gone hard, I assure you. But as I had compassion on his infirmities, and thought he might have learnt no better, I have managed to bring him back to you. Take more care of him for the future.'

'And won't you give me back *my* son?' said the other woman, hastily rising and confronting him. 'Won't you give me back *my* son, sir, who was transported for the same offence?'

'Was *he* deaf and dumb, woman?' asked the gentleman, sternly.

'Was he not, sir?'

'You know he was not.'

'He was,' cried the woman. 'He was deaf, dumb, and blind, to all that was good and right, from his cradle. Her boy may have learnt no better! where did mine learn better? where could he? who was there to teach him better, or where was it to be learnt?'

'Peace, woman,' said the gentleman, 'your boy was in possession of all his senses.'

'He was,' cried the mother; 'and he was the more easy to be led astray because he had them. If you save this boy because he may not know right from wrong, why did you not save mine who was never taught the difference? You gentlemen have as good a right to punish her boy, that God has kept in ignorance of sound and speech, as you have to punish mine, that you kept in ignorance yourselves. How many of the girls and boys—ah, men and women too—that are brought before you and you don't pity, are deaf and dumb in their minds, and go wrong in that state, and are punished in that state, body and soul, while you gentlemen are quarrelling among yourselves whether they ought to learn this or that?—Be a just man, sir, and give me back my son.'

'You are desperate,' said the gentleman, taking out his snuff-box, 'and I am sorry for you.'

'I *am* desperate,' returned the woman, 'and you have made me so. Give me back my son, to work for these helpless children. Be a just man, sir, and, as you have had mercy upon this boy, give me back my son!'

The child had seen and heard enough to know that this was not a place at which to ask for alms. She led the old man softly from the door, and they pursued their journey.

With less and less of hope or strength, as they went on, but with an undiminished resolution not to betray by any word or sigh her sinking state, so long as she had energy to move, the child, throughout the remainder of that hard day, compelled herself to proceed: not even stopping to rest as frequently as usual, to compensate in some measure for the tardy pace at which she was obliged to walk. Evening was drawing on, but had not closed in, when—still travelling among the same dismal objects—they came to a busy town.

Faint and spiritless as they were, its streets were insupportable. After humbly asking for relief at some few doors, and being repulsed, they agreed to make their way out of it as speedily as they could, and try if the inmates of any lone house beyond, would have more pity on their exhausted state.

They were dragging themselves along through the last street, and the child felt that the time was close at hand when her enfeebled powers would bear no more. There appeared before them, at this juncture, going in the same direction as themselves, a traveller on foot, who, with a portmanteau strapped to his back, leaned upon a stout stick as he walked, and read from a book which he held in his other hand.

It was not an easy matter to come up with him, and beseech his aid, for he walked fast, and was a little distance in advance. At length, he stopped, to look more attentively at some passage in his book. Animated with a ray of hope, the child shot on before her grandfather, and, going close to the stranger without rousing him by the sound of her footsteps, began, in a few faint words, to implore his help.

He turned his head. The child clapped her hands together, uttered a wild shriek, and fell senseless at his feet.

CHAPTER XLVI

IT was the poor schoolmaster. No other than the poor schoolmaster. Scarcely less moved and surprised by the sight of the child than she had been on recognising him, he stood, for a moment, silent and confounded by this unexpected apparition, without even the presence of mind to raise her from the ground.

But, quickly recovering his self-possession, he threw down his stick and book, and dropping on one knee beside her, endeavoured, by such simple means as occurred to him, to restore her to herself; while her grandfather, standing idly by, wrung his hands, and implored her with many endearing expressions to speak to him, were it only a word.

'She is quite exhausted,' said the schoolmaster, glancing upward into his face. 'You have taxed her powers too far, friend.'

'She is perishing of want,' rejoined the old man. 'I never thought how weak and ill she was, till now.'

Casting a look upon him, half-reproachful and half-compassionate, the schoolmaster took the child in his arms, and, bidding the old man gather up her little basket and follow him directly, bore her away at his utmost speed.

There was a small inn within sight, to which, it would seem, he had been directing his steps when so unexpectedly overtaken. Towards this place he hurried with his unconscious burden, and rushing into the kitchen, and calling upon the company there assembled to make way for God's sake, deposited it on a chair before the fire.

The company, who rose in confusion on the schoolmaster's entrance, did as people usually do under such circumstances. Everybody called for his or her favourite remedy, which nobody brought; each cried for more air, at the same time carefully excluding what air there was, by closing round the object of sympathy; and all wondered why somebody else didn't do what it never appeared to occur to them might be done by themselves.

The landlady, however, who possessed more readiness and activity than any of them, and who had withal a quicker perception of the merits of the case, soon came running in, with a little hot brandy-and-water, followed by her servant-girl, carrying vinegar, hartshorn, smelling-salts, and such other restoratives;

which, being duly administered, recovered the child so far as to enable her to thank them in a faint voice, and to extend her hand to the poor schoolmaster, who stood with an anxious face, hard by. Without suffering her to speak another word, or so much as to stir a finger any more, the women straightway carried her off to bed; and, having covered her up warm, bathed her cold feet, and wrapped them in flannel, they despatched a messenger for the doctor.

The doctor, who was a red-nosed gentleman with a great bunch of seals dangling below a waistcoat of ribbed black satin, arrived with all speed, and taking his seat by the bedside of poor Nell, drew out his watch, and felt her pulse. Then he looked at her tongue, then he felt her pulse again, and while he did so, he eyed the half-emptied wine-glass as if in profound abstraction.

'I should give her—' said the doctor at length, 'a tea-spoonful, every now and then, of hot brandy-and-water.'

'Why, that's exactly what we've done, sir!' said the delighted landlady.

'I should also,' observed the doctor, who had passed the foot-bath on the stairs, 'I should also,' said the doctor, in the voice of an oracle, 'put her feet in hot water, and wrap them up in flannel. I should likewise,' said the doctor with increased solemnity, 'give her something light for supper—the wing of a roasted fowl now—'

'Why, goodness gracious me, sir, it's cooking at the kitchen fire this instant!' cried the landlady. And so indeed it was, for the schoolmaster had ordered it to be put down, and it was getting on so well that the doctor might have smelt it if he had tried; perhaps he did.

'You may then,' said the doctor, rising gravely, 'give her a glass of hot mulled port wine, if she likes wine—'

'And a toast, sir?' suggested the landlady.

'Ay,' said the doctor, in the tone of a man who makes a dignified concession. 'And a toast—of bread. But be very particular to make it of bread, if you please, ma'am.'

With which parting injunction, slowly and portentously delivered, the doctor departed, leaving the whole house in admiration of that wisdom which tallied so closely with their own. Everybody said he was a very shrewd doctor indeed, and knew perfectly what people's constitutions were; which there appears some reason to suppose he did.

While her supper was preparing, the child fell into a refreshing sleep, from which they were obliged to rouse her when it was ready. As she evinced extraordinary uneasiness on learning that her grandfather was below-stairs, and as she was greatly troubled at the thought of their being apart, he took his supper with her. Finding her still very restless on this head, they made him up a bed in an inner room, to which he presently retired. The key of this chamber happened by good fortune to be on that side of the door which was in Nell's room; she turned it on him when the landlady had withdrawn, and crept to bed again with a thankful heart.

The schoolmaster stood for a long time smoking his pipe by the kitchen fire, which was now deserted, thinking, with a very happy face, on the fortunate chance which had brought him so opportunely to the child's assistance, and parrying, as well as in his simple way he could, the inquisitive cross-examination of the landlady, who had a great curiosity to be made acquainted with every particular of Nell's life and history. The poor schoolmaster was so open-hearted, and so little versed in the most ordinary cunning or deceit, that she could not have failed to succeed in the first five minutes, but that he happened to be unacquainted with what she wished to know; and so he told her. The landlady, by no means satisfied with this assurance, which she considered an ingenious evasion of the question, rejoined that he had his reasons of course. Heaven forbid that she should wish to pry into the affairs of her customers, which indeed were no business of hers, who had so many of her own. She had merely asked a civil question, and to be sure she knew it would meet with a civil answer. She was quite satisfied—quite. She had rather perhaps that he would have said at once that he didn't choose to be communicative, because that would have been plain and intelligible. However, she had no right to be offended of course. He was the best judge, and had a perfect right to say what he pleased; nobody could dispute that for a moment. Oh dear, no!

'I assure you, my good lady,' said the mild schoolmaster, 'that I have told you the plain truth. As I hope to be saved, I have told you the truth.'

'Why then, I do believe you are in earnest,' rejoined the landlady, with ready good-humour, 'and I'm very sorry I have teazed you. But curiosity you know is the curse of our sex, and that's the fact.'

The landlord scratched his head, as if he thought the curse sometimes involved the other sex likewise; but he was prevented from making any remark to that effect, if he had it in contemplation to do so, by the schoolmaster's rejoinder.

'You should question me for half a dozen hours at a sitting, and welcome, and I would answer you patiently for the kindness of heart you have shown to-night, if I could,' he said. 'As it is, please to take care of her in the morning, and let me know early how she is; and to understand that I am paymaster for the three.'

So, parting with them on most friendly terms (not the less cordial perhaps for this last direction), the schoolmaster went to his bed, and the host and hostess to theirs.

The report in the morning was, that the child was better, but was extremely weak, and would at least require a day's rest, and careful nursing, before she could proceed upon her journey. The schoolmaster received this communication with perfect cheerfulness, observing that he had a day to spare—two days for that matter—and could very well afford to wait. As the patient was to sit up in the evening, he appointed to visit her in her room at a certain hour, and rambling out with his book, did not return until the hour arrived.

Nell could not help weeping when they were left alone; whereat, and at sight of her pale face and wasted figure, the simple schoolmaster shed a few tears himself, at the same time showing in very energetic language how foolish it was to do so, and how very easily it could be avoided, if one tried.

'It makes me unhappy even in the midst of all this kindness,' said the child, 'to think that we should be a burden upon you. How can I ever thank you? If I had not met you so far from home, I must have died, and he would have been left alone.'

'We'll not talk about dying,' said the schoolmaster; 'and as to burdens, I have made my fortune since you slept at my cottage.'

'Indeed!' cried the child joyfully.

'Oh yes,' returned her friend. 'I have been appointed clerk and schoolmaster to a village a long way from here—and a long way from the old one as you may suppose—at five-and-thirty pounds a year. Five-and-thirty pounds!'

'I am very glad,' said the child—'so very, very glad.'

'I am on my way there now,' resumed the schoolmaster. 'They allowed me the stage-coach hire—outside stage-coach hire all the way. Bless you, they grudge me nothing. But as the time at which I am expected there, left me ample leisure, I determined to walk instead. How glad I am, to think I did so!'

'How glad should we be!'

'Yes, yes,' said the schoolmaster, moving restlessly in his chair, 'certainly, that's very true. But you— where are you going, where are you coming from, what have you been doing since you left me, what had you been doing before? Now tell me—do tell me. I know very little of the world, and perhaps you are better fitted to advise me in its affairs than I am qualified to give advice to you; but I am very sincere, and I have a reason (you have not forgotten it) for loving you. I have felt since that time as if my love for him who died, had been transferred to you who stood beside his bed. If this,' he added, looking upwards, 'is the beautiful creation that springs from ashes, let its peace prosper with me, as I deal tenderly and compassionately by this young child!'

The plain, frank kindness of the honest schoolmaster, the affectionate earnestness of his speech and manner, the truth which was stamped upon his every word and look, gave the child a confidence in him, which the utmost arts of treachery and dissimulation could never have awakened in her breast. She told him all—that they had no friend or relative—that she had fled with the old man, to save him from a madhouse and all the miseries he dreaded—that she was flying now, to save him from himself—and that she sought an asylum in some remote and primitive place, where the temptation before which he fell would never enter, and her late sorrows and distresses could have no place.

The schoolmaster heard her with astonishment. 'This child!'—he thought—'Has this child heroically persevered under all doubts and dangers, struggled with poverty and suffering, upheld and sustained by strong affection and the consciousness of rectitude alone? And yet the world is full of such heroism. Have I yet to learn that the hardest and best-borne trials are those which are never chronicled in any earthly record, and are suffered every day? And should I be surprised to hear the story of this child?'

What more he thought or said, matters not. It was concluded that Nell and her grandfather should accompany him to the village whither he was bound, and that he should endeavour to find them some humble occupation by which they could subsist. 'We shall be sure to succeed,' said the schoolmaster, heartily. 'The cause is too good a one to fail.'

They arranged to proceed upon their journey next evening, as a stage-waggon, which travelled for some distance on the same road as they must take, would stop at the inn to change horses, and the driver for a small gratuity would give Nell a place inside. A bargain was soon struck when the waggon came; and in due time it rolled away; with the child comfortably bestowed among the softer packages, her grandfather and the schoolmaster walking on beside the driver, and the landlady and all the good folks of the inn screaming out their good wishes and farewells.

What a soothing, luxurious, drowsy way of travelling, to lie inside that slowly-moving mountain, listening to the tinkling of the horses' bells, the occasional smacking of the carter's whip, the smooth rolling of the great broad wheels, the rattle of the harness, the cheery good-nights of passing travellers jogging past on little short-stepped horses—all made pleasantly indistinct by the thick awning, which seemed made for lazy listening under, till one fell asleep! The very going to sleep, still with an indistinct idea, as the head jogged to and fro upon the pillow, of moving onward with no trouble or fatigue, and hearing all these sounds like dreamy music, lulling to the senses—and the slow waking up, and finding one's-self staring out through the breezy curtain half-opened in the front, far up into the cold bright sky with its countless stars, and downward at the driver's lantern dancing on like its namesake Jack of the swamps and marshes, and sideways at the dark grim trees, and forward at the long bare road rising up, up, up, until it stopped abruptly at a sharp high ridge as if there were no more road, and all beyond was sky—and the stopping at the inn to bait, and being helped out, and going into a room with fire and candles, and winking very much, and being agreeably reminded that the night was cold, and anxious for very comfort's sake to think it colder than it was!—What a delicious journey was that journey in the waggon.

Then the going on again—so fresh at first, and shortly afterwards so sleepy. The waking from a sound nap as the mail came dashing past like a highway comet, with gleaming lamps and rattling hoofs, and visions of a guard behind, standing up to keep his feet warm, and of a gentleman in a fur cap opening his eyes and looking wild and stupefied—the stopping at the turnpike where the man was gone to bed, and knocking at the door until he answered with a smothered shout from under the bed-clothes in the little room above, where the faint light was burning, and presently came down, night-capped and shivering, to throw the gate wide open, and wish all waggons off the road except by day. The cold sharp interval between night and morning—the distant streak of light widening and spreading, and turning from grey to white, and from white to yellow, and from yellow to burning red—the presence of day, with all its cheerfulness and life—men and horses at the plough—birds in the trees and hedges, and boys in solitary fields, frightening them away with rattles. The coming to a town—people busy in the markets; light carts and chaises round the tavern yard; tradesmen standing at their doors; men running horses up and down the street for sale; pigs plunging and grunting in the dirty distance, getting off with long strings at their legs, running into clean chemists' shops and being dislodged with brooms by 'prentices; the night coach changing horses—the passengers cheerless, cold, ugly, and discontented, with three months' growth of hair in one night—the coachman fresh as from a bandbox, and exquisitely beautiful by contrast:—so much bustle, so many things in motion, such a variety of incidents—when was there a journey with so many delights as that journey in the waggon?

Sometimes walking for a mile or two while her grandfather rode inside, and sometimes even prevailing upon the schoolmaster to take her place and lie down to rest, Nell travelled on very happily until they came to a large town, where the waggon stopped, and where they spent a night. They passed a large church; and in the streets were a number of old houses, built of a kind of earth or plaster, crossed and re-crossed in a great many directions with black beams, which gave them a remarkable and very ancient look. The doors, too, were arched and low, some with oaken portals and quaint benches, where the former inhabitants had sat on summer evenings. The windows were latticed in little diamond panes, that seemed to wink and blink upon the passengers as if they were dim of sight. They had long since got clear of the smoke and furnaces, except in one or two solitary instances, where a factory planted among fields withered the space about it, like a burning mountain. When they had passed through this town, they entered again upon the country, and began to draw near their place of destination.

It was not so near, however, but that they spent another night upon the road; not that their doing so was quite an act of necessity, but that the schoolmaster, when they approached within a few miles of his village, had a fidgety sense of his dignity as the new clerk, and was unwilling to make his entry in dusty shoes, and travel-disordered dress. It was a fine, clear autumn morning, when they came upon the scene of his promotion, and stopped to contemplate its beauties.

'See—here's the church!' cried the delighted schoolmaster in a low voice; 'and that old building close beside it, is the school-house, I'll be sworn. Five-and-thirty pounds a year in this beautiful place!'

They admired everything—the old grey porch, the mullioned windows, the venerable gravestones dotting the green churchyard, the ancient tower, the very weathercock; the brown thatched roofs of cottage, barn, and homestead, peeping from among the trees; the stream that rippled by the distant water-mill; the blue Welsh mountains far away. It was for such a spot the child had wearied in the dense, dark, miserable haunts of labour. Upon her bed of ashes, and amidst the squalid horrors through which they had forced their way, visions of such scenes—beautiful indeed, but not more beautiful than this sweet reality—

had been always present to her mind. They had
seemed to melt into a dim and airy distance, as the
prospect of ever beholding them again grew fainter;
but, as they receded, she had loved and panted for
them more.

'I must leave you somewhere for a few minutes,'
said the schoolmaster, at length breaking the silence
into which they had fallen in their gladness. 'I have
a letter to present, and inquiries to make, you know.
Where shall I take you? To the little inn yonder?'

'Let us wait here,' rejoined Nell. 'The gate is
open. We will sit in the church porch till you come
back.'

'A good place too,' said the schoolmaster, leading
the way towards it, disencumbering himself of his
portmanteau, and placing it on the stone seat. 'Be
sure that I come back with good news, and am not
long gone!'

So, the happy schoolmaster put on a brand-new pair
of gloves which he had carried in a little parcel in his
pocket all the way, and hurried off, full of ardour and
excitement.

The child watched him from the porch until the intervening foliage hid him from her view, and then
stepped softly out into the old churchyard—so solemn
and quiet that every rustle of her dress upon the fallen
leaves, which strewed the path and made her footsteps noiseless, seemed an invasion of its silence. It
was a very aged, ghostly place; the church had been
built many hundreds of years ago, and had once had
a convent or monastery attached; for arches in ruins,
remains of oriel windows, and fragments of blackened
walls, were yet standing; while other portions of the
old building, which had crumbled away and fallen
down, were mingled with the churchyard earth and
over-grown with grass, as if they too claimed a bury-

ing-place and sought to mix their ashes with the dust of men. Hard by these gravestones of dead years, and forming a part of the ruin which some pains had been taken to render habitable in modern times, were two small dwellings with sunken windows and oaken doors, fast hastening to decay, empty and desolate.

Upon these tenements, the attention of the child became exclusively riveted. She knew not why. The church, the ruin, the antiquated graves, had equal claims at least upon a stranger's thoughts, but from the moment when her eyes first rested on these two dwellings, she could turn to nothing else. Even when she had made the circuit of the enclosure, and, returning to the porch, sat pensively waiting for their friend, she took her station where she could still look upon them, and felt as if fascinated towards that spot.

CHAPTER XLVII

KIT's mother and the single gentleman—upon whose track it is expedient to follow with hurried steps, lest this history should be chargeable with inconstancy, and the offence of leaving its characters in situations of uncertainty and doubt—Kit's mother and the single gentleman, speeding onward in the post-chaise-and-four whose departure from the notary's door we have already witnessed, soon left the town behind them, and struck fire from the flints of the broad highway.

The good woman, being not a little embarrassed by the novelty of her situation, and certain material apprehensions that perhaps by this time little Jacob. or the baby, or both, had fallen into the fire, or tumbled downstairs, or had been squeezed behind doors, or had scalded their windpipes in endeavouring to allay their thirst at the spouts of tea-kettles, preserved an uneasy silence; and meeting from the window the eyes of turnpike-men, omnibus-drivers, and others, felt in the new dignity of her position like a mourner at a funeral, who, not being greatly afflicted by the loss of the departed, recognises his everyday acquaintance from the window of the mourning coach, but is constrained to preserve a decent solemnity, and the appearance of being indifferent to all external objects.

To have been indifferent to the companionship of the single gentleman would have been tantamount to being gifted with nerves of steel.   Never did chaise inclose, or horses draw, such a restless gentleman as he.   He never sat in the same position for two minutes together, but was perpetually tossing his arms and legs about, pulling up the sashes and letting them violently down, or thrusting his head out of one window to draw it in again and thrust it out of another. He carried in his pocket, too, a fire-box of mysterious and unknown construction; and as sure as ever Kit's mother closed her eyes, so surely—whisk, rattle, fizz —there was the single gentleman consulting his watch by a flame of fire, and letting the sparks fall down among the straw as if there were no such thing as a possibility of himself and Kit's mother being roasted alive before the boys could stop their horses. Whenever they halted to change, there he was—out of the carriage without letting down the steps, bursting about the inn-yard like a lighted cracker, pulling out his watch by lamplight and forgetting to look at it before he put it up again, and in short committing so many extravagances that Kit's mother was quite afraid of him.   Then, when the horses were to, in he came like a Harlequin, and before they had gone a mile, out came the watch and the fire-box together, and

Kit's mother was wide-awake again, with no hope of a wink of sleep for that stage.

'Are you comfortable?' the single gentleman would say after one of these exploits, turning sharply round.

'Quite, sir, thank you.'

'Are you sure?   An't you cold?'

'It is a little chilly, sir,' Kit's mother would reply.

'I knew it!' cried the single gentleman, letting down one of the front glasses. 'She wants some brandy-and-water!   Of course she does.   How could I forget it?   Hallo!   Stop at the next inn, and call out for a glass of hot brandy-and-water.'

It was in vain for Kit's mother to protest that she stood in need of nothing of the kind.   The single gentleman was inexorable; and whenever he had exhausted all other modes and fashions of restlessness, it invariably occurred to him that Kit's mother wanted brandy-and-water.

In this way they travelled on until near midnight, when they stopped to supper, for which meal the single gentleman ordered everything eatable that the house contained; and because Kit's mother didn't eat everything at once, and eat it all, he took it into his head that she must be ill.

'You 're faint,' said the single gentleman, who did nothing himself but walk about the room.   'I see what 's the matter with you, ma'am.   You 're faint.'

'Thank you, sir, I 'm not indeed.'

'I know you are.   I 'm sure of it.   I drag this poor woman from the bosom of her family at a minute's notice, and she goes on getting fainter and fainter before my eyes.   I 'm a pretty fellow!   How many children have you got, ma'am?'

'Two, sir, besides Kit.'

'Boys, ma'am?'

'Yes, sir.'

'Are they christened?'

'Only half baptized as yet, sir.'

'I 'm godfather to both of 'em. Remember that, if you please, ma'am. You had better have some mulled wine.'

'I couldn't touch a drop indeed, sir.'

'You must,' said the single gentleman. 'I see you want it. I ought to have thought of it before.'

Immediately flying to the bell, and calling for mulled wine as impetuously as if it had been wanted for instant use in the recovery of some person apparently drowned, the single gentleman made Kit's mother swallow a bumper of it at such a high temperature that the tears ran down her face, and then hustled her off to the chaise again, where—not impossibly from the effects of this agreeable sedative—she soon became insensible to his restlessness, and fell fast asleep. Nor were the happy effects of this prescription of a transitory nature, as, notwithstanding that the distance was greater, and the journey longer, than the single gentleman had anticipated, she did not awake until it was broad day, and they were clattering over the pavement of a town.

'This is the place!' cried her companion, letting down all the glasses. 'Drive to the wax-work!'

The boy on the wheeler touched his hat, and setting spurs to his horse, to the end that they might go in brilliantly, all four broke into a smart canter, and dashed through the streets with a noise that brought the good folks wondering to their doors and windows, and drowned the sober voices of the town-clocks as they chimed out half-past eight. They drove up to a door round which a crowd of persons were collected, and there stopped.

'What 's this?' said the single gentleman thrusting out his head. 'Is anything the matter here?'

'A wedding, sir, a wedding!' cried several voices. 'Hurrah!'

The single gentleman, rather bewildered by finding himself the centre of this noisy throng, alighted with the assistance of one of the postilions, and handed out Kit's mother, at the sight of whom the populace cried out, 'Here 's another wedding!' and roared and leaped for joy.

'The world has gone mad, I think,' said the single gentleman, pressing through the concourse with his supposed bride. 'Stand back here, will you, and let me knock.'

Anything that makes a noise is satisfactory to a crowd. A score of dirty hands were raised directly to knock for him, and seldom has a knocker of equal powers been made to produce more deafening sounds than this particular engine on the occasion in question. Having rendered these voluntary services, the throng modestly retired a little, preferring that the single gentleman should bear their consequences alone.

'Now, sir, what do you want?' said a man with a large white bow at his button-hole, opening the door, and confronting him with a very stoical aspect.

'Who has been married here, my friend?' said the single gentleman.

'I have.'

'You! and to whom, in the devil's name?'

'What right have you to ask?' returned the bridegroom, eyeing him from top to toe.

'What right!' cried the single gentleman, drawing the arm of Kit's mother more tightly through his own, for that good woman evidently had it in contemplation to run away. 'A right you little dream of. Mind, good people, if this fellow has been marrying a minor—tut, tut, that can't be. Where is the child you have here, my good fellow? You call her Nell. Where is she?'

As he propounded this question, which Kit's mother echoed, somebody in a room near at hand, uttered a great shriek, and a stout lady in a white dress came running to the door, and supported herself upon the bridegroom's arm.

'Where is she?' cried this lady. 'What news have you brought me? What has become of her?'

The single gentleman started back, and gazed upon the face of the late Mrs. Jarley (that morning wedded to the philosophic George, to the eternal wrath and despair of Mr. Slum the poet), with looks of conflicting apprehension, disappointment, and incredulity. At length he stammered out—

'I ask *you* where she is? What do you mean?'

'Oh, sir!' cried the bride. 'If you have come here to do her any good, why weren't you here a week ago?'

'She is not—not dead?' said the person to whom she addressed herself, turning very pale.

'No, not so bad as that.'

'I thank God!' cried the single gentleman feebly. 'Let me come in.'

They drew back to admit him, and when he had entered, closed the door.

'You see in me, good people,' he said, turning to the newly-married couple, 'one to whom life itself is not dearer than the two persons whom I seek. They would not know me. My features are strange to them, but if they or either of them are here, take this good woman with you, and let them see her first, for her they both know. If you deny them from any mistaken regard or fear for them, judge of my intentions by their recognition of this person as their old humble friend.'

'I always said it!' cried the bride.   'I knew she was not a common child! Alas, sir! we have no power to help you, for all that we could do, has been tried in vain.'

With that, they related to him, without disguise or concealment, all that they knew of Nell and her grandfather, from their first meeting with them, down to the time of their sudden disappearance; adding (which was quite true) that they had made every possible effort to trace them, but without success; having been at first in great alarm for their safety, as well as on account of the suspicions to which they themselves might one day be exposed in consequence of their abrupt departure.   They dwelt upon the old man's imbecility of mind, upon the uneasiness the child had always testified when he was absent, upon the company he had been supposed to keep, and upon the increased depression which had gradually crept over her and changed her both in health and spirits.   Whether she had missed the old man in the night, and, knowing or conjecturing whither he had bent his steps, had gone in pursuit, or whether they had left the house together, they had no means of determining.   Certain they considered it, that there was but slender prospect left of hearing of them again, and that whether their flight originated with the old man, or with the child, there was now no hope of their return.

To all this, the single gentleman listened with the air of a man quite borne down by grief and disappointment.   He shed tears when they spoke of the grandfather, and appeared in deep affliction.

Not to protract this portion of our narrative, and to make short work of a long story, let it be briefly written that before the interview came to a close, the single gentleman deemed he had sufficient evidence of having been told the truth, and that he endeavoured to force upon the bride and bridegroom an acknowledgment of their kindness to the unfriended child, which, however, they steadily declined accepting. In the end, the happy couple jolted away in the caravan to spend their honeymoon in a country excursion; and the single gentleman and Kit's mother stood ruefully before their carriage-door.

'Where shall we drive you, sir?' said the post-boy.

'You may drive me,' said the single gentleman, 'to the—' He was not going to add 'inn,' but he added it for the sake of Kit's mother; and to the inn they went.

Rumours had already got abroad that the little girl who used to show the waxworks, was the child of great people who had been stolen from her parents in infancy, and had only just been traced. Opinion was divided whether she was the daughter of a prince, a duke, an earl, a viscount, or a baron, but all agreed upon the main fact, and that the single gentleman was her father; and all bent forward to catch a glimpse, though it were only of the tip of his noble nose, as he rode away, desponding, in his four-horse chaise.

What would he have given to know, and what sorrow would have been saved if he had only known, that at that moment both child and grandfather were seated in the old church porch, patiently awaiting the schoolmaster's return!

CHAPTER XLVIII

POPULAR rumour concerning the single gentleman and his errand, travelling from mouth to mouth, and waxing stronger in the marvellous as it was bandied about,—for your popular rumour, unlike the rolling stone of the proverb, is one which gathers a deal of moss in its wanderings up and down,—occasioned his dismounting at the inn-door to be looked upon as an exciting and attractive spectacle, which could scarcely be enough admired; and drew together a large concourse of idlers, who having recently been, as it were, thrown out of employment by the closing of the wax-work and the completion of the nuptial ceremonies, considered his arrival as little else than a special providence, and hailed it with demonstrations of the liveliest joy.

Not at all participating in the general sensation, but wearing the depressed and wearied look of one who sought to meditate on his disappointment in silence and privacy, the single gentleman alighted, and handed out Kit's mother with a gloomy politeness which impressed the lookers-on extremely. That done, he gave her his arm and escorted her into the house, while several active waiters ran on before as a skirmishing party, to clear the way and to show the room which was ready for their reception.

'Any room will do,' said the single gentleman. 'Let it be near at hand, that's all.'

'Close here, sir, if you please to walk this way.'

'Would the gentleman like this room?' said a voice, as a little out-of-the-way door at the foot of the well staircase flew briskly open and a head popped out. 'He's quite welcome to it. He's as welcome as flowers in May, or coals at Christmas. *Would* you like this room, sir? Honour me by walking in. Do me the favour, pray.'

'Goodness gracious me!' cried Kit's mother, falling back in extreme surprise, 'only think of this!'

She had some reason to be astonished, for the person who proffered the gracious invitation was no other than Daniel Quilp. The little door out of which he had thrust his head was close to the inn larder; and there he stood, bowing with grotesque politeness; as much at his ease as if the door were that of his own house; blighting all the legs of mutton and cold roast fowls by his close companionship, and looking like the evil genius of the cellars come from underground upon some work of mischief.

'Would you do me the honour?' said Quilp.

'I prefer being alone,' replied the single gentleman.

'Oh!' said Quilp. And with that, he darted in again with one jerk and clapped the little door to, like a figure in a Dutch clock when the hour strikes.

'Why it was only last night, sir,' whispered Kit's mother, 'that I left him in Little Bethel.'

'Indeed!' said her fellow-passenger. 'When did that person come here, waiter?'

'Come down by the night-coach, this morning, sir.'

'Humph! And when is he going?'

'Can't say, sir, really. When the chambermaid asked him just now if he should want a bed, sir, he first made faces at her, and then wanted to kiss her.'

'Beg him to walk this way,' said the single gentleman. 'I should be glad to exchange a word with him, tell him. Beg him to come at once, do you hear?'

The man stared on receiving these instructions, for the single gentleman had not only displayed as much astonishment as Kit's mother at sight of the dwarf, but, standing in no fear of him, had been at less pains to conceal his dislike and repugnance. He departed on his errand, however, and immediately returned, ushering in its object.

'Your servant, sir,' said the dwarf, 'I encountered your messenger half-way. I thought you'd allow me to pay my compliments to you. I hope you're well. I hope you're very well.'

There was a short pause, while the dwarf, with half-shut eyes and puckered face, stood waiting for an answer. Receiving none, he turned towards his more familiar acquaintance.

'Christopher's mother!' he cried. 'Such a dear lady, such a worthy woman, so blest in her honest son! How is Christopher's mother? Have change of air and scene improved her? Her little family too, and Christopher? Do they thrive? Do they flourish? Are they growing into worthy citizens, eh?'

Making his voice ascend in the scale with every succeeding question, Mr. Quilp finished in a shrill squeak, and subsided into the panting look which was customary with him, and which, whether it were assumed or natural, had equally the effect of banishing all expression from his face, and rendering it, as far as it afforded any index to his mood or meaning, a perfect blank.

'Mr. Quilp,' said the single gentleman.

The dwarf put his hand to his great flapped ear, and counterfeited the closest attention.

'We two have met before—'

'Surely,' cried Quilp, nodding his head. 'Oh surely, sir. Such an honour and pleasure—it's both, Christopher's mother, it's both—is not to be forgotten so soon. By no means!'

'You may remember that the day I arrived in London, and found the house to which I drove, empty and deserted, I was directed by some of the neighbours to

you, and waited upon you without stopping for rest
or refreshment?'

'How precipitate that was, and yet what an earnest
and vigorous measure!' said Quilp, conferring with
himself, in imitation of his friend Mr. Sampson Brass.

'I found,' said the single gentleman, 'you most un-
accountably, in possession of everything that had so
recently belonged to another man, and that other man,
who up to the time of your entering upon his property had been looked upon as affluent, reduced to sudden beggary, and driven from house and home.'

'We had warrant for what we did, my good sir,'
rejoined Quilp, 'we had our warrant. Don't say
driven either. He went of his own accord—vanished
in the night, sir.'

'No matter,' said the single gentleman angrily.
'He was gone.'

'Yes, he was gone,' said Quilp, with the same ex-
asperating composure. 'No doubt he was gone. The
only question was, where. And it's a question still.'

'Now, what am I to think,' said the single gentleman, sternly regarding him, 'of you, who, plainly indisposed to give me any information then—nay, ob-
viously holding back, and sheltering yourself with all
kinds of cunning, trickery, and evasion,—are dogging my footsteps now?'

'I dogging!' cried Quilp.

'Why, are you not?' returned his questioner, fretted
into a state of the utmost irritation. 'Were you not
a few hours since, sixty miles off, and in the chapel
to which this good woman goes to say her prayers?'

'She was there too, I think?' said Quilp, still perfectly unmoved. 'I might say, if I was inclined to be
rude, how do I know but you are dogging *my* footsteps. Yes, I was at chapel. What then? I've
read in books that pilgrims were used to go to chapel

before they went on journeys, to put up petitions for their safe return. Wise men! journeys are very perilous—especially outside the coach. Wheels come off, horses take fright, coachmen drive too fast, coaches overturn. I always go to chapel before I start on journeys. It's the last thing I do on such occasions, indeed.'

That Quilp lied most heartily in this speech, it needed no very great penetration to discover, although for anything that he suffered to appear in his face, voice, or manner, he might have been clinging to the truth with the quiet constancy of a martyr.

'In the name of all that's calculated to drive one crazy, man,' said the unfortunate single gentleman, 'have you not, for some reason of your own, taken upon yourself my errand? don't you know with what object I have come here, and if you do know, can you throw no light upon it?'

'You think I'm a conjuror, sir,' replied Quilp, shrugging up his shoulders. 'If I was, I should tell my own fortune—and make it.'

'Ah! we have said all we need say, I see,' returned the other, throwing himself impatiently upon a sofa. 'Pray leave us, if you please.'

'Willingly,' returned Quilp. 'Most willingly. Christopher's mother, my good soul, farewell. A pleasant journey—*back,* sir. Ahem!'

With these parting words, and with a grin upon his features altogether indescribable, but which seemed to be compounded of every monstrous grimace of which men or monkeys are capable, the dwarf slowly retreated and closed the door behind him.

'Oho!' he said when he had regained his own room, and sat himself down in a chair with his arms akimbo. 'Oho! Are you there, my friend? In-deed!'

Chuckling as though in very great glee, and recompensing himself for the restraint he had lately put upon his countenance by twisting it into all imaginable varieties of ugliness, Mr. Quilp, rocking himself to and fro in his chair and nursing his left leg at the same time, fell into certain meditations, of which it may be necessary to relate the substance.

First, he reviewed the circumstances which had led to his repairing to that spot, which were briefly these. Dropping in at Mr. Sampson Brass's office on the previous evening, in the absence of that gentleman and his learned sister, he had lighted upon Mr. Swiveller, who chanced at the moment to be sprinkling a glass of warm gin-and-water on the dust of the law, and to be moistening his clay, as the phrase goes, rather copiously. But as clay in the abstract, when too much moistened, becomes of a weak and uncertain consistency, breaking down in unexpected places, retaining impressions but faintly, and preserving no strength or steadiness of character, so Mr. Swiveller's clay, having imbibed a considerable quantity of moisture, was in a very loose and slippery state, insomuch that the various ideas impressed upon it were fast losing their distinctive character, and running into each other. It is not uncommon for human clay in this condition to value itself above all things upon its great prudence and sagacity; and Mr. Swiveller, especially prizing himself upon these qualities, took occasion to remark that he had made strange discoveries in connection with the single gentleman who lodged above, which he had determined to keep within his own bosom, and which neither tortures nor cajolery should ever induce him to reveal. Of this determination Mr. Quilp expressed his high approval, and setting himself in the same breath to goad Mr. Swiveller on to further hints, soon made out that the single gentleman had been seen in communication with Kit, and that this was the secret which was never to be disclosed.

Possessed of this piece of information, Mr. Quilp directly supposed that the single gentleman above-stairs must be the same individual who had waited on him, and having assured himself by further inquiries that this surmise was correct, had no difficulty in arriving at the conclusion that the intent and object of his correspondence with Kit was the recovery of his old client and the child. Burning with curiosity to know what proceedings were afoot, he resolved to pounce upon Kit's mother as the person least able to resist his arts, and consequently the most likely to be entrapped into such revelations as he sought; so taking an abrupt leave of Mr. Swiveller, he hurried to her house. The good woman being from home, he made inquiries of a neighbour, as Kit himself did soon afterwards, and being directed to the chapel betook himself there, in order to waylay her, at the conclusion of the service.

He had not sat in the chapel more than a quarter of an hour, and with his eyes piously fixed upon the ceiling was chuckling inwardly over the joke of his being there at all, when Kit himself appeared. Watchful as a lynx, one glance showed the dwarf that he had come on business. Absorbed in appearance, as we have seen, and feigning a profound abstraction, he noted every circumstance of his behaviour, and when he withdrew with his family, shot out after him. In fine, he traced them to the notary's house; learnt the destination of the carriage from one of the postilions; and knowing that a fast night-coach started for the same place at the very hour which was on the point of striking, from a street hard by, darted round to the coach-office without more ado, and took his seat upon the roof. After passing and repassing

the carriage on the road, and being passed and re-
passed by it sundry times in the course of the night,
according as their stoppages were longer or shorter,
or their rate of travelling varied, they reached the
town almost together. Quilp kept the chaise in
sight, mingled with the crowd, learnt the single gentleman's errand, and its failure, and having possessed
himself of all that it was material to know, hurried
off, reached the inn before him, had the interview just
now detailed, and shut himself up in the little room
in which he hastily reviewed all these occurrences.

'You are there, are you, my friend?' he repeated,
greedily biting his nails. 'I am suspected and
thrown aside, and Kit's the confidential agent, is he?
I shall have to dispose of him, I fear. If we had
come up with them this morning,' he continued, after
a thoughtful pause, 'I was ready to prove a pretty
good claim. I could have made my profit. But for
these canting hypocrites, the lad and his mother, I
could get this fiery gentleman as comfortable into
my net as our old friend—our mutual friend, ha! ha!
—and chubby, rosy Nell. At the worst, it 's a golden
opportunity, not to be lost. Let us find them first,
and I 'll find means of draining you of some of your
superfluous cash, sir, while there are prison bars, and
bolts, and locks, to keep your friend or kinsman safely.
I hate your virtuous people!' said the dwarf, throwing off a bumper of brandy, and smacking his lips,
'ah! I hate 'em every one!'

This was not a mere empty vaunt, but a deliberate avowal of his real sentiments; for Mr. Quilp, who
loved nobody, had by little and little come to hate
everybody nearly or remotely connected with his
ruined client:—the old man himself, because he had
been able to deceive him and elude his vigilance—
the child, because she was the object of Mrs. Quilp's

commiseration and constant self-reproach—the single gentleman, because of his unconcealed aversion to himself—Kit and his mother, most mortally, for the reasons shown. Above and beyond that general feeling of opposition to them, which would have been inseparable from his ravenous desire to enrich himself by these altered circumstances, Daniel Quilp hated them every one.

In this amiable mood, Mr. Quilp enlivened himself and his hatreds with more brandy, and then, changing his quarters, withdrew to an obscure alehouse, under cover of which seclusion he instituted all possible inquiries that might lead to the discovery of the old man and his grandchild. But all was in vain. Not the slightest trace or clue could be obtained. They had left the town by night; no one had seen them go; no one had met them on the road; the driver of no coach, cart, or waggon, had seen any travellers answering their description; nobody had fallen in with them, or heard of them. Convinced at last that for the present all such attempts were hopeless, he appointed two or three scouts, with promises of large rewards in case of their forwarding him any intelligence, and returned to London by next day's coach.

It was some gratification to Mr. Quilp to find, as he took his place upon the roof, that Kit's mother was alone inside; from which circumstance he derived in the course of the journey much cheerfulness of spirit, inasmuch as her solitary condition enabled him to terrify her with many extraordinary annoyances; such as hanging over the side of the coach at the risk of his life, and staring in with his great goggle eyes, which seemed in hers the more horrible from his face being upside down; dodging her in this way from one window to another; getting nimbly down whenever they changed horses and thrusting his head in at the window with a dismal squint: which ingenious tortures had such an effect upon Mrs. Nubbles, that she was quite unable for the time to resist the belief that Mr. Quilp did in his own person represent and embody that Evil Power, who was so vigorously attacked at Little Bethel, and who, by reason of her backslidings in respect of Astley's and oysters, was now frolicsome and rampant.

Kit, having been apprised by letter of his mother's intended return, was waiting for her at the coach-office; and great was his surprise when he saw, leering over the coachman's shoulder like some familiar demon, invisible to all eyes but his, the well-known face of Quilp.

'How are you, Christopher?' croaked the dwarf from the coach-top. 'All right, Christopher. Mother's inside.'

'Why, how did he come here, mother?' whispered Kit.

'I don't know how he came or why, my dear,' rejoined Mrs. Nubbles, dismounting with her son's assistance, 'but he has been a terrifying of me out of my seven senses all this blessed day.'

'He has?' cried Kit.

'You wouldn't believe it, that you wouldn't,' replied his mother, 'but don't say a word to him, for I really don't believe he's human. Hush! Don't turn round as if I was talking of him, but he's a squinting at me now in the full blaze of the coach-lamp, quite awful!'

In spite of his mother's injunction, Kit turned sharply round to look. Mr. Quilp was serenely gazing at the stars, quite absorbed in celestial contemplation.

'Oh, he's the artfullest creetur!' cried Mrs. Nubbles.

'But come away. Don't speak to him for the world.'

'Yes I will, mother. What nonsense. I say, sir—'

Mr. Quilp affected to start, and looked smilingly round.

'You let my mother alone, will you?' said Kit. 'How dare you tease a poor lone woman like her, making her miserable and melancholy as if she hadn't got enough to make her so, without you. An't you ashamed of yourself, you little monster?'

'Monster!' said Quilp inwardly, with a smile. 'Ugliest dwarf that could be seen anywhere for a penny—monster—ah!'

'You show her any of your impudence again,' resumed Kit, shouldering the bandbox, 'and I tell you what, Mr. Quilp, I won't bear with you any more. You have no right to do it; I 'm sure we never interfered with you. This isn't the first time; and if ever you worry or frighten her again, you 'll oblige me (though I should be very sorry to do it, on account of your size) to beat you.'

Quilp said not a word in reply, but walking so close to Kit as to bring his eyes within two or three inches of his face, looked fixedly at him, retreated a little distance without averting his gaze, approached again, again withdrew, and so on for half a dozen times, like a head in a phantasmagoria. Kit stood his ground as if in expectation of an immediate assault, but finding that nothing came of these gestures, snapped his fingers and walked away; his mother dragging him off as fast as she could, and, even in the midst of his news of little Jacob and the baby, looking anxiously over her shoulder to see if Quilp were following.

CHAPTER XLIX

KIT's mother might have spared herself the trouble of looking back so often, for nothing was further from Mr. Quilp's thoughts than any intention of pursuing her and her son, or renewing the quarrel with which they had parted. He went his way, whistling from time to time some fragments of a tune; and with a face quite tranquil and composed, jogged pleasantly towards home; entertaining himself as he went with visions of the fears and terrors of Mrs. Quilp, who, having received no intelligence of him for three whole days and two nights, and having had no previous notice of his absence, was doubtless by that time in a state of distraction, and constantly fainting away with anxiety and grief.

This facetious probability was so congenial to the dwarf's humour, and so exquisitely amusing to him, that he laughed as he went along until the tears ran down his cheeks; and more than once, when he found himself in a by-street, vented his delight in a shrill scream, which greatly terrified any lonely passenger, who happened to be walking on before him expecting nothing so little, increased his mirth, and made him remarkably cheerful and light-hearted.

In this happy flow of spirits, Mr. Quilp reached Tower Hill, when, gazing up at the window of his own sitting-room, he thought he descried more light than is usual in a house of mourning. Drawing nearer, and listening attentively, he could hear several voices in earnest conversation, among which he could distinguish, not only those of his wife and mother-in-law, but the tones of men.

'Ha!' cried the jealous dwarf. 'What's this? Do they entertain visitors while I'm away?'

A smothered cough from above, was the reply. He felt in his pockets for his latch-key, but had forgotten it. There was no resource but to knock at the door.

'A light in the passage,' said Quilp, peeping through the key-hole. 'A very soft knock; and, by your leave, my lady, I may yet steal upon you unawares. Soho!'

A very low and gentle rap received no answer from within. But after a second application to the knocker, no louder than the first, the door was softly opened by the boy from the wharf, whom Quilp instantly gagged with one hand, and dragged into the street with the other.

'You 'll throttle me, master,' whispered the boy. 'Let go, will you?'

'Who 's upstairs, you dog?' retorted Quilp in the same tone. 'Tell me. And don't speak above your breath, or I 'll choke you in good earnest.'

The boy could only point to the window, and reply with a stifled giggle, expressive of such intense enjoyment, that Quilp clutched him by the throat and might have carried his threat into execution, or at least have made very good progress towards that end, but for the boy's nimbly extricating himself from his grasp, and fortifying himself behind the nearest post, at which, after some fruitless attempts to catch him by the hair of the head, his master was obliged to come to a parley.

'Will you answer me?' said Quilp. 'What 's going on, above?'

'You won't let one speak,' replied the boy. 'They —ha, ha, ha!—they think you 're—you 're dead. Ha, ha, ha!'

'Dead!' cried Quilp, relaxing into a grim laugh himself. 'No. Do they? Do they really, you dog?'

'They think you 're—you 're drowned,' replied the boy, who in his malicious nature had a strong infusion of his master. 'You was last seen on the brink of the wharf, and they think you tumbled over. Ha ha!'

The prospect of playing the spy under such delicious circumstances, and of disappointing them all by walking in alive, gave more delight to Quilp than the greatest stroke of good fortune could possibly have inspired him with. He was no less tickled than his hopeful assistant, and they both stood for some seconds, grinning and gasping and wagging their heads at each other, on either side of the post, like an unmatchable pair of Chinese idols.

'Not a word,' said Quilp, making towards the door on tip-toe. 'Not a sound, not so much as a creaking board, or a stumble against a cobweb. Drowned, eh, Mrs. Quilp! Drowned!'

So saying, he blew out the candle, kicked off his shoes, and groped his way upstairs; leaving his delighted young friend in an ecstasy of summersets on the pavement.

The bedroom-door on the staircase being unlocked, Mr. Quilp slipped in, and planted himself behind the door of communication between that chamber and the sitting-room, which standing ajar to render both more airy, and having a very convenient chink (of which he had often availed himself for purposes of espial, and had indeed enlarged with his pocket-knife), enabled him not only to hear, but to see distinctly, what was passing.

Applying his eye to this convenient place, he descried Mr. Brass seated at the table with pen, ink, and paper, and the case-bottle of rum—his own case-bottle, and his own particular Jamaica—convenient to his hand; with hot water, fragrant lemons, white lump-sugar, and all things fitting; from which choice materials, Sampson, by no means insensible to their claims upon his attention, had compounded a mighty glass of punch reeking hot; which he was at that very moment stirring up with a tea-spoon, and contemplating with looks in which a faint assumption of sentimental regret, struggled but weakly with a bland and comfortable joy. At the same table, with both her elbows upon it was Mrs. Jiniwin; no longer sipping other people's punch feloniously with teaspoons, but taking deep draughts from a jorum of her own; while her daughter—not exactly with ashes on her head, or sackcloth on her back, but preserving a very decent and becoming appearance of sorrow nevertheless—was reclining in an easy-chair, and soothing her grief with a smaller allowance of the same glib liquid. There were also present, a couple of waterside men, bearing between them certain machines called drags; even these fellows were accommodated with a stiff glass a-piece; and as they drank with a great relish, and were naturally of a red-nosed, pimple-faced, convivial look, their presence rather increased than detracted from that decided appearance of comfort, which was the great characteristic of the party.

'If I could poison that dear old lady's rum-and-water,' murmured Quilp, 'I 'd die happy.'

'Ah!' said Mr. Brass, breaking the silence, and raising his eyes to the ceiling with a sigh, 'who knows but he may be looking down upon us now? Who knows but he may be surveying of us from—from somewheres or another, and contemplating us with a watchful eye? Oh Lor!'

Here Mr. Brass stopped to drink half his punch, and then resumed; looking at the other half, as he spoke, with a dejected smile.

'I can almost fancy,' said the lawyer shaking his

head, 'that I see his eye glistening down at the very bottom of my liquor. When shall we look upon his like again? Never, never! One minute we are here'—holding his tumbler before his eyes—'the next we are there'—gulping down its contents, and striking himself emphatically a little below the chest—'in the silent tomb. To think that I should be drinking his very rum! It seems like a dream.'

With the view, no doubt, of testing the reality of his position, Mr. Brass pushed his tumbler as he spoke towards Mrs. Jiniwin; for the purpose of being replenished; and turned towards the attendant mariners.

'The search has been quite unsuccessful then?'

'Quite, master. But I should say that if he turns up anywhere, he'll come ashore somewhere about Grinidge to-morrow, at ebb-tide, eh, mate?'

The other gentleman assented, observed that he was expected at the Hospital, and that several pensioners would be ready to receive him whenever he arrived.

'Then we have nothing for it but resignation,' said Mr. Brass; 'nothing but resignation, and expectation. It would be a comfort to have his body; it would be a dreary comfort.'

'Oh, beyond a doubt,' assented Mrs. Jiniwin hastily; 'if we once had that, we should be quite sure.'

'With regard to the descriptive advertisement,' said Sampson Brass, taking up his pen. 'It is a melancholy pleasure to recall his traits. Respecting his legs now—?'

'Crooked, certainly,' said Mrs. Jiniwin.

'Do you think they *were* crooked?' said Brass, in an insinuating tone. 'I think I see them now coming up the street very wide apart, in nankeen pantaloons a little shrunk and without straps. Ah! what a vale of tears we live in. Do we say crooked?'

'I think they were a little so,' observed Mrs. Quilp with a sob.

'Legs crooked,' said Brass, writing as he spoke. 'Large head, short body, legs crooked—'

'Very crooked,' suggested Mrs. Jiniwin.

'We'll not say very crooked, ma'am,' said Brass piously. 'Let us not bear hard upon the weaknesses of the deceased. He is gone, ma'am, to where his legs will never come in question.—We will content ourselves with crooked, Mrs. Jiniwin.'

'I thought you wanted the truth,' said the old lady. 'That's all.'

'Bless your eyes, how I love you,' muttered Quilp. 'There she goes again. Nothing but punch!'

'This is an occupation,' said the lawyer, laying down his pen and emptying his glass, 'which seems to bring him before my eyes like the Ghost of Hamlet's father, in the very clothes that he wore on work-a-days. His coat, his waistcoat, his shoes and stockings, his trousers, his hat, his wit and humour, his pathos and his umbrella, all come before me like visions of my youth. His linen!' said Mr. Brass smiling fondly at the wall, 'his linen which was always of a particular colour, for such was his whim and fancy —how plain I see his linen now!'

'You had better go on, sir,' said Mrs. Jiniwin impatiently.

'True, ma'am, true,' cried Mr. Brass. 'Our faculties must not freeze with grief. I'll trouble you for a little more of that, ma'am. A question now arises, with relation to his nose.'

'Flat,' said Mrs. Jiniwin.

'Aquiline!' cried Quilp, thrusting in his head, and striking the feature with his fist. 'Aquiline, you hag. Do you see it? Do you call this flat? Do you? Eh?'

'Oh capital, capital!' shouted Brass, from the mere force of habit. 'Excellent! How very good he is! He's a most remarkable man—so extremely whimsical! Such an amazing power of taking people by surprise!'

Quilp paid no regard whatever to these compliments, nor to the dubious and frightened look into which the lawyer gradually subsided, nor to the shrieks of his wife and mother-in-law, nor to the latter's running from the room, nor to the former's fainting away. Keeping his eye fixed on Sampson Brass, he walked up to the table, and beginning with his glass, drank off the contents, and went regularly round until he had emptied the other two, when he seized the case-bottle, and hugging it under his arm, surveyed him with a most extraordinary leer.

'Not yet, Sampson,' said Quilp. 'Not just yet!'

'Oh very good indeed!' cried Brass, recovering his spirits a little. 'Ha ha ha! Oh exceedingly good! There's not another man alive who could carry it off like that. A most difficult position to carry off. But he has such a flow of good-humour, such an amazing flow!'

'Good-night,' said the dwarf, nodding expressively.

'Good-night, sir, good-night,' cried the lawyer, retreating backwards towards the door. 'This is a joyful occasion indeed, extremely joyful. Ha ha ha! oh very rich, very rich indeed, remarkably so!'

Waiting until Mr. Brass's ejaculations died away in the distance (for he continued to pour them out, all the way downstairs), Quilp advanced towards the two men, who yet lingered in a kind of stupid amazement.

'Have you been dragging the river all day, gentlemen?' said the dwarf, holding the door open with great politeness.

'And yesterday too, master.'

'Dear me, you've had a deal of trouble. Pray consider everything yours that you find upon the—upon the body. Good-night!'

The men looked at each other, but had evidently no inclination to argue the point just then, and shuffled out of the room. The speedy clearance effected, Quilp locked the doors; and still embracing the case-bottle with shrugged-up shoulders and folded arms, stood looking at his insensible wife like a dismounted nightmare.

CHAPTER L

MATRIMONIAL differences are usually discussed by the parties concerned in the form of dialogue, in which the lady bears at least her full half-share. Those of Mr. and Mrs. Quilp, however, were an exception to the general rule; the remarks which they occasioned being limited to a long soliloquy on the part of the gentleman, with perhaps a few deprecatory observations from the lady, not extending beyond a trembling monosyllable uttered at long intervals, and in a very submissive and humble tone. On the present occasion, Mrs. Quilp did not for a long time venture even on this gentle defence, but when she had recovered from her fainting-fit, sat in a tearful silence, meekly listening to the reproaches of her lord and master.

Of these Mr. Quilp delivered himself with the utmost animation and rapidity, and with so many distortions of limb and feature, that even his wife, although tolerably well accustomed to his proficiency in these respects, was well-nigh beside herself with alarm. But the Jamaica rum, and the joy of having occasioned a heavy disappointment, by degrees cooled Mr. Quilp's wrath; which from being at savage heat, dropped slowly to the bantering or chuckling point, at which it steadily remained.

'So you thought I was dead and gone, did you?' said Quilp. 'You thought you were a widow, eh? Ha, ha, ha, you jade!'

'Indeed, Quilp,' returned his wife. 'I'm very sorry—'

'Who doubts it?' cried the dwarf. 'You very sorry! to be sure you are. Who doubts that you're *very* sorry?'

'I don't mean sorry that you have come home again alive and well,' said his wife, 'but sorry that I should have been led into such a belief. I am glad to see you, Quilp; indeed I am.'

In truth Mrs. Quilp did seem a great deal more glad to behold her lord than might have been expected, and did evince a degree of interest in his safety which, all things considered, was rather unaccountable. Upon Quilp, however, this circumstance made no impression, farther than as it moved him to snap his fingers close to his wife's eyes, with divers grins of triumph and derision.

'How could you go away so long, without saying a word to me or letting me hear of you or know anything about you?' asked the poor little woman, sobbing. 'How could you be so cruel, Quilp?'

'How could I be so cruel? cruel?' cried the dwarf. 'Because I was in the humour. I'm in the humour now. I shall be cruel when I like. I'm going away again.'

'Not again.'

'Yes, again. I'm going away now. I'm off directly. I mean to go and live wherever the fancy seizes me—at the wharf—at the counting-house—and

THEY OBEYED MR. QUILP'S DIRECTIONS IN SUBMISSIVE SILENCE.

be a jolly bachelor. You were a widow in anticipation. Damme,' screamed the dwarf, 'I 'll be a bachelor in earnest.'

'You can't be serious, Quilp,' sobbed his wife.

'I tell you,' said the dwarf, exulting in his project, 'that I 'll be a bachelor, a devil-may-care bachelor;
and I 'll have my bachelor's hall at the counting-
house, and at such times come near it if you dare.
And mind too that I don't pounce in upon you at
unseasonable hours again, for I 'll be a spy upon you,
and come and go like a mole or a weazel. Tom Scott
—where 's Tom Scott?'

'Here I am, master,' cried the voice of the boy, as
Quilp threw up the window.

'Wait there, you dog,' returned the dwarf, 'to carry
a bachelor's portmanteau. Pack it up, Mrs. Quilp.
Knock up the dear old lady to help; knock her up.
Halloa there! Halloa!'

With these exclamations, Mr. Quilp caught up the
poker, and hurrying to the door of the good lady's
sleeping-closet, beat upon it therewith until she awoke
in inexpressible terror, thinking that her amiable son-
in-law surely intended to murder her in justification
of the legs she had slandered. Impressed with this
idea, she was no sooner fairly awake than she screamed
violently, and would have quickly precipitated herself out of the window and through a neighbouring
skylight, if her daughter had not hastened in to un-
deceive her, and implore her assistance. Somewhat
reassured by her account of the service she was required to render, Mrs. Jiniwin made her appearance
in a flannel dressing-gown; and both mother and
daughter, trembling with terror and cold—for the
night was now far advanced—obeyed Mr. Quilp's
directions in submissive silence. Prolonging his preparations as much as possible, for their greater com-

fort, that eccentric gentleman superintended the packing of his wardrobe, and having added to it with his own hands, a plate, knife and fork, spoon, tea-cup and saucer, and other small household matters of that nature, strapped up the portmanteau, took it on his shoulders, and actually marched off without another word, and with the case-bottle (which he had never once put down) still tightly clasped under his arm. Consigning his heavier burden to the care of Tom Scott when he reached the street, taking a dram from the bottle for his own encouragement, and giving the boy a rap on the head with it as a small taste for himself, Quilp very deliberately led the way to the wharf, and reached it at between three and four o'clock in the morning.

'Snug!' said Quilp, when he had groped his way to the wooden counting-house, and opened the door with a key he carried about with him. 'Beautifully snug! Call me at eight, you dog.'

With no more formal leave-taking or explanation, he clutched the portmanteau, shut the door on his attendant, and climbing on the desk, and rolling himself up as round as a hedgehog, in an old boat-cloak, fell fast asleep.

Being roused in the morning at the appointed time, and roused with difficulty, after his late fatigues, Quilp instructed Tom Scott to make a fire in the yard of sundry pieces of old timber, and to prepare some coffee for breakfast; for the better furnishing of which repast he entrusted him with certain small moneys, to be expended in the purchase of hot rolls, butter, sugar, Yarmouth bloaters, and other articles of housekeeping; so that in a few minutes a savoury meal was smoking on the board. With this substantial comfort, the dwarf regaled himself to his heart's content; and being highly satisfied with this free and gipsy mode of life (which he had often meditated, as offering, whenever he chose to avail himself of it, an agreeable freedom from the restraints of matrimony, and a choice means of keeping Mrs. Quilp and her mother in a state of incessant agitation and suspense), bestirred himself to improve his retreat, and render it more commodious and comfortable.

With this view, he issued forth to a place hard by, where sea-stores were sold, purchased a second-hand hammock, and had it slung in seamanlike fashion from the ceiling of the counting-house. He also caused to be erected, in the same mouldy cabin, an old ship's stove with a rusty funnel to carry the smoke through the roof; and these arrangements completed, surveyed them with ineffable delight.

'I 've got a country house like Robinson Crusoe,' said the dwarf, ogling the accommodations; 'a solitary, sequestered, desolate-island sort of spot, where I can be quite alone when I have business on hand, and be secure from all spies and listeners. Nobody near me here, but rats, and they are fine stealthy secret fellows. I shall be as merry as a grig among these gentry. I 'll look out for one like Christopher, and poison him—ha, ha, ha! Business though—business —we must be mindful of business in the midst of pleasure, and the time has flown this morning, I declare.'

Enjoining Tom Scott to await his return, and not to stand upon his head, or throw a summerset, or so much as walk upon his hands meanwhile, on pain of lingering torments, the dwarf threw himself into a boat, and crossing to the other side of the river, and then speeding away on foot, reached Mr. Swiveller's usual house of entertainment in Bevis Marks, just as that gentleman sat down alone to dinner in its dusky parlour.

'Dick'—said the dwarf, thrusting his head in at the door, 'my pet, my pupil, the apple of my eye, hey, hey!'

'Oh you 're there, are you?' returned Mr. Swiveller; '*how* are you?'

'How 's Dick?' retorted Quilp. 'How 's the cream of clerkship, eh?'

'Why, rather sour, sir,' replied Mr. Swiveller. 'Beginning to border upon cheesiness, in fact.'

'What 's the matter?' said the dwarf, advancing. 'Has Sally proved unkind? "Of all the girls that are so smart, there 's none like—" eh, Dick?'

'Certainly not,' replied Mr. Swiveller, eating his dinner with great gravity, 'none like her. She 's the sphinx of private life is Sally B.'

'You 're out of spirits,' said Quilp, drawing up a chair. 'What 's the matter?'

'The law don't agree with me,' returned Dick. 'It isn't moist enough, and there 's too much confinement. I have been thinking of running away.'

'Bah!' said the dwarf. 'Where would you run to, Dick?'

'I don't know,' returned Mr. Swiveller. 'Towards Highgate, I suppose. Perhaps the bells might strike up "Turn again, Swiveller, Lord Mayor of London." Whittington's name was Dick. I wish cats were scarcer.'

Quilp looked at his companion with his eyes screwed up into a comical expression of curiosity, and patiently awaited his further explanation; upon which, however, Mr. Swiveller appeared in no hurry to enter, as he ate a very long dinner in profound silence, finally pushed away his plate, threw himself back into his chair, folded his arms, and stared ruefully at the fire, in which some ends of cigars were smoking on their own account, and sending up a fragrant odour.

'Perhaps you'd like a bit of cake'—said Dick, at last turning to the dwarf. 'You're quite welcome to it. You ought to be, for it's of your making.'

'What do you mean?' said Quilp.

Mr. Swiveller replied by taking from his pocket a small and very greasy parcel, slowly unfolding it, and displaying a little slab of plum-cake extremely indigestible in appearance, and bordered with a paste of white sugar an inch and a half deep.

'What should you say this was?' demanded Mr. Swiveller.

'It looks like bride-cake,' replied the dwarf, grinning.

'And whose should you say it was?' inquired Mr. Swiveller, rubbing the pastry against his nose with a dreadful calmness. 'Whose?'

'Not—'

'Yes,' said Dick, 'the same. You needn't mention her name. There's no such name now. Her name is Cheggs now, Sophy Cheggs. Yet loved I as man never loved that hadn't wooden legs, and my heart, my heart is breaking for the love of Sophy Cheggs.'

With this extemporary adaptation of a popular ballad to the distressing circumstances of his own case, Mr. Swiveller folded up the parcel again, beat it very flat between the palms of his hands, thrust it into his breast, buttoned his coat over it, and folded his arms upon the whole.

'Now, I hope you're satisfied, sir,' said Dick; 'and I hope Fred's satisfied. You went partners in the mischief, and I hope you like it. This is the triumph I was to have, is it? It's like the old country-dance of that name, where there are two gentlemen to one lady, and one has her, and the other hasn't, but comes limping up behind to make out the figure. But it's Destiny, and mine's a crusher!'

Disguising his secret joy in Mr. Swiveller's defeat, Daniel Quilp adopted the surest means of soothing him, by ringing the bell, and ordering in a supply of rosy wine (that is to say, of its usual representative), which he put about with great alacrity, calling upon Mr. Swiveller to pledge him in various toasts derisive of Cheggs, and eulogistic of the happiness of single men.   Such was their impression on Mr. Swiveller, coupled with the reflection that no man could oppose his destiny, that in a very short space of time his spirits rose surprisingly, and he was enabled to give the dwarf an account of the receipt of the cake, which, it appeared, had been brought to Bevis Marks by the two surviving Miss Wackleses in person, and delivered at the office-door with much giggling and joyfulness.

'Ha!' said Quilp.   'It will be our turn to giggle soon.   And that reminds me—you spoke of young Trent—where is he?'

Mr. Swiveller explained that his respectable friend had recently accepted a responsible situation in a locomotive gaming-house, and was at that time absent on a professional tour among the adventurous spirits of Great Britain.

'That's unfortunate,' said the dwarf, 'for I came, in fact, to ask you about him.   A thought has occurred to me, Dick; your friend over the way–

'Which friend?'

'In the first-floor.'

'Yes?'

'Your friend in the first-floor, Dick, may know him.'

'No, he don't,' said Mr. Swiveller, shaking his head.

'Don't!   No, because he has never seen him,' rejoined Quilp; 'but if we were to bring them together, who knows, Dick, but Fred, properly introduced, would serve his turn almost as well as little Nell or her grandfather—who knows but it might make the young fellow's fortune, and, through him, yours, eh?'

'Why, the fact is, you see,' said Mr. Swiveller, 'that they *have been* brought together.'

'Have been!' cried the dwarf, looking suspiciously at his companion. 'Through whose means?'

'Through mine,' said Dick, slightly confused. 'Didn't I mention it to you the last time you called over yonder?'

'You know you didn't,' returned the dwarf.

'I believe you 're right,' said Dick. 'No. I didn't, I recollect. Oh yes, I brought 'em together that very day. It was Fred's suggestion.'

'And what came of it?'

'Why, instead of my friend's bursting into tears when he knew who Fred was, embracing him kindly, and telling him that he was his grandfather, or his grandmother in disguise (which we fully expected), he flew into a tremendous passion; called him all manner of names; said it was in a great measure his fault that little Nell and the old gentleman had ever been brought to poverty; didn't hint at our taking anything to drink; and—and in short rather turned us out of the room than otherwise.'

'That 's strange,' said the dwarf, musing.

'So we remarked to each other at the time,' returned Dick coolly, 'but quite true.'

Quilp was plainly staggered by this intelligence, over which he brooded for some time in moody silence, often raising his eyes to Mr. Swiveller's face, and sharply scanning its expression. As he could read in it, however, no additional information or anything to lead him to believe he had spoken falsely; and as Mr. Swiveller, left to his own meditations, sighed deeply, and was evidently growing maudlin on the subject of Mrs. Cheggs; the dwarf soon broke up the conference and took his departure, leaving the bereaved one to his melancholy ruminations.

'Have been brought together, eh?' said the dwarf as he walked the streets alone. 'My friend has stolen a march upon me. It led him to nothing, and therefore is no great matter, save in the intention. I'm glad he has lost his mistress. Ha, ha! The blockhead mustn't leave the law at present. I'm sure of him where he is, whenever I want him for my own purposes, and, besides, he's a good unconscious spy on Brass, and tells, in his cups, all that he sees and hears. You're useful to me, Dick, and cost nothing but a little treating now and then. I am not sure that it may not be worth while, before long, to take credit with the stranger, Dick, by discovering your designs upon the child; but for the present we'll remain the best friends in the world, with your good leave.'

Pursuing these thoughts, and gasping as he went along, after his own peculiar fashion, Mr. Quilp once more crossed the Thames, and shut himself up in his Bachelor's Hall, which, by reason of its newly-erected chimney depositing the smoke inside the room and carrying none of it off, was not quite so agreeable as more fastidious people might have desired. Such inconveniences, however, instead of disgusting the dwarf with his new abode, rather suited his humour; so, after dining luxuriously from the public-house, he lighted his pipe, and smoked against the chimney until nothing of him was visible through the mist but a pair of red and highly inflamed eyes, with sometimes a dim vision of his head and face, as, in a violent fit of coughing, he slightly stirred the smoke and scattered the heavy wreaths by which they were obscured. In the midst of this atmosphere, which must infallibly have smothered any other man, Mr. Quilp passed the evening with great cheerfulness; solacing himself all the time with the pipe and the case-bottle; and occasionally entertaining himself with a melodious howl, intended for a song, but bearing not the faintest resemblance to any scrap of any piece of music, vocal or instrumental, ever invented by man. Thus he amused himself until nearly midnight, when he turned into his hammock with the utmost satisfaction.

The first sound that met his ears in the morning— as he half opened his eyes, and, finding himself so unusually near the ceiling, entertained a drowsy idea that he must have been transformed into a fly or blue-bottle in the course of the night,—was that of a stifled sobbing and weeping in the room. Peeping cautiously over the side of his hammock, he descried Mrs. Quilp, to whom, after contemplating her for some time in silence, he communicated a violent start by suddenly yelling out—

'Halloa!'

'Oh, Quilp!' cried his poor little wife, looking up. 'How you frightened me!'

'I meant to, you jade,' returned the dwarf. 'What do you want here?   I 'm dead, an't I?'

'Oh, please come home, do come home,' said Mrs. Quilp, sobbing; 'we 'll never do so any more, Quilp, and after all it was only a mistake that grew out of our anxiety.'

'Out of your anxiety,' grinned the dwarf. 'Yes, I know that—out of your anxiety for my death. I shall come home when I please, I tell you. I shall come home when I please, and go when I please. I 'll be a Will o' the Wisp, now here, now there, dancing about you always, starting up when you least expect me, and keeping you in a constant state of restlessness and irritation. Will you begone?'

Mrs. Quilp durst only make a gesture of entreaty.

'I tell you no,' cried the dwarf.   'No.   If you dare to come here again unless you 're sent for, I 'll keep watch-dogs in the yard that 'll growl and bite—I 'll have man-traps, cunningly altered and improved for catching women—I 'll have spring guns, that shall explode when you tread upon the wires, and blow you into little pieces.   Will you go?'

'Do forgive me.   Do come back,' said his wife, earnestly.

'No-o-o-o-o!' roared Quilp.   'Not till my own good time, and then I 'll return again as often as I choose, and be accountable to nobody for my goings or comings.   You see the door there.   Will you go?'

Mr. Quilp delivered this last command in such a very energetic voice, and moreover accompanied it with such a sudden gesture, indicative of an intention to spring out of his hammock, and, night-capped as he was, bear his wife home again through the public streets, that she sped away like an arrow.   Her worthy lord stretched his neck and eyes until she had crossed the yard, and then, not at all sorry to have had this opportunity of carrying his point, and asserting the sanctity of his castle, fell into an immoderate fit of laughter, and laid himself down to sleep again.

CHAPTER LI

THE bland and open-hearted proprietor of Bachelor's Hall slept on amidst the congenial accompaniments of rain, mud, dirt, damp, fog, and rats, until late in the day; when, summoning his valet Tom Scott to assist him to rise, and to prepare breakfast, he quitted his couch, and made his toilet.   This duty performed, and his repast ended, he again betook himself to Bevis Marks.

This visit was not intended for Mr. Swiveller, but for his friend and employer Mr. Sampson Brass. Both gentlemen however were from home, nor was the life and light of law, Miss Sally, at her post either.   The fact of their joint desertion of the office was made known to all comers by a scrap of paper in the handwriting of Mr. Swiveller, which was attached to the bell-handle, and which, giving the reader no clue to the time of day when it was first posted, furnished him with the rather vague and unsatisfactory information that that gentleman would 'return in an hour.'

'There's a servant, I suppose,' said the dwarf, knocking at the house-door.   'She 'll do.'

After a sufficiently long interval, the door was opened, and a small voice immediately accosted him with, 'Oh please will you leave a card or message?'

'Eh?' said the dwarf, looking down (it was something quite new to him) upon the small servant.

To this, the child, conducting her conversation as upon the occasion of her first interview with Mr. Swiveller, again replied, 'Oh please will you leave a card or message?'

'I 'll write a note,' said the dwarf, pushing past her into the office; 'and mind your master has it directly he comes home.'   So Mr. Quilp climbed up to the top of a tall stool to write the note, and the small servant, carefully tutored for such emergencies, looked on with her eyes wide open, ready, if he so much as abstracted a wafer, to rush into the street and give the alarm to the police.

As Mr. Quilp folded his note (which was soon written: being a very short one) he encountered the gaze of the small servant. He looked at her, long and earnestly.

'How are you?' said the dwarf, moistening a wafer with horrible grimaces.

The small servant, perhaps frightened by his looks, returned no audible reply; but it appeared from the motion of her lips that she was inwardly repeating the same form of expression concerning the note or message.

'Do they use you ill here? is your mistress a Tartar?' said Quilp with a chuckle.

In reply to the last interrogation, the small servant, with a look of infinite cunning mingled with fear, screwed up her mouth very tight and round, and nodded violently.

Whether there was anything in the peculiar slyness of her action which fascinated Mr. Quilp, or anything in the expression of her features at the moment which attracted his attention for some other reason; or whether it merely occurred to him as a pleasant whim to stare the small servant out of countenance; certain it is, that he planted his elbows square and firmly on the desk, and squeezing up his cheeks with his hands, looked at her fixedly.

'Where do you come from?' he said, after a long pause, stroking his chin.

'I don't know.'

'What's your name?'

'Nothing.'

'Nonsense!' retorted Quilp. 'What does your mistress call you when she wants you?'

'A little devil,' said the child.

She added in the same breath, as if fearful of any further questioning, 'But please will you leave a card or message?'

These unusual answers might naturally have provoked some more inquiries. Quilp, however, without uttering another word, withdrew his eyes from the small servant, stroked his chin more thoughtfully than before, and then, bending over the note as if to direct it with scrupulous and hair-breadth nicety, looked at her, covertly but very narrowly, from under his bushy eyebrows. The result of this secret survey was, that he shaded his face with his hands, and laughed slyly and noiselessly, until every vein in it was swollen almost to bursting. Pulling his hat over his brow to conceal his mirth and its effects, he tossed the letter to the child, and hastily withdrew.

Once in the street, moved by some secret impulse, he laughed, and held his sides, and laughed again, and tried to peer through the dusty area railings as if to catch another glimpse of the child, until he was quite tired out. At last, he travelled back to the Wilderness, which was within rifle-shot of his bachelor retreat, and ordered tea in the wooden summer-house that afternoon for three persons; an invitation to Miss Sally Brass and her brother to partake of that entertainment at that place, having been the object both of his journey and his note.

It was not precisely the kind of weather in which people usually take tea in summer-houses, far less in summer-houses in an advanced state of decay, and overlooking the slimy banks of a great river at low water. Nevertheless, it was in this choice retreat that Mr. Quilp ordered a cold collation to be prepared, and it was beneath its cracked and leaky roof that he, in due course of time, received Mr. Sampson and his sister Sally.

'You 're fond of the beauties of nature,' said Quilp with a grin. 'Is this charming, Brass? Is it unusual, unsophisticated, primitive?'

'It 's delightful indeed, sir,' replied the lawyer.

'Cool?' said Quilp.

'N-not particularly so, I think, sir,' rejoined Brass, with his teeth chattering in his head.

'Perhaps a little damp and ague-ish?' said Quilp.

'Just damp enough to be cheerful, sir,' rejoined Brass. 'Nothing more, sir, nothing more.'

'And Sally?' said the delighted dwarf. 'Does *she* like it?'

'She 'll like it better,' returned that strong-minded lady, 'when she has tea; so let us have it, and don't bother.'

'Sweet Sally!' cried Quilp, extending his arms as if about to embrace her. 'Gentle, charming, over-whelming Sally.'

'He 's a very remarkable man indeed!' soliloquised Mr. Brass. 'He 's quite a Troubadour, you know; quite a Troubadour!'

These complimentary expressions were uttered in a somewhat absent and distracted manner; for the un-fortunate lawyer, besides having a bad cold in his head, had got wet in coming, and would have willingly borne some pecuniary sacrifice if he could have shifted his present raw quarters to a warm room, and dried himself at a fire. Quilp, however,—who, beyond the gratification of his demon whims, owed Sampson some acknowledgment of the part he had played in the mourning scene of which he had been a hidden witness, marked these symptoms of uneasiness with a delight past all expression, and derived from them a secret joy which the costliest banquet could never have afforded him.

It is worthy of remark, too, as illustrating a little feature in the character of Miss Sally Brass, that, although on her own account she would have borne the discomforts of the Wilderness with a very ill grace, and would probably, indeed, have walked off before the tea appeared, she no sooner beheld the latent uneasiness and misery of her brother than she developed a grim satisfaction, and began to enjoy herself after her own manner. Though the wet came stealing through the roof and trickling down upon their heads, Miss Brass uttered no complaint, but presided over the tea equipage with imperturbable composure. While Mr. Quilp, in his uproarious hospitality, seated himself upon an empty beer-barrel, vaunted the place as the most beautiful and comfortable in the three kingdoms, and elevating his glass, drank to their next merry meeting in that jovial spot; and Mr. Brass, with the rain splashing down into his tea-cup, made a dismal attempt to pluck up his spirits and appear at his ease; and Tom Scott, who was in waiting at the door under an old umbrella, exulted in his agonies, and bade fair to split his sides with laughing; while all this was passing, Miss Sally Brass, unmindful of the wet which dripped down upon her own feminine person and fair apparel, sat placidly behind the tea-board erect and grizzly, contemplating the unhappiness of her brother with a mind at ease, and content, in her amiable disregard of self, to sit there all night, witnessing the torments which his avaricious and grovelling nature compelled him to endure and forbade him to resent. And this, it must be observed, or the illustration would be incomplete, although in a business point of view she had the strongest sympathy with Mr. Sampson, and would have been beyond measure indignant if he had thwarted their client in any one respect.

In the height of his boisterous merriment, Mr. Quilp, having on some pretence dismissed his attendant sprite for the moment, resumed his usual manner all at once, dismounted from his cask, and laid his hand upon the lawyer's sleeve.

'A word,' said the dwarf, 'before we go farther. Sally, hark 'ee for a minute.'

Miss Sally drew closer, as if accustomed to business conferences with their host which were the better for not having air.

'Business,' said the dwarf, glancing from brother to sister. 'Very private business. Lay your heads together when you 're by yourselves.'

'Certainly, sir,' returned Brass, taking out his pocket-book and pencil. 'I 'll take down the heads if you please, sir. Remarkable documents,' added the lawyer, raising his eyes to the ceiling, 'most remarkable documents. He states his points so clearly that it 's a treat to have 'em! I don't know any act of parliament that 's equal to him in clearness.'

'I shall deprive you of a treat,' said Quilp. 'Put up your book. We don't want any documents. So. There 's a lad named Kit—'

Miss Sally nodded, implying that she knew of him.

'Kit!' said Mr. Sampson.—'Kit! Ha! I 've heard the name before, but I don't exactly call to mind—I don't exactly—'

'You 're as slow as a tortoise, and more thick-headed than a rhinoceros,' returned his obliging client with an impatient gesture.

'He 's extremely pleasant!' cried the obsequious Sampson. 'His acquaintance with Natural History too is surprising. Quite a Buffoon, quite!'

There is no doubt that Mr. Brass intended some compliment or other; and it has been argued with show of reason that he would have said Buffon, but made use of a superfluous vowel. Be this as it may, Quilp gave him no time for correction, as he performed that office himself by more than tapping him on the head with the handle of his umbrella.

'Don't let's have any wrangling,' said Miss Sally, staying his hand. 'I've showed you that I know him, and that's enough.'

'She's always foremost!' said the dwarf, patting her on the back and looking contemptuously at Sampson. 'I don't like Kit, Sally.'

'Nor I,' rejoined Miss Brass.

'Nor I,' said Sampson.

'Why, that's right!' cried Quilp. 'Half our work is done already. This Kit is one of your honest people; one of your fair characters; a prowling prying hound; a hypocrite; a double-faced, white-livered, sneaking spy; a crouching cur to those that feed and coax him, and a barking yelping dog to all besides.'

'Fearfully eloquent!' cried Brass with a sneeze. 'Quite appalling!'

'Come to the point,' said Miss Sally, 'and don't talk so much.'

'Right again!' exclaimed Quilp, with another contemptuous look at Sampson, 'always foremost! I say, Sally, he is a yelping, insolent dog to all besides, and most of all, to me. In short, I owe him a grudge.'

'That's enough, sir,' said Sampson.

'No, it's not enough, sir,' sneered Quilp; 'will you hear me out? Besides that I owe him a grudge on that account, he thwarts me at this minute, and stands between me and an end which might otherwise prove a golden one to us all. Apart from that, I repeat that he crosses my humour, and I hate him. Now, you know the lad, and can guess the rest. Devise your own means of putting him out of my way, and execute them. Shall it be done?'

'I shall, sir,' said Sampson.

'Then give me your hand,' retorted Quilp. 'Sally, girl, yours. I rely as much, or more, on you than him. Tom Scott comes back. Lantern, pipes, more grog, and a jolly night of it!'

No other word was spoken, no other look exchanged, which had the slightest reference to this, the real occasion of their meeting. The trio were well accustomed to act together, and were linked to each other by ties of mutual interest and advantage, and nothing more was needed. Resuming his boisterous manner with the same ease with which he had thrown it off, Quilp was in an instant the same uproarious, reckless little savage he had been a few seconds before. It was ten o'clock at night before the amiable Sally supported her beloved and loving brother from the Wilderness, by which time he needed the utmost support her tender frame could render; his walk being from some unknown reason anything but steady, and his legs constantly doubling up in unexpected places.

Overpowered, nothwithstanding his late prolonged slumbers, by the fatigues of the last few days, the dwarf lost no time in creeping to his dainty house, and was soon dreaming in his hammock. Leaving him to visions, in which perhaps the quiet figures we quitted in the old church porch were not without their share, be it our task to rejoin them as they sat and watched.

CHAPTER LII

AFTER a long time, the schoolmaster appeared at the wicket-gate of the churchyard, and hurried towards them, jingling in his hand, as he came along, a bundle of rusty keys. He was quite breathless with pleasure and haste when he reached the porch, and at first could only point towards the old building which the child had been contemplating so earnestly.

'You see those two old houses,' he said at last.

'Yes, surely,' replied Nell.   'I have been looking at them nearly all the time you have been away.'

'And you would have looked at them more curiously yet, if you could have guessed what I have to tell you,' said her friend.   'One of those houses is mine.'

Without saying any more, or giving the child time to reply, the schoolmaster took her hand, and, his honest face quite radiant with exultation, led her to the place of which he spoke.

They stopped before its low arched door.   After trying several of the keys in vain, the schoolmaster found one to fit the huge lock, which turned back, creaking, and admitted them into the house.

The room into which they entered was a vaulted chamber once nobly ornamented by cunning archi-tects, and still retaining, in its beautiful groined roof and rich stone tracery, choice remnants of its ancient splendour.   Foliage carved in the stone, and emula-ting the mastery of Nature's hand, yet remained to tell how many times the leaves outside had come and gone, while it lived on unchanged.   The broken figures supporting the burden of the chimney-piece, though mutilated, were still distinguishable for what they had been—far different from the dust without—and showed sadly by the empty hearth, like creatures who had outlived their kind, and mourned their own too slow decay.

In some old time—for even change was old in that old place—a wooden partition had been constructed in one part of the chamber to form a sleeping-closet, into which the light was admitted at the same period by a rude window, or rather niche, cut in the solid wall.   This screen, together with two seats in the broad chimney, had at some forgotten date been part of the church or convent; for the oak, hastily appropriated to its present purpose, had been little altered from its former shape, and presented to the eye a pile of fragments of rich carving from old monkish stalls.

An open door leading to a small room or cell, dim with the light that came through leaves of ivy, completed the interior of this portion of the ruin. It was not quite destitute of furniture. A few strange chairs, whose arms and legs looked as though they had dwindled away with age; a table, the very spectre of its race: a great old chest that had once held records in the church, with other quaintly-fashioned domestic necessaries, and store of fire-wood for the winter, were scattered around, and gave evident tokens of its occupation as a dwelling-place at no very distant time.

The child looked around her, with that solemn feeling with which we contemplate the work of ages that have become but drops of water in the great ocean of eternity. The old man had followed them, but they were all three hushed for a space, and drew their breath softly, as if they feared to break the silence even by so slight a sound.

'It is a very beautiful place!' said the child, in a low voice.

'I almost feared you thought otherwise,' returned the schoolmaster. 'You shivered when we first came in, as if you felt it cold or gloomy.'

'It was not that,' said Nell, glancing round with a slight shudder. 'Indeed I cannot tell you what it was, but when I saw the outside, from the church porch, the same feeling came over me. It is its being so old and grey perhaps.'

'A peaceful place to live in, don't you think so?' said her friend.

'Oh yes,' rejoined the child, clasping her hands earnestly. 'A quiet, happy place—a place to live and learn to die in!' She would have said more, but that the energy of her thoughts caused her voice to falter, and come in trembling whispers from her lips.

'A place to live, and learn to live, and gather health of mind and body in,' said the schoolmaster; 'for this old house is yours.'

'Ours!' cried the child.

'Ay,' returned the schoolmaster gaily, 'for many a merry year to come, I hope. I shall be a close neighbour—only next door—but this house is yours.'

Having now disburdened himself of his great surprise, the schoolmaster sat down, and drawing Nell to his side, told her how he had learnt that that ancient tenement had been occupied for a very long time by an old person, nearly a hundred years of age, who kept the keys of the church, opened and closed it for the services, and showed it to strangers; how she had died not many weeks ago, and nobody had yet been found to fill the office; how, learning all this in an interview with the sexton, who was confined to his bed by rheumatism, he had been bold to make mention of his fellow-traveller, which had been so favourably received by that high authority, that he had taken courage, acting on his advice, to propound the matter to the clergyman. In a word, the result of his exertions was, that Nell and her grandfather were to be carried before the last-named gentleman next day; and, his approval of their conduct and appearance reserved as a matter of form, that they were already appointed to the vacant post.

'There's a small allowance of money,' said the schoolmaster. 'It is not much, but still enough to live upon in this retired spot. By clubbing our funds together, we shall do bravely; no fear of that.'

'Heaven bless and prosper you!' sobbed the child.

'Amen, my dear,' returned her friend cheerfully; 'and all of us, as it will, and has, in leading us through sorrow and trouble to this tranquil life.   But we must look at *my* house now.   Come!'

They repaired to the other tenement; tried the rusty keys as before; at length found the right one; and opened the worm-eaten door.   It led into a chamber, vaulted and old, like that from which they had come, but not so spacious, and having only one other little room attached.   It was not difficult to divine that the other house was of right the schoolmaster's, and that he had chosen for himself the least commodious, in his care and regard for them.   Like the adjoining habitation, it held such old articles of furniture as were absolutely necessary, and had its stack of firewood.

To make these dwellings as habitable and full of comfort as they could, was now their pleasant care. In a short time, each had its cheerful fire glowing and crackling on the hearth, and reddening the pale old wall with a hale and healthy blush.   Nell, busily plying her needle, repaired the tattered window-hangings, drew together the rents that time had worn in the threadbare scraps of carpet, and made them whole and decent.   The schoolmaster swept and smoothed the ground before the door, trimmed the long grass, trained the ivy and creeping plants which hung their drooping heads in melancholy neglect; and gave to the outer walls a cheery air of home.   The old man, sometimes by his side and sometimes with the child, lent his aid to both, went here and there on little patient services, and was happy.   Neighbours, too, as they came from work, proffered their help; or sent their children with such small presents or loans as the strangers needed most.   It was a busy day; and night came on, and found them wondering that there was yet so much to do, and that it should be dark so soon.

They took their supper together, in the house which may be henceforth called the child's; and, when they had finished their meal, drew round the fire, and almost in whispers—their hearts were too quiet and glad for loud expression—discussed their future plans. Before they separated, the schoolmaster read some prayers aloud; and then, full of gratitude and happiness, they parted for the night.

At that silent hour, when her grandfather was sleeping peacefully in his bed, and every sound was hushed, the child lingered before the dying embers, and thought of her past fortunes as if they had been a dream and she only now awoke. The glare of the sinking flame, reflected in the oaken panels whose carved tops were dimly seen in the dusky roof—the aged walls, where strange shadows came and went with every flickering of the fire—the solemn presence, within, of that decay which falls on senseless things the most enduring in their nature: and, without, and round about on every side, of Death—filled her with deep and thoughtful feelings, but with none of terror or alarm. A change had been gradually stealing over her, in the time of her loneliness and sorrow. With failing strength and heightening resolution, there had sprung up a purified and altered mind; there had grown in her bosom blessed thoughts and hopes, which are the portion of few but the weak and drooping. There were none to see the frail, perishable figure, as it glided from the fire and leaned pensively at the open casement; none but the stars, to look into the upturned face and read its history. The old church bell rang out the hour with a mournful sound, as if it had grown sad from so much communing with the dead and unheeded warning to the living; the fallen leaves rustled; the grass stirred upon the graves; all else was still and sleeping.

Some of those dreamless sleepers lay close within the shadow of the church—touching the wall, as if they clung to it for comfort and protection. Others had chosen to lie beneath the changing shade of trees; others by the path, that footsteps might come near them; others, among the graves of little children. Some had desired to rest beneath the very ground they had trodden in their daily walks; some, where the setting sun might shine upon their beds; some, where its light would fall upon them when it rose. Perhaps not one of the imprisoned souls had been able quite to separate itself in living thought from its old companion. If any had, it had still felt for it a love like that which captives have been known to bear towards the cell in which they have been long confined, and, even at parting, hung upon its narrow bounds affectionately.

It was long before the child closed the window, and approached her bed. Again something of the same sensation as before—an involuntary chill—a momentary feeling akin to fear—but vanishing directly, and leaving no alarm behind. Again, too, dreams of the little scholar; of the roof opening, and a column of bright faces, rising far away into the sky, as she had seen in some old scriptural picture once, and looking down on her, asleep. It was a sweet and happy dream. The quiet spot, outside, seemed to remain the same, saving that there was music in the air, and a sound of angels' wings. After a time the sisters came there, hand in hand, and stood among the graves. And then the dream grew dim, and faded.

With the brightness and joy of morning, came the renewal of yesterday's labours, the revival of its pleasant thoughts, the restoration of its energies, cheerfulness, and hope. They worked gaily in ordering and arranging their houses until noon, and then went to visit the clergyman.

He was a simple-hearted old gentleman, of a shrinking, subdued spirit, accustomed to retirement, and very little acquainted with the world, which he had left many years before to come and settle in that place. His wife had died in the house in which he still lived, and he had long since lost sight of any earthly cares or hopes beyond it.

He received them very kindly, and at once showed an interest in Nell; asking her name, and age, her birthplace, the circumstances which had led her there, and so forth. The schoolmaster had already told her story. They had no other friends or home to leave, he said, and had come to share his fortunes. He loved the child as though she were his own.

'Well, well,' said the clergyman. 'Let it be as you desire. She is very young.'

'Old in adversity and trial, sir,' replied the schoolmaster.

'God help her. Let her rest, and forget them,' said the old gentleman. 'But an old church is a dull and gloomy place for one so young as you, my child.'

'Oh no, sir,' returned Nell. 'I have no such thoughts, indeed.'

'I would rather see her dancing on the green at nights,' said the old gentleman, laying his hand upon her head, and smiling sadly, 'than have her sitting in the shadow of our mouldering arches. You must look to this, and see that her heart does not grow heavy among these solemn ruins. Your request is granted, friend.'

After more kind words, they withdrew, and repaired to the child's house; where they were yet in conversation on their happy fortune, when another friend appeared.

This was a little old gentleman, who lived in the parsonage-house, and had resided there (so they learnt soon afterwards) ever since the death of the clergyman's wife, which had happened fifteen years before. He had been his college friend and always his close companion; in the first shock of his grief he had come to console and comfort him; and from that time they had never parted company. The little old gentleman was the active spirit of the place, the adjuster of all differences, the promoter of all merrymakings, the dispenser of his friend's bounty, and of no small charity of his own besides; the universal mediator, comforter, and friend. None of the simple villagers had cared to ask his name, or, when they knew it, to store it in their memory. Perhaps from some vague rumour of his college honours which had been whispered abroad on his first arrival, perhaps because he was an unmarried, unencumbered gentleman, he had been called a bachelor. The name pleased him, or suited him as well as any other, and the Bachelor he had ever since remained. And the bachelor it was, it may be added, who with his own hands had laid in the stock of fuel which the wanderers had found in their new habitation.

The bachelor, then—to call him by his usual appellation—lifted the latch, showed his little round mild face for a moment at the door, and stepped into the room like one who was no stranger to it.

'You are Mr. Marton, the new schoolmaster?' he said, greeting Nell's kind friend.

'I am, sir.'

'You come well recommended, and I am glad to see you. I should have been in the way yesterday, expecting you, but I rode across the country to carry a message for a sick mother to her daughter in service some miles off, and have but just now returned. This is our young church-keeper? You are not the less welcome, friend, for her sake, or for this old man's; nor the worse teacher for having learnt humanity.'

'She has been ill, sir, very lately,' said the schoolmaster, in answer to the look with which their visitor regarded Nell when he had kissed her cheek.

'Yes, yes. I know she has,' he rejoined. 'There have been suffering and heartache here.'

'Indeed there have, sir.'

The little old gentleman glanced at the grandfather, and back again at the child, whose hand he took tenderly in his, and held.

'You will be happier here,' he said; 'we will try, at least, to make you so. You have made great improvements here already. Are they the work of your hands?'

'Yes, sir.'

'We may make some others—not better in themselves, but with better means perhaps,' said the bachelor. 'Let us see now, let us see.'

Nell accompanied him into the other little rooms, and over both the houses, in which he found various small comforts wanting, which he engaged to supply from a certain collection of odds and ends he had at home, and which must have been a very miscellaneous and extensive one, as it comprehended the most opposite articles imaginable. They all came, however, and came without loss of time; for the little old gentleman, disappearing for some five or ten minutes, presently returned, laden with old shelves, rugs, blankets, and other household gear, and followed by a boy bearing a similar load. These being cast on the floor in a promiscuous heap, yielded a quantity of occupation in arranging, erecting, and putting away;

the superintendence of which task evidently afforded the old gentleman extreme delight, and engaged him for some time with great briskness and activity. When nothing more was left to be done, he charged the boy to run off and bring his schoolmates to be marshalled before their new master, and solemnly reviewed.

'As good a set of fellows, Marton, as you 'd wish to see,' he said, turning to the schoolmaster when the boy was gone; 'but I don't let 'em know I think so. That wouldn't do, at all.'

The messenger soon returned at the head of a long row of urchins, great and small, who, being confronted by the bachelor at the house door, fell into various convulsions of politeness; clutching their hats and caps, squeezing them into the smallest possible dimensions, and making all manner of bows and scrapes, which the little old gentleman contemplated with excessive satisfaction, and expressed his approval of by a great many nods and smiles.   Indeed, his approbation of the boys was by no means so scrupulously disguised as he had led the schoolmaster to suppose, inasmuch as it broke out in sundry loud whispers and confidential remarks which were perfectly audible to them every one.

'This first boy, schoolmaster,' said the bachelor, 'is John Owen; a lad of good parts, sir, and frank, honest temper; but too thoughtless, too playful, too light-headed by far.   That boy, my good sir, would break his neck with pleasure, and deprive his parents of their chief comfort—and between ourselves, when you come to see him at hare and hounds, taking the fence and ditch by the finger-post, and sliding down the face of the little quarry, you 'll never forget it.   It 's beautiful!'

John Owen having been thus rebuked, and being in

perfect possession of the speech aside, the bachelor singled out another boy.

'Now, look at that lad, sir,' said the bachelor.   'You see that fellow?   Richard Evans his name is, sir.   An amazing boy to learn, blessed with a good memory, and a ready understanding, and moreover with a good voice and ear for psalm-singing, in which he is the best among us.   Yet, sir, that boy will come to a bad end; he 'll never die in his bed; he 's always falling asleep in sermon-time—and to tell you the truth, Mr. Marton, I always did the same at his age, and feel quite certain that it was natural to my constitution and I couldn't help it.'

This hopeful pupil edified by the above terrible reproval, the bachelor turned to another.

'But if we talk of examples to be shunned,' said he, 'if we come to boys that should be a warning and a beacon to all their fellows, here 's the one, and I hope you won't spare him.   This is the lad, sir; this one with the blue eyes and light hair.   This is a swimmer, sir, this fellow—a diver, Lord save us!   This is a boy, sir, who had a fancy for plunging into eighteen feet of water, with his clothes on, and bringing up a blind man's dog, who was being drowned by the weight of his chain and collar, while his master stood wringing his hands upon the bank, bewailing the loss of his guide and friend.   I sent the boy two guineas anonymously, sir,' added the bachelor, in his peculiar whisper, 'directly I heard of it; but never mention it on any account, for he hasn't the least idea that it came from me.'

Having disposed of this culprit, the bachelor turned to another, and from him to another, and so on through the whole array, laying, for their wholesome restriction within due bounds, the same cutting emphasis on such of their propensities as were dearest to his heart and were unquestionably referable to his own precept and example. Thoroughly persuaded, in the end, that he had made them miserable by his severity, he dismissed them with a small present, and an admonition to walk quietly home, without any leapings, scufflings, or turnings out of the way; which injunction, he informed the schoolmaster in the same audible confidence, he did not think he could have obeyed when he was a boy, had his life depended on it.

Hailing these little tokens of the bachelor's disposition as so many assurances of his own welcome course from that time, the schoolmaster parted from him with a light heart and joyous spirits, and deemed himself one of the happiest men on earth. The windows of the two old houses were ruddy again, that night, with the reflection of the cheerful fires that burnt within; and the bachelor and his friend, pausing to look upon them as they returned from their evening walk, spoke softly together of the beautiful child, and looked round upon the churchyard with a sigh.

CHAPTER LIII

NELL was stirring early in the morning, and having discharged her household tasks, and put everything in order for the good schoolmaster (though sorely against his will, for he would have spared her the pains), took down, from its nail by the fireside, a little bundle of keys with which the bachelor had formally invested her on the previous day, and went out alone to visit the old church.

The sky was serene and bright, the air clear, perfumed with the fresh scent of newly fallen leaves,

and grateful to every sense. The neighbouring
stream sparkled, and rolled onward with a tuneful
sound; the dew glistened on the green mounds, like
tears shed by Good Spirits over the dead.

Some young children sported among the tombs,
and hid from each other, with laughing faces. They
had an infant with them, and had laid it down asleep
upon a child's grave, in a little bed of leaves. It was
a new grave—the resting-place, perhaps, of some little
creature, who, meek and patient in its illness, had
often sat and watched them, and now seemed, to their
minds, scarcely changed.

She drew near and asked one of them whose grave
it was. The child answered that that was not its
name; it was a garden—his brother's. It was green-
er, he said, than all the other gardens, and the birds
loved it better because he had been used to feed them.
When he had done speaking, he looked at her with a
smile, and kneeling down and nestling for a moment
with his cheek against the turf, bounded merrily away.

She passed the church, gazing upward at its old
tower, went through the wicket-gate, and so into the
village. The old sexton, leaning on a crutch, was
taking the air at his cottage door, and gave her good
morrow.

'You are better?' said the child, stopping to speak
with him.

'Ay surely,' returned the old man. 'I'm thankful
to say, much better.'

'You will be quite well soon.'

'With Heaven's leave, and a little patience. But
come in, come in!'

The old man limped on before, and warning her
of the downward step, which he achieved himself with
no small difficulty, led the way into his little cottage.

'It is but one room, you see. There is another up

above, but the stair has got harder to climb of late years, and I never use it.   I 'm thinking of taking to it again, next summer, though.'

The child wondered how a grey-headed man like him—one of his trade too—could talk of time so easily. He saw her eyes wandering to the tools that hung upon the wall, and smiled.

'I warrant now,' he said, 'that you think all those are used in making graves.'

'Indeed, I wondered that you wanted so many.'

'And well you might.   I am a gardener.   I dig the ground, and plant things that are to live and grow. My works don't all moulder away, and rot in the earth. You see that spade in the centre?'

'The very old one—so notched and worn?   Yes.'

'That 's the sexton's spade, and it 's a well-used one, as you see.   We 're healthy people here, but it has done a power of work.   If it could speak now, that spade, it would tell you of many an unexpected job that it and I have done together; but I forget 'em, for my memory 's a poor one.—That 's nothing new,' he added hastily.   'It always was.'

'There are flowers and shrubs to speak to your other work,' said the child.

'Oh yes.   And tall trees.   But they are not so separate from the sexton's labours as you think.'

'No!'

'Not in my mind, and recollection—such as it is,' said the old man.   'Indeed they often help it.   For say that I planted such a tree for such a man.   There it stands, to remind me that he died.   When I look at its broad shadow, and remember what it was in his time, it helps me to the age of my other work, and I can tell you pretty nearly when I made his grave.'

'But it may remind you of one who is still alive,' said the child.

'Of twenty that are dead, in connection with that one who lives, then,' rejoined the old man; 'wife, husband, parents, brothers, sisters, children, friends—a score at least.   So it happens that the sexton's spade gets worn and battered.   I shall need a new one—next summer.'

The child looked quickly towards him, thinking that he jested with his age and infirmity: but the unconscious sexton was quite in earnest.

'Ah!' he said, after a brief silence.   'People never learn.   They never learn.   It's only we who turn up the ground, where nothing grows and everything decays, who think of such things as these—who think of them properly, I mean.   You have been into the church?'

'I am going there now,' the child replied.

'There's an old well there,' said the sexton, 'right underneath the belfry; a deep, dark, echoing well. Forty year ago, you had only to let down the bucket till the first knot in the rope was free of the windlass, and you heard it splashing in the cold dull water. By little and little the water fell away, so that in ten year after that, a second knot was made, and you must unwind so much rope, or the bucket swung tight and empty at the end.   In ten years' time, the water fell again, and a third knot was made.   In ten years more, the well dried up; and now, if you lower the bucket till your arms are tired, and let out nearly all the cord, you'll hear it, of a sudden, clanking and rattling on the ground below; with a sound of being so deep and so far down, that your heart leaps into your mouth, and you start away as if you were falling in.'

'A dreadful place to come on in the dark!' exclaimed the child, who had followed the old man's looks and words until she seemed to stand upon its brink.

'What is it but a grave?' said the sexton.   'What

else? And which of our old folks, knowing all this, thought, as the spring subsided, of their own failing strength, and lessening life? Not one!'

'Are you very old yourself?' asked the child involuntarily.

'I shall be seventy-nine—next summer.'

'You still work when you are well?'

'Work! To be sure. You shall see my gardens hereabout. Look at the window there. I made, and have kept, that plot of ground entirely with my own hands. By this time next year I shall hardly see the sky, the boughs will have grown so thick. I have my winter work at night besides.'

He opened, as he spoke, a cupboard close to where he sat, and produced some miniature boxes, carved in a homely manner and made of old wood.

'Some gentlefolks who are fond of ancient days, and what belongs to them,' he said, 'like to buy these keepsakes from our church and ruins. Sometimes, I make them of scraps of oak, that turn up here and there; sometimes of bits of coffins which the vaults have long preserved. See here—this is a little chest of the last kind, clasped at the edges with fragments of brass plates that had writing on 'em once, though it would be hard to read it now. I haven't many by me at this time of year, but these shelves will be full—next summer.'

The child admired and praised his work, and shortly afterwards departed; thinking, as she went, how strange it was, that this old man, drawing from his pursuits, and everything around him, one stern moral, never contemplated its application to himself; and, while he dwelt upon the uncertainty of human life, seemed both in word and deed to deem himself immortal. But her musings did not stop here, for she was wise enough to think that by a good and merciful adjustment this must be human nature, and that the old sexton, with his plans for next summer, was but a type of all mankind.

Full of these meditations, she reached the church. It was easy to find the key belonging to the outer door, for each was labelled on a scrap of yellow parchment. Its very turning in the lock awoke a hollow sound, and when she entered with a faltering step, the echoes that it raised in closing, made her start.

If the peace of the simple village had moved the child more strongly, because of the dark and troubled ways that lay beyond, and through which she had journeyed with such failing feet, what was the deep impression of finding herself alone in that solemn building, where the very light, coming through sunken windows, seemed old and grey, and the air, redolent of earth and mould, seemed laden with decay, purified by time of all its grosser particles, and sighing through arch and aisle, and clustered pillars, like the breath of ages gone?   Here was the broken pavement, worn, so long ago, by pious feet, that Time, stealing on the pilgrims' steps, had trodden out their track, and left but crumbling stones. Here were the rotten beam, the sinking arch, the sapped and mouldering wall, the lowly trench of earth, the stately tomb on which no epitaph remained,—all,—marble, stone, iron, wood, and dust, one common monument of ruin.   The best work and the worst, the plainest and the richest, the stateliest and the least imposing—both of Heaven's work and Man's—all found one common level here, and told one common tale.

Some part of the edifice had been a baronial chapel, and here were effigies of warriors stretched upon their beds of stone with folded hands—cross-legged, those who had fought in the Holy Wars—girded with their swords, and cased in armour as they had lived.   Some of these knights had their own weapons, helmets, coats of mail, hanging upon the walls hard by, and dangling from rusty hooks.   Broken and dilapidated as they were, they yet retained their ancient form, and something of their ancient aspect.   Thus violent deeds live after men upon the earth, and traces of war and bloodshed will survive in mournful shapes long after those who worked the desolation are but atoms of earth themselves.

The child sat down, in this old, silent place, among the stark figures on the tombs—they made it more quiet there, than elsewhere, to her fancy—and gazing round with a feeling of awe, tempered with a calm delight, felt that now she was happy, and at rest.   She took a Bible from the shelf, and read; then, laying it down, thought of the summer days and the bright springtime that would come—of the rays of sun that would fall in aslant upon the sleeping forms—of the leaves that would flutter at the window, and play in glistening shadows on the pavement—of the songs of birds, and growth of buds and blossoms out of doors —of the sweet air, that would steal in, and gently wave the tattered banners overhead.   What if the spot awakened thoughts of death?   Die who would, it would still remain the same; these sights and sounds would still go on, as happily as ever.   It would be no pain to sleep amidst them.

She left the chapel—very slowly and often turning back to gaze again—and coming to a low door, which plainly led into the tower, opened it, and climbed the winding stair in darkness; save where she looked down, through narrow loopholes, on the place she had left, or caught a glimmering vision of the dusty bells.   At length she gained the end of the ascent and stood upon the turret top.

Oh! the glory of the sudden burst of light; the

freshness of the fields and woods, stretching away on every side, and meeting the bright blue sky; the cattle grazing in the pasturage; the smoke, that, coming from among the trees, seemed to rise upward from the green earth; the children yet at their gambols down below—all, everything, so beautiful and happy! It was like passing from death to life; it was drawing nearer Heaven.

The children were gone, when she emerged into the porch, and locked the door. As she passed the schoolhouse she could hear the busy hum of voices. Her friend had begun his labours only on that day. The noise grew louder, and, looking back, she saw the boys come trooping out and disperse themselves with merry shouts and play. 'It's a good thing,' thought the child, 'I am very glad they pass the church.' And then she stopped, to fancy how the noise would sound inside, and how gently it would seem to die away upon the ear.

Again that day, yes, twice again, she stole back to the old chapel, and in her former seat read from the same book, or indulged the same quiet train of thought. Even when it had grown dusk, and the shadows of coming night made it more solemn still, the child remained, like one rooted to the spot, and had no fear or thought of stirring.

They found her there, at last, and took her home. She looked pale but very happy, until they separated for the night; and then, as the poor schoolmaster stooped down to kiss her cheek, he thought he felt a tear upon his face.

CHAPTER LIV

THE bachelor, among his various occupations, found in the old church a constant source of interest and amusement. Taking that pride in it which men conceive for the wonders of their own little world, he had made its history his study; and many a summer day within its walls, and many a winter's night beside the parsonage fire, had found the bachelor still poring over, and adding to, his goodly store of tale and legend.

As he was not one of those rough spirits who would strip fair Truth of every little shadowy vestment in which time and teeming fancies love to array her—and some of which become her pleasantly enough, serving, like the waters of her well, to add new graces to the charms they half conceal and half suggest, and to awaken interest and pursuit rather than languor and indifference—as, unlike this stern and obdurate class, he loved to see the goddess crowned with those garlands of wildflowers which tradition wreathes for her gentle wearing, and which are often freshest in their homeliest shapes,—he trod with a light step and bore with a light hand upon the dust of centuries, unwilling to demolish any of the airy shrines that had been raised above it, if any good feeling or affection of the human heart were hiding thereabouts. Thus, in the case of an ancient coffin of rough stone, supposed, for many generations, to contain the bones of a certain baron, who, after ravaging, with cut, and thrust, and plunder, in foreign lands, came back with a penitent and sorrowing heart to die at home, but which had been lately shown by learned antiquaries to be no such thing, as the baron in question (so they contended) had died hard in battle, gnashing his teeth and cursing with his latest breath,—the bachelor stoutly maintained that the old tale was the true one; that the baron, repenting him of the evil, had done great charities and meekly given up the ghost; and that, if ever baron went to heaven, that baron was then at peace. In like manner, when the aforesaid antiquaries did argue and contend that a certain secret vault was not the tomb of a grey-haired lady who had been hanged and drawn and quartered by glorious Queen Bess for succouring a wretched priest who fainted of thirst and hunger at her door, the bachelor did solemnly maintain, against all comers, that the church was hallowed by the said poor lady's ashes; that her remains had been collected in the night from four of the city's gates, and thither in secret brought, and there deposited; and the bachelor did further (being highly excited at such times) deny the glory of Queen Bess, and assert the immeasurably greater glory of the meanest woman in her realm, who had a merciful and tender heart. As to the assertion that the flat stone near the door was not the grave of the miser who had disowned his only child and left a sum of money to the church to buy a peal of bells, the bachelor did readily admit the same, and that the place had given birth to no such man. In a word, he would have had every stone, and plate of brass, the monument only of deeds whose memory should survive. All others he was willing to forget. They might be buried in consecrated ground, but he would have had them buried deep, and never brought to light again.

It was from the lips of such a tutor, that the child learnt her easy task. Already impressed beyond all telling, by the silent building and the peaceful beauty of the spot in which it stood—majestic age surrounded by perpetual youth—it seemed to her when she heard these things, sacred to all goodness and virtue. It was another world, where sin and sorrow never came; a tranquil place of rest, where nothing evil entered.

When the bachelor had given her in connection with almost every tomb and flat grave-stone some history of its own, he took her down into the old crypt, now a mere dull vault, and showed her how it had been lighted up in the time of the monks, and how, amid lamps depending from the roof, and swinging censers exhaling scented odours, and habits glittering with gold and silver, and pictures, and precious stuffs, and jewels all flashing and glistening through the low arches, the chaunt of aged voices had been many a time heard there, at midnight, in old days, while hooded figures knelt and prayed around, and told their rosaries of beads. Thence, he took her above ground again, and showed her, high up in the old walls, small galleries, where the nuns had been wont to glide along—dimly seen in their dark dresses so far off—or to pause like gloomy shadows, listening to the prayers. He showed her too, how the warriors, whose figures rested on the tombs, had worn those rotting scraps of armour up above—how this had been a helmet, and that a shield, and that a gauntlet—and how they had wielded the great two-handed swords, and beaten men down with yonder iron mace. All that he told the child she treasured in her mind; and sometimes, when she awoke at night from dreams of those old times, and rising from her bed looked out at the dark church, she almost hoped to see the windows lighted up, and hear the organ's swell, and sound of voices, on the rushing wind.

The old sexton soon got better, and was about again. From him the child learnt many other things, though of a different kind. He was not able to work, but one day there was a grave to be made, and he came to overlook the man who dug it. He was in a talkative mood; and the child, at first standing by his side, and afterwards sitting on the grass at his feet, with her thoughtful face raised towards his, began to converse with him.

Now, the man who did the sexton's duty was a little older than he, though much more active. But he was deaf; and when the sexton (who peradventure, on a pinch, might have walked a mile with great difficulty in half a dozen hours) exchanged a remark with him about his work, the child could not help noticing that he did so with an impatient kind of pity for his infirmity, as if he were himself the strongest and heartiest man alive.

'I'm sorry to see there is this to do,' said the child when she approached. 'I heard of no one having died.'

'She lived in another hamlet, my dear,' returned the sexton. 'Three mile away.'

'Was she young?'

'Ye—yes,' said the sexton; 'not more than sixty-four, I think. David, was she more than sixty-four?'

David, who was digging hard, heard nothing of the question. The sexton, as he could not reach to touch him with his crutch, and was too infirm to rise without assistance, called his attention by throwing a little mould upon his red night-cap.

'What's the matter now?' said David, looking up.

'How old was Becky Morgan?' asked the sexton.

'Becky Morgan?' repeated David.

'Yes,' replied the sexton; adding in a half-compassionate, half-irritable tone, which the old man couldn't hear, 'you're getting very deaf, Davy, very deaf to be sure!'

The old man stopped in his work, and cleansing his spade with a piece of slate he had by him for the purpose—and scraping off, in the process, the essence of

Heaven knows how many Becky Morgans—set himself to consider the subject.

'Let me think,' quoth he. 'I saw last night what they had put upon the coffin—was it seventy-nine?'

'No, no,' said the sexton.

'Ah yes, it was though,' returned the old man with a sigh. 'For I remember thinking she was very near our age. Yes, it was seventy-nine.'

'Are you sure you didn't mistake a figure, Davy?' asked the sexton, with signs of some emotion.

'What?' said the old man. 'Say that again.'

'He's very deaf. He's very deaf indeed,' cried the sexton petulantly; 'are you sure you're right about the figures?'

'Oh quite,' replied the old man. 'Why not?'

'He's exceedingly deaf,' muttered the sexton to himself. 'I think he's getting foolish.'

The child rather wondered what had led him to this belief, as, to say the truth, the old man seemed quite as sharp as he, and was infinitely more robust. As the sexton said nothing more just then, however, she forgot it for the time, and spoke again.

'You were telling me,' she said, 'about your gardening. Do you ever plant things here?'

'In the churchyard?' returned the sexton. 'Not I.'

'I have seen some flowers and little shrubs about,' the child rejoined; 'there are some over there, you see. I thought they were of your rearing, though indeed they grow but poorly.'

'They grow as Heaven wills,' said the old man; 'and it kindly ordains that they shall never flourish here.'

'I do not understand you.'

'Why, this it is,' said the sexton. 'They mark the graves of those who had very tender, loving friends.'

'I was sure they did!' the child exclaimed. 'I am very glad to know they do!'

'Aye,' returned the old man, 'but stay. Look at them. See how they hang their heads, and droop, and wither. Do you guess the reason?'

'No,' the child replied.

'Because the memory of those who lie below, passes away so soon. At first they tend them, morning, noon, and night; they soon begin to come less frequently; from once a day, to once a week; from once a week, to once a month; then, at long and uncertain intervals; then, not at all. Such tokens seldom flourish long. I have known the briefest summer flowers outlive them.'

'I grieve to hear it,' said the child.

'Ah! so say the gentlefolks who come down here to look about them,' returned the old man, shaking his head, 'but I say otherwise. "It 's a pretty custom you have in this part of the country," they say to me sometimes, "to plant the graves, but it 's melancholy to see these things all withering or dead." I crave their pardon and tell them that, as I take it, 'tis a good sign for the happiness of the living. And so it is. It 's nature.'

'Perhaps the mourners learn to look to the blue sky by day, and to the stars by night, and to think that the dead are there, and not in graves,' said the child in an earnest voice.

'Perhaps so,' replied the old man doubtfully. 'It may be.'

'Whether it be as I believe it is, or no,' thought the child within herself, 'I 'll make this place *my* garden. It will be no harm at least to work here day by day, and pleasant thoughts will come of it, I am sure.'

Her glowing cheek and moistened eye passed unnoticed by the sexton, who turned towards old David, and called him by his name. It was plain that Becky Morgan's age still troubled him; though why, the child could scarcely understand.

The second or third repetition of his name attracted the old man's attention. Pausing from his work, he leant on his spade, and put his hand to his dull ear.

'Did you call?' he said.

'I have been thinking, Davy,' replied the sexton, 'that she,' he pointed to the grave, 'must have been a deal older than you or me.'

'Seventy-nine,' answered the old man with a shake of the head, 'I tell you that I saw it.'

'Saw it?' replied the sexton; 'aye, but, Davy, women don't always tell the truth about their age.'

'That's true indeed,' said the other old man, with a sudden sparkle in his eye. 'She might have been older.'

'I'm sure she must have been. Why, only think how old she looked. You and I seemed but boys to her.'

'She did look old,' rejoined David. 'You're right. She did look old.'

'Call to mind how old she looked for many a long, long year, and say if she could be but seventy-nine at last—only our age,' said the sexton.

'Five year older at the very least!' cried the other.

'Five!' retorted the sexton. 'Ten. Good eighty-nine. I call to mind the time her daughter died. She was eighty-nine if she was a day, and tries to pass upon us now, for ten year younger. Oh! human vanity!'

The other old man was not behindhand with some moral reflections on this fruitful theme, and both adduced a mass of evidence, of such weight as to render it doubtful—not whether the deceased was of the age suggested, but whether she had not almost reached the patriarchal term of a hundred. When they had settled this question to their mutual satisfaction, the sexton, with his friend's assistance, rose to go.

'It's chilly, sitting here, and I must be careful—till the summer,' he said, as he prepared to limp away.

'What?' asked old David.

'He's very deaf, poor fellow!' cried the sexton. 'Good-bye!'

'Ah!' said old David, looking after him. 'He's failing very fast. He ages every day.'

And so they parted; each persuaded that the other had less life in him than himself; and both greatly consoled and comforted by the little fiction they had agreed upon, respecting Becky Morgan, whose decease was no longer a precedent of uncomfortable application, and would be no business of theirs for half a score of years to come.

The child remained, for some minutes, watching the deaf old man as he threw out the earth with his shovel, and, often stopping to cough and fetch his breath, still muttered to himself, with a kind of sober chuckle, that the sexton was wearing fast. At length she turned away, and walking thoughtlessly through the churchyard, came unexpectedly upon the schoolmaster, who was sitting on a green grave in the sun, reading.

'Nell here?' he said cheerfully, as he closed his book. 'It does me good to see you in the air and light. I feared you were again in the church, where you so often are.'

'Feared!' replied the child, sitting down beside him. 'Is it not a good place?'

'Yes, yes,' said the schoolmaster. 'But you must be gay sometimes—nay, don't shake your head and smile so sadly.'

'Not sadly, if you knew my heart. Do not look at me as if you thought me sorrowful. There is not a happier creature on earth, than I am now.'

Full of grateful tenderness, the child took his hand, and folded it between her own. 'It's God's will!' she said, when they had been silent for some time.

'What?'

'All this,' she rejoined; 'all this about us. But which of us is sad now? You see that *I* am smiling.'

'And so am I,' said the schoolmaster; 'smiling to think how often we shall laugh in this same place. Were you not talking yonder?'

'Yes,' the child rejoined.

'Of something that has made you sorrowful?'

There was a long pause.

'What was it?' said the schoolmaster, tenderly. 'Come. Tell me what it was.'

'I rather grieve—I *do* rather grieve to think,' said the child, bursting into tears, 'that those who die about us, are so soon forgotten.'

'And do you think,' said the schoolmaster, marking the glance she had thrown around, 'that an unvisited grave, a withered tree, a faded flower or two, are tokens of forgetfulness or cold neglect? Do you think there are no deeds, far away from here, in which these dead may be best remembered? Nell, Nell, there may be people busy in the world, at this instant, in whose good actions and good thoughts these very graves—neglected as they look to us—are the chief instruments.'

'Tell me no more,' said the child quickly. 'Tell me no more. I feel, I know it. How could *I* be unmindful of it, when I thought of you?'

'There is nothing,' cried her friend, 'no, nothing innocent or good, that dies, and is forgotten. Let us hold to that faith, or none. An infant, a prattling child, dying in its cradle, will live again in the better thoughts of those who love it, and will play its part, through them, in the redeeming actions of the world, though its body be burnt to ashes or drowned in the deepest sea.   There is not an angel added to the Host of Heaven but does its blessed work on earth in those that loved it here.   Forgotten! oh, if the good deeds of human creatures could be traced to their source, how beautiful would even death appear; for how much charity, mercy, and purified affection, would be seen to have their growth in dusty graves!'

'Yes,' said the child, 'it is the truth; I know it is. Who should feel its force so much as I, in whom your little scholar lives again?   Dear, dear, good friend, if you knew the comfort you have given me!'

The poor schoolmaster made her no answer, but bent over her in silence; for his heart was full.

They were yet seated in the same place, when the grandfather approached.   Before they had spoken many words together, the church clock struck the hour of school, and their friend withdrew.

'A good man,' said the grandfather, looking after him; 'a kind man.   Surely *he* will never harm us, Nell. We are safe here, at last, eh?   We will never go away from here?'

The child shook her head and smiled.

'She needs rest,' said the old man, patting her cheek; 'too pale—too pale.   She is not like what she was.'

'When?' asked the child.

'Ha!' said the old man, 'to be sure—when?   How many weeks ago?   Could I count them on my fingers?   Let them rest though; they 're better gone.'

'Much better, dear,' replied the child.   'We will forget them; or, if we ever call them to mind, it shall be only as some uneasy dream that has passed away.'

'Hush!' said the old man, motioning hastily to her with his hand and looking over his shoulder; 'no more talk of the dream, and all the miseries it brought. There are no dreams here. 'Tis a quiet place, and they keep away. Let us never think about them, lest they should pursue us again. Sunken eyes and hollow cheeks—wet, cold, and famine—and horrors before them all, that were even worse—we must forget such things if we would be tranquil here.'

'Thank Heaven!' inwardly exclaimed the child, 'for this most happy change!'

'I will be patient,' said the old man, 'humble, very thankful, and obedient, if you will let me stay. But do not hide from me; do not steal away alone; let me keep beside you. Indeed, I will be very true and faithful, Nell.'

'I steal away alone! why that,' replied the child, with assumed gaiety, 'would be a pleasant jest indeed. See here, dear grandfather, we'll make this place our garden—why not! It is a very good one—and to-morrow we'll begin, and work together, side by side.'

'It is a brave thought!' cried her grandfather. 'Mind, darling—we begin to-morrow!'

Who so delighted as the old man, when they next day began their labour! Who so unconscious of all associations connected with the spot, as he! They plucked the long grass and nettles from the tombs, thinned the poor shrubs and roots, made the turf smooth, and cleared it of the leaves and weeds. They were yet in the ardour of their work, when the child, raising her head from the ground over which she bent, observed that the bachelor was sitting on the stile close by, watching them in silence.

'A kind office,' said the little gentleman, nodding

to Nell as she curtsied to him. 'Have you done all that, this morning?'

'It is very little, sir,' returned the child, with downcast eyes, 'to what we mean to do.'

'Good work, good work,' said the bachelor. 'But do you only labour at the graves of children, and young people?'

'We shall come to the others in good time, sir,' replied Nell, turning her head aside, and speaking softly.

It was a slight incident, and might have been design or accident, or the child's unconscious sympathy with youth. But it seemed to strike upon her grandfather, though he had not noticed it before. He looked in a hurried manner at the graves, then anxiously at the child, then pressed her to his side, and bade her stop to rest. Something he had long forgotten, appeared to struggle faintly in his mind. It did not pass away, as weightier things had done; but came uppermost again, and yet again, and many times that day, and often afterwards. Once, while they were yet at work, the child, seeing that he often turned and looked uneasily at her, as though he were trying to resolve some painful doubts or collect some scattered thoughts, urged him to tell the reason. But he said it was nothing—nothing—and, laying her head upon his arm, patted her fair cheek with his hand, and muttered that she grew stronger every day, and would be a woman, soon.

CHAPTER LV

FROM that time, there sprung up in the old man's mind, a solicitude about the child which never slept or left him. There are chords in the human heart—strange, varying strings—which are only struck by accident; which will remain mute and senseless to appeals the most passionate and earnest, and respond at last to the slightest casual touch. In the most insensible or childish minds, there is some train of reflection which art can seldom lead, or skill assist, but which will reveal itself, as great truths have done, by chance, and when the discoverer has the plainest end in view. From that time, the old man never, for a moment, forgot the weakness and devotion of the child; from the time of that slight incident, he who had seen her toiling by his side through so much difficulty and suffering, and had scarcely thought of her otherwise than as the partner of miseries which he felt severely in his own person, and deplored for his own sake at least as much as hers, awoke to a sense of what he owed her, and what those miseries had made her. Never, no, never once, in one unguarded moment from that time to the end, did any care for himself, any thought of his own comfort, any selfish consideration or regard distract his thoughts from the gentle object of his love.

He would follow her up and down, waiting till she should tire and lean upon his arm—he would sit opposite to her in the chimney-corner, content to watch, and look, until she raised her head and smiled upon him as of old—he would discharge by stealth, those household duties which tasked her powers too heavily—he would rise, in the cold dark nights, to listen to her breathing in her sleep, and sometimes crouch for hours by her bedside only to touch her hand.   He who knows all, can only know what hopes, and fears, and thoughts of deep affection, were in that one disordered brain, and what a change had fallen on the poor old man.

Sometimes—weeks had crept on, then—the child, exhausted, though with little fatigue, would pass whole evenings on a couch beside the fire.   At such times, the schoolmaster would bring in books, and read to her aloud; and seldom an evening passed, but the bachelor came in, and took his turn of reading.   The old man sat and listened,—with little understanding for the words, but with his eyes fixed upon the child,—and if she smiled or brightened with the story, he would say it was a good one, and conceive a fondness for the very book.   When, in their evening talk, the bachelor told some tale that pleased her (as his tales were sure to do), the old man would painfully try to store it in his mind; nay, when the bachelor left them, he would sometimes slip out after him, and humbly beg that he would tell him such a part again, that he might learn to win a smile from Nell.

But these were rare occasions, happily; for the child yearned to be out of doors, and walking in her solemn garden.   Parties, too, would come to see the church; and those who came, speaking to others of the child, sent more; so even at that season of the year they had visitors almost daily.   The old man would follow them at a little distance through the building, listening to the voice he loved so well; and when the strangers left, and parted from Nell, he would mingle with them to catch up fragments of their conversation; or he would stand for the same purpose, with his grey head uncovered, at the gate as they passed through.

They always praised the child, her sense and beauty,

and he was proud to hear them! But what was that, so often added, which wrung his heart, and made him sob and weep alone, in some dull corner? Alas! even careless strangers—they who had no feeling for her, but the interest of the moment; they who would go away and forget next week that such a being lived— even they saw it—even they pitied her—even they bade him good day compassionately, and whispered as they passed.

The people of the village, too, of whom there was not one but grew to have a fondness for poor Nell; even among them, there was the same feeling; a tenderness towards her—a compassionate regard for her, increasing every day. The very schoolboys, light-hearted and thoughtless as they were, even they cared for her. The roughest among them was sorry if he missed her in the usual place upon his way to school, and would turn out of the path to ask for her at the latticed window. If she were sitting in the church, they perhaps might peep in softly at the open door; but they never spoke to her, unless she rose and went to speak to them. Some feeling was abroad which raised the child above them all.

So, when Sunday came. They were all poor country people in the church, for the castle in which the old family had lived, was an empty ruin, and there were none but humble folks for seven miles around. There, as elsewhere, they had an interest in Nell. They would gather round her in the porch, before and after service; young children would cluster at her skirts; and aged men and women forsake their gossips, to give her kindly greeting. None of them, young or old, thought of passing the child without a friendly word. Many who came from three or four miles distant, brought her little presents; the humblest and rudest had good wishes to bestow.

She had sought out the young children whom she first saw playing in the churchyard. One of these—he who had spoken of his brother—was her little favourite and friend, and often sat by her side in the church, or climbed with her to the tower-top. It was his delight to help her, or to fancy that he did so, and they soon became close companions.

It happened, that, as she was reading in the old spot by herself one day, this child came running in with his eyes full of tears, and after holding her from him, and looking at her eagerly for a moment, clasped his little arms passionately about her neck.

'What now?' said Nell, soothing him. 'What is the matter?'

'She is not one yet!' cried the boy, embracing her still more closely. 'No, no. Not yet!'

She looked at him wonderingly, and putting his hair back from his face, and kissing him, asked what he meant.

'You must not be one, dear Nell,' cried the boy. 'We can't see them. They never come to play with us, or talk to us. Be what you are. You are better so.'

'I do not understand you,' said the child. 'Tell me what you mean.'

'Why, they say,' replied the boy, looking up into her face, 'that you will be an Angel, before the birds sing again. But you won't be, will you? Don't leave us, Nell, though the sky *is* bright. Do not leave us!'

The child dropped her head, and put her hands before her face.

'She cannot bear the thought!' cried the boy, exulting through his tears. 'You will not go. You know how sorry we should be. Dear Nell, tell me that you 'll stay amongst us. Oh! Pray, pray, tell me that you will.'

The little creature folded his hands, and knelt down at her feet.

'Only look at me, Nell,' said the boy, 'and tell me that you 'll stop, and then I shall know that they are wrong, and will cry no more. Won't you say yes, Nell?'

Still the drooping head and hidden face, and the child quite silent—save for her sobs.

'After a time,' pursued the boy, trying to draw away her hand, 'the kind angels will be glad to think that you are not among them, and that you stayed here to be with us. Willy went away, to join them; but if he had known how I should miss him in our little bed at night, he never would have left me, I am sure.'

Yet the child could make him no answer, and sobbed as though her heart were bursting.

'Why would you go, dear Nell? I know you would not be happy when you heard that we were crying for your loss. They say that Willy is in Heaven now, and that it 's always summer there, and yet I 'm sure he grieves when I lie down upon his garden bed, and he cannot turn to kiss me. But if you do go, Nell,' said the boy, caressing her, and pressing his face to hers, 'be fond of him for my sake. Tell him how I love him still, and how much I loved you; and when I think that you two are together, and are happy, I 'll try to bear it, and never give you pain by doing wrong—indeed I never will!'

The child suffered him to move her hands, and put them round his neck. There was a tearful silence, but it was not long before she looked upon him with a smile, and promised him, in a very gentle, quiet voice, that she would stay, and be his friend, as long as Heaven would let her. He clapped his hands for joy, and thanked her many times; and being charged to tell no person what had passed between them, gave her an earnest promise that he never would.

Nor did he, so far as the child could learn; but was her quiet companion in all her walks and musings, and never again adverted to the theme, which he felt had given her pain, although he was unconscious of its cause. Something of distrust lingered about him still; for he would often come, even in the dark evenings, and call in a timid voice outside the door to know if she were safe within; and being answered yes, and bade to enter, would take his station on a low stool at her feet, and sit there patiently until they came to seek, and take him home. Sure as the morning came, it found him lingering near the house to ask if she were well; and, morning, noon, or night, go where she would, he would forsake his playmates and his sports to bear her company.

'And a good little friend he is, too,' said the old sexton to her once. 'When his elder brother died—elder seems a strange word, for he was only seven years old —I remember this one took it sorely to heart.'

The child thought of what the schoolmaster had told her, and felt how its truth was shadowed out even in this infant.

'It has given him something of a quiet way, I think,' said the old man, 'though for that he is merry enough at times. I'd wager now that you and he have been listening by the old well.'

'Indeed we have not,' the child replied. 'I have been afraid to go near it; for I am not often down in that part of the church, and do not know the ground.'

'Come down with me,' said the old man. 'I have known it from a boy. Come!'

They descended the narrow steps which led into the crypt, and paused among the gloomy arches, in a dim and murky spot.

'This is the place,' said the old man. 'Give me your hand while you throw back the cover, lest you should stumble and fall in. I am too old—I mean rheumatic—to stoop, myself.'

'A black and dreadful place!' exclaimed the child.

'Look in,' said the old man, pointing downward with his finger.

The child complied, and gazed down into the pit.

'It looks like a grave itself,' said the old man.

'It does,' replied the child.

'I have often had the fancy,' said the sexton, 'that it might have been dug at first to make the old place more gloomy, and the old monks more religious.   It's to be closed up and built over.'

The child still stood, looking thoughtfully into the vault.

'We shall see,' said the sexton, 'on what gay heads other earth will have closed, when the light is shut out from here.   God knows!   They'll close it up, next spring.'

'The birds sing again in spring,' thought the child, as she leaned at her casement window, and gazed at the declining sun.   'Spring! a beautiful and happy time!'

CHAPTER LVI

A DAY or two after the Quilp tea-party at the Wilderness, Mr. Swiveller walked into Sampson Brass's office at the usual hour, and being alone in that Temple of Probity, placed his hat upon the desk, and taking from his pocket a small parcel of black crape, applied himself to folding and pinning the same upon it, after the manner of a hatband. Having completed the construction of this appendage, he surveyed

his work with great complacency, and put his hat on
again—very much over one eye, to increase the
mournfulness of the effect. These arrangements
perfected to his entire satisfaction, he thrust his hands
into his pockets, and walked up and down the office
with measured steps.

'It has always been the same with me,' said Mr.
Swiveller, 'always. 'Twas ever thus, from childhood's hour I 've seen my fondest hopes decay, I never
loved a tree or flower but 'twas the first to fade away;
I never nursed a dear Gazelle, to glad me with its
soft black eye, but when it came to know me well, and
love me, it was sure to marry a market-gardener.'

Overpowered by these reflections, Mr. Swiveller
stopped short at the client's chair, and flung himself
into its open arms.

'And this,' said Mr. Swiveller, with a kind of bantering composure, 'is life, I believe. Oh, certainly.
Why not? I 'm quite satisfied. I shall wear,' added
Richard, taking off his hat again and looking hard
at it, as if he were only deterred by pecuniary considerations from spurning it with his foot, 'I shall wear
this emblem of woman's perfidy, in remembrance of
her with whom I shall never again thread the wind-
ings of the mazy; whom I shall never more pledge in
the rosy; who, during the short remainder of my existence, will murder the balmy. Ha, ha, ha!'

It may be necessary to observe, lest there should
appear any incongruity in the close of this soliloquy,
that Mr. Swiveller did not wind up with a cheerful
hilarious laugh, which would have been undoubtedly
at variance with his solemn reflections, but that, being in a theatrical mood, he merely achieved that performance which is designated in melodramas 'laughing like a fiend,'—for it seems that your fiends always
laugh in syllables, and always in three syllables, never

more nor less, which is a remarkable property in such gentry, and one worthy of remembrance.

The baleful sounds had hardly died away, and Mr. Swiveller was still sitting in a very grim state in the client's chair, when there came a ring—or, if we may adapt the sound to his then humour, a knell—at the office-bell. Opening the door with all speed, he beheld the expressive countenance of Mr. Chuckster, between whom and himself a fraternal greeting ensued.

'You 're devilish early at this pestiferous old slaughter-house,' said that gentleman, poising himself on one leg, and shaking the other in an easy manner.

'Rather,' returned Dick.

'Rather,' retorted Mr. Chuckster, with that air of graceful trifling which so well became him. '*I* should think so. Why, my good feller, do you know what o'clock it is—half-past nine A.M. in the morning?'

'Won't you come in?' said Dick. 'All alone. Swiveller solus. " 'Tis now the witching—" '

' "Hour of night!" '

' "When churchyards yawn," '

' "And graves give up their dead." '

At the end of this quotation in dialogue, each gentleman struck an attitude, and immediately subsiding into prose walked into the office. Such morsels of enthusiasm are common among the Glorious Apollos, and were indeed the links that bound them together, and raised them above the cold dull earth.

'Well, and how are you, my buck?' said Mr. Chuckster, taking a stool. 'I was forced to come into the City upon some little private matters of my own, and couldn't pass the corner of the street without looking in, but upon my soul I didn't expect to find you. It is so everlastingly early.'

Mr. Swiveller expressed his acknowledgments; and

it appearing on further conversation that he was in good health, and that Mr. Chuckster was in the like enviable condition, both gentlemen, in compliance with a solemn custom of the ancient Brotherhood to which they belonged, joined in a fragment of the popular duet of 'All 's Well,' with a long shake at the end.

'And what 's the news?' said Richard.

'The town 's as flat, my dear feller,' replied Mr. Chuckster, 'as the surface of a Dutch oven. There 's no news. By the bye, that lodger of yours is a most extraordinary person. He quite eludes the most vigorous comprehension, you know. Never was such a feller!'

'What has he been doing now?' said Dick.

'By Jove, sir,' returned Mr. Chuckster, taking out an oblong snuff-box, the lid whereof was ornamented with a fox's head curiously carved in brass, 'that man is an unfathomable. Sir, that man has made friends with our articled clerk. There 's no harm in him, but he is so amazingly slow and soft. Now, if he wanted a friend, why couldn't he have one that knew a thing or two, and could do him some good by his manners and conversation? I have my faults, sir,' said Mr. Chuckster.

'No, no,' interposed Mr. Swiveller.

'Oh yes, I have, I have my faults, no man knows his faults better than I know mine. But,' said Mr. Chuckster, 'I 'm not meek. My worst enemies—every man has his enemies, sir, and I have mine—never accused me of being meek. And I tell you what, sir, if I hadn't more of these qualities that commonly endear man to man, than our articled clerk has, I 'd steal a Cheshire cheese, tie it round my neck, and drown myself. I 'd die degraded, as I had lived. I would, upon my honour.'

Mr. Chuckster paused, rapped the fox's head ex=
actly on the nose with the knuckle of the fore-finger,
took a pinch of snuff, and looked steadily at Mr.
Swiveller, as much as to say that if he thought he was
going to sneeze, he would find himself mistaken.

'Not contented, sir,' said Mr. Chuckster, 'with
making friends with Abel, he has cultivated the acquaintance of his father and mother.   Since he came
home from that wild-goose chase, he has been there—
actually been there.   He patronises young Snobby
besides; you 'll find, sir, that he 'll be constantly
coming backwards and forwards to this place: yet I
don't suppose that beyond the common forms of
civility, he has ever exchanged half a dozen words
with *me*.   Now, upon my soul, you know,' said Mr.
Chuckster, shaking his head gravely, as men are wont
to do when they consider things are going a little too
far, 'this is altogether such a low-minded affair, that if
I didn't feel for the governor, and know that he could
never get on without me, I should be obliged to cut
the connection.   I should have no alternative.'

Mr. Swiveller, who sat on another stool opposite to
his friend, stirred the fire in an excess of sympathy,
but said nothing.

'As to young Snob, sir,' pursued Mr. Chuckster
with a prophetic look, 'you 'll find he 'll turn out bad.
In our profession we know something of human
nature, and take my word for it, that the feller that
came back to work out that shilling, will show himself
one of these days in his true colours.   He's a low
thief, sir.   He must be.'

Mr. Chuckster being roused, would probably have
pursued this subject further, and in more emphatic
language, but for a tap at the door, which seemed to
announce the arrival of somebody on business, caused
him to assume a greater appearance of meekness than

was perhaps quite consistent with his late declaration. Mr. Swiveller, hearing the same sound, caused his stool to revolve rapidly on one leg until it brought him to his desk, into which, having forgotten in the sudden flurry of his spirits to part with the poker, he thrust it as he cried 'Come in!'

Who should present himself but that very Kit who had been the theme of Mr. Chuckster's wrath! Never did man pluck up his courage so quickly, or look so fierce, as Mr. Chuckster when he found it was he. Mr. Swiveller stared at him for a moment, and then leaping from his stool, and drawing out the poker from its place of concealment, performed the broadsword exercise with all the cuts and guards complete, in a species of frenzy.

'Is the gentleman at home?' said Kit, rather astonished by this uncommon reception.

Before Mr. Swiveller could make any reply, Mr. Chuckster took occasion to enter his indignant protest against this form of inquiry: which he held to be of a disrespectful and snobbish tendency, inasmuch as the inquirer, seeing two gentlemen then and there present, should have spoken of the other gentleman; or rather (for it was not impossible that the object of his search might be of inferior quality) should have mentioned his name, leaving it to his hearers to determine his degree as they thought proper. Mr. Chuckster likewise remarked, that he had some reason to believe this form of address was personal to himself, and that he was not a man to be trifled with—as certain snobs (whom he did not more particularly mention or describe) might find to their cost.

'I mean the gentleman upstairs,' said Kit, turning to Richard Swiveller. 'Is he at home?'

'Why?' rejoined Dick.

'Because if he is, I have a letter for him.'

'From whom?' said Dick.

'From Mr. Garland.'

'Oh!' said Dick with extreme politeness. 'Then you may hand it over, sir. And if you 're to wait for an answer, sir, you may wait in the passage, sir, which is an airy and well-ventilated apartment, sir.'

'Thank you,' returned Kit. 'But I am to give it to himself, if you please.'

The excessive audacity of this retort so overpowered Mr. Chuckster, and so moved his tender regard for his friend's honour, that he declared, if he were not restrained by official considerations, he must certainly have annihilated Kit upon the spot; a resentment of the affront which he did consider, under the extraordinary circumstances of aggravation attending it, could but have met with the proper sanction and approval of a jury of Englishmen, who, he had no doubt, would have returned a verdict of Justifiable Homicide, coupled with a high testimony to the morals and character of the Avenger. Mr. Swiveller, without being quite so hot upon the matter, was rather shamed by his friend's excitement, and not a little puzzled how to act (Kit being quite cool and good-humoured), when the single gentleman was heard to call violently down the stairs.

'Didn't I see somebody for me, come in?' cried the lodger.

'Yes, sir,' replied Dick. 'Certainly, sir.'

'Then where is he?' roared the single gentleman.

'He's here, sir,' rejoined Mr. Swiveller. 'Now, young man, don't you hear you 're to go upstairs? Are you deaf?'

Kit did not appear to think it worth his while to enter into any altercation, but hurried off and left the Glorious Apollos gazing at each other in silence.

'Didn't I tell you so?' said Mr. Chuckster. 'What do you think of that?'

Mr. Swiveller being in the main a good-natured fellow, and not perceiving in the conduct of Kit any villainy of enormous magnitude, scarcely knew what answer to return. He was relieved from his perplexity, however, by the entrance of Mr. Sampson and his sister Sally, at sight of whom Mr. Chuckster precipitately retired.

Mr. Brass and his lovely companion appeared to have been holding a consultation over their temperate breakfast, upon some matter of great interest and importance. On the occasion of such conferences, they generally appeared in the office some half an hour after their usual time, and in a very smiling state, as though their late plots and designs had tranquillised their minds and shed a light upon their toilsome way. In the present instance, they seemed particularly gay; Miss Sally's aspect being of a most oily kind, and Mr. Brass rubbing his hands in an exceedingly jocose and light-hearted manner.

'Well, Mr. Richard,' said Brass. 'How are we this morning? Are we pretty fresh and cheerful, sir —eh, Mr. Richard?'

'Pretty well, sir,' replied Dick.

'That's well,' said Brass. 'Ha ha! We should be as gay as larks, Mr. Richard—why not? It's a pleasant world we live in, sir, a very pleasant world. There are bad people in it, Mr. Richard, but if there were no bad people, there would be no good lawyers. Ha ha! Any letters by the post this morning, Mr. Richard?'

Mr. Swiveller answered in the negative.

'Ha!' said Brass, 'no matter. If there's little business to-day, there'll be more to-morrow. A contented spirit, Mr. Richard, is the sweetness of existence. Anybody been here, sir?'

'Only my friend'—replied Dick. ' "May we ne'er want a—" '

' "Friend," ' Brass chimed in quickly, ' "or a bottle to give him." Ha ha! That's the way the song runs, isn't it? A very good song, Mr. Richard, very good. I like the sentiment of it. Ha ha! Your friend's the young man from Witherden's office, I think—yes—"May we ne'er want a—" Nobody else at all been, Mr. Richard?'

'Only somebody to the lodger,' replied Mr. Swiveller.

'Oh indeed!' cried Brass. 'Somebody to the lodger, eh? Ha ha! "May we ne'er want a friend or a—" Somebody to the lodger, eh, Mr. Richard?'

'Yes,' said Dick, a little disconcerted by the excessive buoyancy of spirits which his employer displayed. 'With him now.'

'With him now!' cried Brass; 'Ha ha! There let 'em be, merry and free, toor rul rol le. Eh, Mr. Richard? Ha ha!'

'Oh certainly,' replied Dick.

'And who,' said Brass, shuffling among his papers, 'who is the lodger's visitor—not a lady visitor, I hope, eh, Mr. Richard? The morals of the Marks you know, sir—"when lovely woman stoops to folly"— and all that—eh, Mr. Richard?'

'Another young man, who belongs to Witherden's too, or half belongs there,' returned Richard. 'Kit, they call him.'

'Kit, eh!' said Brass. 'Strange name—name of a dancing-master's fiddle, eh, Mr. Richard? Ha ha! Kit's there, is he? Oh!'

Dick looked at Miss Sally, wondering that she didn't check this uncommon exuberance on the part of Mr. Sampson; but as she made no attempt to do so, and rather appeared to exhibit a tacit acquiescence in it, he concluded that they had just been cheating somebody, and receiving the bill.

'Will you have the goodness, Mr. Richard,' said Brass, taking a letter from his desk, 'just to step over to Peckham Rye with that? There's no answer, but it's rather particular and should go by hand. Charge the office with your coach-hire back, you know; don't spare the office: get as much out of it as you can—clerk's motto—Eh, Mr. Richard? Ha ha!'

Mr. Swiveller solemnly doffed the aquatic jacket, put on his coat, took down his hat from its peg, pocketed the letter, and departed. As soon as he was gone, up rose Miss Sally Brass, and smiling sweetly at her brother (who nodded and smote his nose in return) withdrew also.

Sampson Brass was no sooner left alone, than he set the office door wide open, and establishing himself at his desk directly opposite, so that he could not fail to see anybody who came downstairs and passed out at the street-door, began to write with extreme cheerfulness and assiduity; humming as he did so, in a voice that was anything but musical, certain vocal snatches which appeared to have reference to the union between Church and State, inasmuch as they were compounded of the Evening Hymn and God save the King.

Thus, the attorney of Bevis Marks sat, and wrote, and hummed, for a long time, except when he stopped to listen with a very cunning face, and hearing nothing, went on humming louder, and writing slower than ever. At length, in one of these pauses, he heard his lodger's door opened and shut, and footsteps coming down the stairs. Then, Mr. Brass left off writing entirely, and, with his pen in his hand, hummed his very loudest; shaking his head meanwhile from side to side, like a man whose whole soul was in the music, and smiling in a manner quite seraphic.

It was towards this moving spectacle that the staircase and the sweet sounds guided Kit; on whose arrival before his door, Mr. Brass stopped his singing, but not his smiling, and nodded affably: at the same time beckoning to him with his pen.

'Kit,' said Mr. Brass, in the pleasantest way imaginable, 'how do you do?'

Kit, being rather shy of his friend, made a suitable reply, and had his hand upon the lock of the street-door when Mr. Brass called him softly back.

'You are not to go, if you please, Kit,' said the attorney in a mysterious and yet business-like way. 'You are to step in here, if you please. Dear me, dear me! When I look at you,' said the lawyer, quitting his stool, and standing before the fire with his back towards it, 'I am reminded of the sweetest little face that ever my eyes beheld. I remember your coming there, twice or thrice, when we were in possession. Ah, Kit, my dear fellow, gentlemen in my profession have such painful duties to perform sometimes, that you needn't envy us—you needn't indeed!'

'I don't, sir,' said Kit, 'though it isn't for the like of me to judge.'

'Our only consolation, Kit,' pursued the lawyer, looking at him in a sort of pensive abstraction, 'is, that although we cannot turn away the wind, we can soften it; we can temper it, if I may say so, to the shorn lambs.'

'Shorn indeed!' thought Kit. 'Pretty close!' But he didn't say so.

'On that occasion, Kit,' said Mr. Brass, 'on that occasion that I have just alluded to, I had a hard battle with Mr. Quilp (for Mr. Quilp is a very hard man) to obtain them the indulgence they had. It might have cost me a client. But suffering virtue inspired me, and I prevailed.'

'He 's not so bad after all,' thought honest Kit, as the attorney pursed up his lips and looked like a man who was struggling with his better feelings.

'I respect *you,* Kit,' said Brass with emotion. 'I saw enough of your conduct, at that time, to respect you, though your station is humble, and your fortune lowly. It isn't the waistcoat that I look at. It is the heart. The checks in the waistcoat are but the wires of the cage. But the heart is the bird. Ah! How many sich birds are perpetually moulting, and putting their beaks through the wires to peck at all mankind!'

This poetic figure, which Kit took to be in special allusion to his own checked waistcoat, quite overcame him; Mr. Brass's voice and manner added not a little to its effect, for he discoursed with all the mild austerity of a hermit, and wanted but a cord round the waist of his rusty surtout, and a skull on the chimneypiece, to be completely set up in that line of business.

'Well, well,' said Sampson, smiling as good men smile when they compassionate their own weakness or that of their fellow-creatures, 'this is wide of the bull's-eye. You 're to take that, if you please.' As he spoke, he pointed to a couple of half-crowns on the desk.

Kit looked at the coins, and then at Sampson, and hesitated.

'For yourself,' said Brass.

'From—'

'No matter about the person they came from,' replied the lawyer. 'Say me, if you like. We have eccentric friends overhead, Kit, and we mustn't ask questions or talk too much—you understand?

You 're to take them, that 's all; and between you and me, I don't think they 'll be the last you 'll have to take from the same place. I hope not. Good-bye, Kit. Good-bye!'

With many thanks, and many more self-reproaches for having on such slight grounds suspected one who in their very first conversation turned out such a different man from what he had supposed, Kit took the money and made the best of his way home. Mr. Brass remained airing himself at the fire, and resumed his vocal exercise, and his seraphic smile, simultaneously.

'May I come in?' said Miss Sally, peeping.

'Oh yes, you may come in,' returned her brother.

'Ahem!' coughed Miss Brass interrogatively.

'Why, yes,' returned Sampson, 'I should say as good as done.'

CHAPTER LVII

MR. CHUCKSTER's indignant apprehensions were not without foundation. Certainly the friendship between the single gentleman and Mr. Garland was not suffered to cool, but had a rapid growth and flourished exceedingly. They were soon in habits of constant intercourse and communication; and the single gentleman labouring at this time under a slight attack of illness—the consequence most probably of his late excited feelings and subsequent disappointment—furnished a reason for their holding yet more frequent correspondence; so that some one of the inmates of Abel Cottage, Finchley, came backwards and forwards between that place and Bevis Marks, almost every day.

As the pony had now thrown off all disguise, and

without any mincing of the matter or beating about the bush, sturdily refused to be driven by anybody but Kit, it generally happened that whether old Mr. Garland came, or Mr. Abel, Kit was of the party. Of all messages and inquiries, Kit was, in right of his position, the bearer; thus it came about that, while the single gentleman remained indisposed, Kit turned into Bevis Marks every morning with nearly as much regularity as the General Postman.

Mr. Sampson Brass, who no doubt had his reasons for looking sharply about him, soon learnt to distinguish the pony's trot and the clatter of the little chaise at the corner of the street. Whenever the sound reached his ears, he would immediately lay down his pen and fall to rubbing his hands and exhibiting the greatest glee.

'Ha ha!' he would cry. 'Here's the pony again! Most remarkable pony, extremely docile, eh, Mr. Richard, eh, sir?'

Dick would return some matter-of-course reply, and Mr. Brass standing on the bottom rail of his stool, so as to get a view of the street over the top of the window-blind, would take an observation of the visitors.

'The old gentleman again!' he would exclaim, 'a very prepossessing old gentleman, Mr. Richard—charming countenance, sir—extremely calm—benevolence in every feature, sir. He quite realises my idea of King Lear, as he appeared when in possession of his kingdom, Mr. Richard—the same good-humour, the same white hair and partial baldness, the same liability to be imposed upon. Ah! A sweet subject for contemplation, sir, very sweet!'

Then Mr. Garland having alighted and gone upstairs, Sampson would nod and smile to Kit from the window, and presently walk out into the street to greet him, when some such conversation as the following would ensue.

'Admirably groomed, Kit'—Mr. Brass is patting the pony—'does you great credit—amazingly sleek and bright to be sure.   He literally looks as if he had been varnished all over.'

Kit touches his hat, smiles, pats the pony himself, and expresses his conviction, 'that Mr. Brass will not find many like him.'

'A beautiful animal indeed!' cried Brass.   'Sagacious too?'

'Bless you!' replies Kit, 'he knows what you say to him as well as a Christian does.'

'Does he indeed!' cries Brass, who has heard the same thing in the same place from the same person in the same words a dozen times, but is paralysed with astonishment notwithstanding.   'Dear me!'

'I little thought the first time I saw him, sir,' says Kit, pleased with the attorney's strong interest in his favourite, 'that I should come to be as intimate with him as I am now.'

'Ah!' rejoins Mr. Brass, brimful of moral precepts and love of virtue.   'A charming subject of reflection for you, very charming.   A subject of proper pride and congratulation, Christopher.   Honesty is the best policy.—I always find it so myself.   I lost forty-seven pound ten by being honest this morning.   But it's all gain, it's gain!'

Mr. Brass slyly tickles his nose with his pen, and looks at Kit with the water standing in his eyes.   Kit thinks that if ever there was a good man who belied his appearance, that man is Sampson Brass.

'A man,' says Sampson, 'who loses forty-seven pound ten in one morning by his honesty, is a man to be envied.   If it had been eighty pound, the luxuriousness of feeling would have been increased.   Every pound lost, would have been a hundredweight of happiness gained. The still small voice, Christopher,' cries Brass, smiling, and tapping himself on the bosom, 'is a singing comic songs within me, and all is happiness and joy!'

Kit so improved by the conversation, and finds it go so completely home to his feelings, that he is considering what he shall say, when Mr. Garland appears. The old gentleman is helped into the chaise with great obsequiousness by Mr. Sampson Brass; and the pony, after shaking his head several times, and standing for three or four minutes with all his four legs planted firmly on the ground, as if he had made up his mind never to stir from that spot, but there to live and die, suddenly darts off, without the smallest notice, at the rate of twelve English miles an hour. Then, Mr. Brass and his sister (who has joined him at the door) exchange an odd kind of smile—not at all a pleasant one in its expression—and return to the society of Mr. Richard Swiveller, who, during their absence, has been regaling himself with various feats of pantomime, and is discovered at his desk, in a very flushed and heated condition, violently scratching out nothing with half a penknife.

Whenever Kit came alone, and without the chaise, it always happened that Sampson Brass was reminded of some mission, calling Mr. Swiveller, if not to Peckham Rye again, at all events to some pretty distant place from which he could not be expected to return for two or three hours, or in all probability a much longer period, as that gentleman was not, to say the truth, renowned for using great expedition on such occasions, but rather for protracting and spinning out the time to the very utmost limit of possibility. Mr. Swiveller out of sight, Miss Sally immediately withdrew. Mr. Brass would then set the office-door wide open, hum his old tune with great gaiety of heart, and smile seraphically as before. Kit coming downstairs would be called in; entertained with some moral and agreeable conversation; perhaps entreated to mind the office for an instant while Mr. Brass stepped over the way; and afterwards presented with one or two half-crowns as the case might be. This occurred so often, that Kit, nothing doubting but that they came from the single gentleman who had already rewarded his mother with great liberality, could not enough admire his generosity; and bought so many cheap presents for her, and for little Jacob, and for the baby, and for Barbara to boot, that one or other of them was having some new trifle every day of their lives.

While these acts and deeds were in progress in and out of the office of Sampson Brass, Richard Swiveller, being often left alone therein, began to find the time hang heavy on his hands. For the better preservation of his cheerfulness, therefore, and to prevent his faculties from rusting, he provided himself with a cribbage-board and pack of cards, and accustomed himself to play at cribbage with a dummy, for twenty, thirty, or sometimes even fifty thousand pounds a side, besides many hazardous bets to a considerable amount.

As these games were very silently conducted, notwithstanding the magnitude of the interests involved, Mr. Swiveller began to think that on those evenings when Mr. and Miss Brass were out (and they often went out now) he heard a kind of snorting or hardbreathing sound in the direction of the door, which it occurred to him, after some reflection, must proceed from the small servant, who always had a cold from damp living. Looking intently that way one night, he plainly distinguished an eye gleaming and glistening at the key-hole; and having now no doubt that his suspicions were correct, he stole softly to the door, and pounced upon her before she was aware of his approach.

'Oh! I didn't mean any harm indeed, upon my word I didn't,' cried the small servant, struggling like a much larger one. 'It's so very dull downstairs. Please don't you tell upon me, please don't.'

'Tell upon you!' said Dick. 'Do you mean to say you were looking through the key-hole for company?'

'Yes, upon my word I was,' replied the small servant.

'How long have you been cooling your eye there?' said Dick.

'Oh ever since you first began to play them cards, and long before.'

Vague recollections of several fantastic exercises with which he had refreshed himself after the fatigues of business, and to all of which, no doubt, the small servant was a party, rather disconcerted Mr. Swiveller; but he was not very sensitive on such points, and recovered himself speedily.

'Well,—come in'—he said, after a little consideration. 'Here—sit down, and I'll teach you how to play.'

'Oh! I dursn't do it,' rejoined the small servant; 'Miss Sally 'ud kill me, if she know'd I come up here.'

'Have you got a fire downstairs?' said Dick.

'A very little one,' replied the small servant.

'Miss Sally couldn't kill me if she know'd I went down there, so I'll come,' said Richard, putting the cards into his pocket. 'Why, how thin you are! What do you mean by it?'

'It an't my fault.'

'Could you eat any bread and meat?' said Dick, taking down his hat. 'Yes? Ah! I thought so. Did you ever taste beer?'

'I had a sip of it once,' said the small servant.

'Here's a state of things!' cried Mr. Swiveller, raising his eyes to the ceiling. 'She *never* tasted it—it can't be tasted in a sip! Why, how old are you?'

'I don't know.'

Mr. Swiveller opened his eyes very wide, and appeared thoughtful for a moment; then, bidding the child mind the door until he came back, vanished straightway.

Presently, he returned, followed by the boy from the public-house, who bore in one hand a plate of bread and beef, and in the other a great pot, filled with some very fragrant compound, which sent forth a grateful steam, and was indeed choice purl, made after a particular recipe which Mr. Swiveller had imparted to the landlord, at a period when he was deep in his books and desirous to conciliate his friendship. Relieving the boy of his burden at the door, and charging his little companion to fasten it to prevent surprise, Mr. Swiveller followed her into the kitchen.

'There!' said Richard, putting the plate before her. 'First of all clear that off, and then you'll see what's next.'

The small servant needed no second bidding, and the plate was soon empty.

'Next,' said Dick, handing the purl, 'take a pull at that; but moderate your transports, you know, for you're not used to it. Well, is it good?'

'Oh! isn't it?' said the small servant.

Mr. Swiveller appeared gratified beyond all expression by this reply, and took a long draught himself: steadfastly regarding his companion while he did so. These preliminaries disposed of, he applied himself to teaching her the game, which she soon learnt tolerably well, being both sharp-witted and cunning.

'Now,' said Mr. Swiveller, putting two sixpences into a saucer, and trimming the wretched candle, when the cards had been cut and dealt, 'those are the stakes. If you win, you get 'em all.   If I win, I get 'em. To make it seem more real and pleasant, I shall call you the Marchioness, do you hear?'

The small servant nodded.

'Then, Marchioness,' said Mr. Swiveller, 'fire away!'

The Marchioness, holding her cards very tight in both hands, considered which to play, and Mr. Swiveller, assuming the gay and fashionable air which such society required, took another pull at the tankard, and waited for her lead.

CHAPTER LVIII

MR. SWIVELLER and his partner played several rubbers with varying success, until the loss of three sixpences, the gradual sinking of the purl, and the striking of ten o'clock, combined to render that gentleman mindful of the flight of Time, and the expediency of withdrawing before Mr. Sampson and Miss Sally Brass returned.

'With which object in view, Marchioness,' said Mr. Swiveller gravely, 'I shall ask your ladyship's permission to put the board in my pocket, and to retire from the presence when I have finished this tankard; merely observing, Marchioness, that since life like a river is flowing, I care not how fast it rolls on, ma'am, on, while such purl on the bank still is growing, and such eyes light the waves as they run.   Marchioness, your health.   You will excuse my wearing my hat, but the palace is damp, and the marble floor is—if I may be allowed the expression—sloppy.'

As a precaution against this latter inconvenience,

Mr. Swiveller had been sitting for some time with his feet on the hob, in which attitude he now gave utterance to these apologetic observations, and slowly sipped the last choice drops of nectar.

'The Baron Sampsono Brasso and his fair sister are (you tell me) at the Play?' said Mr. Swiveller, leaning his left arm heavily upon the table, and raising his voice and his right leg after the manner of a theatrical bandit.

The Marchioness nodded.

'Ha!' said Mr. Swiveller, with a portentous frown. '' 'Tis well. Marchioness!—but no matter. Some wine there. Ho!' He illustrated these melodramatic morsels, by handing the tankard to himself with great humility, receiving it haughtily, drinking from it thirstily, and smacking his lips fiercely.

The small servant, who was not so well acquainted with theatrical conventionalities as Mr. Swiveller (having indeed never seen a play, or heard one spoken of, except by chance through chinks of doors and in other forbidden places), was rather alarmed by demonstrations so novel in their nature, and showed her concern so plainly in her looks, that Mr. Swiveller felt it necessary to discharge his brigand manner for one more suitable to private life, as he asked—

'Do they often go where glory waits 'em, and leave you here?'

'Oh, yes; I believe you they do,' returned the small servant. 'Miss Sally's such a one-er for that, she is.'

'Such a what?' said Dick.

'Such a one-er,' returned the Marchioness.

After a moment's reflection, Mr. Swiveller determined to forego his responsible duty of setting her right, and to suffer her to talk on; as it was evident that her tongue was loosened by the purl, and her opportunities for conversation were not so frequent as to render a momentary check of little consequence.

'They sometimes go to see Mr. Quilp,' said the small servant with a shrewd look; 'they go to a many places, bless you!'

'Is Mr. Brass a wunner?' said Dick.

'Not half what Miss Sally is, he isn't' replied the small servant, shaking her head. 'Bless you, he'd never do anything without her.'

'Oh!   He wouldn't, wouldn't he?' said Dick.

'Miss Sally keeps him in such order,' said the small servant; 'he always asks her advice, he does; and he catches it sometimes.   Bless you, you wouldn't believe how much he catches it.'

'I suppose,' said Dick, 'that they consult together, a good deal, and talk about a great many people—about me for instance, sometimes, eh, Marchioness?'

The Marchioness nodded amazingly.

'Complimentary?' said Mr. Swiveller.

The Marchioness changed the motion of her head, which had not yet left off nodding, and suddenly began to shake it from side to side, with a vehemence which threatened to dislocate her neck.

'Humph!' Dick muttered.   'Would it be any breach of confidence, Marchioness, to relate what they say of the humble individual who has now the honour to—?'

'Miss Sally says you're a funny chap,' replied his friend.

'Well, Marchioness,' said Mr. Swiveller, 'that's not uncomplimentary.   Merriment, Marchioness, is not a bad or a degrading quality.   Old King Cole was himself a merry old soul, if we may put any faith in the pages of history.'

'But she says,' pursued his companion, 'that you an't to be trusted.'

'Why, really, Marchioness,' said Mr. Swiveller,

thoughtfully; 'several ladies and gentlemen—not exactly professional persons, but tradespeople, ma'am, tradespeople—have made the same remark. The obscure citizen who keeps the hotel over the way, inclined strongly to that opinion to-night when I ordered him to prepare the banquet. It's a popular prejudice, Marchioness; and yet I am sure I don't know why, for I have been trusted in my time to a considerable amount, and I can safely say that I never forsook my trust until it deserted me—never. Mr. Brass is of the same opinion, I suppose?'

His friend nodded again, with a cunning look which seemed to hint that Mr. Brass held stronger opinions on the subject than his sister; and seeming to recollect herself, added imploringly, 'But don't you ever tell upon me, or I shall be beat to death.'

'Marchioness,' said Mr. Swiveller, rising, 'the word of a gentleman is as good as his bond—sometimes better, as in the present case, where his bond might prove but a doubtful sort of security. I am your friend, and I hope we shall play many more rubbers together in this same saloon. But, Marchioness,' added Richard, stopping in his way to the door, and wheeling slowly round upon the small servant, who was following with the candle; 'it occurs to me that you must be in the constant habit of airing your eye at key-holes, to know all this.'

'I only wanted,' replied the trembling Marchioness, 'to know where the key of the safe was hid; that was all; and I wouldn't have taken much, if I had found it—only enough to squench my hunger.'

'You didn't find it then?' said Dick. 'But of course you didn't, or you'd be plumper. Good-night, Marchioness. Fare thee well, and if for ever, then for ever fare thee well—and put up the chain, Marchioness, in case of accidents.'

With this parting injunction, Mr. Swiveller emerged from the house; and feeling that he had by this time taken quite as much to drink as promised to be good for his constitution (purl being a rather strong and heady compound), wisely resolved to betake himself to his lodgings, and to bed at once. Homeward he went therefore; and his apartments (for he still retained the plural fiction) being at no great distance from the office, he was soon seated in his own bedchamber, where, having pulled off one boot and forgotten the other, he fell into deep cogitation.

'This Marchioness,' said Mr. Swiveller, folding his arms, 'is a very extraordinary person—surrounded by mysteries, ignorant of the taste of beer, unacquainted with her own name (which is less remarkable), and taking a limited view of society through the key-holes of doors—can these things be her destiny, or has some unknown person started an opposition to the decrees of fate?   It is a most inscrutable and unmitigated staggerer!'

When his meditations had attained this satisfactory point, he became aware of his remaining boot, of which, with unimpaired solemnity he proceeded to divest himself; shaking his head with exceeding gravity all the time, and sighing deeply.

'These rubbers,' said Mr. Swiveller, putting on his night-cap in exactly the same style as he wore his hat, 'remind me of the matrimonial fireside. Cheggs's wife plays cribbage; all-fours likewise. She rings the changes on 'em now.   From sport to sport they hurry her, to banish her regrets, and when they win a smile from her, they think that she forgets— but she don't.   By this time, I should say,' added Richard, getting his left cheek into profile, and looking complacently at the reflection of a very little scrap of whisker in the looking-glass; 'by this time, I should say, the iron has entered into her soul. It serves her right!'

Melting from this stern and obdurate, into the tender and pathetic mood, Mr. Swiveller groaned a little, walked wildly up and down, and even made a show of tearing his hair, which, however, he thought better of, and wrenched the tassel from his nightcap instead. At last, undressing himself with a gloomy resolution, he got into bed.

Some men in his blighted position would have taken to drinking, but as Mr. Swiveller had taken to that before, he only took, on receiving the news that Sophy Wackles was lost to him for ever, to playing the flute; thinking after mature consideration that it was a good, sound, dismal occupation, not only in unison with his own sad thoughts, but calculated to awaken a fellow-feeling in the bosoms of his neighbours. In pursuance of this resolution, he now drew a little table to his bedside, and arranging the light and a small oblong music-book to the best advantage, took his flute from its box, and began to play most mournfully.

The air was 'Away with melancholy'—a composition, which, when it is played very slowly on the flute, in bed, with the further disadvantage of being performed by a gentleman but imperfectly acquainted with the instrument, who repeats one note a great many times before he can find the next, has not a lively effect. Yet, for half the night, or more, Mr. Swiveller, lying sometimes on his back with his eyes upon the ceiling, and sometimes half out of bed to correct himself by the book, played this unhappy tune over and over again; never leaving off, save for a minute or two at a time to take breath and soliloquise

THE AIR WAS, "AWAY WITH MELANCHOLY."

about the Marchioness, and then beginning again with renewed vigour. It was not until he had quite exhausted his several subjects of meditation, and had breathed into the flute the whole sentiment of the purl down to its very dregs, and had nearly maddened the people of the house, and at both the next doors, and over the way,—that he shut up the music-book, extinguished the candle, and finding himself greatly lightened and relieved in his mind, turned round and fell asleep.

He awoke in the morning, much refreshed; and having taken half an hour's exercise at the flute, and graciously received a notice to quit from his landlady, who had been in waiting on the stairs for that purpose since the dawn of day, repaired to Bevis Marks; where the beautiful Sally was already at her post, bearing in her looks a radiance, mild as that which beameth from the virgin moon.

Mr. Swiveller acknowledged her presence by a nod, and exchanged his coat for the aquatic jacket; which usually took some time fitting on, for in consequence of a tightness in the sleeves, it was only to be got into by a series of struggles. This difficulty overcome, he took his seat at the desk.

'I say,' quoth Miss Brass, abruptly breaking silence, 'you haven't seen a silver pencil-case this morning, have you?'

'I didn't meet many in the street,' rejoined Mr. Swiveller. 'I saw one—a stout pencil-case of respectable appearance—but as he was in company with an elderly penknife, and a young toothpick with whom he was in earnest conversation, I felt a delicacy in speaking to him.'

'No, but have you?' returned Miss Brass. 'Seriously, you know.'

'What a dull dog you must be to ask me such a question seriously,' said Mr. Swiveller. 'Haven't I this moment come?'

'Well, all I know is,' replied Miss Sally, 'that it's not to be found, and that it disappeared one day this week, when I left it on the desk.'

'Halloa!' thought Richard, 'I hope the Marchioness hasn't been at work here.'

'There was a knife too,' said Miss Sally, 'of the same pattern. They were given to me by my father, years ago, and are both gone. You haven't missed anything yourself, have you?'

Mr. Swiveller involuntarily clapped his hands to the jacket to be quite sure that it *was* a jacket and not a skirted coat; and having satisfied himself of the safety of this, his only moveable in Bevis Marks, made answer in the negative.

'It's a very unpleasant thing, Dick,' said Miss Brass, pulling out the tin box and refreshing herself with a pinch of snuff; 'but between you and me—between friends you know, for if Sammy knew it, I should never hear the last of it—some of the office-money, too, that has been left about, has gone in the same way. In particular, I have missed three half-crowns at three different times.'

'You don't mean that?' cried Dick. 'Be careful what you say, old boy, for this is a serious matter. Are you quite sure? Is there no mistake?'

'It is so, and there can't be any mistake at all,' rejoined Miss Brass emphatically.

'Then, by Jove,' thought Richard, laying down his pen, 'I am afraid the Marchioness is done for!'

The more he discussed the subject in his thoughts, the more probable it appeared to Dick that the miserable little servant was the culprit. When he considered on what a spare allowance of food she lived, how neglected and untaught she was, and how her natural cunning had been sharpened by necessity and privation, he scarcely doubted it.   And yet he pitied her so much, and felt so unwilling to have a matter of such gravity disturbing the oddity of their acquaintance, that he thought, and thought truly, that rather than receive fifty pounds down, he would have the Marchioness proved innocent.

While he was plunged in very profound and serious meditation upon this theme, Miss Sally sat shaking her head with an air of great mystery and doubt; when the voice of her brother Sampson, carolling a cheerful strain, was heard in the passage, and that gentleman himself, beaming with virtuous smiles, appeared.

'Mr. Richard sir, good morning!   Here we are again, sir, entering upon another day, with our bodies strengthened by slumber and breakfast, and our spirits fresh and flowing.   Here we are, Mr. Richard, rising with the sun to run our little course—our course of duty, sir—and, like him, to get through our day's work with credit to ourselves and advantage to our fellow-creatures.   A charming reflection, sir, very charming!'

While he addressed his clerk in these words, Mr. Brass was, somewhat ostentatiously, engaged in minutely examining and holding up against the light a five-pound bank-note, which he had brought in, in his hand.

Mr. Richard not receiving his remarks with anything like enthusiasm, his employer turned his eyes to his face, and observed that it wore a troubled expression.

'You 're out of spirits, sir,' said Brass.   'Mr. Richard sir, we should fall to work cheerfully, and not in a despondent state. It becomes us, Mr. Richard sir, to—'

Here the chaste Sarah heaved a loud sigh.

'Dear me!' said Mr. Sampson, 'You too! Is anything the matter? Mr. Richard sir—'

Dick, glancing at Miss Sally, saw that she was making signals to him, to acquaint her brother with the subject of their recent conversation. As his own position was not a very pleasant one until the matter was set at rest one way or other, he did so; and Miss Brass, plying her snuff-box at a most wasteful rate corroborated his account.

The countenance of Sampson fell, and anxiety overspread his features. Instead of passionately bewailing the loss of his money, as Miss Sally had expected, he walked on tip-toe to the door, opened it, looked outside, shut it softly, returned on tip-toe, and said in a whisper—

'This is a most extraordinary and painful circumstance—Mr. Richard sir, a most painful circumstance. The fact is, that I myself have missed several small sums from the desk, of late, and have refrained from mentioning it, hoping that accident would discover the offender; but it has not done so—it has not done so. Sally—Mr. Richard sir—this is a particularly distressing affair!'

As Sampson spoke, he laid the bank-note upon the desk among some papers, in an absent manner, and thrust his hands into his pockets. Richard Swiveller pointed to it, and admonished him to take it up.

'No, Mr. Richard sir,' rejoined Brass with emotion, 'I will not take it up. I will let it lie there, sir. To take it up, Mr. Richard sir, would imply a doubt of you; and in you, sir, I have unlimited confidence. We will let it lie there, sir, if you please, and we will not take it up by any means.' With that, Mr. Brass patted him twice or thrice on the shoulder, in a most friendly manner, and entreated him to believe that he had as much faith in his honesty as he had in his own.

Although at another time Mr. Swiveller might have looked upon this as a doubtful compliment, he felt it, under the then-existing circumstances, a great relief to be assured that he was not wrongfully suspected. When he had made a suitable reply, Mr. Brass wrung him by the hand, and fell into a brown study, as did Miss Sally likewise. Richard too remained in a thoughtful state; fearing every moment to hear the Marchioness impeached, and unable to resist the conviction that she must be guilty.

When they had severally remained in this condition for some minutes, Miss Sally all at once gave a loud rap upon the desk with her clenched fist, and cried, 'I 've hit it!'—as indeed she had, and chipped a piece out of it too; but that was not her meaning.

'Well,' cried Brass anxiously. 'Go on, will you?'

'Why,' replied his sister with an air of triumph, 'hasn't there been somebody always coming in and out of this office for the last three or four weeks; hasn't that somebody been left alone in it sometimes —thanks to you; and do you mean to tell me that that somebody isn't the thief?'

'What somebody?' blustered Brass.

'Why, what do you call him—Kit.'

'Mr. Garland's young man?'

'To be sure.'

'Never!' cried Brass. 'Never. I 'll not hear of it. Don't tell me—'said Sampson, shaking his head, and working with both his hands as if he were clearing away ten thousand cobwebs. 'I 'll never believe it of him. Never!'

'I say,' repeated Miss Brass, taking another pinch of snuff, 'that he's the thief.'

'I say,' returned Sampson violently, 'that he is *not*. What do you mean? How dare you? Are characters to be whispered away like this? Do you know that he's the honestest and faithfullest fellow that ever lived, and that he has an irreproachable good name? Come in, come in!'

These last words were not addressed to Miss Sally, though they partook of the tone in which the indignant remonstrances that preceded them had been uttered. They were addressed to some person who had knocked at the office-door; and they had hardly passed the lips of Mr. Brass, when this very Kit himself looked in.

'Is the gentleman upstairs, sir, if you please?'

'Yes, Kit,' said Brass, still fired with an honest indignation, and frowning with knotted brows upon his sister; 'Yes, Kit, he is. I am glad to see you, Kit, I am rejoiced to see you. Look in again, as you come downstairs, Kit. *That* lad a robber!' cried Brass when he had withdrawn, 'with that frank and open countenance! I'd trust him with untold gold. Mr. Richard sir, have the goodness to step directly to Wrasp and Co.'s in Broad Street, and inquire if they have had instructions to appear in Carkem and Painter. *That* lad a robber,' sneered Sampson, flushed and heated with his wrath. 'Am I blind, deaf, silly; do I know nothing of human nature when I see it before me? Kit a robber! Bah!'

Flinging this final interjection at Miss Sally with immeasurable scorn and contempt, Sampson Brass thrust his head into his desk, as if to shut the base world from his view, and breathed defiance from under its half-closed lid.

CHAPTER LIX

W<small>HEN</small> Kit, having discharged his errand, came downstairs from the single gentleman's apartment after the lapse of a quarter of an hour or so, Mr. Sampson Brass was alone in the office.   He was not singing as usual, nor was he seated at his desk.   The open door showed him standing before the fire with his back towards it, and looking so very strange that Kit supposed he must have been suddenly taken ill.

'Is anything the matter, sir?' said Kit.

'Matter!' cried Brass.   'No.   Why anything the matter?'

'You are so very pale,' said Kit, 'that I should hardly have known you.'

'Pooh pooh! mere fancy,' cried Brass, stooping to throw up the cinders.   'Never better, Kit, never better in all my life.   Merry too.   Ha ha!   How's our friend above-stairs, eh?'

'A great deal better,' said Kit.

'I'm glad to hear it,' rejoined Brass; 'thankful, I may say.   An excellent gentleman—worthy, liberal, generous, gives very little trouble—an admirable lodger.   Ha ha! Mr. Garland—he's well, I hope, Kit—and the pony—my friend, my particular friend you know.   Ha ha!'

Kit gave a satisfactory account of all the little household at Abel Cottage.   Mr. Brass, who seemed remarkably inattentive and impatient, mounted on his stool, and beckoning him to come nearer, took him by the button-hole.

'I have been thinking, Kit,' said the lawyer, 'that I could throw some little emoluments in your mother's way—You have a mother, I think?   If I recollect right, you told me—'

'Oh yes, sir, yes certainly.'

'A widow, I think? an industrious widow?'

'A harder-working woman or a better mother never lived, sir.'

'Ah!' cried Brass.   'That's affecting, truly affecting.   A poor widow struggling to maintain her orphans in decency and comfort, is a delicious picture of human goodness.—Put down your hat, Kit.'

'Thank you, sir, I must be going directly.'

'Put it down while you stay, at any rate,' said Brass, taking it from him and making some confusion among the papers, in finding a place for it on the desk.   'I was thinking, Kit, that we have often houses to let for people we are concerned for, and matters of that sort.   Now you know we 're obliged to put people into those houses to take care of 'em—very often undeserving people that we can't depend upon.   What 's to prevent our having a person that we *can* depend upon, and enjoying the delight of doing a good action at the same time?   I say, what 's to prevent our employing this worthy woman, your mother?   What with one job and another, there 's lodging—and good lodging too—pretty well all the year round, rent free, and a weekly allowance besides, Kit, that would provide her with a great many comforts she don't at present enjoy.   Now what do you think of that?   Do you see any objection?   My only desire is to serve you, Kit; therefore if you do, say so freely.'

As Brass spoke, he moved the hat twice or thrice, and shuffled among the papers again, as if in search of something.

'How can I see any objection to such a kind offer, sir?' replied Kit with his whole heart.   'I don't know how to thank you, sir, I don't indeed.'

'Why then,' said Brass, suddenly turning upon him and thrusting his face close to Kit's with such a re-

pulsive smile that the latter, even in the very height
of his gratitude, drew back, quite startled. 'Why
then, *it's done.*'

Kit looked at him in some confusion.

'Done, I say,' added Sampson, rubbing his hands
and veiling himself again in his usual oily manner.
'Ha ha! and so you shall find, Kit, so you shall find.
But dear me,' said Brass, 'what a time Mr. Richard
is gone! A sad loiterer to be sure! Will you mind
the office one minute, while I run upstairs? Only
one minute. I'll not detain you an instant longer,
on any account, Kit.'

Talking as he went, Mr. Brass bustled out of the
office, and in a very short time returned. Mr. Swiveller came back, almost at the same instant; and as Kit
was leaving the room hastily, to make up for lost time,
Miss Brass encountered him in the doorway.

'Oh!' sneered Sally, looking after him as she entered. 'There goes your pet, Sammy, eh?'

'Ah! There he goes,' replied Brass. 'My pet, if
you please. An honest fellow, Mr. Richard sir—a
worthy fellow indeed!'

'Hem!' coughed Miss Brass.

'I tell you, you aggravating vagabond,' said the
angry Sampson, 'that I'd stake my life upon his
honesty. Am I never to hear the last of this? Am
I always to be baited, and beset, by your mean suspicions? Have you no regard for true merit, you
malignant fellow? If you come to that, I'd sooner
suspect your honesty than his.'

Miss Sally pulled out the tin snuff-box, and took a
long, slow pinch: regarding her brother with a steady
gaze all the time.

'She drives me wild, Mr. Richard sir,' said Brass,
'she exasperates me beyond all bearing. I am heated
and excited, sir, I know I am. These are not business

manners, sir, nor business looks, but she carries me out of myself.'

'Why don't you leave him alone?' said Dick.

'Because she can't, sir,' retorted Brass; 'because to chafe and vex me is a part of her nature, sir, and she will and must do it, or I don't believe she'd have her health. But never mind,' said Brass, 'never mind. I've carried my point. I've shown my confidence in the lad. He has minded the office again. Ha ha! Ugh, you viper!'

The beautiful virgin took another pinch, and put the snuff-box in her pocket; still looking at her brother with perfect composure.

'He has minded the office again,' said Brass triumphantly; 'he has had my confidence, and he shall continue to have it; he—why, where's the—'

'What have you lost?' inquired Mr. Swiveller.

'Dear me!' said Brass, slapping all his pockets, one after another, and looking into his desk, and under it, and upon it, and wildly tossing the papers about, 'the note, Mr. Richard sir, the five-pound note—what can have become of it? I laid it down here—God bless me!'

'What?' cried Miss Sally, starting up, clapping her hands, and scattering the papers on the floor. 'Gone! Now who's right? Now who's got it? Never mind five pounds—what's five pounds? He's honest you know, quite honest. It would be mean to suspect *him*. Don't run after him. No, no, not for the world!'

'Is it really gone though?' said Dick, looking at Brass with a face as pale as his own.

'Upon my word, Mr. Richard sir,' replied the lawyer, feeling in all his pockets with looks of the greatest agitation, 'I fear this is a black business. It's certainly gone, sir. What's to be done?'

'Don't run after him,' said Miss Sally, taking more snuff. 'Don't run after him on any account. Give him time to get rid of it, you know. It would be cruel to find him out!'

Mr. Swiveller and Sampson Brass looked from Miss Sally to each other, in a state of bewilderment, and then, as by one impulse, caught up their hats and rushed out into the street—darting along in the middle of the road, and dashing aside all obstructions, as though they were running for their lives.

It happened that Kit had been running too, though not so fast, and having the start of them by some few minutes, was a good distance ahead. As they were pretty certain of the road he must have taken, however, and kept on at a great pace, they came up with him, at the very moment when he had taken breath, and was breaking into a run again.

'Stop!' cried Sampson, laying his hand on one shoulder, while Mr. Swiveller pounced upon the other. 'Not so fast, sir. You're in a hurry?'

'Yes, I am,' said Kit, looking from one to the other in great surprise.

'I—I—can hardly believe it,' panted Sampson, 'but something of value is missing from the office. I hope you don't know what.'

'Know what! good Heaven, Mr. Brass!' cried Kit, trembling from head to foot; 'you don't suppose—'

'No, no,' rejoined Brass quickly, 'I don't suppose anything. Don't say *I* said you did. You'll come back quietly, I hope?'

'Of course I will,' returned Kit. 'Why not?'

'To be sure!' said Brass. 'Why not? I hope there may turn out to be no why not. If you knew the trouble I've been in, this morning, through taking your part, Christopher, you'd be sorry for it.'

'And I am sure you'll be sorry for having suspected

me, sir,' replied Kit. 'Come. Let us make haste back.'

'Certainly!' cried Brass, 'the quicker, the better. Mr. Richard—have the goodness, sir, to take that arm. I'll take this one. It's not easy walking three abreast, but under these circumstances it must be done, sir; there's no help for it.'

Kit did turn from white to red, and from red to white again, when they secured him thus, and for a moment seemed disposed to resist. But, quickly recollecting himself, and remembering that if he made any struggle, he would perhaps be dragged by the collar through the public streets, he only repeated, with great earnestness and with the tears standing in his eyes, that they would be sorry for this—and suffered them to lead him off. While they were on the way back, Mr. Swiveller, upon whom his present function sat very irksomely, took an opportunity of whispering in his ear that if he would confess his guilt, even by so much as a nod, and promise not to do so any more, he would connive at his kicking Sampson Brass on the shins and escaping up a court; but Kit indignantly rejecting this proposal, Mr. Richard had nothing for it, but to hold him tight until they reached Bevis Marks, and ushered him into the presence of the charming Sarah, who immediately took the precaution of locking the door.

'Now, you know,' said Brass, 'if this is a case of innocence, it is a case of that description, Christopher, where the fullest disclosure is the best satisfaction for everybody. Therefore if you'll consent to an examination,' he demonstrated what kind of examination he meant by turning back the cuffs of his coat, 'it will be a comfortable and pleasant thing for all parties.'

'Search me,' said Kit, proudly holding up his arms.

'But mind, sir—I know you'll be sorry for this, to the last day of your life.'

'It is certainly a very painful occurrence,' said Brass with a sigh, as he dived into one of Kit's pockets, and fished up a miscellaneous collection of small articles; 'very painful. Nothing here, Mr. Richard sir, all perfectly satisfactory. Nor here, sir. Nor in the waistcoat, Mr. Richard, nor in the coat-tails. So far, I am rejoiced, I am sure.'

Richard Swiveller, holding Kit's hat in his hand, was watching the proceedings with great interest, and bore upon his face the slightest possible indication of a smile, as Brass, shutting one of his eyes, looked with the other up the inside of one of the poor fellow's sleeves as if it were a telescope—when Sampson turning hastily to him, bade him search the hat.

'Here's a handkerchief,' said Dick.

'No harm in that, sir,' rejoined Brass, applying his eye to the other sleeve, and speaking in the voice of one who was contemplating an immense extent of prospect. 'No harm in a handkerchief, sir, whatever. The faculty don't consider it a healthy custom, I believe, Mr. Richard, to carry one's handkerchief in one's hat—I have heard that it keeps the head too warm—but in every other point of view, its being there, is extremely satisfactory—ex-tremely so.'

An exclamation, at once from Richard Swiveller, Miss Sally, and Kit himself, cut the lawyer short. He turned his head, and saw Dick standing with the bank-note in his hand.

'In the hat?' cried Brass in a sort of shriek.

'Under the handkerchief, and tucked beneath the lining,' said Dick, aghast at the discovery.

Mr. Brass looked at him, at his sister, at the walls, at the ceiling, at the floor—everywhere but at Kit, who stood quite stupefied and motionless.

'And this,' cried Sampson, clasping his hands, 'is the world that turns upon its own axis, and has Lunar influences, and revolutions round Heavenly Bodies, and various games of that sort!   This is human natur, is it?   Oh, natur, natur!   This is the miscreant that I was going to benefit with all my little arts, and that, even now, I feel so much for, as to wish to let him go!   But,' added Mr. Brass with greater fortitude, 'I am myself a lawyer, and bound to set an example in carrying the laws of my happy country into effect. Sally my dear, forgive me, and catch hold of him on the other side.   Mr. Richard sir, have the goodness to run and fetch a constable.   The weakness is past and over, sir, and moral strength returns.   A constable, sir, if *you* please!'

CHAPTER LX

KIT stood as one entranced, with his eyes opened wide and fixed upon the ground, regardless alike of the tremulous hold which Mr. Brass maintained on one side of his cravat, and of the firmer grasp of Miss Sally upon the other; although this latter detention was in itself no small inconvenience, as that fascinating woman, besides screwing her knuckles inconveniently into his throat from time to time, had fastened upon him in the first instance with so tight a grip that even in the disorder and distraction of his thoughts he could not divest himself of an uneasy sense of choking.   Between the brother and sister he remained in this posture, quite unresisting and passive, until Mr. Swiveller returned, with a police-constable at his heels.

This functionary, being, of course, well used to such scenes; looking upon all kinds of robbery, from petty larceny up to housebreaking or ventures on the highway, as matters in the regular course of business; and regarding the perpetrators in the light of so many customers coming to be served at the wholesale and retail shop of criminal law where he stood behind the counter; received Mr. Brass's statement of facts with about as much interest and surprise, as an undertaker might evince if required to listen to a circumstantial account of the last illness of a person whom he was called in to wait upon professionally; and took Kit into custody with a decent indifference.

'We had better,' said this subordinate minister of justice, 'get to the office while there's a magistrate sitting.   I shall want you to come along with us, Mr. Brass, and the—' he looked at Miss Sally as if in some doubt whether she might not be a griffin or other fabulous monster.

'The lady, eh?' said Sampson.

'Ah!' replied the constable. 'Yes—the lady. Likewise the young man that found the property.'

'Mr. Richard sir,' said Brass in a mournful voice. 'A sad necessity.   But the altar of our country, sir—'

'You'll have a hackney-coach, I suppose?' interrupted the constable, holding Kit (whom his other captors had released) carelessly by the arm, a little above the elbow.   'Be so good as to send for one, will you?'

'But, hear me speak a word,' cried Kit, raising his eyes and looking imploringly about him.   'Hear me speak a word.   I am no more guilty than any one of you.   Upon my soul I am not.   I a thief!   Oh, Mr. Brass, you know me better.   I am sure you know me better.   This is not right of you, indeed.'

'I give you my word, constable—' said Brass.   But here the constable interposed with the constitutional principle 'words be blowed'; observing that words were but spoonmeat for babes and sucklings, and that oaths were the food for strong men.

'Quite true, constable,' assented Brass in the same mournful tone. 'Strictly correct. I give you my oath, constable, that down to a few minutes ago, when this fatal discovery was made, I had such confidence in that lad, that I'd have trusted him with—a hackney-coach, Mr. Richard sir; you're very slow, sir.'

'Who is there that knows me,' cried Kit, 'that would not trust me—that does not? ask anybody whether they have ever doubted me; whether I have ever wronged them of a farthing. Was I ever once dishonest when I was poor and hungry, and is it likely I would begin now? Oh consider what you do. How can I meet the kindest friends that ever human creature had, with this dreadful charge upon me?'

Mr. Brass rejoined that it would have been well for the prisoner if he had thought of that, before, and was about to make some other gloomy observations when the voice of the single gentleman was heard, demanding from above-stairs what was the matter, and what was the cause of all that noise and hurry. Kit made an involuntary start towards the door in his anxiety to answer for himself, but being speedily detained by the constable, had the agony of seeing Sampson Brass run out alone to tell the story in his own way.

'And he can hardly believe it, either,' said Sampson, when he returned, 'nor nobody will. I wish I could doubt the evidence of my senses, but their depositions are unimpeachable. It's of no use cross-examining my eyes,' cried Sampson, winking and rubbing them, 'they stick to their first account, and will. Now, Sarah, I hear the coach in the Marks; get on your bonnet, and we'll be off. A sad errand! a moral funeral, quite!'

'Mr. Brass,' said Kit, 'do me one favour.   Take me to Mr. Witherden's first.'

Sampson shook his head irresolutely.

'Do,' said Kit.   'My master's there.   For Heaven's sake, take me there, first.'

'Well, I don't know,' stammered Brass, who perhaps had his reasons for wishing to show as fair as possible in the eyes of the notary.   'How do we stand in point of time, constable, eh?'

The constable, who had been chewing a straw all this while with great philosophy, replied that if they went away at once they would have time enough, but that if they stood shilly-shallying there, any longer, they must go straight to the Mansion House; and finally expressed his opinion that that was where it was, and that was all about it.

Mr. Richard Swiveller having arrived inside the coach, and still remaining immovable in the most commodious corner with his face to the horses, Mr. Brass instructed the officer to remove his prisoner, and declared himself quite ready.   Therefore, the constable, still holding Kit in the same manner, and pushing him on a little before him, so as to keep him at about three-quarters of an arm's-length in advance (which is the professional mode), thrust him into the vehicle and followed himself.   Miss Sally entered next; and there being now four inside, Sampson Brass got upon the box, and made the coachman drive on.

Still completely stunned by the sudden and terrible change which had taken place in his affairs, Kit sat gazing out of the coach-window, almost hoping to see some monstrous phenomenon in the streets which might give him reason to believe he was in a dream. Alas!   Everything was too real and familiar: the same succession of turnings, the same houses, the same streams of people running side by side in different directions upon the pavement, the same bustle of carts and carriages in the road, the same well-remembered objects in the shop-windows: a regularity in the very noise and hurry which no dream ever mirrored. Dreamlike as the story was, it was true. He stood charged with robbery; the note had been found upon him, though he was innocent in thought and deed; and they were carrying him back, a prisoner.

Absorbed in these painful ruminations, thinking with a drooping heart of his mother and little Jacob, feeling as though even the consciousness of innocence would be insufficient to support him in the presence of his friends if they believed him guilty, and sinking in hope and courage more and more as they drew nearer to the notary's, poor Kit was looking earnestly out of the window, observant of nothing,—when all at once, as though it had been conjured up by magic, he became aware of the face of Quilp.

And what a leer there was upon the face! It was from the open window of a tavern that it looked out; and the dwarf had so spread himself over it, with his elbows on the window-sill and his head resting on both his hands, that what between this attitude and his being swoln with suppressed laughter, he looked puffed and bloated into twice his usual breadth. Mr. Brass, on recognising him, immediately stopped the coach. As it came to a halt directly opposite to where he stood, the dwarf pulled off his hat, and saluted the party with a hideous and grotesque politeness.

'Aha!' he cried. 'Where now, Brass? where now? Sally with you too? Sweet Sally! And Dick? Pleasant Dick! And Kit? Honest Kit!'

'He's extremely cheerful!' said Brass to the coach-man. 'Very much so! Ah, sir—a sad business! Never believe in honesty any more, sir.'

'Why not?' returned the dwarf. 'Why not, you rogue of a lawyer, why not?'

'Bank-note lost in our office, sir,' said Brass, shaking his head. 'Found in his hat, sir—he previously left alone there—no mistake at all, sir—chain of evidence complete—not a link wanting.'

'What?' cried the dwarf, leaning half his body out of the window. 'Kit a thief! Kit a thief! Ha ha ha! Why, he's an uglier-looking thief than can be seen anywhere for a penny. Eh, Kit—eh? Ha ha ha! Have you taken Kit into custody before he had time and opportunity to beat me? Eh, Kit, eh?' And with that, he burst into a yell of laughter, manifestly to the great terror of the coachman, and pointed to a dyer's pole hard by, where a dangling suit of clothes bore some resemblance to a man upon a gibbet.

'Is it coming to that, Kit?' cried the dwarf, rubbing his hands violently. 'Ha ha ha ha! What a disappointment for little Jacob, and for his darling mother! Let him have the Bethel minister to comfort and console him, Brass. Eh, Kit, eh? Drive on coachey, drive on. Bye-bye, Kit; all good go with you; keep up your spirits; my love to the Garlands—the dear old lady and gentleman. Say I inquired after 'em, will you? Blessings on 'em, on you, and on everybody, Kit. Blessings on all the world!'

With such good wishes and farewells, poured out in a rapid torrent until they were out of hearing, Quilp suffered them to depart; and when he could see the coach no longer, drew in his head, and rolled upon the ground in an ecstasy of enjoyment.

When they reached the notary's, which they were not long in doing, for they had encountered the dwarf in a by-street at a very little distance from the house, Mr. Brass dismounted; and opening the coach-door

with a melancholy visage, requested his sister to accompany him into the office, with a view of preparing the good people within, for the mournful intelligence that awaited them.   Miss Sally complying, he
desired Mr. Swiveller to accompany them.   So, into
the office they went; Mr. Sampson and his sister arm-
in-arm; and Mr. Swiveller following, alone.

The notary was standing before the fire in the outer
office, talking to Mr. Abel and the elder Mr. Garland, while Mr. Chuckster sat writing at the desk,
picking up such crumbs of their conversation as happened to fall in his way.   This posture of affairs Mr.
Brass observed through the glass-door as he was turning the handle, and seeing that the notary recognised
him, he began to shake his head and sigh deeply while
that partition yet divided them.

'Sir,' said Sampson, taking off his hat, and kissing
the two fore-fingers of his right hand beaver glove,
'my name is Brass—Brass of Bevis Marks, sir.   I
have had the honour and pleasure, sir, of being concerned against you in some little testamentary matters.
How do you do, sir?'

'My clerk will attend to any business you may have
come upon, Mr. Brass,' said the notary, turning away.

'Thank you, sir,' said Brass, 'thank you, I am sure.
Allow me, sir, to introduce my sister—quite one of us,
sir, although of the weaker sex—of great use in my
business, sir, I assure you.   Mr. Richard sir, have the
goodness to come forward if you please—No really,'
said Brass, stepping between the notary and his
private office (towards which he had begun to retreat),
and speaking in the tone of an injured man, 'really,
sir, I must, under favour, request a word or two with
you, indeed.'

'Mr. Brass,' said the other, in a decided tone, 'I am
engaged.   You see that I am occupied with these gen-

tlemen. If you will communicate your business to Mr. Chuckster yonder, you will receive every attention.'

'Gentlemen,' said Brass, laying his right hand on his waistcoat, and looking towards the father and son with a smooth smile—'Gentlemen, I appeal to you— really, gentlemen—consider, I beg of you. I am of the law. I am styled "gentleman" by Act of Parliament. I maintain the title by the annual payment of twelve pound sterling for a certificate. I am not one of your players of music, stage actors, writers of books, or painters of pictures, who assume a station that the laws of their country don't recognise. I am none of your strollers or vagabonds. If any man brings his action against me, he must describe me as a gentleman, or his action is null and void. I appeal to you—is this quite respectful? Really, gentlemen —'

'Well, will you have the goodness to state your business then, Mr. Brass?' said the notary.

'Sir,' rejoined Brass, 'I will. Ah, Mr. Witherden! you little know the—but I will not be tempted to travel from the point, sir. I believe the name of one of these gentlemen is Garland.'

'Of both,' said the notary.

'In-deed!' rejoined Brass, cringing excessively. 'But I might have known that, from the uncommon likeness. Extremely happy, I am sure, to have the honour of an introduction to two such gentlemen, although the occasion is a most painful one. One of you gentlemen has a servant called Kit?'

'Both,' replied the notary.

'Two Kits?' said Brass smiling. 'Dear me!'

'One Kit, sir,' returned Mr. Witherden angrily, 'who is employed by both gentlemen. What of him?'

'This of him, sir,' rejoined Brass, dropping his

voice impressively. 'That young man, sir, that I have felt unbounded and unlimited confidence in, and always behaved to as if he was my equal—that young man has this morning committed a robbery in my office, and been taken almost in the fact.'

'This must be some falsehood!' cried the notary.

'It is not possible,' said Mr. Abel.

'I 'll not believe one word of it,' exclaimed the old gentleman.

Mr. Brass looked mildly round upon them, and rejoined—

'Mr. Witherden sir, *your* words are actionable, and if I was a man of low and mean standing, who couldn't afford to be slandered, I should proceed for damages. Hows'ever, sir, being what I am, I merely scorn such expressions. The honest warmth of the other gentleman I respect, and I 'm truly sorry to be the messenger of such unpleasant news. I shouldn't have put myself in this painful position, I assure you, but that the lad himself desired to be brought here in the first instance, and I yielded to his prayers. Mr. Chuckster sir, will you have the goodness to tap at the window for the constable that 's waiting in the coach?'

The three gentlemen looked at each other with blank faces when these words were uttered, and Mr. Chuckster, doing as he was desired, and leaping off his stool with something of the excitement of an inspired prophet whose foretellings had in the fulness of time been realised, held the door open for the entrance of the wretched captive.

Such a scene as there was, when Kit came in, and bursting into the rude eloquence with which Truth at length inspired him, called Heaven to witness that he was innocent, and that how the property came to be found upon him he knew not! Such a confusion of tongues, before the circumstances were related, and the proofs disclosed! Such a dead silence when all was told, and the three friends exchanged looks of doubt and amazement!

'Is it not possible,' said Mr. Witherden, after a long pause, 'that this note may have found its way into the hat by some accident,—such as the removal of the papers on the desk, for instance?'

But, this was clearly shown to be quite impossible. Mr. Swiveller, though an unwilling witness, could not help proving to demonstration, from the position in which it was found, that it must have been designedly secreted.

'It's very distressing,' said Brass, 'immensely distressing, I am sure. When he comes to be tried, I shall be very happy to recommend him to mercy on account of his previous good character. I did lose money before, certainly, but it doesn't quite follow that he took it. The presumption's against him—strongly against him—but we're Christians, I hope?'

'I suppose,' said the constable, looking round, 'that no gentleman here, can give evidence as to whether he's been flush of money of late. Do you happen to know, sir?'

'He has had money from time to time, certainly,' returned Mr. Garland, to whom the man had put the question. 'But that, as he always told me, was given him by Mr. Brass himself.'

'Yes to be sure,' said Kit eagerly. 'You can bear me out in that, sir?'

'Eh?' cried Brass, looking from face to face with an expression of stupid amazement.

'The money you know, the half-crowns, that you gave me—from the lodger,' said Kit.

'Oh dear me!' cried Brass, shaking his head and frowning heavily. 'This is a bad case, I find; a very bad case indeed.'

'What? Did you give him no money on account of anybody, sir?' asked Mr. Garland, with great anxiety.

'*I* give him money, sir!' returned Sampson. 'Oh, come you know, this is too barefaced. Constable, my good fellow, we had better be going.'

'What?' shrieked Kit. 'Does he deny that he did? ask him, somebody, pray. Ask him to tell you whether he did or not!'

'Did you, sir?' asked the notary.

'I tell you what, gentlemen,' replied Brass, in a very grave manner, 'he 'll not serve his case this way, and really, if you feel any interest in him, you had better advise him to go upon some other tack. Did I, sir? Of course I never did.'

'Gentlemen,' cried Kit, on whom a light broke suddenly, 'Master, Mr. Abel, Mr. Witherden, every one of you—he did it! What I have done to offend him, I don't know, but this is a plot to ruin me. Mind, gentlemen, it 's a plot, and whatever comes of it, I will say with my dying breath that he put that note in my hat himself! Look at him, gentlemen! see how he changes colour. Which of us looks the guilty person—he or I?'

'You hear him, gentlemen?' said Brass, smiling, 'you hear him. Now, does this case strike you as assuming rather a black complexion, or does it not? Is it all a treacherous case, do you think, or is it one of mere ordinary guilt? Perhaps, gentlemen, if he had not said this in your presence and I had reported it, you 'd have held this to be impossible, likewise, eh?'

With such pacific and bantering remarks did Mr. Brass refute the foul aspersion on his character; but the virtuous Sarah, moved by stronger feelings, and having at heart, perhaps, a more jealous regard for the honour of her family, flew from her brother's side, without any previous intimation of her design, and darted at the prisoner with the utmost fury. It would undoubtedly have gone hard with Kit's face, but that the wary constable, foreseeing her design, drew him aside at the critical moment, and thus placed Mr. Chuckster in circumstances of some jeopardy; for that gentleman happening to be next the object of Miss Brass's wrath; and rage being, like love and fortune, blind; was pounced upon by the fair enslaver, and had a false collar plucked up by the roots, and his hair very much dishevelled, before the exertions of the company could make her sensible of her mistake.

The constable, taking warning by this desperate attack, and thinking perhaps that it would be more satisfactory to the ends of justice if the prisoner were taken before a magistrate, whole, rather than in small pieces, led him back to the hackney-coach without more ado, and moreover insisted on Miss Brass becoming an outside passenger; to which proposal the charming creature, after a little angry discussion, yielded her consent; and so took her brother Sampson's place upon the box: Mr. Brass with some reluctance agreeing to occupy her seat inside. Those arrangements perfected, they drove to the justice-room with all speed, followed by the notary and his two friends in another coach. Mr. Chuckster alone was left behind—greatly to his indignation; for he held the evidence he could have given, relative to Kit's returning to work out the shilling, to be so very material as bearing upon his hypocritical and designing character, that he considered its suppression little better than a compromise of felony.

At the justice-room, they found the single gentleman, who had gone straight there, and was expecting them with desperate impatience. But, not fifty single gentlemen rolled into one could have helped poor Kit, who in half an hour afterwards was committed

for trial, and was assured by a friendly officer on his
way to prison that there was no occasion to be cast
down, for the sessions would soon be on, and he would,
in all likelihood, get his little affair disposed of, and
be comfortably transported, in less than a fortnight.

CHAPTER LXI

LET moralists and philosophers say what they may, it
is very questionable whether a guilty man would have
felt half as much misery that night, as Kit did, being
innocent. The world, being in constant commission
of vast quantities of injustice, is a little too apt to
comfort itself with the idea that if the victim of its
falsehood and malice have a clear conscience, he cannot fail to be sustained under his trials, and some-
how or other to come right at last; 'in which case,'
say they who have hunted him down, '—though we
certainly don't expect it—nobody will be better pleased
than we.' Whereas, the world would do well to re-
flect, that injustice is in itself, to every generous and
properly constituted mind, an injury, of all others the
most insufferable, the most torturing, and the most
hard to bear; and that many clear consciences have
gone to their account elsewhere, and many sound
hearts have broken, because of this very reason; the
knowledge of their own deserts only aggravating their
sufferings, and rendering them the less endurable.

The world, however, was not in fault in Kit's case.
But, Kit was innocent; and knowing this, and feeling
that his best friends deemed him guilty—that Mr.
and Mrs. Garland would look upon him as a monster
of ingratitude—that Barbara would associate him with
all that was bad and criminal—that the pony would
consider himself forsaken—and that even his own

mother might perhaps yield to the strong appearances against him, and believe him to be the wretch he seemed—knowing and feeling all this, he experienced, at first, an agony of mind which no words can describe, and walked up and down the little cell in which he was locked up for the night, almost beside himself with grief.

Even when the violence of these emotions had in some degree subsided, and he was beginning to grow more calm, there came into his mind a new thought, the anguish of which was scarcely less. The child— the bright star of the simple fellow's life—she, who always came back upon him like a beautiful dream,— who had made the poorest part of his existence, the happiest and best—who had ever been so gentle, and considerate, and good—if she were ever to hear of this, what would she think? As this idea occurred to him, the walls of the prison seemed to melt away, and the old place to reveal itself in their stead, as it was wont to be on winter nights—the fireside, the little supper-table, the old man's hat, and coat, and stick—the half-opened door, leading to her little room —they were all there. And Nell herself was there, and he—both laughing heartily as they had often done —and when he had got as far as this, Kit could go no farther, but flung himself upon his poor bedstead and wept.

It was a long night, which seemed as though it would have no end; but he slept too, and dreamed— always of being at liberty, and roving about, now with one person and now with another, but ever with a vague dread of being recalled to prison; not that prison, but one which was in itself a dim idea—not of a place, but of a care and sorrow: of something oppressive and always present, and yet impossible to define. At last, the morning dawned, and there was the jail itself—cold, black, and dreary, and very real indeed.

He was left to himself, however, and there was comfort in that. He had liberty to walk in a small paved yard at a certain hour, and learnt from the turnkey, who came to unlock his cell and show him where to wash, that there was a regular time for visiting, every day, and that if any of his friends came to see him, he would be fetched down to the grate. When he had given him this information, and a tin porringer containing his breakfast, the man locked him up again; and went clattering along the stone passage, opening and shutting a great many other doors, and raising numberless loud echoes which resounded through the building for a long time, as if they were in prison too, and unable to get out.

This turnkey had given him to understand that he was lodged, like some few others in the jail, apart from the mass of prisoners; because he was not supposed to be utterly depraved and irreclaimable, and had never occupied apartments in that mansion before. Kit was thankful for this indulgence, and sat reading the church catechism very attentively (though he had known it by heart from a little child), until he heard the key in the lock, and the man entered again.

'Now then,' he said, 'come on!'

'Where to, sir?' asked Kit.

The man contented himself by briefly replying 'Wisitors'; and taking him by the arm in exactly the same manner as the constable had done the day before, led him, through several winding ways and strong gates, into a passage, where he placed him at a grating and turned upon his heel. Beyond this grating, at the distance of about four or five feet, was another exactly like it. In the space between, sat a turnkey reading a newspaper, and outside the further railing, Kit saw, with a palpitating heart, his mother with the baby in her arms; Barbara's mother with her never-failing umbrella; and poor little Jacob, staring in with all his might, as though he were looking for the bird, or the wild beast, and thought the men were mere accidents with whom the bars could have no possible concern.

But, when little Jacob saw his brother, and, thrusting his arms between the rails to hug him, found that he came no nearer, but still stood afar off with his head resting on the arm by which he held to one of the bars, he began to cry most piteously; whereupon, Kit's mother and Barbara's mother, who had restrained themselves as much as possible, burst out sobbing and weeping afresh. Poor Kit could not help joining them, and not one of them could speak a word.

During this melancholy pause, the turnkey read his newspaper with a waggish look (he had evidently got among the facetious paragraphs) until, happening to take his eyes off for an instant, as if to get by dint of contemplation at the very marrow of some joke of a deeper sort than the rest, it appeared to occur to him, for the first time, that somebody was crying.

'Now, ladies, ladies,' he said, looking round with surprise, 'I'd advise you not to waste time like this. It's allowanced here, you know. You mustn't let that child make that noise either. It's against all rules.'

'I'm his poor mother, sir,' sobbed Mrs. Nubbles, curtseying humbly, 'and this is his brother, sir. Oh dear me, dear me!'

'Well!' replied the turnkey, folding his paper on his knee, so as to get with greater convenience at the

top of the next column.   'It can't be helped you know.
He ain't the only one in the same fix.   You mustn't
make a noise about it!'

With that he went on reading.   The man was not
unnaturally cruel or hard-hearted.   He had come to
look upon felony as a kind of disorder, like the scarlet
fever or erysipelas; some people had it—some hadn't
—just as it might be.

'Oh! my darling Kit,' said his mother, whom Barbara's mother had charitably relieved of the baby,
'that I should see my poor boy here!'

'You don't believe that I did what they accuse me
of, mother dear?' cried Kit, in a choking voice.

'*I* believe it!' exclaimed the poor woman, '*I* that
never knew you tell a lie, or do a bad action from your
cradle—that have never had a moment's sorrow on
your account, except it was for the poor meals that
you have taken with such good-humour and content,
that I forgot how little there was, when I thought how
kind and thoughtful you were, though you were but
a child!—I believe it of the son that 's been a comfort
to me from the hour of his birth until this time, and
that I never laid down one night in anger with!   I
believe it of you, Kit!—'

'Why then, thank God!' said Kit, clutching the bars
with an earnestness that shook them, 'and I can bear
it, mother!   Come what may, I shall always have one
drop of happiness in my heart when I think that you
said that.'

At this the poor woman fell a crying again, and
Barbara's mother too.   And little Jacob, whose dis-
jointed thoughts had by this time resolved themselves
into a pretty distinct impression that Kit couldn't go
out for a walk if he wanted, and that there were no
birds, lions, tigers, or other natural curiosities behind those bars—nothing indeed, but a caged brother

—added his tears to theirs with as little noise as possible.

Kit's mother, drying her eyes (and moistening them, poor soul, more than she dried them), now took from the ground a small basket, and submissively addressed herself to the turnkey, saying, would he please to listen to her for a minute? The turnkey, being in the very crisis and passion of a joke, motioned to her with his hand to keep silent one minute longer, for her life. Nor did he remove his hand into its former posture, but kept it in the same warning attitude until he had finished the paragraph, when he paused for a few seconds, with a smile upon his face, as who should say 'this editor is a comical blade—a funny dog,' and then asked her what she wanted.

'I have brought him a little something to eat,' said the good woman. 'If you please, sir, might he have it?'

'Yes,—he may have it. There's no rule against that. Give it to me when you go, and I'll take care he has it.'

'No, but if you please, sir—don't be angry with me, sir—I am his mother, and you had a mother once—if I might only see him eat a little bit, I should go away, so much more satisfied that he was all comfortable.'

And again the tears of Kit's mother burst forth, and of Barbara's mother, and of little Jacob. As to the baby, it was crowing and laughing with all its might—under the idea, apparently, that the whole scene had been invented and got up for its particular satisfaction.

The turnkey looked as if he thought the request a strange one and rather out of the common way, but nevertheless he laid down his paper, and coming round to where Kit's mother stood, took the basket from her, and after inspecting its contents, handed it to Kit, and went back to his place. It may be easily conceived that the prisoner had no great appetite, but he sat down on the ground, and ate as hard as he could, while, at every morsel he put into his mouth, his mother sobbed and wept afresh, though with a softened grief that bespoke the satisfaction the sight afforded her.

While he was thus engaged, Kit made some anxious inquiries about his employers, and whether they had expressed any opinion concerning him; but all he could learn was that Mr. Abel had himself broken the intelligence to his mother, with great kindness and delicacy, late on the previous night, but had himself expressed no opinion of his innocence or guilt. Kit was on the point of mustering courage to ask Barbara's mother about Barbara, when the turnkey who had conducted him, reappeared, a second turnkey appeared behind his visitors, and the third turnkey with the newspaper cried 'Time 's up!'—adding in the same breath 'Now for the next party!' and then plunging deep into his newspaper again. Kit was taken off in an instant, with a blessing from his mother, and a scream from little Jacob, ringing in his ears. As he was crossing the next yard with the basket in his hand, under the guidance of his former conductor, another officer called to them to stop, and came up with a pint-pot of porter in his hand.

'This is Christopher Nubbles, isn't it, that come in last night for felony?' said the man.

His comrade replied that this was the chicken in question.

'Then here 's your beer,' said the other man to Christopher. 'What are you looking at? There an't a discharge in it.'

'I beg your pardon,' said Kit. 'Who sent it me?'

'Why, your friend,' replied the man. 'You 're to

have it every day, he says.   And so you will, if he pays for it.'

'My friend!' repeated Kit.

'You 're all abroad, seemingly,' returned the other man.   'There 's his letter.   Take hold!'

Kit took it, and when he was locked up again, read as follows.

'Drink of this cup, you 'll find there 's a spell in its every drop 'gainst the ills of mortality.   Talk of the cordial that sparkled for Helen!   *Her* cup was a fiction, but this is reality (Barclay and Co.'s).   If they ever send it in a flat state, complain to the Governor. Yours, R. S.'

'R. S.!' said Kit, after some consideration.   'It must be Mr. Richard Swiveller.   Well, it 's very kind of him, and I thank him heartily.'

CHAPTER LXII

A FAINT light, twinkling from the window of the counting-house on Quilp's wharf, and looking inflamed and red through the night-fog, as though it suffered from it like an eye, forewarned Mr. Sampson Brass, as he approached the wooden cabin with a cautious step, that the excellent proprietor, his esteemed client, was inside, and probably waiting with his accustomed patience and sweetness of temper the fulfilment of the appointment which now brought Mr. Brass within his fair domain.

'A treacherous place to pick one's steps in, of a dark night,' muttered Sampson, as he stumbled for the twentieth time over some stray lumber, and limped in pain.   'I believe that boy strews the ground differently every day, on purpose to bruise and maim one;

unless his master does it with his own hands, which is more than likely. I hate to come to this place without Sally. She 's more protection than a dozen men.'

As he paid this compliment to the merit of the absent charmer, Mr. Brass came to a halt; looking doubtfully towards the light, and over his shoulder.

'What 's he about, I wonder?' murmured the lawyer, standing on tip-toe and endeavouring to obtain a glimpse of what was passing inside, which at that distance was impossible—'drinking, I suppose,—making himself more fiery and furious, and heating his malice and mischievousness till they boil. I 'm always afraid to come here by myself, when his account 's a pretty large one. I don't believe he 'd mind throttling me, and dropping me softly into the river when the tide was at its strongest, any more than he 'd mind killing a rat—indeed I don't know whether he wouldn't consider it a pleasant joke. Hark! Now he 's singing!'

Mr. Quilp was certainly entertaining himself with vocal exercise, but it was rather a kind of chant than a song; being a monotonous repetition of one sentence in a very rapid manner, with a long stress upon the last word, which he swelled into a dismal roar. Nor did the burden of this performance bear any reference to love, or war, or wine, or loyalty, or any other, the standard topics of song, but to a subject not often set to music or generally known in ballads; the words being these:—'The worthy magistrate, after remarking that the prisoner would find some difficulty in persuading a jury to believe his tale, committed him to take his trial at the approaching sessions; and directed the customary recognisances to be entered into for the pros-e-cu-tion.'

Every time he came to this concluding word, and

had exhausted all possible stress upon it, Quilp burst into a shriek of laughter, and began again.

'He's dreadfully imprudent,' muttered Brass, after he had listened to two or three repetitions of the chant. 'Horribly inprudent. I wish he was dumb. I wish he was deaf. I wish he was blind. Hang him,' cried Brass, as the chant began again. 'I wish he was dead!'

Giving utterance to these friendly aspirations in behalf of his client, Mr. Sampson composed his face into its usual state of smoothness, and waiting until the shriek came again and was dying away, went up to the wooden house, and knocked at the door.

'Come in!' cried the dwarf.

'How do you do to-night, sir?' said Sampson, peeping in. 'Ha ha ha! How do you do, sir? Oh dear me, how very whimsical! Amazingly whimsical to be sure!'

'Come in, you fool!' returned the dwarf, 'and don't stand there shaking your head and showing your teeth. Come in, you false witness, you perjurer, you suborner of evidence, come in!'

'He has the richest humour!' cried Brass, shutting the door behind him; 'the most amazing vein of comicality! But isn't it *rather* injudicious, sir—?'

'What?' demanded Quilp. 'What, Judas?'

'Judas!' cried Brass. 'He has such extraordinary spirits! His humour is so extremely playful! Judas! Oh yes—dear me, how very good! Ha ha ha!'

All this time, Sampson was rubbing his hands, and staring, with ludicrous surprise and dismay, at a great, goggle-eyed, blunt-nosed figure-head of some old ship, which was reared up against the wall in a corner near the stove, looking like a goblin or hideous idol whom the dwarf worshipped.   A mass of timber on its head, carved into the dim and distant semblance of a cocked hat, together with a representation of a star on the left breast and epaulettes on the shoulders, denoted that it was intended for the effigy of some famous admiral; but, without those helps, any observer might have supposed it the authentic portrait of a distinguished merman, or great sea-monster.   Being originally much too large for the apartment which it was now employed to decorate, it had been sawn short off at the waist.   Even in this state it reached from floor to ceiling; and thrusting itself forward, with that excessively wide-awake aspect, and air of somewhat obstrusive politeness, by which figure-heads are usually characterised, seemed to reduce everything else to mere pigmy proportions.

'Do you know it?' said the dwarf, watching Sampson's eyes.   'Do you see the likeness?'

'Eh?' said Brass, holding his head on one side and throwing it a little back, as connoisseurs do.   'Now I look at it again, I fancy I see a—yes, there certainly is something in the smile that reminds me of—and yet upon my word I—'

Now, the fact was, that Sampson, having never seen anything in the smallest degree resembling this substantial phantom, was much perplexed; being uncertain whether Mr. Quilp considered it like himself, and had therefore bought it for a family portrait; or whether he was pleased to consider it as the likeness of some enemy.   He was not very long in doubt; for, while he was surveying it with that knowing look which people assume when they are contemplating for the first time portraits which they ought to recognise but don't, the dwarf threw down the newspaper from which he had been chanting the words already quoted, and seizing a rusty iron bar, which he used in lieu of poker, dealt the figure such a stroke on the nose that it rocked again.

'Is it like Kit—is it his picture, his image, his very self?' cried the dwarf, aiming a shower of blows at the insensible countenance, and covering it with deep dimples. 'Is it the exact model and counterpart of the dog—is it—is it—is it?' And with every repetition of the question, he battered the great image, until the perspiration streamed down his face with the violence of the exercise.

Although this might have been a very comical thing to look at from a secure gallery, as a bull-fight is found to be a comfortable spectacle by those who are not in the arena, and a house on fire is better than a play to people who don't live near it, there was something in the earnestness of Mr. Quilp's manner which made his legal adviser feel that the counting-house was a little too small, and a deal too lonely, for the complete enjoyment of these humours. Therefore, he stood as far off as he could, while the dwarf was thus engaged; whimpering out but feeble applause; and when Quilp left off and sat down again from pure exhaustion, approached with more obsequiousness than ever.

'Excellent indeed!' cried Brass. 'He he! Oh, very good, sir. You know,' said Sampson, looking round as if in appeal to the bruised animal, 'he's quite a remarkable man—quite!'

'Sit down,' said the dwarf. 'I bought the dog yesterday. I've been screwing gimlets into him, and sticking forks in his eyes, and cutting my name on him. I mean to burn him at last.'

'Ha ha!' cried Brass. 'Extremely entertaining, indeed!'

'Come here,' said Quilp, beckoning him to draw near. 'What's injudicious, hey?'

'Nothing, sir—nothing. Scarcely worth mentioning, sir; but I thought that song—admirably humorous in itself you know—was perhaps rather—'

'Yes,' said Quilp, 'rather what?'

'Just bordering, or as one may say remotely verging, upon the confines of injudiciousness perhaps, sir,' returned Brass, looking timidly at the dwarf's cunning eyes, which were turned towards the fire and reflected its red light.

'Why?' inquired Quilp, without looking up.

'Why, you know, sir,' returned Brass, venturing to be more familiar: '—the fact is, sir, that any allusion to these little combinings together, of friends, for objects in themselves extremely laudable, but which the law terms conspiracies, are—you take me, sir?—best kept snug and among friends, you know.'

'Eh?' said Quilp, looking up with a perfectly vacant countenance. 'What do you mean?'

'Cautious, exceedingly cautious, very right and proper!' cried Brass, nodding his head. 'Mum, sir, even here—my meaning, sir, exactly.'

'*Your* meaning exactly, you brazen scarecrow,—what 's your meaning?' retorted Quilp. 'Why do you talk to me of combining together? Do *I* combine? Do I know anything about your combinings?'

'No no, sir—certainly not; not by any means,' returned Brass.

'If you so wink and nod at me,' said the dwarf, looking about him as if for his poker, 'I 'll spoil the expression of your monkey's face, I will.'

'Don't put yourself out of the way I beg, sir,' rejoined Brass, checking himself with great alacrity. 'You 're quite right, sir, quite right. I shouldn't have mentioned the subject, sir. It 's much better not to. You 're quite right, sir. Let us change it, if you please. You were asking, sir, Sally told me, about our lodger. He has not returned, sir.'

'No?' said Quilp, heating some rum in a little saucepan, and watching it to prevent its boiling over. 'Why not?'

'Why, sir,' returned Brass, 'he—dear me, Mr. Quilp sir—'

'What 's the matter?' said the dwarf, stopping his hand in the act of carrying the saucepan to his mouth.

'You have forgotten the water, sir,' said Brass. 'And—excuse me, sir—but it 's burning hot.'

Deigning no other than a practical answer to this remonstrance, Mr. Quilp raised the hot saucepan to his lips, and deliberately drank off all the spirit it contained, which might have been in quantity about half a pint, and had been but a moment before, when he took it off the fire, bubbling and hissing fiercely. Having swallowed this gentle stimulant, and shaken his fist at the admiral, he bade Mr. Brass proceed.

'But first,' said Quilp, with his accustomed grin, 'have a drop yourself—a nice drop—a good, warm, fiery drop.'

'Why, sir,' replied Brass, 'if there was such a thing as a mouthful of water that could be got without trouble—'

'There 's no such thing to be had here,' cried the dwarf. 'Water for lawyers! Melted lead and brimstone, you mean, nice hot blistering pitch and tar—that 's the thing for them—eh, Brass, eh?'

'Ha ha ha!' laughed Mr. Brass. 'Oh very biting! and yet it 's like being tickled—there 's a pleasure in it too, sir!'

'Drink that,' said the dwarf, who had by this time heated some more. 'Toss it off, don't leave any heeltap, scorch your throat and be happy!'

The wretched Sampson took a few short sips of the liquor, which immediately distilled itself into burning tears, and in that form came rolling down his cheeks into the pipkin again, turning the colour of his face and eye-lids to a deep red, and giving rise to a violent fit of coughing, in the midst of which he was still heard to declare, with the constancy of a martyr, that it was 'beautiful indeed!' While he was yet in unspeakable agonies, the dwarf renewed their conversation.

'The lodger,' said Quilp,—'what about him?'

'He is still, sir,' returned Brass, with intervals of coughing, 'stopping with the Garland family. He has only been home once, sir, since the day of the examination of that culprit. He informed Mr. Richard, sir, that he couldn't bear the house after what had taken place; that he was wretched in it; and that he looked upon himself as being in a certain kind of way the cause of the occurrence.—A very excellent lodger, sir. I hope we may not lose him.'

'Yah!' cried the dwarf. 'Never thinking of anybody but yourself—why don't you retrench then—scrape up, hoard, economise, eh?'

'Why, sir,' replied Brass, 'upon my word I think Sarah's as good an economiser as any going. I do indeed, Mr. Quilp.'

'Moisten your clay, wet the other eye, drink, man!' cried the dwarf. 'You took a clerk to oblige me.'

'Delighted, sir, I am sure, at any time,' replied Sampson. 'Yes, sir, I did.'

'Then now you may discharge him,' said Quilp. 'There's a means of retrenchment for you at once.'

'Discharge Mr. Richard, sir?' cried Brass.

'Have you more than one clerk, you parrot, that you ask the question? Yes.'

'Upon my word, sir,' said Brass, 'I wasn't prepared for this—'

'How could you be?' sneered the dwarf, 'when *I* wasn't? How often am I to tell you that I brought him to you that I might always have my eye on him and know where he was—and that I had a plot, a scheme, a little quiet piece of enjoyment afoot, of which the very cream and essence was, that this old man and grandchild (who have sunk underground I think) should be, while he and his precious friend believed them rich, in reality as poor as frozen rats.'

'I quite understood that, sir,' rejoined Brass. 'Thoroughly.'

'Well, sir,' retorted Quilp, 'and do you understand now, that they're *not* poor—that they can't be, if they have such men as your lodger searching for them, and scouring the country far and wide?'

'Of course I do, sir,' said Sampson.

'Of course you do,' retorted the dwarf, viciously snapping at his words. 'Of course do you understand then, that it's no matter what comes of this fellow? of course do you understand that for any other purpose he's no man for me, nor for you?'

'I have frequently said to Sarah, sir,' returned Brass, 'that he was of no use at all in the business. You can't put any confidence in him, sir. If you'll believe me I've found that fellow, in the commonest little matters of the office that have been trusted to him, blurting out the truth, though expressly cautioned. The aggravation of that chap, sir, has exceeded anything you can imagine, it has indeed. Nothing but the respect and obligation I owe to you, sir—'

As it was plain that Sampson was bent on a complimentary harangue, unless he received a timely interruption, Mr. Quilp politely tapped him on the crown of his head with the little saucepan, and requested that he would be so obliging as to hold his peace.

'Practical, sir, practical,' said Brass, rubbing the place and smiling; 'but still extremely pleasant—immensely so!'

'Hearken to me, will you?' returned Quilp, 'or I 'll be a little more pleasant, presently. There's no chance of his comrade and friend returning. The scamp has been obliged to fly, as I learn, for some knavery, and has found his way abroad. Let him rot there.'

'Certainly, sir. Quite proper.—Forcible!' cried Brass, glancing at the admiral again, as if he made a third in company. 'Extremely forcible!'

'I hate him,' said Quilp between his teeth, 'and have always hated him for family reasons. Besides he was an intractable ruffian; otherwise *he* would have been of use. This fellow is pigeon-hearted, and light-headed. I don't want him any longer. Let him hang or drown—starve—go to the devil.'

'By all means, sir,' returned Brass. 'When would you wish him, sir, to—ha ha!—to make that little excursion?'

'When this trial's over,' said Quilp. 'As soon as that's ended, send him about his business.'

'It shall be done, sir,' returned Brass; 'by all means. It will be rather a blow to Sarah, sir, but she has all her feelings under control. Ah, Mr. Quilp, I often think, sir, if it had only pleased Providence to bring you and Sarah together, in earlier life, what blessed results would have flowed from such a union! You never saw our dear father, sir?—A charming gentleman. Sarah was his pride and joy, sir. He would have closed his eyes in bliss, would Foxey, Mr.

Quilp, if he could have found her such a partner. You esteem her, sir?'

'I love her,' croaked the dwarf.

'You 're very good, sir,' returned Brass, 'I am sure. Is there any other order, sir, that I can take note of, besides this little matter of Mr. Richard?'

'None,' replied the dwarf, seizing the saucepan. 'Let us drink the lovely Sarah.'

'If we could do it in something, sir, that wasn't quite boiling,' suggested Brass humbly, 'perhaps it would be better. I think it will be more agreeable to Sarah's feelings, when she comes to hear from me of the honour you have done her, if she learns it was in liquor rather cooler than the last, sir.'

But to these remonstrances, Mr. Quilp turned a deaf ear. Sampson Brass, who was, by this time, anything but sober, being compelled to take further draughts of the same strong bowl, found that, instead of at all contributing to his recovery, they had the novel effect of making the counting-house spin round and round with extreme velocity, and causing the floor and ceiling to heave in a very distressing manner. After a brief stupor, he awoke to a consciousness of being partly under the table and partly under the grate. This position not being the most comfortable one he could have chosen for himself, he managed to stagger to his feet, and, holding on by the admiral, looked round for his host.

Mr. Brass's first impression was, that his host was gone and had left him there alone—perhaps locked him in for the night. A strong smell of tobacco, however, suggested a new train of ideas, he looked upward, and saw that the dwarf was smoking in his hammock.

'Good-bye, sir,' cried Brass faintly. 'Good-bye, sir.'

'Won't you stop all night?' said the dwarf, peeping out. 'Do stop all night!'

'I couldn't indeed, sir,' replied Brass, who was almost dead from nausea and the closeness of the room. 'If you'd have the goodness to show me a light, so that I may see my way across the yard, sir—'

Quilp was out in an instant; not with his legs first, or his head first, or his arms first, but bodily—altogether.

'To be sure,' he said, taking up a lantern, which was now the only light in the place. 'Be careful how you go, my dear friend. Be sure to pick your way among the timber, for all the rusty nails are upwards. There's a dog in the lane. He bit a man last night, and a woman the night before, and last Tuesday he killed a child—but that was in play. Don't go too near him.'

'Which side of the road is he, sir?' asked Brass, in great dismay.

'He lives on the right-hand,' said Quilp, 'but sometimes he hides on the left, ready for a spring. He's uncertain in that respect. Mind you take care of yourself. I'll never forgive you if you don't. There's the light out—never mind—you know the way—straight on!'

Quilp had slightly shaded the light by holding it against his breast, and now stood chuckling and shaking from head to foot in rapture of delight, as he heard the lawyer stumbling up the yard, and now and then falling heavily down. At length, however, he got quit of the place, and was out of hearing.

The dwarf shut himself up again, and sprang once more into his hammock.

CHAPTER LXIII

THE professional gentleman who had given Kit that consolatory piece of information relative to the settlement of his trifle of business at the Old Bailey, and the probability of its being very soon disposed of, turned out to be quite correct in his prognostications. In eight days' time, the sessions commenced. In one day afterwards, the Grand Jury found a True Bill against Christopher Nubbles for felony; and in two days from that finding, the aforesaid Christopher Nubbles was called upon to plead Guilty or Not Guilty to an Indictment for that he the said Christopher did feloniously abstract and steal from the dwelling-house and office of one Sampson Brass, gentleman, one Bank-note for Five Pounds issued by the Governor and Company of the Bank of England; in contravention of the Statutes in that case made and provided, and against the peace of our Sovereign Lord the King, his crown and dignity.

To this indictment Christopher Nubbles, in a low and trembling voice, pleaded Not Guilty; and here, let those who are in the habit of forming hasty judgments from appearances, and who would have had Christopher, if innocent, speak out very strong and loud, observe, that confinement and anxiety will subdue the stoutest hearts; and that to one who has been close shut up, though it be only for ten or eleven days, seeing but stone walls and a very few stony faces, the sudden entrance into a great hall filled with life, is a rather disconcerting and startling circumstance. To this, it must be added, that life in a wig, is, to a large class of people, much more terrifying and impressive than life with its own head of hair; and if, in addition to these considerations, there be taken into account

Kit's natural emotion on seeing the two Mr. Garlands and the little notary looking on with pale and anxious faces, it will perhaps seem matter of no very great wonder that he should have been rather out of sorts, and unable to make himself quite at home.

Although he had never seen either of the Mr. Garlands, or Mr. Witherden, since the time of his arrest, he had been given to understand that they had employed counsel for him. Therefore, when one of the gentlemen in wigs got up and said 'I am for the prisoner, my Lord,' Kit made him a bow; and when another gentleman in a wig got up and said 'And I 'm against him, my Lord,' Kit trembled very much, and bowed to him too. And didn't he hope in his own heart that his gentleman was a match for the other gentleman, and would make him ashamed of himself in no time!

The gentleman who was against him had to speak first, and being in dreadfully good spirits (for he had, in the last trial, very nearly procured the acquittal of a young gentleman who had had the misfortune to murder his father) he spoke up, you may be sure; telling the Jury that if they acquitted this prisoner they must expect to suffer no less pangs and agonies that he had told the other Jury they would certainly undergo if they convicted that prisoner. And when he had told them all about the case, and that he had never known a worse case, he stopped a little while, like a man who had something terrible to tell them, and then said that he understood an attempt would be made by his learned friend (and here he looked sideways at Kit's gentleman) to impeach the testimony of those immaculate witnesses whom he should call before them; but he did hope and trust that his learned friend would have a greater respect and veneration for the character of the prosecutor; than whom, as he well knew, there did not exist, and never had existed, a more honourable member of that most honourable profession to which he was attached. And then he said, did the Jury know Bevis Marks? And if they did know Bevis Marks (as he trusted for their own character, they did) did they know the historical and elevating associations connected with that most remarkable spot? Did they believe that a man like Brass could reside in a place like Bevis Marks, and not be a virtuous and most upright character? And when he had said a great deal to them on this point, he remembered that it was an insult to their understandings to make any remarks on what they must have felt so strongly without him, and therefore called Sampson Brass into the witness-box, straightway.

Then up comes Mr. Brass, very brisk and fresh; and, having bowed to the judge, like a man who has had the pleasure of seeing him before, and who hopes he has been pretty well since their last meeting, folds his arms, and looks at his gentleman as much as to say 'Here I am—full of evidence—Tap me!' And the gentleman does tap him presently, and with great discretion too; drawing off the evidence by little and little, and making it run quite clear and bright in the eyes of all present. Then, Kit's gentleman takes him in hand, but can make nothing of him; and after a great many very long questions and very short answers, Mr. Sampson Brass goes down in glory.

To him succeeds Sarah, who in like manner is easy to be managed by Mr. Brass's gentleman, but very obdurate to Kit's. In short, Kit's gentleman can get nothing out of her but a repetition of what she has said before (only a little stronger this time, as against his client), and therefore lets her go, in some confusion. Then, Mr. Brass's gentleman calls Richard Swiveller, and Richard Swiveller appears accordingly.

Now, Mr. Brass's gentleman has it whispered in his ear that this witness is disposed to be friendly to the prisoner—which, to say the truth, he is rather glad to hear, as his strength is considered to lie in what is familiarly termed badgering. Wherefore, he begins by requesting the officer to be quite sure that this witness kisses the book, and then goes to work at him, tooth and nail.

'Mr. Swiveller,' says this gentleman to Dick, when he had told his tale with evident reluctance and a desire to make the best of it: 'Pray, sir, where did you dine yesterday?'—'Where did I dine yesterday?'—'Aye, sir, where did you dine yesterday—was it near here, sir?'—'Oh to be sure—yes—just over the way.'—'To be sure. Yes. Just over the way,' repeats Mr. Brass's gentleman, with a glance at the court—'Alone, sir?'—'I beg your pardon,' says Mr. Swiveller, who has not caught the question—'*Alone,* sir?' repeats Mr. Brass's gentleman in a voice of thunder, 'did you dine alone? Did you treat anybody, sir? Come!'—'Oh yes, to be sure—yes, I did,' says Mr. Swiveller with a smile. 'Have the goodness to banish a levity, sir, which is very ill-suited to the place in which you stand (though perhaps you have reason to be thankful that it's only that place),' said Mr. Brass's gentleman, with a nod of the head, insinuating that the dock is Mr. Swiveller's legitimate sphere of action; 'and attend to me. You were waiting about here, yesterday, in expectation that this trial was coming on. You dined over the way. You treated somebody. Now, was that somebody brother to the prisoner at the bar?'—Mr. Swiveller is proceeding to explain—'Yes or No, sir,' cries Mr. Brass's gentleman—'But will you allow me—'—'Yes or No, sir'—'Yes it was, but—'—'Yes it was,' cries the gentleman, taking him up short—'And a very pretty witness *you* are!'

Down sits Mr. Brass's gentleman. Kit's gentleman, not knowing how the matter really stands, is afraid to pursue the subject. Richard Swiveller retires abashed. Judge, jury, and spectators have visions of his lounging about, with an ill-looking, large-whiskered, dissolute young fellow of six feet high. The reality is, little Jacob, with the calves of his legs exposed to the open air, and himself tied up in a shawl. Nobody knows the truth; everybody believes a falsehood; and all because of the ingenuity of Mr. Brass's gentleman.

Then, come the witnesses to character, and here Mr. Brass's gentleman shines again. It turns out that Mr. Garland has had no character with Kit, no recommendation of him but from his own mother, and that he was suddenly dismissed by his former master for unknown reasons. 'Really, Mr. Garland,' says Mr. Brass's gentleman, 'for a person who has arrived at your time of life, you are, to say the least of it, singularly indiscreet, I think.' The Jury think so too, and find Kit guilty. He is taken off, humbly protesting his innocence. The spectators settle themselves in their places with renewed attention, for there are several female witnesses to be examined in the next case, and it has been rumoured that Mr. Brass's gentleman will make great fun in cross-examining them for the prisoner.

Kit's mother, poor woman, is waiting at the grate below-stairs, accompanied by Barbara's mother (who, honest soul! never does anything but cry, and hold the baby), and a sad interview ensues. The newspaper-reading turnkey has told them all. He don't think it will be transportation for life, because there's time to prove the good character yet, and that is sure to serve him. He wonders what he did it for. 'He never did it!' cries Kit's mother. 'Well,' said the turnkey, 'I won't contradict you. It's all one, now, whether he did it or not.'

Kit's mother can reach his hand through the bars, and she clasps it—God, and those to whom he has given such tenderness, only know in how much agony. Kit bids her keep a good heart, and, under pretence of having the children lifted up to kiss him, prays Barbara's mother in a whisper to take her home.

'Some friend will rise up for us, mother,' cried Kit, 'I am sure. If not now, before long. My innocence will come out, mother, and I shall be brought back again; I feel confidence in that. You must teach little Jacob and the baby how all this was, for if they thought I had ever been dishonest, when they grew old enough to understand, it would break my heart to know it, if I was thousands of miles away.—Oh! is there no good gentleman here, who will take care of her?'

The hand slips out of his, for the poor creature sinks down upon the earth, insensible, Richard Swiveller comes hastily up, elbows the bystanders out of the way, takes her (after some trouble) in one arm after the manner of theatrical ravishers, and, nodding to Kit, and commanding Barbara's mother to follow, for he has a coach waiting, bears her swiftly off.

Well; Richard took her home. And what astonishing absurdities in the way of quotation from song and poem, he perpetrated on the road, no man knows. He took her home, and stayed till she was recovered; and, having no money to pay the coach, went back in state to Bevis Marks, bidding the driver (for it was Saturday night) wait at the door while he went in for 'change.'

'Mr. Richard sir,' said Brass cheerfully, 'good-evening!'

Monstrous as Kit's tale had appeared, at first, Mr. Richard did, that night, half suspect his affable employer of some deep villainy. Perhaps it was but the misery he had just witnessed which gave his careless nature this impulse; but, be that as it may, it was very strong upon him, and he said in as few words as possible, what he wanted.

'Money?' cried Brass, taking out his purse. 'Ha ha! To be sure, Mr. Richard, to be sure, sir. All men must live. You haven't change for a five-pound note, have you, sir?'

'No,' returned Dick, shortly.

'Oh!' said Brass, 'here's the very sum. That saves trouble. You're very welcome I'm sure.—Mr. Richard sir—'

Dick, who had by this time reached the door, turned round.

'You needn't,' said Brass, 'trouble yourself to come back any more, sir.'

'Eh?'

'You see, Mr. Richard,' said Brass, thrusting his hands in his pockets, and rocking himself to and fro on his stool, 'the fact is, that a man of your abilities is lost, sir, quite lost, in our dry and mouldy line. It's terrible drudgery—shocking. I should say, now, that the stage, or the—or the army, Mr. Richard—or something very superior in the licensed victualling way—was the kind of thing that would call out the genius of such a man as you. I hope you'll look in to see us now and then. Sally, sir, will be delighted I'm sure. She's extremely sorry to lose you, Mr.

Richard, but a sense of her duty to society reconciles her.   An amazing creature that, sir!   You 'll find the money quite correct, I think.   There 's a cracked window, sir, but I 've not made any deduction on that account.   Whenever we part with friends, Mr. Richard, let us part liberally.   A delightful sentiment, sir!'

To all these rambling observations, Mr. Swiveller answered not one word, but, returning for the aquatic jacket, rolled it into a tight round ball: looking steadily at Brass meanwhile as if he had some intention of bowling him down with it.   He only took it under his arm, however, and marched out of the office in profound silence.   When he had closed the door, he reopened it, stared in again for a few moments with the same portentous gravity, and nodding his head once, in a slow and ghost-like manner, vanished.

He paid the coachman, and turned his back on Bevis Marks, big with great designs for the comforting of Kit's mother and the aid of Kit himself.

But the lives of gentlemen devoted to such pleasures as Richard Swiveller, are extremely precarious.   The spiritual excitement of the last fortnight, working upon a system affected in no slight degree by the spirituous excitement of some years, proved a little too much for him.   That very night, Mr. Richard was seized with an alarming illness, and in twenty-four hours was stricken with a raging fever.

CHAPTER LXIV

TOSSING to and fro upon his hot, uneasy bed; tormented by a fierce thirst which nothing could appease; unable to find, in any change of posture, a moment's peace or ease; and rambling, ever, through deserts of thought where there was no resting-place, no sight or sound suggestive of refreshment or repose, nothing but a dull eternal weariness, with no change but the restless shiftings of his miserable body, and the weary wandering of his mind, constant still to one ever-present anxiety—to a sense of something left undone, of some fearful obstacle to be surmounted, of some carking care that would not be driven away, and which haunted the distempered brain, now in this form, now in that, always shadowy and dim, but recognisable for the same phantom in every shape it took: darkening every vision like an evil conscience, and making slumber horrible—in these slow tortures of his dread disease, the unfortunate Richard lay wasting and consuming inch by inch, until, at last, when he seemed to fight and struggle to rise up, and to be held down by devils, he sank into a deep sleep, and dreamed no more.

He awoke.   With a sensation of most blissful rest, better than sleep itself, he began gradually to remember something of these sufferings, and to think what a long night it had been, and whether he had not been delirious twice or thrice.   Happening, in the midst of these cogitations, to raise his hand, he was astonished to find how heavy it seemed, and yet how thin and light it really was.   Still, he felt indifferent and happy; and having no curiosity to pursue the subject, remained in the same waking slumber until his attention was attracted by a cough.   This made him doubt whether he had locked his door last night, and feel a little surprised at having a companion in the room.   Still, he lacked energy to follow up this train of thought; and unconsciously fell, in a luxury of repose, to staring at some green stripes on the bed-furniture, and associating them strangely with patches of fresh turf, while the yellow ground between, made gravel-walks, and so helped out a long perspective of trim gardens.

He was rambling in imagination on these terraces, and had quite lost himself among them indeed, when he heard the cough once more.   The walks shrunk into stripes again at the sound, and raising himself a little in the bed, and holding the curtain open with one hand, he looked out.

The same room certainly, and still by candlelight; but with what unbounded astonishment did he see all those bottles, and basins, and articles of linen airing by the fire, and such-like furniture of a sick-chamber —all very clean and neat, but all quite different from anything he had left there, when he went to bed! The atmosphere, too, filled with a cool smell of herbs and vinegar; the floor newly sprinkled; the—the what? The Marchioness?

Yes; playing cribbage with herself at the table. There she sat, intent upon her game, coughing now and then in a subdued manner as if she feared to disturb him—shuffling the cards, cutting, dealing, playing, counting, pegging—going through all the mysteries of cribbage as if she had been in full practice from her cradle!

Mr. Swiveller contemplated these things for a short time, and suffering the curtain to fall into its former position, laid his head on the pillow again.

'I 'm dreaming,' thought Richard, 'that 's clear. When I went to bed, my hands were not made of eggshells; and now I can almost see through 'em.   If this is not a dream, I have woke up, by mistake, in an Arabian Night, instead of a London one.   But I have no doubt I 'm asleep.   Not the least.'

Here the small servant had another cough.

'Very remarkable!' thought Mr. Swiveller.   'I never dreamt such a real cough as that, before.   I

THE MARCHIONESS JUMPED UP QUICKLY AND CLAPPED HER HANDS.

don't know, indeed, that I ever dreamt either a cough or a sneeze. Perhaps it's part of the philosophy of dreams that one never does. There's another—and another—I say!—I'm dreaming rather fast!'

For the purpose of testing his real condition, Mr. Swiveller, after some reflection, pinched himself in the arm.

'Queerer still!' he thought. 'I came to bed rather plump than otherwise, and now there's nothing to lay hold of. I'll take another survey.'

The result of this additional inspection was, to convince Mr. Swiveller that the objects by which he was surrounded were real, and that he saw them, beyond all question, with his waking eyes.

'It's an Arabian Night; that's what it is,' said Richard. 'I'm in Damascus or Grand Cairo. The Marchioness is a Genie, and having had a wager with another Genie about who is the handsomest young man alive, and the worthiest to be the husband of the Princess of China, has brought me away, room and all, to compare us together. Perhaps,' said Mr. Swiveller, turning languidly round on his pillow, and looking on that side of his bed which was next the wall, 'the Princess may be still—No, she's gone.'

Not feeling quite satisfied with this explanation, as, even taking it to be the correct one, it still involved a little mystery and doubt, Mr. Swiveller raised the curtain again, determined to take the first favourable opportunity of addressing his companion. An occasion soon presented itself. The Marchioness dealt, turned up a knave, and omitted to take the usual advantage; upon which Mr. Swiveller called out as loud as he could—'Two for his heels!'

The Marchioness jumped up quickly, and clapped her hands. 'Arabian Night, certainly,' thought Mr. Swiveller; 'they always clap their hands instead of ringing the bell. Now for the two thousand black slaves, with jars of jewels on their heads!'

It appeared, however, that she had only clapped her hands for joy; as, directly afterwards she began to laugh, and then to cry; declaring, not in choice Arabic but in familiar English, that she was 'so glad, she didn't know what to do.'

'Marchioness,' said Mr. Swiveller, thoughtfully, 'be pleased to draw nearer. First of all, will you have the goodness to inform me where I shall find my voice; and secondly, what has become of my flesh?'

The Marchioness only shook her head mournfully, and cried again; whereupon Mr. Swiveller (being very weak) felt his own eyes affected likewise.

'I begin to infer, from your manner, and these appearances, Marchioness,' said Richard after a pause, and smiling with a trembling lip, 'that I have been ill.'

'You just have!' replied the small servant, wiping her eyes. 'And haven't you been a talking nonsense!'

'Oh!' said Dick. 'Very ill, Marchioness, have I been?'

'Dead, all but,' replied the small servant. 'I never thought you'd get better. Thank Heaven you have!'

Mr. Swiveller was silent for a long while. By and by, he began to talk again: inquiring how long he had been there.

'Three weeks to-morrow,' replied the small servant.

'Three what?' said Dick.

'Weeks,' returned the Marchioness emphatically; 'three long, slow weeks.'

The bare thought of having been in such extremity, caused Richard to fall into another silence, and to lie flat down again, at his full length. The Marchioness, having arranged the bed-clothes more comfortably, and felt that his hands and forehead were quite cool —a discovery that filled her with delight—cried a little more, and then applied herself to getting tea ready, and making some thin dry toast. While she was thus engaged, Mr. Swiveller looked on with a grateful heart, very much astonished to see how thoroughly at home she made herself, and attributing this attention, in its origin, to Sally Brass, whom, in his own mind, he could not thank enough. When the Marchioness had finished her toasting, she spread a clean cloth on a tray, and brought him some crisp slices and a great basin of weak tea, with which (she said) the doctor had left word he might refresh himself when he awoke. She propped him up with pillows, if not as skilfully as if she had been a professional nurse all her life, at least as tenderly; and looked on with unutterable satisfaction while the patient—stopping every now and then to shake her by the hand—took his poor meal with an appetite and relish, which the greatest dainties of the earth, under any other circumstances, would have failed to provoke. Having cleared away, and disposed everything comfortably about him again, she sat down at the table to take her own tea.

'Marchioness,' said Mr. Swiveller, 'how's Sally?'

The small servant screwed her face into an expression of the very uttermost entanglement of slyness, and shook her head.

'What, haven't you seen her lately?' said Dick.

'Seen her!' cried the small servant. 'Bless you, I've run away!'

Mr. Swiveller immediately laid himself down again quite flat, and so remained for about five minutes. By slow degrees he resumed his sitting posture after that lapse of time, and inquired—

'And where do you live, Marchioness?'

'Live!' cried the small servant. 'Here!'

'Oh!' said Mr. Swiveller.

And with that he fell down flat again, as suddenly as if he had been shot. Thus he remained, motionless and bereft of speech, until she had finished her meal, put everything in its place, and swept the hearth; when he motioned her to bring a chair to the bedside, and, being propped up again, opened a farther conversation.

'And so,' said Dick, 'you have run away?'

'Yes,' said the Marchioness, 'and they've been a tizing of me.'

'Been—I beg your pardon,' said Dick—'what have they been doing?'

'Been a tizing of me—tizing you know—in the newspapers,' rejoined the Marchioness.

'Aye, aye,' said Dick, 'advertising?'

The small servant nodded, and winked. Her eyes were so red with waking and crying, that the Tragic Muse might have winked with greater consistency. And so Dick felt.

'Tell me,' said he, 'how it was that you thought of coming here.'

'Why, you see,' returned the Marchioness, 'when you was gone, I hadn't any friend at all, because the lodger he never come back, and I didn't know where either him or you was to be found, you know. But one morning, when I was—'

'Was near a key-hole?' suggested Mr. Swiveller, observing that she faltered.

'Well then,' said the small servant, nodding; 'when I was near the office key-hole—as you see me through, you know—I heard somebody saying that she lived here, and was the lady whose house you lodged at, and that you was took very bad, and wouldn't nobody come and take care of you. Mr. Brass, he says, "It's no business of mine," he says;

and Miss Sally, she says, "He's a funny chap, but it's no business of mine"; and the lady went away, and slammed the door to, when she went out, I can tell you. So I run away that night, and come here, and told 'em you was my brother, and they believed me, and I've been here ever since.'

'This poor little Marchioness has been wearing herself to death!' cried Dick.

'No I haven't,' she returned, 'not a bit of it. Don't you mind about me. I like sitting up, and I've often had a sleep, bless you, in one of them chairs. But if you could have seen how you tried to jump out o' winder, and if you could have heard how you used to keep on singing and making speeches, you wouldn't have believed it—I'm so glad you're better, Mr. Liverer.'

'Liverer indeed!' said Dick thoughtfully. 'It's well I *am* a liverer. I strongly suspect I should have died, Marchioness, but for you.'

At this point, Mr. Swiveller took the small servant's hand in his, again, and being, as we have seen, but poorly, might in struggling to express his thanks have made his eyes as red as hers, but that she quickly changed the theme by making him lie down, and urging him to keep very quiet.

'The doctor,' she told him, 'said you was to be kept quite still, and there was to be no noise nor nothing. Now, take a rest, and then we'll talk again. I'll sit by you, you know. If you shut your eyes, perhaps you'll go to sleep. You'll be all the better for it, if you do.'

The Marchioness, in saying these words, brought a little table to the bedside, took her seat at it, and began to work away at the concoction of some cooling drink, with the address of a score of chemists. Richard

Swiveller, being indeed fatigued, fell into a slumber, and waking in about half an hour, inquired what time it was.

'Just gone half after six,' replied his small friend, helping him to sit up again.

'Marchioness,' said Richard, passing his hand over his forehead and turning suddenly round, as though the subject but that moment flashed upon him, 'what has become of Kit?'

He had been sentenced to transportation for a great many years, she said.

'Has he gone?' asked Dick—'his mother—how is she,—what has become of her?'

His nurse shook her head, and answered that she knew nothing about them. 'But if I thought,' said she, very slowly, 'that you 'd keep quiet, and not put yourself into another fever, I could tell you—but I won't now.'

'Yes, do,' said Dick. 'It will amuse me.'

'Oh! would it though?' rejoined the small servant, with a horrified look. 'I know better than that. Wait till you 're better and then I 'll tell you.'

Dick looked very earnestly at his little friend: and his eyes, being large and hollow from illness, assisted the expression so much, that she was quite frightened, and besought him not to think any more about it. What had already fallen from her, however, had not only piqued his curiosity, but seriously alarmed him, wherefore he urged her to tell him the worst at once.

'Oh there 's no worst in it,' said the small servant. 'It hasn't anything to do with you.'

'Has it anything to do with—is it anything you heard through chinks or key-holes—and that you were not intended to hear?' asked Dick, in a breathless state.

'Yes,' replied the small servant.

'In—in Bevis Marks?' pursued Dick hastily. 'Conversations between Brass and Sally?'

'Yes,' cried the small servant again.

Richard Swiveller thrust his lank arm out of bed, and, gripping her by the wrist and drawing her close to him, bade her out with it, and freely too, or he would not answer for the consequences; being wholly unable to endure that state of excitement and expectation. She, seeing that he was greatly agitated, and that the effects of postponing her revelation might be much more injurious than any that were likely to ensue from its being made at once, promised compliance, on condition that the patient kept himself perfectly quiet, and abstained from starting up or tossing about.

'But if you begin to do that,' said the small servant, 'I'll leave off. And so I tell you.'

'You can't leave off, till you have gone on,' said Dick. 'And do go on, there's a darling. Speak, sister, speak. Pretty Polly say. Oh tell me when, and tell me where, pray, Marchioness, I beseech you!'

Unable to resist these fervent adjurations, which Richard Swiveller poured out as passionately as if they had been of the most solemn and tremendous nature, his companion spoke thus—

'Well! Before I run away, I used to sleep in the kitchen—where we played cards, you know. Miss Sally used to keep the key of the kitchen-door in her pocket, and she always come down at night to take away the candle and rake out the fire. When she had done that, she left me to go to bed in the dark, locked the door on the outside, put the key in her pocket again, and kept me locked up till she come down in the morning—very early I can tell you—and let me out. I was terrible afraid of being kept like this, because if there was a fire, I thought they might forget me and only take care of themselves you know. So, whenever I see an old rusty key anywhere, I picked it up and tried if it would fit the door, and at last I found in the dust cellar a key that *did* fit it.'

Here, Mr. Swiveller made a violent demonstration with his legs. But the small servant immediately pausing in her talk, he subsided again, and pleading a momentary forgetfulness of their compact, entreated her to proceed.

'They kept me very short,' said the small servant. 'Oh! you can't think how short they kept me! So I used to come out at night after they'd gone to bed, and feel about in the dark for bits of biscuit, or sang-witches that you'd left in the office, or even pieces of orange-peel to put into cold water and make believe it was wine. Did you ever taste orange-peel and water?'

Mr. Swiveller replied that he had never tasted that ardent liquor; and once more urged his friend to resume the thread of her narrative.

'If you make believe very much, it's quite nice,' said the small servant, 'but if you don't, you know, it seems as if it would bear a little more seasoning, certainly. Well, sometimes I used to come out after they'd gone to bed, and sometimes before, you know; and one or two nights before there was all that precious noise in the office—when the young man was took, I mean—I come upstairs while Mr. Brass and Miss Sally was a sittin' at the office fire; and I'll tell you the truth, that I come to listen again, about the key of the safe.'

Mr. Swiveller gathered up his knees so as to make a great cone of the bed-clothes, and conveyed into his countenance an expression of the utmost concern. But, the small servant pausing, and holding up her finger, the cone gently disappeared, though the look of concern did not.

'There was him and her,' said the small servant, 'a sittin' by the fire, and talking softly together. Mr. Brass says to Miss Sally, "Upon my word," he says, "it's a dangerous thing, and it might get us into a world of trouble, and I don't half like it." She says —you know her way—she says, "You're the chickenest-hearted, feeblest, faintest man I ever see, and I think," she says, "that I ought to have been the brother and you the sister. Isn't Quilp," she says, "our principal support?" "He certainly is," says Mr. Brass. "And an't we," she says, "constantly ruining somebody or other in the way of business?" "We certainly are," says Mr. Brass. "Then does it signify," she says, "about ruining this Kit when Quilp desires it?" "It certainly does not signify," says Mr. Brass. Then, they whispered and laughed for a long time about there being no danger if it was well done, and then Mr. Brass pulls out his pocket-book, and says, "Well," he says, "here it is—Quilp's own five-pound note. We'll agree that way, then," he says. "Kit's coming to-morrow morning, I know. While he's upstairs, you'll get out of the way, and I'll clear off Mr. Richard. Having Kit alone, I'll hold him in conversation, and put this property in his hat. I'll manage so, besides," he says, "that Mr. Richard shall find it there, and be the evidence. And if that don't get Christopher out of Mr. Quilp's way, and satisfy Mr. Quilp's grudges," he says, "the Devil's in it." Miss Sally laughed, and said that was the plan, and as they seemed to be moving away, and I was afraid to stop any longer, I went downstairs again.—There!'

The small servant had gradually worked herself into as much agitation as Mr. Swiveller, and therefore made no effort to restrain him when he sat up in bed and hastily demanded whether this story had been told to anybody.

'How could it be?' replied his nurse. 'I was almost afraid to think about it, and hoped the young man would be let off. When I heard 'em say they had found him guilty of what he didn't do, you was gone, and so was the lodger—though I think I should have been frightened to tell him, even if he 'd been there. Ever since I come here, you 've been out of your senses, and what would have been the good of telling you then?'

'Marchioness,' said Mr. Swiveller, plucking off his night-cap and flinging it to the other end of the room; 'if you 'll do me the favour to retire for a few minutes and see what sort of a night it is, I 'll get up.'

'You mustn't think of such a thing,' cried his nurse.

'I must indeed,' said the patient, looking round the room. 'Whereabouts are my clothes?'

'Oh I 'm so glad—you haven't got any,' replied the Marchioness.

'Ma'am!' said Mr. Swiveller, in great astonishment.

'I 've been obliged to sell them, every one, to get the things that was ordered for you. But don't take on about that,' urged the Marchioness, as Dick fell back upon his pillow. 'You 're too weak to stand indeed.'

'I 'm afraid,' said Richard dolefully, 'that you 're right. What ought I to do? what is to be done?'

It naturally occurred to him on very little reflection, that the first step to take would be to communicate with one of the Mr. Garlands instantly. It was very possible that Mr. Abel had not yet left the office. In as little time as it takes to tell it, the small servant had the address in pencil on a piece of paper; a verbal description of father and son, which would enable her to recognise either, without difficulty; and a special caution to be shy of Mr. Chuckster, in consequence of that gentleman's known antipathy to Kit. Armed with these slender powers, she hurried away, commissioned to bring either old Mr. Garland or Mr. Abel, bodily, to that apartment.

'I suppose,' said Dick, as she closed the door slowly, and peeped into the room again, to make sure that he was comfortable, 'I suppose there's nothing left—not so much as a waistcoat even?'

'No, nothing.'

'It's embarrassing,' said Mr. Swiveller, 'in case of fire—even an umbrella would be something—but you did quite right, dear Marchioness. I should have died without you!'

CHAPTER LXV

IT was well for the small servant that she was of a sharp, quick nature, or the consequence of sending her out alone, from the very neighbourhood in which it was most dangerous for her to appear, would probably have been the restoration of Miss Sally Brass to the supreme authority over her person. Not unmindful of the risk she ran, however, the Marchioness no sooner left the house than she dived into the first dark by-way that presented itself, and, without any present reference to the point to which her journey tended, made it her first business to put two good miles of brick and mortar between herself and Bevis Marks.

When she had accomplished this object, she began to shape her course for the notary's office, to which—shrewdly inquiring of apple-women and oyster-sellers at street-corners, rather than in lighted shops or of well-dressed people, at the hazard of attracting notice—she easily procured a direction. As carrier-pigeons,

on being first let loose in a strange place, beat the air
at random for a short time, before darting off towards the spot for which they are designed, so did the
Marchioness flutter round and round until she believed herself in safety, and then bear swiftly down
upon the port for which she was bound.

She had no bonnet—nothing on her head but a great
cap which, in some old time, had been worn by Sally
Brass, whose taste in head-dresses was, as we have
seen, peculiar—and her speed was rather retarded
than assisted by her shoes, which, being extremely
large and slipshod, flew off every now and then, and
were difficult to find again, among the crowd of
passengers. Indeed, the poor little creature experienced so much trouble and delay from having to grope
for these articles of dress in mud and kennel, and suffered in these researches so much jostling, pushing,
squeezing, and bandying from hand to hand, that by
the time she reached the street in which the notary
lived, she was fairly worn out and exhausted, and
could not refrain from tears.

But to have got there at last, was a great comfort,
especially as there were lights still burning in the
office-window, and therefore some hope that she was
not too late. So, the Marchioness dried her eyes with
the backs of her hands, and, stealing softly up the
steps, peeped in through the glass door.

Mr. Chuckster was standing behind the lid of his
desk, making such preparations towards finishing off
for the night, as pulling down his wristbands and
pulling up his shirt-collar, settling his neck more
gracefully in his stock, and secretly arranging his
whiskers by the aid of a little triangular bit of looking-glass. Before the ashes of the fire, stood two
gentlemen, one of whom she rightly judged to be the

notary, and the other (who was buttoning his great-coat and was evidently about to depart immediately) Mr. Abel Garland.

Having made these observations, the small spy took counsel with herself, and resolved to wait in the street until Mr. Abel came out, as there would be then no fear of having to speak before Mr. Chuckster, and less difficulty in delivering her message. With this purpose she slipped out again, and crossing the road, sat down upon a door-step just opposite.

She had hardly taken this position, when there came dancing up the street, with his legs all wrong, and his head everywhere by turns, a pony. This pony had a little phaeton behind him, and a man in it; but neither man nor phaeton seemed to embarrass him in the least as he reared up on his hind-legs, or stopped, or went on, or stood still again, or backed, or went side-ways, without the smallest reference to them,—just as the fancy seized him, and as if he were the freest animal in creation. When they came to the notary's door, the man called out in a very respectful manner, 'Woa then,'—intimating that if he might venture to express a wish, it would be that they stopped there. The pony made a moment's pause; but, as if it occurred to him that to stop when he was required might be to establish an inconvenient and dangerous prece-dent, he immediately started off again, rattled at a fast trot to the street corner, wheeled round, came back, and then stopped of his own accord.

'Oh! you 're a precious creatur!' said the man—who didn't venture by the bye to come out in his true colours until he was safe on the pavement. 'I wish I had the rewarding of you,—I do.'

'What has he been doing?' said Mr. Abel, tying a shawl round his neck as he came down the steps.

'He 's enough to fret a man's heart out,' replied the hostler. 'He is the most wicious rascal— Woa then, will you?'

'He 'll never stand still, if you call him names,' said Mr. Abel, getting in, and taking the reins. 'He 's a very good fellow if you know how to manage him. This is the first time he has been out, this long while, for he has lost his old driver and wouldn't stir for anybody else, till this morning.   The lamps are right, are they?   That 's well.   Be here to take him to-morrow, if you please.   Good-night!'

And, after one or two strange plunges, quite of his own invention, the pony yielded to Mr. Abel's mildness, and trotted gently off.

All this time Mr. Chuckster had been standing at the door, and the small servant had been afraid to approach.   She had nothing for it now, therefore, but to run after the chaise, and to call to Mr. Abel to stop. Being out of breath when she came up with it, she was unable to make him hear.   The case was desperate; for the pony was quickening his pace.   The Marchioness hung on behind for a few moments, and, feeling that she could go no farther, and must soon yield, clambered by a vigorous effort into the hinder seat, and in so doing lost one of the shoes for ever.

Mr. Abel being in a thoughtful frame of mind, and having quite enough to do to keep the pony going, went jogging on without looking round: little dreaming of the strange figure that was close behind him, until the Marchioness, having in some degree recovered her breath, and the loss of her shoe, and the novelty of her position, uttered close into his ear, the words—

'I say, sir—'

He turned his head quickly enough then, and stopping the pony, cried, with some trepidation, 'God bless me, what is this?'

'Don't be frightened, sir,' replied the still panting messenger. 'Oh I 've run such a way after you!'

'What do you want with me?' said Mr. Abel. 'How did you come here?'

'I got in behind,' replied the Marchioness. 'Oh please drive on, sir—don't stop—and go towards the City, will you? And oh do please make haste, because it 's of consequence. There 's somebody wants to see you there. He sent me to say would you come directly, and that he knowed all about Kit, and could save him yet, and prove his innocence.'

'What do you tell me, child?'

'The truth, upon my word and honour I do. But please to drive on—quick, please! I 've been such a time gone, he 'll think I 'm lost.'

Mr. Abel involuntarily urged the pony forward. The pony, impelled by some secret sympathy or some new caprice, burst into a great pace, and neither slackened it, nor indulged in any eccentric performances, until they arrived at the door of Mr. Swiveller's lodging, where, marvellous to relate, he consented to stop when Mr. Abel checked him.

'See! It 's that room up there,' said the Marchioness, pointing to one where there was a faint light. 'Come!'

Mr. Abel, who was one of the simplest and most retiring creatures in existence, and naturally timid withal, hesitated; for he had heard of people being decoyed into strange places to be robbed and murdered, under circumstances very like the present, and, for anything he knew to the contrary, by guides very like the Marchioness. His regard for Kit, however, overcame every other consideration. So, entrusting

Whisker to the charge of a man who was lingering hard by in expectation of the job, he suffered his companion to take his hand, and to lead him up the dark and narrow stairs.

He was not a little surprised to find himself conducted into a dimly-lighted sick-chamber, where a man was sleeping tranquilly in bed.

'An't it nice to see him lying there so quiet?' said his guide, in an earnest whisper. 'Oh! you'd say it was, if you had only seen him two or three days ago.'

Mr. Abel made no answer, and, to say the truth, kept a long way from the bed and very near the door. His guide, who appeared to understand his reluctance, trimmed the candle, and taking it in her hand, approached the bed. As she did so, the sleeper started up, and he recognised in the wasted face the features of Richard Swiveller.

'Why, how is this?' said Mr. Abel kindly, as he hurried towards him. 'You have been ill?'

'Very,' replied Dick. 'Nearly dead. You might have chanced to hear of your Richard on his bier, but for the friend I sent to fetch you. Another shake of the hand, Marchioness, if you please. Sit down, sir.'

Mr. Abel seemed rather astonished to hear of the quality of his guide, and took a chair by the bedside.

'I have sent for you, sir,' said Dick—'but she told you on what account?'

'She did. I am quite bewildered by all this. I really don't know what to say or think,' replied Mr. Abel.

'You'll say that presently,' retorted Dick. 'Marchioness, take a seat on the bed, will you? Now, tell this gentleman all that you told me; and be particular. Don't you speak another word, sir.'

The story was repeated; it was, in effect, exactly the same as before, without any deviation or omission.

Richard Swiveller kept his eyes fixed on his visitor during its narration, and directly it was concluded, took the word again.

'You have heard it all, and you 'll not forget it. I 'm too giddy and too queer to suggest anything; but you and your friends will know what to do. After this long delay, every minute is an age. If ever you went home fast in your life, go home fast to-night. Don't stop to say one word to me, but go. She will be found here, whenever she 's wanted; and as to me, you 're pretty sure to find me at home, for a week or two. There are more reasons than one for that. Marchioness, a light! If you lose another minute in looking at me, sir, I 'll never forgive you!'

Mr. Abel needed no more remonstrance or persuasion. He was gone in an instant; and the Marchioness, returning from lighting him downstairs, reported that the pony, without any preliminary objection whatever, had dashed away at full gallop.

'That 's right!' said Dick; 'and hearty of him; and I honour him from this time. But get some supper and a mug of beer, for I am sure you must be tired. Do have a mug of beer. It will do me as much good to see you take it as if I might drink it myself.'

Nothing but this assurance could have prevailed upon the small nurse to indulge in such a luxury. Having eaten and drunk to Mr. Swiveller's extreme contentment, given him his drink, and put everything in neat order, she wrapped herself in an old coverlet and lay down upon the rug before the fire.

Mr. Swiveller was by that time murmuring in his sleep, 'Strew then, oh strew, a bed of rushes. Here will we stay, till morning blushes. Good-night, Marchioness!'

CHAPTER LXVI

On awakening in the morning, Richard Swiveller became conscious, by slow degrees, of whispering voices in his room. Looking out between the curtains, he espied Mr. Garland, Mr. Abel, the notary, and the single gentleman, gathered round the Marchioness, and talking to her with great earnestness but in very subdued tones—fearing, no doubt, to disturb him. He lost no time in letting them know that this precaution was unnecessary, and all four gentlemen directly approached his bedside. Old Mr. Garland was the first to stretch out his hand, and inquire how he felt.

Dick was about to answer that he felt much better, though still as weak as need be, when his little nurse, pushing the visitors aside and pressing up to his pillow as if in jealousy of their interference, set his breakfast before him, and insisted on his taking it before he underwent the fatigue of speaking or of being spoken to. Mr. Swiveller, who was perfectly ravenous, and had had, all night, amazingly distinct and consistent dreams of mutton-chops, double stout, and similar delicacies, felt even the weak tea and dry toast such irresistible temptations, that he consented to eat and drink on one condition.

'And that is,' said Dick, returning the pressure of Mr. Garland's hand, 'that you answer me this question truly, before I take a bit or drop. Is it too late?'

'For completing the work you began so well last night?' returned the old gentleman. 'No. Set your mind at rest on that point. It is not, I assure you.'

Comforted by this intelligence, the patient applied himself to his food with a keen appetite, though evidently not with a greater zest in the eating than his nurse appeared to have in seeing him eat. The manner of his meal was this:—Mr. Swiveller, holding the slice of toast or cup of tea in his left hand, and taking a bite or drink, as the case might be, constantly kept, in his right, one palm of the Marchioness tight locked; and to shake, or even to kiss this imprisoned hand, he would stop every now and then, in the very act of swallowing, with perfect seriousness of intention, and the utmost gravity. As often as he put anything into his mouth, whether for eating or drinking, the face of the Marchioness lighted up beyond all description; but, whenever he gave her one or other of these tokens of recognition, her countenance became overshadowed, and she began to sob. Now, whether she was in her laughing joy, or in her crying one, the Marchioness could not help turning to the visitors with an appealing look, which seemed to say, 'You see this fellow—can I help this?'—and they, being thus made, as it were, parties to the scene, as regularly answered by another look, 'No. Certainly not.' This dumb-show, taking place during the whole time of the invalid's breakfast, and the invalid himself, pale and emaciated, performing no small part of the same, it may be fairly questioned whether at any meal, where no word, good or bad, was spoken from beginning to end, so much was expressed by gestures in themselves so slight and unimportant.

At length—and to say the truth before very long— Mr. Swiveller had despatched as much toast and tea as in that stage of his recovery it was discreet to let him have. But, the cares of the Marchioness did not stop here; for, disappearing for an instant and presently returning with a basin of fair water, she laved his face and hands, brushed his hair, and in short made him as spruce and smart as anybody under such circumstances could be made; and all this, in as brisk and business-like a manner, as if he were a very little boy, and she his grown-up nurse. To these various attentions, Mr. Swiveller submitted in a kind of grateful astonishment beyond the reach of language. When they were at last brought to an end, and the Marchioness had withdrawn into a distant corner to take her own poor breakfast (cold enough by that time), he turned his face away for some few moments, and shook hands heartily with the air.

'Gentlemen,' said Dick, rousing himself from this pause, and turning round again, 'you'll excuse me. Men who have been brought so low as I have been, are easily fatigued. I am fresh again now, and fit for talking. We're short of chairs here, among other trifles, but if you'll do me the favour to sit upon the bed—'

'What can we do for you?' said Mr. Garland, kindly.

'If you could make the Marchioness yonder, a Marchioness, in real, sober earnest,' returned Dick, 'I'd thank you to get it done off-hand. But as you can't, and as the question is not what you will do for me, but what you will do for somebody else who has a better claim upon you, pray, sir, let me know what you intend doing.'

'It's chiefly on that account that we have come just now,' said the single gentleman, 'for you will have another visitor presently. We feared you would be anxious unless you knew from ourselves what steps we intended to take, and therefore came to you before we stirred in the matter.'

'Gentlemen,' returned Dick, 'I thank you. Anybody in the helpless state that you see me in, is naturally anxious. Don't let me interrupt you, sir.'

'Then, you see, my good fellow,' said the single

gentleman, 'that while we have no doubt whatever of the truth of this disclosure, which has so providentially come to light—'

'Meaning hers?' said Dick, pointing towards the Marchioness.

'—Meaning hers, of course. While we have no doubt of that, or that a proper use of it would procure the poor lad's immediate pardon and liberation, we have a great doubt whether it would, by itself, enable us to reach Quilp, the chief agent in this villainy. I should tell you that this doubt has been confirmed into something very nearly approaching certainty by the best opinions we have been enabled, in this short space of time, to take upon the subject. You 'll agree with us, that to give him even the most distant chance of escape, if we could help it, would be monstrous. You say with us, no doubt, if somebody must escape, let it be any one but he.'

'Yes,' returned Dick, 'certainly. That is if somebody *must*—but upon my word, I 'm unwilling that anybody should. Since laws were made for every degree, to curb vice in others as well as in me—and so forth, you know—doesn't it strike you in that light?'

The single gentleman smiled as if the light in which Mr. Swiveller had put the question were not the clearest in the world, and proceeded to explain that they contemplated proceeding by stratagem in the first instance; and that their design was to endeavour to extort a confession from the gentle Sarah.

'When she finds how much we know, and how we know it,' he said, 'and that she is clearly compromised already, we are not without strong hopes that we may be enabled through her means to punish the other two effectually. If we could do that, she might go scot-free for aught I cared.'

Dick received this project in anything but a gracious manner, representing with as much warmth as he was then capable of showing, that they would find the old buck (meaning Sarah) more difficult to manage than Quilp himself—that, for any tampering, terrifying, or cajolery, she was a very unpromising and unyielding subject—that, she was of a kind of brass not easily melted or moulded into shape—in short, that they were no match for her, and would be signally defeated. But, it was in vain to urge them to adopt some other course. The single gentleman has been described as explaining their joint intentions, but it should have been written that they all spoke together; that if any one of them by chance held his peace for a moment, he stood gasping and panting for an opportunity to strike in again: in a word, that they had reached that pitch of impatience and anxiety where men can neither be persuaded nor reasoned with; and that it would have been as easy to turn the most impetuous wind that ever blew, as to prevail on them to reconsider their determination. So, after telling Mr. Swiveller how they had not lost sight of Kit's mother and the children; how they had never once even lost sight of Kit himself, but had been unremitting in their endeavours to procure a mitigation of his sentence; how they had been perfectly distracted between the strong proofs of his guilt, and their own fading hopes of his innocence; and how he, Richard Swiveller, might keep his mind at rest, for everything should be happily adjusted between that time and night;—after telling him all this, and adding a great many kind and cordial expressions, personal to himself, which it is unnecessary to recite, Mr. Garland, the notary, and the single gentleman, took their leaves at a very critical time, or Richard Swiveller must assuredly have been driven into another fever, whereof the results might have been fatal.

Mr. Abel remained behind, very often looking at his watch and at the room-door, until Mr. Swiveller was roused from a short nap, by the setting-down on the landing-place outside, as from the shoulders of a porter, of some giant load, which seemed to shake the house, and make the little physic-bottles on the mantel-shelf ring again. Directly this sound reached his ears, Mr. Abel started up, and hobbled to the door, and opened it; and behold! there stood a strong man, with a mighty hamper, which, being hauled into the room and presently unpacked, disgorged such treasures of tea, and coffee, and wine, and rusks, and oranges, and grapes, and fowls ready trussed for boiling, and calves'-foot jelly, and arrow-foot, and sago, and other delicate restoratives, that the small servant, who had never thought it possible that such things could be, except in shops, stood rooted to the spot in her one shoe, with her mouth and eyes watering in unison, and her power of speech quite gone. But, not so Mr. Abel; or the strong man who emptied the hamper, big as it was, in a twinkling; and not so the nice old lady, who appeared so suddenly that she might have come out of the hamper too (it was quite large enough), and who, bustling about on tip-toe and without noise—now here, now there, now everywhere at once—began to fill out the jelly in tea-cups, and to make chicken-broth in small saucepans, and to peel oranges for the sick man and to cut them up in little pieces, and to ply the small servant with glasses of wine and choice bits of everything until more substantial meat could be prepared for her refreshment. The whole of which appearances were so unexpected and bewildering, that Mr. Swiveller, when he had taken two oranges and a little jelly, and had seen

the strong man walk off with the empty basket, plainly leaving all that abundance for his use and benefit, was fain to lie down and fall asleep again, from
sheer inability to entertain such wonders in his mind.

Meanwhile, the single gentleman, the notary, and
Mr. Garland, repaired to a certain coffee-house, and
from that place indited and sent a letter to Miss
Sally Brass, requesting her, in terms mysterious and
brief, to favour an unknown friend who wished to
consult her, with her company there, as speedily as
possible.   The communication performed its errand
so well, that within ten minutes of the messenger's
return and report of its delivery, Miss Brass herself
was announced.

'Pray, ma'am,' said the single gentleman, whom she
found alone in the room, 'take a chair.'

Miss Brass sat herself down, in a very stiff and
frigid state, and seemed—as indeed she was—not a little astonished to find that the lodger and her mysterious correspondent were one and the same person.

'You did not expect to see me?' said the single
gentleman.

'I didn't think much about it,' returned the beauty.
'I supposed it was business of some kind or other.   If
it's about the apartments, of course you'll give my
brother regular notice, you know—or money.   That's
very easily settled.   You're a responsible party, and
in such a case lawful money and lawful notice are
pretty much the same.'

'I am obliged to you for your good opinion,' retorted the single gentleman, 'and quite concur in these
sentiments.   But, that is not the subject on which I
wish to speak with you.'

'Oh!' said Sally.   'Then just state the particulars,
will you?   I suppose it's professional business?'

'Why it *is* connected with the law, certainly.'

'Very well,' returned Miss Brass. 'My brother and I are just the same. I can take any instructions, or give you any advice.'

'As there are other parties interested besides myself,' said the single gentleman, rising and opening the door of an inner room, 'we had better confer together. Miss Brass is here, gentlemen.'

Mr. Garland and the notary walked in, looking very grave: and, drawing up two chairs, one on each side of the single gentleman, formed a kind of fence round the gentle Sarah, and penned her into a corner. Her brother Sampson under such circumstances would certainly have evinced some confusion or anxiety, but she—all composure—pulled out the tin box, and calmly took a pinch of snuff.

'Miss Brass,' said the notary, taking the word at this crisis, 'we professional people understand each other, and, when we choose, can say what we have to say, in very few words. You advertised a runaway servant, the other day?'

'Well,' returned Miss Sally, with a sudden flush overspreading her features, 'what of that?'

'She is found, ma'am,' said the notary, pulling out his pocket-handkerchief with a flourish. 'She is found.'

'Who found her?' demanded Sarah hastily.

'We did, ma'am—we three. Only last night, or you would have heard from us before.'

'And now I *have* heard from you,' said Miss Brass, folding her arms as though she were about to deny something to the death, 'what have you got to say? Something you have got into your heads about her, of course. Prove it, will you—that's all. Prove it. You have found her, you say. I can tell you (if you don't know it) that you have found the most artful, lying, pilfering, devilish little minx that was ever born.

—Have you got her here?' she added, looking sharply round.

'No, she is not here at present,' returned the notary. 'But she is quite safe.'

'Ha!' cried Sally, twitching a pinch of snuff out of her box, as spitefully as if she were in the very act of wrenching off the small servant's nose; 'she shall be safe enough from this time, I warrant you.'

'I hope so,' replied the notary.—'Did it occur to you for the first time, when you found she had run away, that there were two keys to your kitchen-door?'

Miss Sally took another pinch, and putting her head on one side, looked at her questioner, with a curious kind of spasm about her mouth, but with a cunning aspect of immense expression.

'Two keys,' repeated the notary; 'one of which gave her the opportunities of roaming through the house at nights when you supposed her fast locked up, and of overhearing confidential consultations—among others, that particular conference, to be described to-day before a justice, which you will have an opportunity of hearing her relate; that conference which you and Mr. Brass held together, on the night before that most unfortunate and innocent young man was accused of robbery, by a horrible device of which I will only say that it may be characterised by the epithets which you have applied to this wretched little witness, and by a few stronger ones besides.'

Sally took another pinch. Although her face was wonderfully composed, it was apparent that she was wholly taken by surprise, and that what she had expected to be taxed with, in connection with her small servant, was something very different from this.

'Come, come, Miss Brass,' said the notary, 'you have great command of feature, but you feel, I see, that by a chance which never entered your imagination, this base design is revealed, and two of its plotters must be brought to justice. Now, you know the pains and penalties you are liable to, and so I need not dilate upon them, but I have a proposal to make to you. You have the honour of being sister to one of the greatest scoundrels unhung; and, if I may venture to say so to a lady, you are in every respect quite worthy of him. But, connected with you two is a third party, a villain of the name of Quilp, the prime mover of the whole diabolical device, who I believe to be worse than either. For his sake, Miss Brass, do us the favour to reveal the whole history of this affair. Let me remind you that your doing so, at our instance, will place you in a safe and comfortable position— your present one is not desirable—and cannot injure your brother; for against him and you we have quite sufficient evidence (as you hear) already. I will not say to you that we suggest this course in mercy (for, to tell you the truth, we do not entertain any regard for you), but it is a necessity to which we are reduced, and I recommend it to you as a matter of the very best policy. Time,' said Mr. Witherden, pulling out his watch, 'in a business like this, is exceedingly precious. Favour us with your decision as speedily as possible, ma'am.'

With a smile upon her face, and looking at each of the three by turns, Miss Brass took two or three more pinches of snuff, and having by this time very little left, travelled round and round the box with her forefinger and thumb, scraping up another. Having disposed of this likewise and put the box carefully in her pocket, she said—

'I am to accept or reject at once, am I?'

'Yes,' said Mr. Witherden.

The charming creature was opening her lips to speak in reply, when the door was hastily opened too, and the head of Sampson Brass was thrust into the room.

'Excuse me,' said that gentleman hastily.   'Wait a bit!'

So saying, and quite indifferent to the astonishment his presence occasioned, he crept in, shut the door, kissed his greasy glove as servilely as if it were the dust, and made a most abject bow.

'Sarah,' said Brass, 'hold your tongue if you please, and let me speak.   Gentlemen, if I could express the pleasure it gives me to see three such men in a happy unity of feeling and concord of sentiment, I think you would hardly believe me.   But though I am unfortunate—nay, gentlemen, criminal, if we are to use harsh expressions in a company like this—still, I have my feelings like other men.   I have heard of a poet, who remarked that feelings were the common lot of all.   If he could have been a pig, gentlemen, and have uttered that sentiment, he would still have been immortal.'

'If you 're not an idiot,' said Miss Brass harshly, 'hold your peace.'

'Sarah, my dear,' returned her brother, 'thank you. But I know what I am about, my love, and will take the liberty of expressing myself accordingly.   Mr. Witherden, sir, your handkerchief is hanging out of your pocket—would you allow me to—'

As Mr. Brass advanced to remedy this accident, the notary shrunk from him with an air of disgust. Brass, who over and above his usual prepossessing qualities, had a scratched face, a green shade over one eye, and a hat grievously crushed, stopped short, and looked round with a pitiful smile.

'He shuns me,' said Sampson, 'even when I would, as I may say, heap coals of fire upon his head.   Well! Ah!   But I am a falling house, and the rats (if I may be allowed the expression in reference to a gentleman I respect and love beyond everything) fly from me! Gentlemen—regarding your conversation just now, I happened to see my sister on her way here, and, wondering where she could be going to, and being—may I venture to say?—naturally of a suspicious turn, followed her. Since then, I have been listening.'

'If you're not mad,' interposed Miss Sally, 'stop there, and say no more.'

'Sarah, my dear,' rejoined Brass with undiminished politeness, 'I thank you kindly, but will still proceed. Mr. Witherden, sir, as we have the honour to be members of the same profession—to say nothing of that other gentleman having been my lodger, and having partaken, as one may say, of the hospitality of my roof—I think you might have given me the refusal of this offer in the first instance. I do indeed. Now, my dear sir,' cried Brass, seeing that the notary was about to interrupt him, 'suffer me to speak, I beg.'

Mr. Witherden was silent, and Brass went on.

'If you will do me the favour,' he said, holding up the green shade, and revealing an eye most horribly discoloured, 'to look at this, you will naturally inquire, in your own minds, how did I get it. If you look from that, to my face, you will wonder what could have been the cause of all these scratches. And if from them to my hat, how it came into the state in which you see it. Gentlemen,' said Brass, striking the hat fiercely with his clenched hand, 'to all these questions I answer—Quilp!'

The three gentlemen looked at each other, but said nothing.

'I say,' pursued Brass, glancing aside, at his sister, as though he were talking for her information, and speaking with a snarling malignity, in violent contrast to his usual smoothness, 'that I answer to all these questions,—Quilp—Quilp, who deludes me into his infernal den, and takes a delight in looking on and chuckling while I scorch and burn, and bruise, and maim myself—Quilp, who never once, no never once, in all our communications together, has treated me otherwise than as a dog—Quilp, whom I have always hated with my whole heart, but never so much as lately. He gives me the cold shoulder on this very matter as if he had had nothing to do with it, instead of being the first to propose it. I can't trust him. In one of his howling, raving, blazing humours, I believe he 'd let it out, if it was murder, and never think of himself so long as he could terrify me. Now,' said Brass, picking up his hat again and replacing the shade over his eye, and actually crouching down, in the excess of his servility, 'What does all this lead to? —what should you say it led me to, gentlemen?— could you guess at all near the mark?'

Nobody spoke. Brass stood smirking for a little while, as if he had propounded some choice conundrum; and then said—

'To be short with you, then, it leads me to this. If the truth has come out, as it plainly has in a manner that there 's no standing up against—and a very sublime and grand thing is Truth, gentlemen, in its way, though like other sublime and grand things, such as thunderstorms and that, we 're not always over and above glad to see it—I had better turn upon this man than let this man turn upon me. It 's clear to me that I am done for. Therefore, if anybody is to split, I had better be the person and have the advantage of it. Sarah, my dear, comparatively speaking you 're safe. I relate these circumstances for my own profit.'

With that, Mr. Brass, in a great hurry, revealed the whole story; bearing as heavily as possible on his amiable employer, and making himself out to be rather a saintlike and holy character, though subject—he acknowledged—to human weaknesses. He concluded thus—

'Now, gentlemen, I am not a man who does things by halves. Being in for a penny, I am ready, as the saying is, to be in for a pound. You must do with me what you please, and take me where you please. If you wish to have this in writing, we'll reduce it into manuscript immediately. You will be tender with me, I am sure. I am quite confident you will be tender with me. You are men of honour, and have feeling hearts. I yielded from necessity to Quilp, for though necessity has no law, she has her lawyers. I yield to you from necessity too; from policy besides; and because of feelings that have been a pretty long time working within me. Punish Quilp, gentlemen. Weigh heavily upon him. Grind him down. Tread him under foot. He has done as much by me, for many and many a day.'

Having now arrived at the conclusion of his discourse, Sampson checked the current of his wrath, kissed his glove again, and smiled as only parasites and cowards can.

'And this,' said Miss Brass, raising her head, with which she had hitherto sat resting on her hands, and surveying him from head to foot with a bitter sneer, 'this is my brother, is it? This is my brother, that I have worked and toiled for, and believed to have had something of the man in him!'

'Sarah, my dear,' returned Sampson, rubbing his hands feebly; 'you disturb our friends. Besides you —you're disappointed, Sarah, and, not knowing what you say, expose yourself.'

'Yes, you pitiful dastard,' retorted the lovely damsel, 'I understand you. You feared that I should be beforehand with you. But do you think that *I* would have been enticed to say a word!   I 'd have scorned it, if they had tried and tempted me for twenty years.'

'He he!' simpered Brass, who, in his deep debasement, really seemed to have changed sexes with his sister, and to have made over to her any spark of manliness he might have possessed.   'You think so, Sarah, you think so perhaps; but you would have acted quite different, my good fellow.   You will not have forgotten that it was a maxim with Foxey—our revered father, gentlemen—"Always suspect everybody." That 's the maxim to go through life with!   If you were not actually about to purchase your own safety when I showed myself, I suspect you 'd have done it by this time.   And therefore I 've done it myself, and spared you the trouble as well as the shame.   The shame, gentlemen,' added Brass, allowing himself to be slightly overcome, 'if there is any, is mine.   It 's better that a female should be spared it.'

With deference to the better opinion of Mr. Brass, and more particularly to the authority of his Great Ancestor, it may be doubted, with humility, whether the elevating principle laid down by the latter gentleman, and acted upon by his descendant, is always a prudent one, or attended in practice with the desired results.   This is, beyond question, a bold and presumptuous doubt, inasmuch as many distinguished characters, called men of the world, long-headed customers, knowing dogs, shrewd fellows, capital hands at business, and the like, have made, and do daily make, this axiom their polar star and compass.   Still, the doubt may be gently insinuated.   And in illustration it may be observed, that if Mr. Brass, not being over-suspicious, had without prying and listening, left his sister to manage the conference on their joint behalf, or prying and listening, had not been in such a mighty hurry to anticipate her (which he would not have been, but for his distrust and jealousy), he would probably have found himself much better off in the end.   Thus, it will always happen that these men of the world who go through it in armour, defend themselves from quite as much good as evil; to say nothing of the inconvenience and absurdity of mounting guard with a microscope at all times, and of wearing a coat of mail on the most innocent occasions.

The three gentlemen spoke together apart, for a few moments.   At the end of their consultation, which was very brief, the notary pointed to the writing materials on the table, and informed Mr. Brass that if he wished to make any statement in writing, he had the opportunity of doing so.   At the same time he felt bound to tell him that they would require his attendance, presently, before a justice of the peace, and that in what he did or said, he was guided entirely by his own discretion.

'Gentlemen,' said Brass, drawing off his gloves, and crawling in spirit upon the ground before them, 'I will justify the tenderness with which I know I shall be treated; and as, without tenderness, I should, now that this discovery has been made, stand in the worst position of the three, you may depend upon it I will make a clean breast.   Mr. Witherden, sir, a kind of faintness is upon my spirits—if you would do me the favour to ring the bell and order up a glass of something warm and spicy, I shall, notwithstanding what has passed, have a melancholy pleasure in drinking your good health.   I had hoped,' said Brass, looking round with a mournful smile, 'to have seen you three gentlemen, one day or another, with your legs under the mahogany in my humble parlour in the Marks.   But hopes are fleeting.   Dear me!'

Mr. Brass found himself so exceedingly affected, at

this point, that he could say or do nothing more until some refreshment arrived. Having partaken of it, pretty freely for one in his agitated state, he sat down to write.

The lovely Sarah, now with her arms folded, and now with her hands clasped behind her, paced the room with manly strides while her brother was thus employed, and sometimes stopped to pull out her snuff-box and bite the lid. She continued to pace up and down until she was quite tired, and then fell asleep on a chair near the door.

It has been since supposed, with some reason, that this slumber was a sham or feint, as she contrived to slip away unobserved in the dusk of the afternoon. Whether this was an intentional and waking departure, or a somnambulistic leave-taking and walking in her sleep, may remain a subject of contention; but, on one point (and indeed the main one) all parties are agreed. In whatever state she walked away, she certainly did not walk back again.

Mention having been made of the dusk of the afternoon, it will be inferred that Mr. Brass's task occupied some time in the completion. It was not finished until evening; but, being done at last, that worthy person and the three friends adjourned in a hackney-coach to the private office of a Justice, who, giving Mr. Brass a warm reception and detaining him in a secure place that he might insure to himself the pleasure of seeing him on the morrow, dismissed the others with the cheering assurance that a warrant could not fail to be granted next day for the apprehension of Mr. Quilp, and that a proper application and statement of all the circumstances to the secretary of state (who was fortunately in town), would no doubt procure Kit's free pardon and liberation without delay.

And now, indeed, it seemed that Quilp's malignant

career was drawing to a close, and that retribution, which often travels slowly—especially when heaviest—had tracked his footsteps with a sure and certain scent and was gaining on him fast. Unmindful of her stealthy tread, her victim holds his course in fancied triumph. Still at his heels she comes, and once afoot, is never turned aside!

Their business ended, the three gentlemen hastened back to the lodgings of Mr. Swiveller, whom they found progressing so favourably in his recovery as to have been able to sit up for half an hour, and to have conversed with cheerfulness. Mrs. Garland had gone home some time since, but Mr. Abel was still sitting with him. After telling him all they had done, the two Garlands and the single gentleman, as if by some previous understanding, took their leaves for the night, leaving the invalid alone with the notary and the small servant.

'As you are so much better,' said Mr. Witherden, sitting down at the bedside, 'I may venture to communicate to you a piece of news which has come to me professionally.'

The idea of any professional intelligence from a gentleman connected with legal matters, appeared to afford Richard anything but a pleasing anticipation. Perhaps he connected it in his own mind with one or two outstanding accounts, in reference to which he had already received divers threatening letters. His countenance fell as he replied—

'Certainly, sir. I hope it's not anything of a very disagreeable nature, though?'

'If I thought it so, I should choose some better time for communicating it,' replied the notary. 'Let me tell you, first, that my friends who have been here to-day, know nothing of it, and that their kindness to you has been quite spontaneous and with no hope of return. It may do a thoughtless, careless man, good, to know that.'

Dick thanked him, and said he hoped it would.

'I have been making some inquiries about you,' said Mr. Witherden, 'little thinking that I should find you under such circumstances as those which have brought us together. You are the nephew of Rebecca Swiveller, spinster, deceased, of Cheselbourne in Dorsetshire.'

'Deceased!' cried Dick.

'Deceased. If you had been another sort of nephew, you would have come into possession (so says the will, and I see no reason to doubt it) of five-and-twenty thousand pounds. As it is, you have fallen into an annuity of one hundred and fifty pounds a year; but I think I may congratulate you even upon that.'

'Sir,' said Dick, sobbing and laughing together, 'you may. For, please God, we'll make a scholar of the poor Marchioness yet! And she shall walk in silk attire, and siller have to spare, or may I never rise from this bed again!'

CHAPTER LXVII

UNCONSCIOUS of the proceedings faithfully narrated in the last chapter, and little dreaming of the mine which had been sprung beneath him (for, to the end that he should have no warning of the business afoot, the profoundest secrecy was observed in the whole transaction) Mr. Quilp remained shut up in his hermitage, undisturbed by any suspicion, and extremely well satisfied with the result of his machinations. Being engaged in the adjustment of some accounts—an occupation to which the silence and solitude of his retreat were very favourable—he had not strayed from his den for two whole days. The third day of his devotion to this pursuit found him still hard at work, and little disposed to stir abroad.

It was the day next after Mr. Brass's confession, and, consequently, that which threatened the restriction of Mr. Quilp's liberty, and the abrupt communication to him of some very unpleasant and unwelcome facts. Having no intuitive perception of the cloud which lowered upon his house, the dwarf was in his ordinary state of cheerfulness; and, when he found he was becoming too much engrossed by business with a due regard to his health and spirits, he varied its monotonous routine with a little screeching, or howling, or some other innocent relaxation of that nature.

He was attended, as usual, by Tom Scott, who sat crouching over the fire after the manner of a toad, and, from time to time, when his master's back was turned, imitating his grimaces with a fearful exactness. The figure-head had not yet disappeared, but remained in its old place. The face, horribly seared by the frequent application of the red-hot poker, and further ornamented by the insertion, in the tip of the nose, of a tenpenny nail, yet smiled blandly in its less lacerated parts, and seemed, like a sturdy martyr, to provoke its tormentor to the commission of new outrages and insults.

The day, in the highest and brightest quarters of the town, was damp, dark, cold, and gloomy. In that low and marshy spot, the fog filled every nook and corner with a thick dense cloud. Every object was obscure at one or two yards' distance. The warning lights and fires upon the river were powerless beneath this pall, and, but for a raw and piercing chillness in the air, and now and then the cry of some bewildered boatman as he rested on his oars and tried to make out where he was, the river itself might have been miles away.

The mist, though sluggish and slow to move, was of a keenly searching kind. No muffling up in furs and broadcloth kept it out. It seemed to penetrate into the very bones of the shrinking wayfarers, and to rack them with cold and pains. Everything was wet and clammy to the touch. The warm blaze alone defied it, and leaped and sparkled merrily. It was a day to be at home, crowding about the fire, telling stories of travellers who had lost their way in such weather on heaths and moors; and to love a warm hearth more than ever.

The dwarf's humour, as we know, was to have a fireside to himself; and when he was disposed to be convivial, to enjoy himself alone. By no means insensible to the comfort of being within doors, he ordered Tom Scott to pile the little stove with coals, and, dismissing his work for that day, determined to be jovial.

To this end, he lighted up fresh candles and heaped more fuel on the fire; and having dined off a beefsteak, which he cooked himself in somewhat of a savage and cannibal-like manner, brewed a great bowl of hot punch, lighted his pipe, and sat down to spend the evening.

At this moment, a low knocking at the cabin-door arrested his attention. When it had been twice or thrice repeated, he softly opened the little window, and thrusting his head out, demanded who was there.

'Only me, Quilp,' replied a woman's voice.

'Only you!' cried the dwarf, stretching his neck to obtain a better view of his visitor. 'And what brings you here, you jade? How dare you approach the ogre's castle, eh?'

'I have come with some news,' rejoined his spouse. 'Don't be angry with me.'

'Is it good news, pleasant news, news to make a man skip and snap his fingers?' said the dwarf. 'Is the dear old lady dead?'

'I don't know what news it is, or whether it's good or bad,' rejoined his wife.

'Then she's alive,' said Quilp, 'and there's nothing the matter with her. Go home again, you bird of evil note, go home!'

'I have brought a letter,' cried the meek little woman.

'Toss it in at the window here, and go your ways,' said Quilp, interrupting her, 'or I'll come out and scratch you.'

'No, but please, Quilp—do hear me speak,' urged his submissive wife, in tears. 'Please do!'

'Speak then,' growled the dwarf with a malicious grin. 'Be quick and short about it. Speak, will you?'

'It was left at our house this afternoon,' said Mrs. Quilp, trembling, 'by a boy who said he didn't know from whom it came, but that it was given to him to leave, and that he was told to say it must be brought on to you directly, for it was of the very greatest consequence.—But please,' she added, as her husband stretched out his hand for it, 'please let me in. You don't know how wet and cold I am, or how many times I have lost my way in coming here through this thick fog. Let me dry myself at the fire for five minutes. I'll go away directly you tell me to, Quilp. Upon my word I will.'

Her amiable husband hesitated for a few moments; but, bethinking himself that the letter might require some answer, of which she could be the bearer, closed the window, opened the door, and bade her enter. Mrs. Quilp obeyed right willingly, and, kneeling down before the fire to warm her hands, delivered into his, a little packet.

'I'm glad you're wet,' said Quilp, snatching it, and squinting at her. 'I'm glad you're cold. I'm glad you lost your way. I'm glad your eyes are red with crying. It does my heart good to see your little nose so pinched and frosty.'

'Oh Quilp!' sobbed his wife. 'How cruel it is of you!'

'Did she think I was dead?' said Quilp, wrinkling his face into a most extraordinary series of grimaces. 'Did she think she was going to have all the money, and to marry somebody she liked? Ha ha ha! Did she?'

These taunts elicited no reply from the poor little woman, who remained on her knees, warming her hands, and sobbing, to Mr. Quilp's great delight. But, just as he was contemplating her, and chuckling excessively, he happened to observe that Tom Scott was delighted too; wherefore, that he might have no presumptuous partner in his glee, the dwarf instantly collared him, dragged him to the door, and after a short scuffle, kicked him into the yard. In return for this mark of attention, Tom immediately walked upon his hands to the window, and—if the expression be allowable—looked in with his shoes: besides rattling his feet upon the glass like a Banshee upside down. As a matter of course, Mr. Quilp lost no time in resorting to the infallible poker, with which, after some dodging and lying in ambush, he paid his young friend one or two such unequivocal compliments that he vanished precipitately, and left him in quiet possession of the field.

'So! That little job being disposed of,' said the

dwarf, coolly, 'I 'll read my letter.   Humph!' he muttered, looking at the direction.   'I ought to know this
writing.   Beautiful Sally!'

Opening it, he read, in a fair, round, legal hand,
as follows—

'Sammy has been practised upon, and has broken
confidence.   It has all come out.   You had better not
be in the way, for strangers are going to call upon
you.   They have been very quiet as yet, because they
mean to surprise you.   Don't lose time.   I didn't.   I
am not to be found anywhere.   If I was you, I
wouldn't be, either.   S. B., late of B. M.'

To describe the changes that passed over Quilp's
face, as he read this letter half a dozen times, would
require some new language: such, for power of expression, as was never written, read, or spoken.   For
a long time he did not utter one word; but, after a considerable interval, during which Mrs. Quilp was almost paralysed with the alarm his looks engendered,
he contrived to gasp out—

'If I had him here.   If I only had him here—'

'Oh Quilp!' said his wife, 'what 's the matter?   Who
are you angry with?'

'—I should drown him,' said the dwarf, not heeding
her.   'Too easy a death, too short, too quick—but the
river runs close at hand.   Oh! if I had him here!
Just to take him to the brink coaxingly and pleasantly,
—holding him by the button-hole—joking with him,
—and, with a sudden push, to send him splashing
down!   Drowning men come to the surface three
times they say.   Ah!   To see him those three times,
and mock him as his face came bobbing up,—oh, what
a rich treat that would be!'

'Quilp!' stammered his wife, venturing at the same
time to touch him on the shoulder: 'what has gone
wrong?'

She was so terrified by the relish with which he pictured this pleasure to himself, that she could scarcely make herself intelligible.

'Such a bloodless cur!' said Quilp, rubbing his hands very slowly, and pressing them tight together. 'I thought his cowardice and servility were the best guarantee for his keeping silence. Oh Brass, Brass—my dear, good, affectionate, faithful, complimentary, charming friend—if I only had you here!'

His wife, who had retreated lest she should seem to listen to these mutterings, ventured to approach him again, and was about to speak, when he hurried to the door, and called Tom Scott, who, remembering his latest gentle admonition, deemed it prudent to appear immediately.

'There!' said the dwarf, pulling him in. 'Take her home. Don't come here to-morrow, for this place will be shut up. Come back no more till you hear from me or see me. Do you mind?'

Tom nodded sulkily, and beckoned Mrs. Quilp to lead the way.

'As for you,' said the dwarf, addressing himself to her, 'ask no questions about me, make no search for me, say nothing concerning me. I shall not be dead, mistress, and that 'll comfort you. He 'll take care of you.'

'But, Quilp? What is the matter? Where are you going? Do say something more?'

'I 'll say that,' said the dwarf, seizing her by the arm, 'and do that too, which undone and unsaid would be best for you, unless you go directly.'

'Has anything happened?' cried his wife. 'Oh! Do tell me that?'

'Yes,' snarled the dwarf. 'No. What matter which? I have told you what to do. Woe betide you if you fail to do it, or disobey me by a hair's breadth. Will you go?'

'I am going, I'll go directly; but,' faltered his wife, 'answer me one question first. Has this letter any connection with dear little Nell? I must ask you that—I must indeed, Quilp. You cannot think what days and nights of sorrow I have had through having once deceived that child. I don't know what harm I may have brought about, but, great or little, I did it for you, Quilp. My conscience misgave me when I did it. Do answer me this question, if you please?'

The exasperated dwarf returned no answer, but turned round and caught up his usual weapon with such vehemence, that Tom Scott dragged his charge away, by main force, and as swiftly as he could. It was well he did so, for Quilp, who was nearly mad with rage, pursued them to the neighbouring lane, and might have prolonged the chase but for the dense mist which obscured them from his view, and appeared to thicken every moment.

'It will be a good night for travelling anonymously,' he said, as he returned slowly: being pretty well breathed with his run. 'Stay. We may look better here. This is too hospitable and free.'

By a great exertion of strength, he closed the two old gates, which were deeply sunken in the mud, and barred them with a heavy beam. That done, he shook his matted hair from about his eyes, and tried them. —Strong and fast.

'The fence between this wharf and the next is easily climbed,' said the dwarf, when he had taken these precautions. 'There's a back-lane, too, from there. That shall be my way out. A man need know his road well, to find it in this lovely place to-night. I need fear no unwelcome visitors while this lasts, I think.'

Almost reduced to the necessity of groping his way with his hands (it had grown so dark and the fog had so much increased), he returned to his lair; and, after musing for some time over the fire, busied himself in preparations for a speedy departure.

While he was collecting a few necessaries and cramming them into his pockets, he never once ceased communing with himself in a low voice, or unclenched his teeth: which he had ground together on finishing Miss Brass's note.

'Oh Sampson!' he muttered, 'good worthy creature —if I could but hug you! If I could only fold you in my arms, and squeeze your ribs, as I *could* squeeze them if I once had you tight—what a meeting there would be between us! If we ever do cross each other again, Sampson, we'll have a greeting not easily to be forgotten, trust me. This time, Sampson, this moment when all had gone on so well, was so nicely chosen! It was so thoughtful of you, so penitent, so good. Oh, if we were face to face in this room again, my white-livered man of law, how well contented one of us would be!'

There he stopped; and raising the bowl of punch to his lips, drank a long deep draught, as if it were fair water and cooling to his parched mouth. Setting it down abruptly, and resuming his preparations, he went on with his soliloquy.

'There's Sally,' he said, with flashing eyes; 'the woman has spirit, determination, purpose—was she asleep, or petrified? She could have stabbed him— poisoned him safely. She might have seen this coming on. Why does she give me notice when it's too late? When he sat there,—yonder there, over there, —with his white face, and red head, and sickly smile, why didn't I know what was passing in his heart? It should have stopped beating, that night, if I had been in his secret, or there are no drugs to lull a man to sleep, or no fire to burn him!'

Another draught from the bowl; and, cowering over the fire with a ferocious aspect, he muttered to himself again.

'And this, like every other trouble and anxiety I have had of late times, springs from that old dotard and his darling child—two wretched feeble wanderers! I 'll be their evil genius yet. And you, sweet Kit, honest Kit, virtuous, innocent Kit, look to yourself. Where I hate, I bite. I hate you, my darling fellow, with good cause, and proud as you are to-night, I 'll have my turn.—What 's that?'

A knocking at the gate he had closed. A loud and violent knocking. Then, a pause; as if those who knocked had stopped to listen. Then, the noise again, more clamorous and importunate than before.

'So soon!' said the dwarf. 'And so eager! I am afraid I shall disappoint you. It 's well I 'm quite prepared. Sally, I thank you!'

As he spoke, he extinguished the candle. In his impetuous attempts to subdue the brightness of the fire, he overset the stove, which came tumbling forward, and fell with a crash upon the burning embers it had shot forth in its descent, leaving the room in pitchy darkness. The noise at the gate still continuing, he felt his way to the door, and stepped into the open air.

At that moment the knocking ceased. It was about eight o'clock; but the dead of the darkest night would have been as noon-day in comparison with the thick cloud which then rested upon the earth, and shrouded everything from view. He darted forward for a few paces, as if into the mouth of some dim, yawning cavern; then, thinking he had gone wrong, changed the direction of his steps; then, stood still, not knowing where to turn.

'If they would knock again,' said Quilp, trying to peer into the gloom by which he was surrounded, 'the sound might guide me! Come! Batter the gate once more!'

He stood listening intently, but the noise was not renewed. Nothing was to be heard in that deserted place, but, at intervals, the distant barking of dogs. The sound was far away—now in one quarter, now answered in another—nor was it any guide, for it often came from shipboard, as he knew.

'If I could find a wall or fence,' said the dwarf, stretching out his arms, and walking slowly on, 'I should know which way to turn. A good, black, devil's night this, to have my dear friend here! If I had but that wish, it might, for anything I cared, never be day again.'

As the word passed his lips, he staggered and fell —and next moment was fighting with the cold dark water!

For all its bubbling up and rushing in his ears, he could hear the knocking at the gate again—could hear a shout that followed it—could recognise the voice. For all his struggling and splashing, he could understand that they had lost their way, and had wandered back to the point from which they started; that they were all but looking on, while he was drowned; that they were close at hand, but could not make an effort to save him; that he himself had shut and barred them out. He answered the shout—with a yell, which seemed to make the hundred fires that danced before his eyes tremble and flicker, as if a gust of wind had stirred them. It was of no avail. The strong tide filled his throat, and bore him on, upon its rapid current.

Another mortal struggle, and he was up again, beating the water with his hands, and looking out, with wild and glaring eyes that showed him some black object he was drifting close upon. The hull of a ship! He could touch its smooth and slippery surface with his hand. One loud cry now—but the resistless water bore him down before he could give it utterance, and driving him under it, carried away a corpse.

It toyed and sported with its ghastly freight, now bruising it against the slimy piles, now hiding it in mud or long rank grass, now dragging it heavily over rough stones and gravel, now feigning to yield it to its own element, and in the same action luring it away, until, tired of the ugly plaything, it flung it on a swamp—a dismal place where pirates had swung in chains, through many a wintry night—and left it there to bleach.

And there it lay, alone. The sky was red with flame, and the water that bore it there had been tinged with the sullen light as it flowed along. The place the deserted carcase had left so recently, a living man, was now a blazing ruin. There was something of the glare upon its face. The hair, stirred by the damp breeze, played in a kind of mockery of death—such a mockery as the dead man himself would have delighted in when alive—about its head, and its dress fluttered idly in the night wind.

CHAPTER LXVIII

LIGHTED rooms, bright fires, cheerful faces, the music of glad voices, words of love and welcome, warm hearts, and tears of happiness—what a change is this! But it is to such delights that Kit is hastening. They are awaiting him, he knows. He fears he will die of joy, before he gets among them.

They have prepared him for this, all day. He is not to be carried off to-morrow with the rest, they tell him first. By degrees they let him know that doubts have arisen, that inquiries are to be made, and perhaps he may be pardoned after all. At last, the evening being come, they bring him to a room where some gentlemen are assembled. Foremost among them is his good old master, who comes and takes him by the hand. He hears that his innocence is established, and that he is pardoned. He cannot see the speaker, but he turns towards the voice, and in trying to answer, falls down insensible.

They recover him again, and tell him he must be composed, and bear this like a man. Somebody says he must think of his poor mother. It is because he does think of her so much, that the happy news has overpowered him. They crowd about him, and tell him that the truth has gone abroad, and that all the town and country ring with sympathy for his misfortunes. He has no ears for this. His thoughts, as yet, have no wider range than home. Does *she* know it? what did she say? who told her? He can speak of nothing else.

They make him drink a little wine, and talk kindly to him for a while, until he is more collected, and can listen, and thank them. He is free to go. Mr. Garland thinks, if he feels better, it is time they went away.   The gentlemen cluster round him, and shake hands with him.   He feels very grateful to them for the interest they have in him, and for the kind promises they make; but the power of speech is gone again, and he has much ado to keep his feet, even though leaning on his master's arm.

As they come through the dismal passages, some officers of the jail who are in waiting there, congratulate him, in their rough way, on his release.   The newsmonger is of the number, but his manner is not quite hearty—there is something of surliness in his compliments.   He looks upon Kit as an intruder, as one who has obtained admission to that place on false pretences, who has enjoyed a privilege without being duly qualified.   He may be a very good sort of young man, he thinks, but he has no business there, and the sooner he is gone, the better.

The last door shuts behind them.   They have passed the outer wall, and stand in the open air—in the street to be.   The night is bad, and yet how cheerful and gay the gloomy stones, and which has been in all his dreams.   It seems wider and more busy than it used to be.   The night is bad, and yet how cheerful and gay in his eyes!   One of the gentlemen, in taking leave of him, pressed some money into his hand.   He has not counted it; but when they have gone a few paces beyond the box for poor Prisoners, he hastily returns and drops it in.

Mr. Garland has a coach waiting in a neighbouring street, and, taking Kit inside with him, bids the man drive home.   At first, they can only travel at a footpace, and then with torches going on before, because of the heavy fog.   But, as they get farther from the river, and leave the closer portions of the town behind, they are able to dispense with this precaution and to proceed at a brisker rate.   On the road, hard galloping would be too slow for Kit; but, when they are drawing near their journey's end, he begs that they may go more slowly, and, when the house appears in sight, that they may stop—only for a minute or two, to give him time to breathe.

But there is no stopping then, for the old gentleman speaks stoutly to him, the horses mend their pace, and they are already at the garden-gate. Next minute, they are at the door. There is a noise of tongues, and tread of feet, inside. It opens. Kit rushes in, and finds his mother clinging round his neck.

And there, too, is the ever-faithful Barbara's mother, still holding the baby as if she had never put it down since that sad day when they little hoped to have such joy as this—there she is, Heaven bless her, crying her eyes out, and sobbing as never woman sobbed before; and there is little Barbara—poor little Barbara, so much thinner and so much paler, and yet so very pretty—trembling like a leaf and supporting herself against the wall; and there is Mrs. Garland, neater and nicer than ever, fainting away stone-dead with nobody to help her; and there is Mr. Abel, violently blowing his nose, and wanting to embrace everybody; and there is the single gentleman hovering round them all, and constant to nothing for an instant; and there is that good, dear, thoughtful little Jacob, sitting all alone by himself on the bottom stair, with his hands on his knees like an old man, roaring fearfully without giving any trouble to anybody; and each and all of them are for the time clean out of their wits, and do jointly and severally commit all manner of follies.

And even when the rest have in some measure come to themselves again, and can find words and smiles, Barbara—that soft-hearted, gentle, foolish little Bar-

bara—is suddenly missed, and found to be in a swoon
by herself in the back-parlour, from which swoon she
falls into hysterics, and from which hysterics into a
swoon again, and is, indeed, so bad, that despite a
mortal quantity of vinegar and cold water she is hardly
a bit better at last than she was at first.   Then, Kit's
mother comes in and says, will he come in and speak
to her; and Kit says 'Yes,' and goes; and he says in a
kind voice, 'Barbara!' and Barbara's mother tells her
that 'it 's only Kit'; and Barbara says (with her eyes
closed all the time) 'Oh! but is it him indeed?' and
Barbara's mother says 'To be sure it is, my dear;
there 's nothing the matter now.'   And in further assurance that he 's safe and sound, Kit speaks to her
again; and then Barbara goes off into another fit of
laughter, and then into another fit of crying; and
then Barbara's mother and Kit's mother nod to each
other and pretend to scold her—but only to bring her
to herself the faster, bless you!—and being experienced matrons, and acute at perceiving the first dawn-
ing symptoms of recovery, they comfort Kit with the
assurance that 'she 'll do now,' and so dismiss him to the
place from whence he came.

Well!   In that place (which is the next room)
there are decanters of wine, and all that sort of thing,
set out as grand as if Kit and his friends were first-
rate company; and there is little Jacob, walking, as
the popular phrase is, into a home-made plum-cake,
at a most surprising pace, and keeping his eye on the
figs and oranges which are to follow, and making the
best use of his time, you may believe.   Kit no sooner
comes in, then that single gentleman (never was such
a busy gentleman) charges all the glasses—bumpers
—and drinks his health, and tells him he shall never
want a friend while *he* lives; and so does Mr. Garland,
and so does Mrs. Garland, and so does Mr. Abel.

But, even this honour and distinction is not all, for the single gentleman forthwith pulls out of his pocket a massive silver watch—going hard, and right to half a second—and upon the back of this watch is engraved Kit's name, with flourishes all over; and in short it is Kit's watch, bought expressly for him, and presented to him on the spot. You may rest assured that Mr. and Mrs. Garland can't help hinting about their present, in store, and that Mr. Abel tells outright that he has his; and that Kit is the happiest of the happy.

There is one friend he has not seen yet, and as he cannot be conveniently introduced into the family circle, by reason of his being an iron-shod quadruped, Kit takes the first opportunity of slipping away and hurrying to the stable. The moment he lays his hand upon the latch, the pony neighs the loudest pony's greeting; before he has crossed the threshold, the pony is capering about his loose box (for he brooks not the indignity of a halter), mad to give him welcome; and when Kit goes up to caress and pat him, the pony rubs his nose against his coat, and fondles him more lovingly than ever pony fondled man. It is the crowning circumstance of his earnest, heartfelt reception; and Kit fairly puts his arm round Whisker's neck and hugs him.

But how comes Barbara to trip in there? and how smart she is again! she has been at her glass since she recovered. How comes Barbara in the stable, of all places in the world? Why, since Kit has been away, the pony would take his food from nobody but her, and Barbara, you see, not dreaming that Christopher was there, and just looking in, to see that everything was right, has come upon him unawares. Blushing little Barbara!

It may be that Kit has caressed the pony enough; it may be that there are even better things to caress than ponies. He leaves him for Barbara at any rate, and hopes she is better. Yes. Barbara is a great deal better. She is afraid—and here Barbara looks down and blushes more—that he must have thought her very foolish. 'Not at all,' says Kit. Barbara is very glad of that and coughs—Hem!—just the slightest cough possible—not more than that.

What a discreet pony when he chooses! He is as quiet now as if he were of marble. He has a very knowing look, but that he always has. 'We have hardly had time to shake hands, Barbara,' says Kit. Barbara gives him hers. Why, she is trembling now! Foolish, fluttering Barbara!

Arm's length? The length of an arm is not much. Barbara's was not a long arm, by any means, and besides, she didn't hold it out straight, but bent a little. Kit was so near her when they shook hands, that he could see a small tiny tear, yet trembling on an eyelash. It was natural that he should look at it, unknown to Barbara. It was natural that Barbara should raise her eyes unconsciously, and find him out. Was it natural that at that instant, without any previous impulse or design, Kit should kiss Barbara? He did it, whether or no. Barbara said 'for shame,' but let him do it too—twice. He might have done it thrice, but the pony kicked up his heels and shook his head, as if he were suddenly taken with convulsions of delight, and Barbara being frightened, ran away— not straight to where her mother and Kit's mother were, though, lest they should see how red her cheeks were, and should ask her why. Sly little Barbara!

When the first transports of the whole party had subsided, and Kit and his mother, and Barbara and her mother, with little Jacob and the baby to boot, had had their suppers together—which there was no hurrying over, for they were going to stop there all night—Mr. Garland called Kit to him, and taking him into a room where they could be alone, told him that he had something yet to say, which would surprise him greatly. Kit looked so anxious and turned so pale on hearing this, that the old gentleman hastened to add, he would be agreeably surprised; and asked him if he would be ready next morning for a journey.

'For a journey, sir!' cried Kit.

'In company with me and my friend in the next room. Can you guess its purpose?'

Kit turned paler yet, and shook his head.

'Oh yes. I think you do already,' said his master. 'Try.'

Kit murmured something rather rambling and unintelligible, but he plainly pronounced the words 'Miss Nell,' three or four times—shaking his head while he did so, as if he would add that there was no hope of that.

But Mr. Garland, instead of saying 'Try again,' as Kit had made sure he would, told him very seriously, that he had guessed right.

'The place of their retreat is indeed discovered,' he said, 'at last. And that is our journey's end.'

Kit faltered out such questions as, where was it, and how had it been found, and how long since, and was she well and happy?

'Happy she is, beyond all doubt,' said Mr. Garland. 'And well, I—I trust she will be soon. She has been weak and ailing, as I learn, but she was better when I heard this morning, and they were full of hope. Sit you down, and you shall hear the rest.'

Scarcely venturing to draw his breath, Kid did as he was told. Mr. Garland then related to him, how he had a brother (of whom he would remember to have heard him speak, and whose picture, taken when he was a young man, hung in the best room), and how this brother lived a long way off, in a country-place, with an old clergyman who had been his early friend. How, although they loved each other as brothers should, they had not met for many years, but had communicated by letter from time to time, always looking forward to some period when they would take each other by the hand once more, and still letting the Present time steal on, as it was the habit for men to do, and suffering the Future to melt into the Past. How this brother, whose temper was very mild and quiet and retiring—such as Mr. Abel's—was greatly beloved by the simple people among whom he dwelt, who quite revered the Bachelor (for so they called him), and had every one experienced his charity and benevolence. How even those slight circumstances had come to his knowledge, very slowly and in course of years, for the Bachelor was one of those whose goodness shuns the light, and who have more pleasure in discovering and extolling the good deeds of others, than in trumpeting their own, be they never so commendable. How, for that reason, he seldom told them of his village friends; but how, for all that, his mind had become so full of two among them—a child and an old man, to whom he had been very kind—that, in a letter received a few days before, he had dwelt upon them from first to last, and had told such a tale of their wandering, and mutual love, that few could read it without being moved to tears. How he, the recipient of that letter, was directly led to the belief that these must be the very wanderers for whom so much search had been made, and whom Heaven had directed to his brother's care. How he had written for such further information as would put the fact beyond all doubt; how it had that morning arrived; had confirmed his first impression into a certainty; and was the immediate cause of that journey being planned, which they were to take to-morrow.

'In the meantime,' said the old gentleman rising, and laying his hand on Kit's shoulder, 'you have a great need of rest; for such a day as this would wear out the strongest man. Good-night, and Heaven send our journey may have a prosperous ending!'

CHAPTER LXIX

KIT was no sluggard next morning, but, springing from his bed some time before day, began to prepare for his welcome expedition. The hurry of spirits consequent upon the events of yesterday, and the unexpected intelligence he had heard at night, had troubled his sleep through the long dark hours, and summoned such uneasy dreams about his pillow that it was rest to rise.

But, had it been the beginning of some great labour with the same end in view—had it been the commencement of a long journey, to be performed on foot in that inclement season of the year, to be pursued under every privation and difficulty, and to be achieved only with great distress, fatigue, and suffering—had it been the dawn of some painful enterprise, certain to task his utmost powers of resolution and endurance, and to need his utmost fortitude, but only likely to end, if happily achieved, in good fortune and delight to Nell—Kit's cheerful zeal would have been as highly roused: Kit's ardour and impatience would have been, at least, the same.

Nor was he alone excited and eager. Before he had been up a quarter of an hour the whole house were astir and busy. Everybody hurried to do something towards facilitating the preparations. The single gentleman, it is true, could do nothing himself, but he overlooked everybody else and was more locomotive than anybody. The work of packing and making ready went briskly on, and by daybreak every preparation for the journey was completed. Then, Kit began to wish they had not been quite so nimble; for the travelling-carriage which had been hired for the occasion was not to arrive until nine o'clock, and there was nothing but breakfast to fill up the intervening blank of one hour and a half.

Yes there was, though. There was Barbara. Barbara was busy, to be sure, but so much the better— Kit could help her, and that would pass away the time better than any means that could be devised. Barbara had no objection to this arrangement, and Kit, tracking out the idea which had come upon him so suddenly overnight, began to think that surely Barbara was fond of him, and surely he was fond of Barbara.

Now, Barbara, if the truth must be told—as it must and ought to be—Barbara seemed, of all the little household, to take least pleasure in the bustle of the occasion; and when Kit, in the openness of his heart, told her how glad and overjoyed it made him, Barbara became more downcast still, and seemed to have even less pleasure in it than before!

'You have not been home so long, Christopher,' said Barbara—and it is impossible to tell how carelessly she said it—'You have not been home so long, that you need be glad to go away again, I should think.'

'But for such a purpose,' returned Kit. 'To bring back Miss Nell! To see her again! Only think of that! I am so pleased too, to think that *you* will see her, Barbara, at last.'

Barbara did not absolutely say that she felt no gratification on this point, but she expressed the sentiment so plainly by one little toss of her head, that Kit was quite disconcerted, and wondered, in his simplicity, why she was so cool about it.

'You 'll say she has the sweetest and beautifullest face you ever saw, I know,' said Kit, rubbing his hands. 'I 'm sure you 'll say that.'

Barbara tossed her head again.

'What 's the matter, Barbara?' said Kit.

'Nothing,' cried Barbara. And Barbara pouted— not sulkily, or in an ugly manner, but just enough to make her look more cherry-lipped than ever.

There is no school in which a pupil gets on so fast, as that in which Kit became a scholar when he gave Barbara the kiss. He saw what Barbara meant now —he had his lesson by heart all at once—she was the book—there it was before him, as plain as print.

'Barbara,' said Kit, 'you 're not cross with me?'

Oh dear no! Why should Barbara be cross? And what right had she to be cross? And what did it matter whether she was cross or not? Who minded *her?*

'Why, *I* do,' said Kit. 'Of course I do.'

Barbara didn't see why it was of course, at all.

Kit was sure she must. Would she think again?

Certainly, Barbara would think again. No, she didn't see why it was of course. She didn't understand what Christopher meant. And besides she was sure they wanted her upstairs by this time, and she must go, indeed—

'No, but Barbara,' said Kit, detaining her gently, 'let us part friends. I was always thinking of you, in my troubles. I should have been a great deal more miserable than I was, if it hadn't been for you.'

Goodness gracious, how pretty Barbara was when she coloured—and when she trembled, like a little shrinking bird!

'I am telling you the truth, Barbara, upon my word, but not half so strong as I could wish,' said Kit. 'When I want you to be pleased to see Miss Nell, it's only because I like you to be pleased with what pleases me—that's all. As to her, Barbara, I think I could almost die to do her service, but you would think so too, if you knew her as I do. I am sure you would.'

Barbara was touched, and sorry to have appeared indifferent.

'I have been used, you see,' said Kit, 'to talk and think of her, almost as if she was an angel. When I look forward to meeting her again, I think of her smiling as she used to do, and being glad to see me, and putting out her hand and saying, "It's my own old Kit," or some such words as those—like what she used to say. I think of seeing her happy, and with friends about her, and brought up as she deserves, and as she ought to be. When I think of myself, it's as her old servant, and one that loved her dearly, as his kind, good, gentle mistress; and who would have gone—yes, and still would go—through any harm to serve her. Once, I couldn't help being afraid that if she came back with friends about her she might forget, or be ashamed of having known, a humble lad like me, and so might speak coldly, which would have cut me, Barbara, deeper than I can tell. But when I came to think again, I felt sure that I was doing her wrong in this; and so I went on, as I did at first, hoping to see her once more, just as she used to be. Hoping this, and remembering what she was, has made me feel as if I would always try to please her, and always be what I should like to seem to her if I was still her servant. If I'm the better for that—and I don't think I'm the worse—I am grateful to

her for it, and love and honour her the more.   That 's
the plain honest truth, dear Barbara, upon my word
it is!'

Little Barbara was not of a wayward or capricious
nature, and, being full of remorse, melted into tears.
To what more conversation this might have led, we
need not stop to inquire; for the wheels of the carriage were heard at that moment, and, being followed
by a smart ring at the garden-gate, caused the bustle
in the house, which had lain dormant for a short time,
to burst again into tenfold life and vigour.

Simultaneously with the travelling equipage, arrived Mr. Chuckster in a hackney-cab, with certain
papers and supplies of money for the single gentleman, into whose hands he delivered them.   This duty
discharged, he subsided into the bosom of the family;
and, entertaining himself with a strolling or peri-
patetic breakfast, watched, with genteel indifference,
the process of loading the carriage.

'Snobby 's in this, I see, sir?' he said to Mr. Abel
Garland.   'I thought he wasn't in the last trip because
it was expected that his presence wouldn't be ac-
ceptable to the ancient buffalo.'

'To whom, sir,' demanded Mr. Abel.

'To the old gentleman,' returned Mr. Chuckster,
slightly abashed.

'Our client prefers to take him now,' said Mr. Abel,
drily.   'There is no longer any need for that precaution, as my father's relationship to a gentleman in
whom the objects of his search have full confidence,
will be a sufficient guarantee for the friendly nature
of their errand.'

'Ah!' thought Mr. Chuckster, looking out of window, 'anybody but me!   Snobby before me, of course.
He didn't happen to take that particular five-pound
note, but I have not the smallest doubt that he 's al-

ways up to something of that sort. I always said it, long before this came out. Devilish pretty girl that! 'Pon my soul, an amazing little creature!'

Barbara was the subject of Mr. Chuckster's commendations; and as she was lingering near the carriage (all being now ready for its departure), that gentleman was suddenly seized with a strong interest in the proceedings, which impelled him to swagger down the garden, and take up his position at a convenient ogling distance. Having had great experience of the sex, and being perfectly acquainted with all those little artifices which find the readiest road to their hearts, Mr. Chuckster, on taking his ground, planted one hand on his hip, and with the other adjusted his flowing hair. This is a favourite attitude in the polite circles, and, accompanied with a graceful whistling, has been known to do immense execution.

Such, however, is the difference between town and country, that nobody took the smallest notice of this insinuating figure; the wretches being wholly engaged in bidding the travellers farewell, in kissing hands to each other, waving handkerchiefs, and the like tame and vulgar practices. For, now, the single gentleman and Mr. Garland were in the carriage, and the post-boy was in the saddle, and Kit, well wrapped and muffled up, was in the rumble behind; and Mrs. Garland was there, and Mr. Abel was there, and Kit's mother was there, and little Jacob was there, and Barbara's mother was visible in remote perspective, nursing the ever-wakeful baby; and all were nodding, beckoning, curtseying, or crying out, 'Good-bye!' with all the energy they could express. In another minute the carriage was out of sight; and Mr. Chuckster remained alone on the spot where it had lately been, with a vision of Kit standing up in the rumble waving his hand to Barbara, and of Barbara in the full light and lustre of his eyes—*his* eyes—Chuckster's—Chuckster the successful—on whom ladies of quality had looked with favour from phaetons in the parks on Sundays—waving hers to Kit!

How Mr. Chuckster, entranced by this monstrous fact, stood for some time rooted to the earth, protesting within himself that Kit was the Prince of felonious characters, and very Emperor or Great Mogul of Snobs, and how he clearly traced this revolting circumstance back to that old villainy of the shilling, are matters foreign to our purpose, which is to track the rolling wheels, and bear the travellers company on their cold, bleak journey.

It was a bitter day. A keen wind was blowing, and rushed against them fiercely: bleaching the hard ground, shaking the white frost from the trees and hedges, and whirling it away like dust. But, little cared Kit for weather. There was a freedom and freshness in the wind, as it came howling by, which, let it cut never so sharp, was welcome. As it swept on with its cloud of frost, bearing down the dry twigs and boughs and withered leaves, and carrying them away pell-mell, it seemed as though some general sympathy had got abroad, and everything was in a hurry, like themselves. The harder the gusts, the better progress they appeared to make. It was a good thing to go struggling and fighting forwards, vanquishing them one by one; to watch them driving up, gathering strength and fury as they came along; to bend for a moment, as they whistled past; and then, to look back and see them speed away, their hoarse noise dying in the distance, and the stout trees cowering down before them.

All day long, it blew without cessation. The night was clear and starlight, but the wind had not fallen, and the cold was piercing. Sometimes—towards the end of a long stage—Kit could not help wishing it were a little warmer: but when they stopped to change horses, and he had had a good run, and what with that, and the bustle of paying the old postilion, and rousing the new one, and running to and fro again until the horses were put to, he was so warm that the blood tingled and smarted in his fingers' ends—then, he felt as if to have it one degree less cold would be to lose half the delight and glory of the journey: and up he jumped again, right cheerily, singing to the merry music of the wheels as they rolled away, and, leaving the townspeople in their warm beds, pursued their course along the lonely road.

Meantime the two gentlemen inside, who were little disposed to sleep, beguiled the time with conversation. As both were anxious and expectant, it naturally turned upon the subject of their expedition, on the manner in which it had been brought about, and on the hopes and fears they entertained respecting it. Of the former they had many, of the latter few—none perhaps beyond that indefinable uneasiness which is inseparable from suddenly awakened hope, and protracted expectation.

In one of the pauses of their discourse, and when half the night had worn away, the single gentleman, who had gradually become more and more silent and thoughtful, turned to his companion and said abruptly—

'Are you a good listener?'

'Like most other men, I suppose,' returned Mr. Garland, smiling. 'I can be, if I am interested; and if not interested, I should still try to appear so. Why do you ask?'

'I have a short narrative on my lips,' rejoined his friend, 'and will try you with it. It is very brief.'

Pausing for no reply, he laid his hand on the old gentleman's sleeve, and proceeded thus—

'There were once two brothers, who loved each other dearly. There was a disparity in their ages—some twelve years. I am not sure but they may insensibly have loved each other the better for that reason. Wide as the interval between them was, however, they became rivals too soon. The deepest and strongest affection of both their hearts settled upon one object.

'The youngest—there were reasons for *his* being sensitive and watchful—was the first to find this out. I will not tell you what misery he underwent, what agony of soul he knew, how great his mental struggle was. He had been a sickly child. His brother, patient and considerate in the midst of his own high health and strength, had many and many a day denied himself the sports he loved, to sit beside his couch, telling him old stories till his pale face lighted up with an unwonted glow; to carry him in his arms to some green spot, where he could tend the poor pensive boy as he looked upon the bright summer day, and saw all nature healthy but himself; to be, in any way, his fond and faithful nurse. I may not dwell on all he did, to make the poor, weak creature love him, or my tale would have no end. But when the time of trial came, the younger brother's heart was full of those old days. Heaven strengthened it to repay the sacrifices of inconsiderate youth by one of thoughtful manhood. He left his brother to be happy. The truth never passed his lips, and he quitted the country, hoping to die abroad.

'The elder brother married her. She was in Heaven before long, and left him with an infant daughter.

'If you have seen the picture-gallery of any one old family, you will remember how the same face and figure—often the fairest and slightest of them all—

come upon you in different generations; and how you trace the same sweet girl through a long line of portraits—never growing old or changing—the Good Angel of the race—abiding by them in all reverses—redeeming all their sins—

'In this daughter the mother lived again. You may judge with what devotion he who lost that mother almost in the winning, clung to this girl, her breathing image. She grew to womanhood, and gave her heart to one who could not know its worth. Well! Her fond father could not see her pine and droop. He might be more deserving than he thought him. He surely might become so, with a wife like her. He joined their hands, and they were married.

'Through all the misery that followed this union; through all the cold neglect and undeserved reproach; through all the poverty he brought upon her; through all the struggles of their daily life, too mean and pitiful to tell, but dreadful to endure; she toiled on, in the deep devotion of her spirit, and in her better nature, as only women can. Her means and substance wasted; her father nearly beggared by her husband's hand, and the hourly witness (for they lived now under one roof) of her ill-usage and unhappiness, —she never, but for him, bewailed her fate. Patient, and upheld by strong affection to the last, she died a widow of some three weeks' date, leaving to her father's care two orphans; one a son of ten or twelve years old; the other a girl—such another infant child —the same in helplessness, in age, in form, in feature —as she had been herself when her young mother died.

'The elder brother, grandfather to these two children, was now a broken man; crushed and borne down, less by the weight of years than by the heavy hand of sorrow. With the wreck of his possessions, he began to trade—in pictures first, and then in curious ancient things.   He had entertained a fondness for such mat-ters from a boy, and the tastes he had cultivated were now to yield him an anxious and precarious subsist-ence.

'The boy grew like his father in mind and person; the girl so like her mother, that when the old man had her on his knee, and looked into her mild blue eyes, he felt as if awakening from a wretched dream, and his daughter were a little child again.   The wayward boy soon spurned the shelter of his roof, and sought associates more congenial to his taste.   The old man and the child dwelt alone together.

'It was then, when the love of two dead people who had been nearest and dearest to his heart, was all transferred to this slight creature; when her face, con-stantly before him, reminded him, from hour to hour, of the too early change he had seen in such another— of all the sufferings he had watched and known, and all his child had undergone; when the young man's profligate and hardened course drained him of money as his father's had, and even sometimes occasioned them temporary privation and distress; it was then that there began to beset him, and to be ever in his mind, a gloomy dread of poverty and want.   He had no thought for himself in this.   His fear was for the child.   It was a spectre in his house, and haunted him night and day.

'The younger brother had been a traveller in many countries, and had made his pilgrimage through life alone.   His voluntary banishment had been miscon-strued, and he had borne (not without pain) reproach and slight for doing that which had wrung his heart, and cast a mournful shadow on his path.   Apart from this, communication between him and the elder was difficult, and uncertain, and often failed; still, it was not so wholly broken off but that he learnt—with long

blanks and gaps between each interval of information
—all that I have told you now.

'Then, dreams of their young, happy life—happy
to him though laden with pain and early care—visited
his pillow yet oftener than before; and every night, a
boy again, he was at his brother's side. With the utmost speed he could exert, he settled his affairs; con-
verted into money all the goods he had; and, with
honourable wealth enough for both, with open heart
and hand, with limbs that trembled as they bore him
on, with emotion such as men can hardly bear and
live, arrived one evening at his brother's door!'

The narrator, whose voice had faltered lately,
stopped. 'The rest,' said Mr. Garland, pressing his
hand after a pause, 'I know.'

'Yes,' rejoined his friend, 'we may spare ourselves
the sequel. You know the poor result of all my
search. Even when by dint of such inquiries as the
utmost vigilance and sagacity could set on foot, we
found they had been seen with two poor travelling
showmen—and in time discovered the men themselves
—and in time, the actual place of their retreat; even
then, we were too late. Pray God we are not too late
again!'

'We cannot be,' said Mr. Garland. 'This time we
must succeed!'

'I have believed and hoped so,' returned the other.
'I try to believe and hope so still. But a heavy weight
has fallen on my spirits, my good friend, and the sad-
ness that gathers over me, will yield to neither hope
nor reason.'

'That does not surprise me,' said Mr. Garland; 'it
is a natural consequence of the events you have recalled; of this dreary time and place; and above all,
of this wild and dismal night. A dismal night indeed!
Hark! how the wind is howling!'

CHAPTER LXX

Day broke, and found them still upon their way. Since leaving home, they had halted here and there for necessary refreshment, and had frequently been delayed, especially in the night-time, by waiting for fresh horses. They had made no other stoppages, but the weather continued rough, and the roads were often steep and heavy. It would be night again before they reached their place of destination.

Kit, all bluff and hardened with the cold, went on manfully; and, having enough to do to keep his blood circulating, to picture to himself the happy end of this adventurous journey, and to look about him and be amazed at everything, had little spare time for thinking of discomforts. Though his impatience, and that of his fellow-travellers, rapidly increased as the day waned, the hours did not stand still. The short daylight of winter soon faded away, and it was dark again when they had yet many miles to travel.

As it grew dusk, the wind fell; its distant moanings were more low and mournful; and, as it came creeping up the road, and rattling covertly among the dry brambles on either hand, it seemed like some great phantom for whom the way was narrow, whose garments rustled as it stalked along. By degrees it lulled and died away, and then it came on to snow.

The flakes fell fast and thick, soon covering the ground some inches deep, and spreading abroad a solemn stillness. The rolling wheels were noiseless, and the sharp ring and clatter of the horses' hoofs, became a dull, muffled tramp. The life of their progress seemed to be slowly hushed, and something death-like to usurp its place.

Shading his eyes from the falling snow, which froze

upon their lashes and obscured his sight, **Kit** often tried to catch the earliest glimpse of twinkling lights denoting their approach to some not distant town. He could descry objects enough at such times, but none correctly.   Now, a tall church spire appeared in view, which presently became a tree, a barn, a shadow on the ground, thrown on it by their own bright lamps. Now, there were horsemen, foot-passengers, carriages, going on before, or meeting them in narrow ways; which, when they were close upon them, turned to shadows too.   A wall, a ruin, a sturdy gable end, would rise up in the road; and, when they were plunging headlong at it, would be the road itself.   Strange turnings too, bridges, and sheets of water, appeared to start up here and there, making the way doubtful and uncertain; and yet they were on the same bare road, and these things, like the others, as they were passed, turned into dim illusions.

He descended slowly from his seat—for his limbs were numbed—when they arrived at a lone posting-house, and inquired how far they had to go to reach their journey's end.   It was a late hour in such by-places, and the people were abed; but a voice answered from an upper window, Ten miles.   The ten minutes that ensued appeared an hour; but at the end of that time, a shivering figure led out the horses they required, and after another brief delay they were again in motion.

It was a cross-country road, full, after the first three or four miles, of holes and cart-ruts, which, being covered by the snow, were so many pitfalls to the trembling horses, and obliged them to keep a foot-pace.   As it was next to impossible for men so much agitated as they were by this time, to sit still and move so slowly, all three got out and plodded on behind the carriage.   The distance seemed interminable, and the walk was most laborious. As each was thinking within himself that the driver must have lost his way, a church bell, close at hand, struck the hour of midnight, and the carriage stopped. It had moved softly enough, but when it ceased to crunch the snow, the silence was as startling as if some great noise had been replaced by perfect stillness.

'This is the place, gentlemen,' said the driver, dismounting from his horse, and knocking at the door of a little inn. 'Holloa! Past twelve o'clock is the dead of night here.'

The knocking was loud and long, but it failed to rouse the drowsy inmates. All continued dark and silent as before. They fell back a little, and looked up at the windows, which were mere black patches in the whitened house front. No light appeared. The house might have been deserted, or the sleepers dead, for any air of life it had about it.

They spoke together with a strange inconsistency in whispers; unwilling to disturb again the dreary echoes they had just now raised.

'Let us go on,' said the younger brother, 'and leave this good fellow to wake them, if he can. I cannot rest until I know that we are not too late. Let us go on, in the name of Heaven!'

They did so, leaving the postilion to order such accommodation as the house afforded, and to renew his knocking. Kit accompanied them with a little bundle, which he had hung in the carriage when they left home, and had not forgotten since—the bird in his old cage—just as she had left him. She would be glad to see her bird, he knew.

The road wound gently downward. As they proceeded, they lost sight of the church whose clock they had heard, and of the small village clustering round it. The knocking, which was now renewed, and which in that stillness they could plainly hear, troubled them. They wished the man would forbear, or that they had told him not to break the silence until they returned.

The old church tower, clad in a ghostly garb of pure cold white, again rose up before them, and a few moments brought them close beside it. A venerable building—grey, even in the midst of the hoary landscape. An ancient sun-dial on the belfry wall was nearly hidden by the snow-drift, and scarcely to be known for what it was. Time itself seemed to have grown dull and old, as if no day were ever to displace the melancholy night.

A wicket-gate was close at hand, but there was more than one path across the churchyard to which it led, and, uncertain which to take, they came to a stand again.

The village street—if street that could be called which was an irregular cluster of poor cottages of many heights and ages, some with their fronts, some with their backs, and some with gable ends towards the road, with here and there a sign-post, or a shed encroaching on the path—was close at hand. There was a faint light in a chamber-window not far off, and Kit ran towards that house to ask their way.

His first shout was answered by an old man within, who presently appeared at the casement, wrapping some garment round his throat as a protection from the cold, and demanded who was abroad at that unseasonable hour, wanting him.

' 'Tis hard weather this,' he grumbled, 'and not a night to call me up in. My trade is not of that kind that I need be roused from bed. The business on which folks want me, will keep cold, especially at this season. What do you want?'

'I would not have roused you, if I had known you were old and ill,' said Kit.

'Old!' repeated the other peevishly. 'How do you know I am old? Not so old as you think, friend, perhaps. As to being ill, you will find many young people in worse case than I am. More 's the pity that it should be so—not that I should be strong and hearty for my years, I mean, but that they should be weak and tender. I ask your pardon though,' said the old man, 'if I spoke rather rough at first. My eyes are not good at night—that 's neither age nor illness; they never were—and I didn't see you were a stranger.'

'I am sorry to call you from your bed,' said Kit, 'but those gentlemen you may see by the churchyard-gate, are strangers too, who have just arrived from a long journey, and seek the parsonage-house. You can direct us?'

'I should be able to,' answered the old man, in a trembling voice, 'for, come next summer, I have been sexton here, good fifty years. The right-hand path, friend, is the road.—There is no ill news for our good gentleman, I hope?'

Kit thanked him, and made him a hasty answer in the negative; he was turning back, when his attention was caught by the voice of a child. Looking up, he saw a very little creature at a neighbouring window.

'What is that?' cried the child, earnestly. 'Has my dream come true? Pray speak to me, whoever that is, awake and up.'

'Poor boy!' said the sexton, before Kit could answer, 'how goes it, darling?'

'Has my dream come true?' exclaimed the child again, in a voice so fervent that it might have thrilled to the heart of any listener. 'But no, that can never be! How could it be—Oh! how could it?'

'I guess his meaning,' said the sexton. 'To bed again, poor boy!'

'Aye!' cried the child, in a burst of despair. 'I knew it could never be, I felt too sure of that, before I asked! But, all to-night, and last night too, it was the same. I never fall asleep, but that cruel dream comes back.'

'Try to sleep again,' said the old man, soothingly. 'It will go in time.'

'No no, I would rather that it staid—cruel as it is, I would rather that it staid,' rejoined the child. 'I am not afraid to have it in my sleep, but I am so sad —so very, very sad.'

The old man blessed him, the child in tears replied Good-night, and Kit was again alone.

He hurried back, moved by what he had heard, though more by the child's manner than by anything he had said, as his meaning was hidden from him. They took the path indicated by the sexton, and soon arrived before the parsonage wall. Turning round to look about them when they had got thus far, they saw, among some ruined buildings at a distance, one single solitary light.

It shone from what appeared to be an old oriel window, and being surrounded by the deep shadows of overhanging walls, sparkled like a star. Bright and glimmering as the stars above their heads, lonely and motionless as they, it seemed to claim some kindred with the eternal lamps of Heaven, and to burn in fellowship with them.

'What light is that!' said the younger brother.

'It is surely,' said Mr. Garland, 'in the ruin where they live. I see no other ruin hereabouts.'

'They cannot,' returned the brother hastily, 'be waking at this late hour—'

Kit interposed directly, and begged that, while

they rang and waited at the gate, they would let him make his way to where this light was shining, and try to ascertain if any people were about.   Obtaining the permission he desired, he darted off with breathless eagerness, and, still carrying the birdcage in his hand, made straight towards the spot.

It was not easy to hold that pace among the graves, and at another time he might have gone more slowly, or round by the path.   Unmindful of all obstacles, however, he pressed forward without slackening his speed, and soon arrived within a few yards of the window.

He approached as softly as he could, and advancing so near the wall as to brush the whitened ivy with his dress, listened.   There was no sound inside.   The church itself was not more quiet.   Touching the glass with his cheek, he listened again.   No.   And yet there was such a silence all around, that he felt sure he could have heard even the breathing of a sleeper, if there had been one there.

A strange circumstance, a light in such a place at that time of night, with no one near it.

A curtain was drawn across the lower portion of the window, and he could not see into the room.   But there was no shadow thrown upon it from within. To have gained a footing on the wall and tried to look in from above, would have been attended with some danger—certainly with some noise, and the chance of terrifying the child, if that really were her habitation. Again and again he listened; again and again the same wearisome blank.

Leaving the spot with slow and cautious steps, and skirting the ruin for a few paces, he came at length to a door.   He knocked.   No answer.   But there was a curious noise inside.   It was difficult to determine what it was.   It bore a resemblance to the low moaning of one in pain, but it was not that, being far too regular and constant.   Now it seemed a kind of song, now a wail—seemed, that is, to his changing fancy, for the sound itself was never changed or checked.   It was unlike anything he had ever heard; and in its tone there was something fearful, chilling, and unearthly.

The listener's blood ran colder now, than ever it had done in frost and snow, but he knocked again. There was no answer, and the sound went on without any interruption.   He laid his hand softly upon the latch, and put his knee against the door.   It was secured on the inside, but yielded to the pressure, and turned upon its hinges.   He saw the glimmering of a fire upon the old walls, and entered.

CHAPTER LXXI

THE dull, red glow of a wood fire—for no lamp or candle burnt within the room—showed him a figure, seated on the hearth with its back towards him, bending over the fitful light.   The attitude was that of one who sought the heat.   It was, and yet was not. The stooping posture and the cowering form were there, but no hands were stretched out to meet the grateful warmth, no shrug or shiver compared its luxury with the piercing cold outside.   With limbs huddled together, head bowed down, arms crossed upon the breast, and fingers tightly clenched, it rocked to and fro upon its seat without a moment's pause, accompanying the action with the mournful sound he had heard.

The heavy door had closed behind him on his entrance, with a crash that made him start.   The figure neither spoke, nor turned to look, nor gave in any other way the faintest sign of having heard the noise. The form was that of an old man, his white head akin in colour to the mouldering embers upon which he gazed. He, and the failing light and dying fire, the time-worn room, the solitude, the wasted life, and gloom, were all in fellowship. Ashes, and dust, and ruin!

Kit tried to speak, and did pronounce some words, though what they were he scarcely knew. Still the same terrible low cry went on—still the same rocking in the chair—the same stricken figure was there, unchanged and heedless of his presence.

He had his hand upon the latch, when something in the form—distinctly seen as one log broke and fell, and, as it fell, blazed up—arrested it. He returned to where he had stood before—advanced a pace—another—another still. Another, and he saw the face. Yes! Changed as it was, he knew it well.

'Master!' he cried, stooping on one knee and catching at his hand. 'Dear master. Speak to me!'

The old man turned slowly towards him; and muttered in a hollow voice—

'This is another!—How many of these spirits there have been to-night!'

'No spirit, master. No one but your old servant. You know me now, I am sure? Miss Nell—where is she—where is she?'

'They all say that!' cried the old man. 'They all ask the same question. A spirit!'

'Where is she?' demanded Kit. 'Oh tell me but that, but that, dear master!'

'She is asleep—yonder—in there.'

'Thank God!'

'Aye! Thank God!' returned the old man. 'I have prayed to Him, many, and many, and many a livelong night, when she has been asleep, He knows. Hark! Did she call?'

'I heard no voice.'

'You did. You hear her now. Do you tell me that you don't hear *that?*'

He started up, and listened again.

'Nor that?' he cried, with a triumphant smile. 'Can anybody know that voice so well as I! Hush! hush!'

Motioning to him to be silent, he stole away into another chamber. After a short absence (during which he could be heard to speak in a softened soothing tone) he returned, bearing in his hand a lamp.

'She is still asleep,' he whispered. 'You were right. She did not call—unless she did so in her slumber. She has called to me in her sleep before now, sir; as I have sat by, watching, I have seen her lips move, and have known, though no sound came from them, that she spoke of me. I feared the light might dazzle her eyes and wake her, so I brought it here.'

He spoke rather to himself than to the visitor, but when he had put the lamp upon the table, he took it up, as if impelled by some momentary recollection or curiosity, and held it near his face. Then, as if forgetting his motive in the very action, he turned away and put it down again.

'She is sleeping soundly,' he said; 'but no wonder. Angel hands have strewn the ground deep with snow, that the lightest footstep may be lighter yet; and the very birds are dead, that they may not wake her. She used to feed them, sir. Though never so cold and hungry, the timid things would fly from us. They never flew from her!'

Again he stopped to listen, and scarcely drawing breath, listened for a long, long time. That fancy past, he opened an old chest, took out some clothes as fondly as if they had been living things, and began to smooth and brush them with his hand.

'Why dost thou lie so idle there, dear Nell,' he murmured, 'when there are bright red berries out of doors waiting for thee to pluck them? Why dost thou lie so idle there, when thy little friends come creeping to the door, crying "Where is Nell—sweet Nell?"—and sob, and weep, because they do not see thee? She was always gentle with children. The wildest would do her bidding—she had a tender way with them, indeed she had!'

Kit had no power to speak. His eyes were filled with tears.

'Her little homely dress,—her favourite!' cried the old man, pressing it to his breast, and patting it with his shrivelled hand. 'She will miss it when she wakes. They have hid it here in sport, but she shall have it— she shall have it. I would not vex my darling, for the wide world's riches. See here—these shoes—how worn they are—she kept them to remind her of our last long journey. You see where the little feet went bare upon the ground. They told me, afterwards, that the stones had cut and bruised them. *She* never told me that. No, no, God bless her! and, I have remembered since, she walked behind me, sir, that I might not see how lame she was—but yet she had my hand in hers, and seemed to lead me still.'

He pressed them to his lips, and having carefully put them back again, went on communing with himself—looking wistfully from time to time towards the chamber he had lately visited.

'She was not wont to be a lie-abed; but she was well then. We must have patience. When she is well again, she will rise early, as she used to do, and ramble abroad in the healthy morning time. I often tried to track the way she had gone, but her small footstep left no print upon the dewy ground, to guide me. Who is that? Shut the door. Quick!—Have we not enough to do to drive away that marble cold, and keep her warm?'

The door was indeed opened, for the entrance of Mr. Garland and his friend, accompanied by two other persons. These were the schoolmaster, and the bachelor. The former held a light in his hand. He had, it seemed, but gone to his own cottage to replenish the exhausted lamp, at the moment when Kit came up and found the old man alone.

He softened again at sight of these two friends, and, laying aside the angry manner—if to anything so feeble and so sad the term can be applied—in which he had spoken when the door opened, resumed his former seat, and subsided, by little and little, into the old action, and the old, dull, wandering sound.

Of the strangers, he took no heed whatever. He had seen them, but appeared quite incapable of interest or curiosity. The younger brother stood apart. The bachelor drew a chair towards the old man, and sat down close beside him. After a long silence, he ventured to speak.

'Another night, and not in bed!' he said softly; 'I hoped you would be more mindful of your promise to me. Why do you not take some rest?'

'Sleep has left me,' returned the old man. 'It is all with her!'

'It would pain her very much to know that you were watching thus,' said the bachelor. 'You would not give her pain?'

'I am not so sure of that, if it would only rouse her. She has slept so very long. And yet I am rash to say so. It is a good and happy sleep—eh?'

'Indeed it is,' returned the bachelor. 'Indeed, indeed, it is!'

'That's well!—and the waking'—faltered the old man.

'Happy too. Happier than tongue can tell, or heart of man conceive.'

They watched him as he rose and stole on tip-toe to the other chamber where the lamp had been replaced. They listened as he spoke again within its silent walls. They looked into the faces of each other, and no man's cheek was free from tears. He came back, whispering that she was still asleep, but that he thought she had moved. It was her hand, he said— a little—a very, very little—but he was pretty sure she had moved it—perhaps in seeking his. He had known her do that, before now, though in the deepest sleep the while. And when he had said this, he dropped into his chair again, and clasping his hands above his head, uttered a cry never to be forgotten.

The poor schoolmaster motioned to the bachelor that he would come on the other side, and speak to him. They gently unlocked his fingers, which he had twisted in his grey hair, and pressed them in their own.

'He will hear me,' said the schoolmaster, 'I am sure. He will hear either me or you if we beseech him. She would, at all times.'

'I will hear any voice she liked to hear,' cried the old man. 'I love all she loved!'

'I know you do,' returned the schoolmaster. 'I am certain of it. Think of her; think of all the sorrows and afflictions you have shared together; of all the trials, and all the peaceful pleasures, you have jointly known.'

'I do. I do. I think of nothing else.'

'I would have you think of nothing else to-night—

of nothing but those things which will soften your heart, dear friend, and open it to old affections and old times. It is so that she would speak to you herself, and in her name it is that I speak now.'

'You do well to speak softly,' said the old man. 'We will not wake her. I should be glad to see her eyes again, and to see her smile. There is a smile upon her young face now, but it is fixed and changeless. I would have it come and go. That shall be in Heaven's good time. We will not wake her.'

'Let us not talk of her in her sleep, but as she used to be when you were journeying together, far away—as she was at home, in the old house from which you fled together—as she was, in the old cheerful time,' said the schoolmaster.

'She was always cheerful—very cheerful,' cried the old man, looking steadfastly at him. 'There was ever something mild and quiet about her, I remember, from the first; but she was of a happy nature.'

'We have heard you say,' pursued the schoolmaster, 'that in this and in all goodness, she was like her mother. You can think of, and remember her?'

He maintained his steadfast look, but gave no answer.

'Or even one before her,' said the bachelor. 'It is many years ago, and affliction makes the time longer, but you have not forgotten her whose death contributed to make this child so dear to you, even before you knew her worth or could read her heart? Say, that you could carry back your thoughts to very distant days—to the time of your early life—when, unlike this fair flower, you did not pass your youth alone. Say, that you could remember, long ago, another child who loved you dearly, you being but a child yourself. Say, that you had a brother, long forgotten, long unseen, long separated from you, who now, at last, in your utmost need came back to comfort and console you'—

'To be to you what you were once to him,' cried the younger, falling on his knee before him; 'to repay your old affection, brother dear, by constant care, solicitude, and love; to be, at your right hand, what he has never ceased to be when oceans rolled between us; to call to witness his unchanging truth and mindfulness of bygone days, whole years of desolation. Give me but one word of recognition, brother—and never—no never, in the brightest moment of our youngest days, when, poor silly boys, we thought to pass our lives together—have we been half as dear and precious to each other as we shall be from this time hence!'

The old man looked from face to face, and his lips moved; but no sound came from them in reply.

'If we were knit together then,' pursued the younger brother, 'what will be the bond between us now? Our love and fellowship began in childhood, when life was all before us, and will be resumed when we have proved it, and are but children at the last. As many restless spirits, who have hunted fortune, fame, or pleasure through the world, retire in their decline to where they first drew breath, vainly seeking to be children once again before they die, so we, less fortunate than they in early life, but happier in its closing scenes, will set up our rest again among our boyish haunts, and going home with no hope realised, that had its growth in manhood—carrying back nothing that we brought away, but our old yearnings to each other—saving no fragment from the wreck of life, but that which first endeared it—may be, indeed, but children as at first. And even,' he added in an altered voice, 'even if what I dread to name has come to pass—even if that be so, or is to be (which Heaven forbid and spare us!)—still, dear brother, we are not apart, and have that comfort in our great affliction.'

By little and little, the old man had drawn back towards the inner chamber, while these words were spoken. He pointed there, as he replied, with trembling lips—

'You plot among you to wean my heart from her. You never will do that—never while I have life. I have no relative or friend but her—I never had—I never will have. She is all in all to me. It is too late to part us now.'

Waving them off with his hand, and calling softly to her as he went, he stole into the room. They who were left behind, drew close together, and after a few whispered words—not unbroken by emotion, or easily uttered—followed him. They moved so gently, that their footsteps made no noise; but there were sobs from among the group, and sounds of grief and mourning.

For she was dead. There, upon her little bed, she lay at rest. The solemn stillness was no marvel now.

She was dead. No sleep so beautiful and calm, so free from trace of pain, so fair to look upon. She seemed a creature fresh from the hand of God, and waiting for the breath of life; not one who had lived and suffered death.

Her couch was dressed with here and there some winter berries and green leaves, gathered in a spot she had been used to favour. 'When I die, put near me something that has loved the light, and had the sky above it always.' Those were her words.

She was dead. Dear, gentle, patient, noble Nell was dead. Her little bird—a poor slight thing the pressure of a finger would have crushed—was stirring nimbly in its cage; and the strong heart of its child mistress was mute and motionless for ever.

Where were the traces of her early cares, her sufferings, and fatigues? All gone. Sorrow was dead indeed in her, but peace and perfect happiness were born; imaged in her tranquil beauty and profound repose.

And still her former self lay there, unaltered in this change. Yes. The old fireside had smiled upon that same sweet face; it had passed, like a dream, through haunts of misery and care; at the door of the poor schoolmaster on the summer evening, before the furnace fire upon the cold wet night, at the still bedside of the dying boy, there had been the same mild lovely look. So shall we know the angels in their majesty, after death.

The old man held one languid arm in his, and had the small hand tight folded to his breast, for warmth. It was the hand she had stretched out to him with her last smile—the hand that had led him on, through all their wanderings. Ever and anon he pressed it to his lips; then hugged it to his breast again, murmuring that it was warmer now; and, as he said it, he looked, in agony, to those who stood around, as if imploring them to help her.

She was dead, and past all help, or need of it. The ancient rooms she had seemed to fill with life, even while her own was waning fast—the garden she had tended—the eyes she had gladdened—the noiseless haunts of many a thoughtful hour—the paths she had trodden as it were but yesterday—could know her never more.

'It is not,' said the schoolmaster, as he bent down to kiss her on the cheek, and gave his tears free vent, 'it is not on earth that Heaven's justice ends. Think what earth is, compared with the World to which her young spirit has winged its early flight; and say, if one deliberate wish expressed in solemn terms above this bed could call her back to life, which of us would utter it!'

CHAPTER LXXII

WHEN morning came, and they could speak more calmly on the subject of their grief, they heard how her life had closed.

She had been dead two days. They were all about her at the time, knowing that the end was drawing on. She died soon after daybreak. They had read and talked to her in the earlier portion of the night, but as the hours crept on, she sunk to sleep. They could tell, by what she faintly uttered in her dreams, that they were of her journeyings with the old man; they were of no painful scenes, but of people who had helped and used them kindly, for she often said 'God bless you!' with great fervour. Waking, she never wandered in her mind but once, and that was of beautiful music which she said was in the air. God knows. It may have been.

Opening her eyes at last, from a very quiet sleep, she begged that they would kiss her once again. That done, she turned to the old man with a lovely smile upon her face—such, they said, as they had never seen, and never could forget—and clung with both her arms about his neck. They did not know that she was dead, at first.

She had spoken very often of the two sisters, who, she said, were like dear friends to her. She wished they could be told how much she thought about them, and how she had watched them as they walked together, by the riverside at night. She would like to see poor Kit, she had often said of late. She wished there was somebody to take her love to Kit. And, even then, she never thought or spoke about him, but with something of her old, clear, merry laugh.

For the rest, she had never murmured or complained; but with a quiet mind, and manner quite unaltered—save that she every day became more earnest and more grateful to them—faded like the light upon a summer's evening.

The child who had been her little friend came there, almost as soon as it was day, with an offering of dried flowers which he begged them to lay upon her breast. It was he who had come to the window over-night and spoken to the sexton, and they saw in the snow traces of small feet, where he had been lingering near the room in which she lay, before he went to bed. He had a fancy, it seemed, that they had left her there alone; and could not bear the thought.

He told them of his dream again, and that it was of her being restored to them, just as she used to be. He begged hard to see her, saying that he would be very quiet, and that they need not fear his being alarmed, for he had sat alone by his young brother all day long when *he* was dead, and had felt glad to be so near him. They let him have his wish; and indeed he kept his word, and was, in his childish way, a lesson to them all.

Up to that time, the old man had not spoken once—except to her—or stirred from the bedside. But, when he saw her little favourite, he was moved as they had not seen him yet, and made as though he would have him come nearer. Then, pointing to the bed, he burst into tears for the first time, and they who stood by, knowing that the sight of this child had done him good, left them alone together.

Soothing him with his artless talk of her, the child persuaded him to take some rest, to walk abroad, to do almost as he desired him. And when the day came on, which must remove her in her earthly shape from earthly eyes for ever, he led him away, that he might not know when she was taken from him.

They were to gather fresh leaves and berries for her bed. It was Sunday—a bright, clear, wintry afternoon—and as they traversed the village street, those who were walking in their path drew back to make way for them, and gave them a softened greeting. Some shook the old man kindly by the hand, some stood uncovered while he tottered by, and many cried 'God help him!' as he passed along.

'Neighbour!' said the old man, stopping at the cottage where his young guide's mother dwelt, 'how is it that the folks are nearly all in black to-day? I have seen a mourning ribbon or a piece of crape on almost every one.'

She could not tell, the woman said.

'Why, you yourself—you wear the colour too?' he said. 'Windows are closed that never used to be by day. What does this mean?'

Again the woman said she could not tell.

'We must go back,' said the old man, hurriedly. 'We must see what this is?'

'No, no,' cried the child, detaining him. 'Remember what you promised. Our way is to the old green lane, where she and I so often were, and where you found us, more than once, making those garlands for her garden. Do not turn back!'

'Where is she now?' said the old man. 'Tell me that.'

'Do you not know?' returned the child. 'Did we not leave her, but just now?'

'True. True. It *was* her we left—was it?'

He pressed his hand upon his brow, looked vacantly round, and as if impelled by a sudden thought, crossed the road, and entered the sexton's house. He and his deaf assistant were sitting before the fire. Both rose up, on seeing who it was.

The child made a hasty sign to them with his hand. It was the action of an instant, but that, and the old man's look, were quite enough.

'Do you—do you bury any one to-day?' he said, eagerly.

'No, no! Who should we bury, sir?' returned the sexton.

'Aye, who indeed! I say with you, who indeed?'

'It is a holiday with us, good sir,' returned the sexton mildly. 'We have no work to do to-day.'

'Why then, I'll go where you will,' said the old man, turning to the child. 'You're sure of what you tell me? You would not deceive me? I am changed, even in the little time since you last saw me.'

'Go thy ways with him, sir,' cried the sexton, 'and Heaven be with ye both!'

'I am quite ready,' said the old man, meekly. 'Come, boy, come—' and so submitted to be led away.

And now the bell—the bell she had so often heard, by night and day, and listened to with solemn pleasure almost as a living voice—rung its remorseless toll, for her, so young, so beautiful, so good. Decrepit age, and vigorous life, and blooming youth, and helpless infancy, poured forth—on crutches, in the pride of strength and health, in the full blush of promise, in the mere dawn of life—to gather round her tomb. Old men were there, whose eyes were dim and senses failing—grandmothers, who might have died ten years ago, and still been old—the deaf, the blind, the lame, the palsied, the living dead in many shapes and forms, to see the closing of that early grave. What was the death it would shut in, to that which still could crawl and creep above it?

Along the crowded path they bore her now; pure

as the newly-fallen snow that covered it; whose day on earth had been as fleeting. Under the porch, where she had sat when Heaven in its mercy brought her to that peaceful spot, she passed again; and the old church received her in its quiet shade.

They carried her to one old nook, where she had many and many a time sat musing, and laid their burden softly on the pavement. The light streamed on it through the coloured window—a window, where the boughs of trees were ever rustling in the summer, and where the birds sang sweetly all day long. With every breath of air that stirred among those branches in the sunshine, some trembling, changing light would fall upon her grave.

Earth to earth, ashes to ashes, dust to dust! Many a young hand dropped in its little wreath, many a stifled sob was heard. Some—and they were not a few—knelt down. All were sincere and truthful in their sorrow.

The service done, the mourners stood apart, and the villagers closed round to look into the grave before the pavement-stone should be replaced. One, called to mind how he had seen her sitting on that very spot, and how her book had fallen on her lap, and she was gazing with a pensive face upon the sky. Another, told how he had wondered much that one so delicate as she, should be so bold; how she had never feared to enter the church alone at night, but had loved to linger there when all was quiet, and even to climb the tower stair, with no more light than that of the moon-rays stealing through the loopholes in the thick old wall. A whisper went about among the oldest, that she had seen and talked with angels; and when they called to mind how she had looked, and spoken, and her early death, some thought it might be so, indeed. Thus, coming to the grave in little knots, and glancing down, and giving place to others, and falling off in whispering groups of three or four, the church was cleared in time, of all but the sexton and the mourning friends.

They saw the vault covered, and the stone fixed down. Then, when the dusk of evening had come on, and not a sound disturbed the sacred stillness of the place—when the bright moon poured in her light on tomb and monument, on pillar, wall, and arch, and most of all (it seemed to them) upon her quiet grave —in that calm time, when outward things and inward thoughts teem with assurances of immortality, and worldly hopes and fears are humbled in the dust before them—then, with tranquil and submissive hearts they turned away, and left the child with God.

Oh! it is hard to take to heart the lesson that such deaths will teach, but let no man reject it, for it is one that all must learn, and is a mighty universal Truth. When Death strikes down the innocent and young, for every fragile form from which he lets the panting spirit free, a hundred virtues rise, in shapes of mercy, charity, and love, to walk the world, and bless it. Of every tear that sorrowing mortals shed on such green graves, some good is born, some gentler nature comes. In the Destroyer's steps there spring up bright creations that defy his power, and his dark path becomes a way of light to Heaven.

It was late when the old man came home. The boy had led him to his own dwelling, under some pretence, on their way back; and, rendered drowsy by his long ramble and late want of rest, he had sunk into a deep sleep by the fireside. He was perfectly exhausted, and they were careful not to rouse him. The slumber held him a long time, and when he at length awoke the moon was shining.

The younger brother, uneasy at his protracted absence, was watching at the door for his coming, when he appeared in the pathway with his little guide. He advanced to meet them, and tenderly obliging the old man to lean upon his arm, conducted him with slow and trembling steps towards the house.

He repaired to her chamber, straight. Not finding what he had left there, he returned with distracted looks to the room in which they were assembled. From that, he rushed into the schoolmaster's cottage, calling her name. They followed close upon him, and when he had vainly searched it, brought him home.

With such persuasive words as pity and affection could suggest, they prevailed upon him to sit among them, and hear what they should tell him. Then endeavouring by every little artifice to prepare his mind for what must come, and dwelling with many fervent words upon the happy lot to which she had been removed, they told him, at last, the truth. The moment it had passed their lips, he fell down among them like a murdered man.

For many hours, they had little hope of his surviving; but grief is strong, and he recovered.

If there be any who have never known the blank that follows death—the weary void—the sense of desolation that will come upon the strongest minds, when something familiar and beloved is missed at every turn—the connection between inanimate and senseless things, and the object of recollection, when every household god becomes a monument and every room a grave—if there be any who have not known this, and proved it by their own experience, they can never faintly guess how, for many days, the old man pined and moped away the time, and wandered here and there as seeking something, and had no comfort.

Whatever power of thought or memory he retained,

was all bound up in her. He never understood, or seemed to care to understand, about his brother. To every endearment and attention he continued listless. If they spoke to him on this, or any other theme—save one—he would hear them patiently for awhile, then turn away, and go on seeking as before.

On that one theme, which was in his and all their minds, it was impossible to touch. Dead! He could not hear or bear the word. The slightest hint of it would throw him into a paroxysm, like that he had had when it was first spoken. In what hope he lived, no man could tell; but, that he had some hope of finding her again—some faint and shadowy hope, deferred from day to day, and making him from day to day more sick and sore at heart—was plain to all.

They bethought them of a removal from the scene of this last sorrow; of trying whether change of place would rouse or cheer him. His brother sought the advice of those who were accounted skilful in such matters, and they came and saw him. Some of the number staid upon the spot, conversed with him when he would converse, and watched him as he wandered up and down, alone and silent. Move him where they might, they said, he would ever seek to get back there. His mind would run upon that spot. If they confined him closely, and kept a strict guard upon him, they might hold him prisoner, but if he could by any means escape, he would surely wander back to that place, or die upon the road.

The boy, to whom he had submitted at first, had no longer any influence with him. At times he would suffer the child to walk by his side, or would even take such notice of his presence as giving him his hand, or would stop to kiss his cheek, or pat him on the head. At other times, he would entreat him—not unkindly—to be gone, and would not brook him near.

But, whether alone, or with this pliant friend, or with those who would have given him, at any cost or sacrifice, some consolation or some peace of mind, if happily the means could have been devised; he was at all times the same—with no love or care for anything in life—a broken-hearted man.

At length, they found, one day, that he had risen early, and, with his knapsack on his back, his staff in hand, her own straw hat, and little basket full of such things as she had been used to carry, was gone. As they were making ready to pursue him far and wide, a frightened schoolboy came who had seen him, but a moment before, sitting in the church, upon her grave, he said.

They hastened there, and going softly to the door, espied him in the attitude of one who waited patiently. They did not disturb him then, but kept a watch upon him all that day. When it grew quite dark, he rose and returned home, and went to bed, murmuring to himself, 'She will come to-morrow!'

Upon the morrow he was there again from sunrise until night; and still at night he laid him down to rest, and murmured, 'She will come to-morrow!'

And thenceforth, every day, and all day long, he waited at her grave, for her. How many pictures of new journeys over pleasant country, of resting-places under the free broad sky, of rambles in the fields and woods, and paths not often trodden—how many tones of that one well-remembered voice, how many glimpses of the form, the fluttering dress, the hair that waved so gaily in the wind—how many visions of what had been, and what he hoped was yet to be— rose up before him, in the old, dull, silent church? He never told them what he thought, or where he went. He would sit with them at night, pondering with a secret satisfaction, they could see, upon the flight that he and she would take before night came again; and still they would hear him whisper in his prayers, 'Lord! let her come to-morrow!'

The last time was on a genial day in spring. He did not return at the usual hour, and they went to seek him. He was lying dead upon the stone.

They laid him by the side of her whom he had loved so well; and, in the church where they had often prayed, and mused, and lingered hand in hand, the child and the old man slept together.

CHAPTER THE LAST

THE magic reel, which, rolling on before, has led the chronicler thus far, now slackens in its pace, and stops. It lies before the goal; the pursuit is at an end.

It remains but to dismiss the leaders of the little crowd who have borne us company upon the road, and so to close the journey.

Foremost among them, smooth Sampson Brass and Sally, arm-in-arm, claim our polite attention.

Mr. Sampson, then, being detained, as already has been shown, by the justice upon whom he called, and being so strongly pressed to protract his stay that he could by no means refuse, remained under his protection for a considerable time, during which the great attention of his entertainer kept him so extremely close, that he was quite lost to society, and never even went abroad for exercise saving into a small paved yard. So well, indeed, was his modest and retiring temper understood by those with whom he had to deal, and so jealous were they of his absence, that they required a kind of friendly bond to be entered into by two substantial housekeepers, in the sum of fifteen hundred pounds a-piece, before they would suffer him to quit their hospitable roof—doubting, it appeared, that he would return, if once let loose, on any other terms.   Mr. Brass, struck with the humour of this jest, and carrying out its spirit to the utmost, sought from his wide connection a pair of friends whose joint possessions fell some halfpence short of fifteen-pence, and proffered them as bail—for that was the merry word agreed upon on both sides.   These gentlemen being rejected after twenty-four hours' pleasantry, Mr. Brass consented to remain, and did remain, until a club of choice spirits called a Grand Jury (who were in the joke) summoned him to a trial before twelve other wags for perjury and fraud, who in their turn found him guilty with a most facetious joy,—nay, the very populace entered into the whim, and when Mr. Brass was moving in a hackney-coach towards the building where these wags assembled, saluted him with rotten eggs and carcases of kittens, and feigned to wish to tear him into shreds, which greatly increased the comicality of the thing, and made him relish it the more, no doubt.

To work this sportive vein still further, Mr. Brass, by his counsel, moved in arrest of judgment that he had been led to criminate himself, by assurances of safety and promises of pardon, and claimed the leniency which the law extends to such confiding natures as are thus deluded.   After solemn argument, this point (with others of a technical nature, whose humorous extravagance it would be difficult to exaggerate) was referred to the judges for their decision, Sampson being meantime removed to his former quarters.   Finally, some of the points were given in Sampson's favour, and some against him; and the upshot was, that, instead of being desired to travel for a time in foreign parts, he was permitted to grace the mother-country under certain insignificant restrictions.

These were, that he should, for a term of years, reside in a spacious mansion where several other gentlemen were lodged and boarded at the public charge, who went clad in a sober uniform of grey turned up with yellow, had their hair cut extremely short, and chiefly lived on gruel and light soup. It was also required of him that he should partake of their exercise of constantly ascending an endless flight of stairs; and, lest his legs, unused to such exertion, should be weakened by it, that he should wear upon one ankle an amulet or charm of iron. These conditions being arranged, he was removed one evening to his new abode, and enjoyed, in common with nine other gentlemen, and two ladies, the privilege of being taken to his place of retirement in one of Royalty's own carriages.

Over and above these trifling penalties, his name was erased and blotted out from the roll of attorneys; which erasure has been always held in these latter times to be a great degradation and reproach, and to imply the commission of some amazing villainy—as indeed it would seem to be the case, when so many worthless names remain among its better records, unmolested.

Of Sally Brass, conflicting rumours went abroad. Some said with confidence that she had gone down to the docks in male attire, and had become a female sailor; others darkly whispered that she had enlisted as a private in the second regiment of Foot Guards, and had been seen in uniform, and on duty, to wit, leaning on her musket and looking out of a sentry-box in St. James's Park, one evening. There were many such whispers as these in circulation; but the truth appears to be that, after the lapse of some five years (during which there is no direct evidence of her having been seen at all), two wretched people were more than once observed to crawl at dusk from the inmost recesses of St. Giles's, and to take their way along the streets, with shuffling steps and cowering shivering forms, looking into the roads and kennels as they went in search of refuse food or disregarded offal. These forms were never beheld but in those nights of cold and gloom, when the terrible spectres, who lie at all other times in the obscene hiding-places of London, in archways, dark vaults and cellars, venture to creep into the streets; the embodied spirits of Disease, and Vice, and Famine. It was whispered by those who should have known, that these were Sampson and his sister Sally; and to this day, it is said, they sometimes pass, on bad nights, in the same loathsome guise, close at the elbow of the shrinking passenger.

The body of Quilp being found—though not until some days had elapsed—an inquest was held on it near the spot where it had been washed ashore. The general supposition was that he had committed suicide, and, this appearing to be favoured by all the circumstances of his death, the verdict was to that effect. He was left to be buried with a stake through his heart in the centre of four lonely roads.

It was rumoured afterwards that this horrible and barbarous ceremony had been dispensed with, and that the remains had been secretly given up to Tom Scott. But even here, opinion was divided; for some said Tom dug them up at midnight, and carried them to a place indicated to him by the widow. It is probable that both these stories may have had their origin in the simple fact of Tom's shedding tears upon the inquest—which he certainly did, extraordinary as it may appear.   He manifested besides, a strong desire to assault the jury; and being restrained and conducted out of court, darkened its only window by standing on his head upon the sill, until he was dexterously tilted upon his feet again by a cautious beadle.

Being cast upon the world by his master's death, he determined to go through it upon his head and hands, and accordingly began to tumble for his bread.   Finding, however, his English birth an insurmountable obstacle to his advancement in this pursuit (notwithstanding that his art was in high repute and favour), he assumed the name of an Italian image lad, with whom he had become acquainted; and afterwards tumbled with extraordinary success, and to overflowing audiences.

Little Mrs. Quilp never quite forgave herself the one deceit that lay so heavy on her conscience, and never spoke or thought of it but with bitter tears. Her husband had no relations, and she was rich.   He had made no will, or she would probably have been poor.   Having married the first time at her mother's instigation, she consulted in her second choice nobody but herself.   It fell upon a smart young fellow enough; and as he made it a preliminary condition that Mrs. Jiniwin should be thenceforth an outpensioner, they lived together after marriage with no more than the average amount of quarrelling, and led a merry life upon the dead dwarf's money.

Mr. and Mrs. Garland, and Mr. Abel, went out as usual (except that there was a change in their household, as will be seen presently), and in due time the latter went into partnership with his friend the notary, on which occasion there was a dinner, and a ball, and great extent of dissipation.   Unto this ball there happened to be invited the most bashful young lady that was ever seen, with whom Mr. Abel happened to fall in love. *How* it happened, or how they found it out, or which of them first communicated the discovery to the other, nobody knows. But, certain it is that in course of time they were married; and equally certain it is that they were the happiest of the happy; and no less certain it is that they deserved to be so. And it is pleasant to write down that they reared a family; because any propagation of goodness and benevolence is no small addition to the aristocracy of nature, and no small subject of rejoicing for mankind at large.

The pony preserved his character for independence and principle down to the last moment of his life; which was an unusually long one, and caused him to be looked upon, indeed, as the very Old Parr of ponies. He often went to and fro with the little phaeton between Mr. Garland's and his son's, and, as the old people and the young were frequently together, had a stable of his own at the new establishment, into which he would walk of himself with surprising dignity. He condescended to play with the children, as they grew old enough to cultivate his friendship, and would run up and down the little paddock with them like a dog; but though he relaxed so far, and allowed them such small freedoms as caresses, or even to look at his shoes or hang on by his tail, he never permitted any one among them to mount his back or drive him; thus showing that even their familiarity must have its limits, and that there were points between them far too serious for trifling.

He was not unsusceptible of warm attachments in his later life, for when the good bachelor came to live with Mr. Garland upon the clergyman's decease, he conceived a great friendship for him, and amiably submitted to be driven by his hands without the least resistance. He did no work for two or three years before he died, but lived in clover; and his last act (like a choleric old gentleman) was to kick his doctor.

Mr. Swiveller, recovering very slowly from his illness, and entering into the receipt of his annuity, bought for the Marchioness a handsome stock of clothes, and put her to school forthwith, in redemption of the vow he had made upon his fevered bed.   After casting about for some time for a name which should be worthy of her, he decided in favour of Sophronia Sphynx, as being euphonious and genteel, and furthermore indicative of mystery.   Under this title the Marchioness repaired, in tears, to the school of his selection, from which, as she soon distanced all competitors, she was removed before the lapse of many quarters to one of a higher grade.   It is but bare justice to Mr. Swiveller to say, that, although the expenses of her education kept him in straitened circumstances for half a dozen years, he never slackened in his zeal, and always held himself sufficiently repaid by the accounts he heard (with great gravity) of her advancement, on his monthly visits to the governess, who looked upon him as a literary gentleman of eccentric habits, and of a most prodigious talent in quotation.

In a word, Mr. Swiveller kept the Marchioness at this establishment until she was, at a moderate guess, full nineteen years of age—good-looking, clever, and good-humoured; when he began to consider seriously what was to be done next.   On one of his periodical visits, while he was revolving this question in his mind, the Marchioness came down to him, alone, looking more smiling and more fresh than ever.   Then, it occurred to him, but not for the first time, that if she would marry him, how comfortable they might be! So Richard asked her; whatever she said, it wasn't No; and they were married in good earnest that day week. Which gave Mr. Swiveller frequent occasion to remark at divers subsequent periods that there had been a young lady saving up for him after all.

A little cottage at Hampstead being to let, which had in its garden a smoking-box, the envy of the civilised world, they agreed to become its tenants, and, when the honeymoon was over, entered upon its occupation. To this retreat Mr. Chuckster repaired regularly every Sunday to spend the day—usually beginning with breakfast—and here he was the great purveyor of general news and fashionable intelligence. For some years he continued a deadly foe to Kit, protesting that he had a better opinion of him when he was supposed to have stolen the five-pound note, than when he was shown to be perfectly free of the crime; inasmuch as his guilt would have had in it something daring and bold, whereas his innocence was but another proof of a sneaking and crafty disposition. By slow degrees, however, he was reconciled to him in the end; and even went so far as to honour him with his patronage, as one who had in some measure reformed, and was therefore to be forgiven. But he never forgot or pardoned that circumstance of the shilling; holding that if he had come back to get another he would have done well enough, but that his returning to work out the former gift was a stain upon his moral character which no penitence or contrition could ever wash away.

Mr. Swiveller, having always been in some measure of a philosophic and reflective turn, grew immensely contemplative, at times, in the smoking-box, and was accustomed at such periods to debate in his own mind the mysterious question of Sophronia's parentage. Sophronia herself supposed she was an orphan; but Mr. Swiveller, putting various slight circumstances together, often thought Miss Brass must know better than that; and, having heard from his wife of her strange interview with Quilp, entertained sundry mis-givings whether that person, in his lifetime, might not also have been able to solve the riddle, had he chosen. These speculations, however, gave him no uneasiness; for Sophronia was ever a most cheerful, affectionate, and provident wife to him; and Dick (excepting for an occasional outbreak with Mr. Chuckster, which she had the good sense rather to encourage than oppose) was to her an attached and domesticated husband. And they played many hundred thousand games of cribbage together. And let it be added, to Dick's honour, that, though we have called her Sophronia, he called her the Marchioness from first to last; and that upon every anniversary of the day on which he found her in his sick-room, Mr. Chuckster came to dinner, and there was great glorification.

The gamblers, Isaac List and Jowl, with their trusty confederate Mr. James Groves of unimpeach-able memory, pursued their course with varying suc-cess, until the failure of a spirited enterprise in the way of their profession, dispersed them in various directions, and caused their career to receive a sudden check from the long and strong arm of the law. This defeat had its origin in the untoward detection of a new associate—young Frederick Trent—who thus became the unconscious instrument of their punishment and his own.

For the young man himself he rioted abroad for a brief term, living by his wits—which means by the abuse of every faculty that worthily employed raises man above the beasts, and so degraded, sinks him far below them. It was not long before his body was recognised by a stranger, who chanced to visit that hospital in Paris where the drowned are laid out to be owned; despite the bruises and disfigurements which were said to have been occasioned by some previous scuffle. But the stranger kept his own counsel until he returned home, and it was never claimed or cared for.

The young brother, or the single gentleman, for that designation is more familiar, would have drawn the poor schoolmaster from his lone retreat, and made him his companion and friend. But the humble village teacher was timid of venturing into the noisy world, and had become fond of his dwelling in the old churchyard. Calmly happy in his school, and in the spot, and in the attachment of Her little mourner, he pursued his quiet course in peace; and was, through the righteous gratitude of his friend—let this brief mention suffice for that—a *poor* schoolmaster no more.

That friend—single gentleman, or younger brother, which you will—had at his heart a heavy sorrow; but it bred in him no misanthropy or monastic gloom. He went forth into the world, a lover of his kind. For a long, long time, it was his chief delight to travel in the steps of the old man and the child (so far as he could trace them from her last narrative), to halt where they had halted, sympathise where they had suffered, and rejoice where they had been made glad. Those who been kind to them, did not escape his search. The sisters at the school—they who were her friends, because themselves so friendless—Mrs. Jarley of the wax-work, Codlin, Short—he found them all; and trust me, the man who fed the furnace fire was not forgotten.

Kit's story having got abroad, raised him up a host of friends, and many offers of provision for his future life. He had no idea at first of ever quitting Mr. Garland's service; but, after serious remonstrance and advice from that gentleman, began to contemplate the possibility of such a change being brought about in time. A good post was procured for him, with a rapidity which took away his breath, by some of the gentlemen who had believed him guilty of the offence laid to his charge, and who had acted upon that belief. Through the same kind agency, his mother was secured from want, and made quite happy. Thus, as Kit often said, his great misfortune turned out to be the source of all his subsequent prosperity.

Did Kit live a single man all his days, or did he marry? Of course he married, and who should be his wife but Barbara? And the best of it was, he married so soon that little Jacob was an uncle, before the calves of his legs, already mentioned in this history, had ever been encased in broadcloth pantaloons, —though that was not quite the best either, for of necessity the baby was an uncle too. The delight of Kit's mother and of Barbara's mother upon the great occasion is past all telling; finding they agreed so well on that, and on all other subjects, they took up their abode together, and were a most harmonious pair of friends from that time forth. And hadn't Astley's cause to bless itself for their all going together once a quarter to the pit—and didn't Kit's mother always say, when they painted the outside, that Kit's last treat had helped to that, and wonder what the manager would feel if he but knew it as they passed his house?

When Kit had children six and seven years old, there was a Barbara among them, and a pretty Barbara she was. Nor was there wanting an exact facsimile and copy of little Jacob, as he appeared in those remote times when they taught him what oysters meant. Of course there was an Abel, own godson to the Mr. Garland of that name; and there was a Dick, whom Mr. Swiveller did especially favour. The little group would often gather round him of a night and beg him to tell again that story of good

Miss Nell who died. This, Kit would do; and when they cried to hear it, wishing it longer too, he would teach them how she had gone to Heaven, as all good people did; and how, if they were good, like her, they might hope to be there too, one day, and to see and know her as he had done when he was quite a boy. Then, he would relate to them how needy he used to be, and how she had taught him what he was otherwise too poor to learn, and how the old man had been used to say 'she always laughs at Kit'; at which they would brush away their tears, and laugh themselves to think that she had done so, and be again quite merry.

He sometimes took them to the street where she had lived; but new improvements had altered it so much, it was not like the same. The old house had been long ago pulled down, and a fine broad road was in its place. At first he would draw with his stick a square upon the ground to show them where it used to stand. But, he soon became uncertain of the spot, and could only say it was thereabouts, he thought, and these alterations were confusing.

Such are the changes which a few years bring about, and so do things pass away, like a tale that is told!

THE END